W9-BRH-462

Also by Harold Robbins

Memories

SIMON AND SCHUSTER • *New York*

# of Another Day

a novel by

Harold Robbins

Designed by Irving Perkins
Manufactured in the United States of America
Typography by Dix Typesetting
Printed and bound by The Book Press

1 2 3 4 5 6 7 8 9 10

Library of Congress Cataloging in Publication Data
Robbins, Harold, date.
    Memories of another day.

    I. Title.
PZ3.R53564Me   [PS3568.0224]   813'.5'4   79-20774
ISBN 0-671-22585-5

For Grazia Maria
con amore

Now

THE LAST time I saw my father, he was lying quietly on his back in his coffin, his eyes closed, an unaccustomed blandness on his strong features, his thick white hair and heavy eyebrows neatly brushed. I stood there in the silence of the funeral chapel staring down at him. There was something wrong. All wrong. After a moment I realized what it was. My father had never slept on his back. Not once in all the years I knew him.

Usually my father slept balanced on his side, his barrel chest and big belly sinking into the mattress, one arm thrown over his eyes to shield them from the light, a scowl of concentration fierce even in sleep on his face. Now there was nothing there. Not even the hatred of the morning that would come to tear him from his private world. Then the lid of the coffin came down and I never saw him again.

I was flooded with a sense of relief. It was over. I was free. I tore my eyes away from the burnished copper-and-mahogany coffin and looked up.

The minister gestured for us to leave. I started off. My brother, D.J., short for Daniel, Junior, pulled me back.

"Take your mother's arm," he whispered hoarsely. "And

wipe that stupid smile off your face. There are a million photographers out there."

I stared up at him. He was thirty-seven years old—twenty years older than I—and we were worlds apart. He came out of my father's first marriage and I came out of his last. In between my father had other women but no other children. I pulled my arm free. "Fuck you," I said.

I walked out into the small antechamber off the chapel where the family was supposed to wait until the funeral limousines were ready and lit a cigarette. Several close friends and associates of my father's were already there.

Moses Barrington, my father's executive assistant, came up to me, his black face shining with the heat. "How's your mother taking it?"

I sucked on the cigarette, taking the smoke deep into my lungs before I answered him. "Okay."

He watched the smoke curling out from my nose. "You can get cancer from those things."

"Yeah," I said. "I read the warning on the package."

The door opened and everyone's eyes turned toward it. My mother came in, leaning on D.J.'s arm. He had his other arm around her back as if supporting her. He looked more like a big brother than a stepson. Which somehow seemed okay, since he was three years older than she was.

The widow's black made my mother look even younger. It made her white skin seem more translucent and the long blond hair paler. When the door had closed behind them, her widow's frailty disappeared. She stepped free of D.J.'s arm and came toward me. "Jonathan, my baby. You're all I have left."

I managed to avoid her reach. That couldn't be true. Not if I could believe half the shit I read in the newspapers about my father. Somewhere along the line he had to have socked away a bundle. Union or no union. Justice Department or no Justice Department. Jail or no jail.

My mother stood there a moment, her hands grabbing at empty air. Then she dropped them to her side. "Give me a cigarette."

I held out the pack, then lit one for her. She dragged on it. "That's better," she said.

12

I watched some color come back into her face. She was a pretty lady, my mother, and she knew it. "When we get back to the house we'll have to have a talk."

"Okay." I ground out my cigarette in a sandbox. "I'll wait there for you."

"You'll wait there for me?" Her voice was an echo.

I nodded. "I'm not going to the cemetery."

"What do you mean you're not going?" D.J. had come up behind her. "How do you think it will look?"

"I don't give a damn how it looks," I said.

"But it's important," D.J. said. "The funeral will be on the national newscasts. Union members all over the country will see it."

"Then just make sure *you're* up front where they can see you. That's all that matters. You're the one who is going to be their next national president, not me."

He turned to my mother. "Margaret, you'd better make him come."

"Jonathan—"

I cut her off. "No, Mother. It's just a waste of time. I didn't like him when he was alive, and now that he's dead there's no point in pretending that I like him any better. It's a barbaric, hypocritical custom and I want no part of it."

There was dead silence in the room as I walked out. When I turned to close the door behind me, I could see the others cluster around my mother. Only Jack Haney hung back against the wall and watched. There was no rush on his part. He would get her later. In the sack. That is, if he still wanted to, now that she was no longer the wife of the national president and could no longer do him any good. His eyes caught mine and he nodded. I nodded back and silently closed the door.

He wasn't so bad. No worse than any of the others around my father. I couldn't blame him for what he did any more than I could blame my mother. My father had corrupted the world around him.

I went out through a side entrance to avoid the crowds around the funeral parlor. D.J. was right. There were hundreds of people out there. And the television cameras were right up front with the newspapermen right behind them. I leaned on the wall and watched.

The mourners were coming out of the chapel now and getting into their big black limousines. The Vice President of the United States was first. He paused in front of the TV cameras, his hawklike face arranged in properly somber lines. His lips moved. I couldn't hear what he was saying, but didn't doubt that it was all the proper things. After all, union members were still allowed to vote. After him came governors, senators, congressmen, mayors, other officials and union leaders. One by one they took their turn in the spotlight, hoping that when running the newscast the local station would at least feature the hometown product.

A truck ground to a stop in the alleyway behind me. There was the sound of footsteps, and I could smell the man before I turned to see him. I didn't have to be told it was a garbage truck.

"Is that Big Dan's funeral?"

I looked at him. The small blue-and-white union button was pinned to the pocket of his grimy, grease-stained blouse. "Yes."

"Big crowd."

"Uh-huh."

"Any interesting pussy around?"

"What makes you ask?" I asked.

"Big Dan was supposed to be big with the ladies too," he answered. "Our shop steward was out with him a couple of times. He said there was always lots of pussy and lots of whiskey whenever Big Dan was around."

"I didn't see any," I said.

"Oh." He sounded disappointed. Then his voice brightened. "Any truth to the talk there was a young girl in the plane with him when he crashed?"

I looked at him and decided not to disappoint him any more that day. I lowered my voice to a whisper, even though there was no need to do so. There was no one within a hundred feet of us. "I got the real scoop."

He fished a pack of cigarettes out of his pocket and held it toward me. We both lit up. He looked expectantly at me.

"Ever hear of the Mile High Club?" I asked.

He shook his head. "What's that?"

14

"If you ball a chick in an airplane, you're automatically a member."

"Sweet Jesus," he said reverently. "Was that what he was doin'?"

"Better than that," I said. "She was a blond chick with big tits. She was kneeling down in front of him, her tits out on his lap, his cock coming up between them, and she was blowing him when they came down out of the clouds with the mountain in front of them. He tried pulling the wheel back toward him to lift the plane up, but no use. Her head was blocking it so the wheel didn't move."

"Sweet Jesus," he said again. "What a way to go!"

I didn't answer.

He looked over the fence at the crowd. "Big turnout."

"Yeah."

"He had to be the greatest," he said admiringly. "My old man told me during the Depression he got nine dollars a week for the same job I'm doing, an' I'm pullin' down a hunnert and ninety-five per. He was the best friend a workingman ever had."

"He was a shit," I said. "All the workingman ever meant to him was power."

"Wait a minute," he said, his fist doubling threateningly. "You got no right to say things like that."

"I have every right in the world," I said. "He was my father."

A strange look came over his face. Then his fist relaxed. "I'm sorry, kid," he said, and went back to his truck.

I watched him climb into the cab and start off, then turned back to look over the fence. Mother and D.J. were coming out. The photographers pushed forward trying to get their pictures. I turned and walked away down the alley just as they were getting into the limousine.

"That's no way to talk about your father."

"Go away, Old Man. You're dead."

"I'm not dead. I'll be alive as long as you're alive, as long as your children and their children are alive. There is something of me in

every cell of your body and there is no way you can get rid of me."

"You're dead, dead, dead."

"You're seventeen and you don't believe in anything, do you?"

"No."

"Would you really like to know what happened in that plane before it crashed?"

"Yes."

"You already do. You told that garbageman."

"I made that up."

"No, you didn't. I put the words into your mouth. Don't forget your brain is made up of cells too."

"I don't believe you. You're lying to me. You've always lied to me."

"I never lied to you. There was no way I could. You were part of me. You were my truth. You were not like your brother. He is a copy of me. But you—you are yourself. You are my truth."

"Lies, lies, lies. Even the grave doesn't stop you."

"That is nothing they are carrying to the grave. A body, an empty shell. I am here. Inside you."

"I don't feel you, Father. I never felt you. I don't feel you now."

"In time you will."

"Never."

"Jonathan, my son."

"Go away, Old Man. You're dead."

I turned the corner onto my street. The first thing I saw was the cars parked in front of my house. Several men were standing there in the shade of the trees. Reporters. I'd thought they would be gone by now. But they were waiting. Apparently Big Dan was news even after he was dead and buried.

I cut back to the street behind my house and went up through the Forbeses' driveway. Our back door was right behind the fence that separated the two houses.

I was carefully stepping over the flower bed against the fence, knowing that Mrs. Forbes was hysterical about her flowers. I had one foot on the fence when Anne called me. Just as carefully, I put my foot down again and turned. She was sitting on the back porch, a glass of wine in her hand.

"I thought you'd be at the funeral," she said.

"I went to the service," I said. "I didn't go out to the cemetery. It was too much of a drag. I came this way because the reporters are still out front and I didn't want to talk to them."

"I know," she said. "They came around here this morning. They wanted to know what kind of a neighbor your father was."

"What did you tell them?"

"I didn't talk to them. My mother and father did." She giggled. "They told them what a great man he was. You know."

I had to smile at that. There was no love lost between the Forbeses and my father. When we moved into the neighborhood, the Forbeses had led the fight against him. They didn't want a labor-racketeering Communist polluting their clean Westchester air. "Where are your folks?" I asked.

She giggled again. "At the funeral. Where did you think they would be?"

I laughed. The whole world was full of shit and hypocrites.

"Want a glass of wine?" she asked.

"No. But I'll take a can of beer if you got one."

"I got one." She disappeared through the kitchen door as I climbed up on the porch. She was back in a moment with a cold can of Miller's.

I pulled the tab, and the cold beer came gushing over my hand. I raised it quickly to my mouth. I didn't know how dry and thirsty I had been until I felt the icy tang in my throat. I was halfway through the can before I came up for air. I leaned back against the porch railing.

"You're all strung out," she said.

"Not too bad."

"Bad enough." Her eyes went down to the can of beer in my hand. "Your hands are shaking."

I held up the can of beer. She was right. "I didn't sleep much last night," I said.

"Want a tranq?" she asked.

I shook my head. I wasn't a pill popper.

"I've got some real good shit," she said. "I can roll you a joint."

"No, thanks," I said. "I'm not in the mood."

"Mind if I smoke, then?"

"Go ahead."

I watched her pick up the small Bulldog pouch from the floor beside her chair and deftly roll a ZigZag. She tamped the ends down neatly and lit up. She took a deep toke, then a sip of wine, then another deep toke.

A bright shine came into her eyes. She didn't need much to trip off—she was into it all the time. "I've been thinking about your father."

"Yes?"

"I've been horny all afternoon thinking about him. There's something about death that turns you on."

I took another swig of the beer. "I don't know."

"It's true," she said. "I read somewhere that when the bombs were falling during the last war, everybody turned on. It's got something to do with immortality, I think."

"That's deep. Ever stop to think that maybe people just like to fuck and that it was a good excuse for them to break the rules?"

"It's more than just that," she said. "When I woke up this morning I thought how sad it was that he was gone and that he would never have another chance to leave more of himself behind. Then I began to think how nice it would have been if we had made it just once and he had planted a baby in my belly. It made me so horny that I took myself off three times today."

I laughed. "That's horny."

She looked at me resentfully. "You don't understand."

"My father was seventy-four years old," I said. "You're nineteen."

"Age doesn't matter," she said. "You're seventeen; you were fourteen when we first made it and that didn't stop us."

"That was different."

"No, it's not. I've made it with older men. It's the same thing. All in the way you feel." She took another drag on the joint and another sip of wine. "But he's gone now and all I can do is be sorry we missed it."

I finished the beer and crumpled the can in my hand. "Thanks for the beer."

"It's okay."

18

I turned to go. She called me back. "What are you going to do now? This summer, I mean."

"I figured on goin' hitching until school opened in the fall. But now I don't know."

"You'll be eighteen soon," she said.

"That's right. Vote, all that shit. Another two months I'll be all grown up. Seven weeks." I looked at the smoke curling out of her nose. "Tell me something."

"Yes?"

"If you had the hots for my father, why didn't you do something about it?"

"I was afraid, I guess."

"Of what?"

Her eyes were thoughtful. "Of rejection. That he might laugh at me. Think I was a silly kid." She hesitated a moment. "That happened to me once. With another man. It took me months to get over it."

"That wouldn't have happened with my father," I said. I vaulted the porch rail and landed on the soft earth.

"Jonathan." She came to the rail and looked down at me. "Don't you feel alone? Terribly alone?"

"I always did," I said. "Even when he was alive."

I took the key from under the doormat and let myself in. I went through the back hallway into the kitchen. The only sound in the house was my footsteps. There were pots on the stove and dishes placed neatly on the counter near the sink. The world might come to an end, but Mamie would have everything ready for dinner at seven o'clock. That was the time my father liked to eat. I wondered whether it would change now.

Suddenly I was hungry. I opened the refrigerator door, found the ham and cheese and made myself a sandwich. I pulled out a can of beer and sat down at the kitchen table. I took the first bite of the sandwich before I realized what was wrong. There was not another sound in the house.

I got up and turned on the kitchen TV. The warming buzz followed me back to my chair. A moment later the screen flashed into life and my father's face scowled at me. His hoarse voice filled the kitchen.

It was his most famous speech. The Challenge to Democracy. "A man is born, he works and he dies. Then there is nothing. . . ."

I got up again and switched channels. I'd heard that speech before. A rerun of *Star Trek* was on Channel 11. I settled into that one. Monsters on other worlds were much more palatable than the monsters on this one. Mr. Spock did his number. He never cracked a smile.

I finished the sandwich and walked out of the kitchen, leaving the set on. The noise trailed me through the house. I peeked out the windows before going upstairs to my room. The reporters were still there.

I got out of my suit and into a pair of jeans and a sweat shirt. I changed the black leather shoes for a pair of sneakers. Then I went into the bathroom and rubbed all the gook out of my hair. I looked into the mirror. My face stared back at me critically.

Not bad. No pimples.

I nodded to my reflection and went downstairs. The door to my father's study was open. I stood there for a moment and then went into the room.

Already there was something musty about it. As if suddenly it were yesterday's room. You could feel somehow that it was no longer his room.

I walked over and looked down at the desk. It was covered with papers and reports. Several ashtrays still held the butts of cigars, and the wastebasket was full. Idly, I went behind the desk and sat in the oversize leather chair. It was still shaped by my father's big ass, and I sank right into it. I pulled myself forward and began looking through some of the papers.

Most of them were reports from various locals around the country. Dues collections, arrears, contract notices. All dull stuff. I wondered why my father had wasted his time going through each and every one of them with all the other things he had to do.

Once I had asked. Now I remembered his reply. "You can't run a big business, son, without knowing your finances every minute. And don't you forget, this union is one of the biggest in the country. Our pension fund alone has a surplus of almost two hundred million dollars, and we have investments in everything from government bonds to Las Vegas."

"Then you're no different than any of the companies you fight," I said. "All you care about is profits."

"We have different motivations, son."

"I can't see the difference," I said. "When it comes to your money, you're just as reactionary as anyone else."

My father took his heavy reading glasses off and put them on the desk. "I never knew you were interested in what we do."

"I'm not," I said quickly. "It's just that from what I see, big labor and big business are one and the same thing. Money is all that matters."

My father's piercing blue eyes searched my face. At last he spoke. "Someday, when I have time, we'll go into that. I think I'll be able to convince you that you're wrong."

But as usual when my turn came, he never had the time. Now it was too late. I put the papers back on the desk and began to open the drawers.

The center drawer was filled with more papers. So was the left-hand top drawer. But the right-hand top drawer had nothing in it. Absolutely nothing.

It didn't make sense. All the other drawers were packed to overflowing. I put my hand in the drawer and fished around. Still nothing. Then I noticed a small catch. I pressed it and the bottom of the drawer slid forward.

I looked down into the false bottom. There, blue-black, oily and deadly, was a big Colt Government Model Automatic. Slowly I picked it up. It weighed a ton in my hand. This was no toy; this was serious business. Somewhere I had read that a bullet from a Colt .45-caliber automatic makes a hole as big as a silver dollar when it comes out the other side.

I put it back in the drawer and shut it. I sat there staring at the closed drawer, and after a while I got to my feet and left the room. I took another can of beer from the fridge and went out on the back porch.

Anne was still sitting where I had left her. She waved to me. I waved back, then sat down on the swing chair. I took a sip of the beer and we sat there, each of us, just staring at each other across the fence that separated our backyards.

21

"Why did you go through my desk?"
"I don't know. It was there, that's all."
"I don't object. I was just curious."
"You're dead. It shouldn't matter to you anymore. The dead have no privacy."
"I'm not dead. I thought you were beginning to understand that."
"That's a lot of shit. Dead is dead."
"Dead is never. You're still alive."
"But you're not."
"Why did you switch to Star Trek? *Were you afraid to look at me?"*
"It was a better program."
"Why are you sitting here? I thought you were going away."
"I haven't made up my mind yet."
"You're going."
"What makes you so sure?"
"That girl over there. I haven't finished with her yet."
"You haven't changed, have you?"
"Why should I? You're still alive."

The beer can was empty. I got to my feet and threw it into the plastic garbage pail near the kitchen door. I pulled open the door and started to go back into the house. I looked back at her.

She hadn't moved. The smoke from her cigarette was curling up around her face, and her eyes were watching me. She had to be stoned by this time. Then I saw her nod and rise slowly to her feet. I watched her disappear behind the screen door and heard the click of its latch. The sound seemed to hang there until I closed the door behind me. I went upstairs to my room, threw myself on the bed and almost instantly fell asleep.

The hum of voices rising through the floor woke me up. I opened my eyes. The afternoon sun had moved away from the windows. I stared up at the ceiling, listening to the drone of voices beneath me.

22

It was familiar and oddly comforting. There had been so many nights when I had fallen asleep just like this with the sounds of muted conversation in my ears. My bedroom was just over my father's study.

It was familiar, but there was something different about it this time, something missing. It took a moment before I realized what it was: his voice. Somehow I had always been able to hear it above all the others.

I got out of bed and went downstairs. The study door was closed; the voices filtered through the wood. I opened it and looked in. The room was suddenly silent.

D.J. was in the chair behind the desk, with Moses standing beside him as he used to stand with my father. Jack was seated at the side of the desk on D.J.'s right, and three other men, their backs to me, were sitting in front of the desk. They turned and looked at me silently. I didn't know them.

"My brother, Jonathan," D.J. said. It was more an explanation than an introduction.

The strangers nodded cautiously, their eyes guarded.

D.J. didn't bother to introduce them. "I didn't know you were home."

"I came right from the funeral parlor." I stayed in the open doorway. "Where's my mother?"

"The doctor gave her a pill and sent her to bed. She's had a rough day."

I nodded.

"I thought we'd come in here. There were some things to straighten out before I went home. I'm booked on an eight-o'clock flight, and we have an executive-council meeting first thing in the morning."

I stepped into the room. "Getting it together?"

Dan looked at me. "What do you mean?"

"Carving up the world and all that." I walked over to the desk and looked down at it. All the papers I had seen in the drawers were now spread across the desk top. The gun wasn't there. I wondered if they had found it.

"The work doesn't stop just because . . ." D.J.'s voice trailed off.

I finished it for him. "The King is dead. Long live the King."

D.J. flushed. Moses' voice was gentle. "Jonathan, we really have a great deal of work to do."

I looked at him. There was a strain in his eyes I had never seen before. An uncertainty. I looked around at the others. Suddenly I knew what it was. The foundation had gone and they were afraid that the house might crumble.

I felt sorry for them. They were on their own now. My father wasn't around to tell them what to do.

"I'll get out of your way." I looked down at my brother. "Don't worry," I said. "It will come out all right."

He didn't answer.

I held out my hand. "Good luck."

He looked at my hand, then up at me. His voice was husky as he took it, and there was something very close to tears behind his eyes. "Thank you, Jonathan." He blinked rapidly. "Thank you."

"You'll do okay."

"I hope so," he said. "But it won't be easy. Things won't be the same."

"They never are," I said, and left the room. I closed the door behind me and leaned against it for a moment. The voices began again. I closed my eyes, searching for my father's voice. But it wasn't there.

D.J. had loved him. I hadn't. Why? Why was it different for the two of us? We were both his sons. What had D.J. seen in him that I hadn't?

I went through the hall to the kitchen. Mamie was in there fussing with her pots and pans, muttering to herself. "What time is dinner?" I asked.

"I doan know," she answered. "I doan know nothin' 'bout this house no more. Ever'thing's topsy-turvy. Your brother doan want dinner an' your mother upstairs cryin' her eyes out."

"I thought the doctor gave her a pill to sleep."

"Maybe he did. But it ain't workin', that's all I know." She dipped a ladle into a pot and held it steaming in front of me. "Taste it," she commanded. "But blow on it fust. It's hot."

I blew and tasted. Good beef stew. "Needs more salt."

She laughed and took the ladle away. "I might've expected

it. Just like your pappy. That's what he always used to say."

I stared at her. "Did you like my father?"

She put the ladle down on the sink and turned to me. "That's the stupidest question I ever heard, Jonathan. I adored your pappy. He was the greatest man who ever lived."

"Why do you say that?"

"Because that's the truth, that's why. You ask anyone back home. They all tell you the same thing. He treated niggers like people before they became blacks." She went back to the stove and took the cover off the pot and looked inside. "More salt, you say?"

"Yes," I said, and went out the door. I went upstairs and stood outside my mother's door.

Mamie was wrong.

There was not a sound.

Jack Haney came into the kitchen, where I was having dinner alone. "I'll join you for a cup of coffee," he said, pulling up a chair.

"Have some stew," I said. "There's enough here to feed an army."

"No, thanks," he answered as Mamie put the coffee in front of him. "We're grabbing a bite on the plane."

I watched him raise the coffee cup to his mouth. "You're going down to Washington?"

He nodded. "Dan wants me with him at the executive meeting tomorrow. There could be some legal questions."

Suddenly it was no longer D.J., not even Daniel, Junior—it was Dan.

"Any problems?"

"I don't think so," he said. "Your father had it all pretty well worked out."

"Then what's D.J. worried about?"

"There's a lot of old-timers around who might resent having a young man like him take over."

"Why should they? They knew about it all the time."

"True enough. But while your father was alive they

wouldn't stand up to him. Now it's another story. What they don't understand is that for the first time they're getting someone who is trained for the job and doesn't have to learn it as he goes along and that it doesn't really matter whether he ever worked in the field or organized or walked a picket line. Running a union is much like running a big business. It needs trained men. That's why the corporations compete for the top men in colleges and universities. Your father always thought that was what we should do. That's why he pushed Dan through all those schools."

I knew what he meant. He had been after me to do the same thing. First Harvard Law, then the Business School. He had had it all figured out. Everything except that I wasn't about to be pushed. I wiped up the last bit of gravy on my plate with a piece of bread.

Mamie stood over my empty plate. "More?"

I shook my head.

She picked up the plate. "'Nough salt?"

"Perfect."

She laughed and put the coffee down in front of me. "Jus' like your pappy. Fust complainin' there's not enough salt, then lovin' it 'thout my having to add any."

I looked at Jack. "Exactly what's happening tomorrow?"

"The executive committee is supposed to appoint Dan acting president until the next general election. That's nine months away, next spring. By then we expect to have everything under control."

I nodded. If my father had planned it, it would work. Father's plans always worked.

Jack finished his coffee and got to his feet. "Would you explain to your mother why I left and tell her that I'll call her in the morning?

I looked up at him. "Okay."

"Thanks," he said, starting for the door. A few minutes later I heard a car door slam out in the driveway. I went over to the window and looked out. The big black Cadillac limousine was just moving off. I watched until its red lights turned into the street. Then I went upstairs and stood outside my mother's door. There was still nothing but silence.

26

I turned the doorknob softly and looked into the room. In the fading light of the day, I could make out her outline on the bed. Quietly I walked into the room and looked down at her.

There was something pale and helpless about her asleep that I had never seen in her awake. Gently I straightened the sheet around her. She didn't move.

I tiptoed out of the room and went down the hall. I pulled my knapsack out of the closet and began to pack. I was finished in ten minutes. There wasn't very much I had to take.

I awoke one minute before the alarm went off. I reached out and turned it off. No point in waking the whole house. I dressed quickly and went downstairs.

The halls were dark, but the kitchen, facing east, caught the first morning light. I turned the switch on the percolator. As usual, Mamie had everything ready.

My father had been an early riser. He would come downstairs alone in the morning and sit and drink coffee until the rest of the house was awake. Those were his thinking hours, he used to say. The alone time. And whatever his problem was, big or little, by the time the rest of the house was awake he had thought it through until it was no longer a problem, but just a task to be done.

I went back to my room and took down the backpack. The study door was open, and on an impulse I went into the room and pulled open the drawer.

The pistol was still there. They had missed the false bottom. I took it out and looked at it. It was well oiled and held a full clip. It still didn't make sense. Guns were for frightened people, and my father hadn't known the meaning of fear.

I pulled open a flap of the pack and shoved the gun inside between my underwear and my shirts. I pushed the drawer shut with my knee. The coffee should be about ready by now.

"Jonathan." My mother was standing in the doorway. "What are you doing?"

"Nothing." The classic answer of a child whose parents

27

have caught him with his hand in the cookie jar. I wondered how long she had been standing there.

She came into the study. "I can still smell his cigars," she said, almost to herself.

"Airwick'll get rid of it, if you can believe the commercials," I said.

She turned to me. "Will it be that easy?"

I took a long moment. "No. Not until they make one that can air out the inside of your head."

She noticed the pack. "You're leaving, so soon?"

"There's nothing to hang around for," I said. "And only seven weeks left of the summer."

"Can't you wait a little while?" she asked. "There's so much we have to talk about."

"Like what?"

"School. What college you want to go to, what you're going to do with your life."

I laughed. "Small choice. My draft board will tell me."

"Your father says . . ." She corrected herself. "Your father said that you wouldn't be drafted."

"Sure. He had it fixed. Like he did with everything else."

"Isn't it time you stopped fighting him, Jonathan? He's dead now and there's nothing he can do." Her voice broke.

"What about you?" I asked. "You don't believe that any more than I do. He provided for everything. Even death."

She still didn't speak, but just stood there with the tears running silently down her cheeks. I walked over to her and awkwardly put my arms around her shoulders. She buried her face against my chest. "Jonathan, Jonathan."

"Take it easy, Mother," I said, stroking her hair. "It's over."

"I feel so guilty." Her voice was muffled against my shirt. "I never loved him. I worshiped him, but I never loved him. Can you understand that?"

"Then why did you marry him?" I asked.

"Because of you."

"Me? I wasn't born yet."

"I was seventeen and pregnant," she whispered.

"Even in those days you could have done something about it," I said.

28

She slipped out of my arms. "Give me a cigarette."

I lit the cigarette for her. "Did you turn on the coffee?" she asked.

I nodded and followed her into the kitchen. She filled two mugs and we sat down at the table.

"You didn't answer my question. You didn't have to marry him."

"He wouldn't hear of it. He wanted a son, he said."

"Why? He already had one."

"Dan was not enough for him. He knew it, and sometimes I think even Dan knew it. That's why he always tried so hard to please his father. But Dan was soft, and your father was not." Even Mother no longer called him D.J. "Your father got what he wanted. Whether you like it or not, you're exactly like him."

I got to my feet and brought the percolator over to the table. "More coffee?"

She shook her head. I refilled my cup. "You drink too much coffee," she said.

I laughed. "Think it will stunt my growth?" I stood just over six feet. Even she had to smile. "You know, Mother, you're a very pretty lady."

She shook her head. "I don't feel like one just now."

"Give yourself time," I said. "You will."

She hesitated a moment; then her eyes met mine. "You know about Jack and me?"

I nodded.

"I thought you did," she said. "But you never said anything."

"Not my place."

"Now he wants to get married," she said. "But I don't know."

"You don't have to rush," I said. "Nobody's pressing this time."

A shade of wonder came into her eyes. "You looked just like your father when you said that."

I laughed. "I couldn't have. If I were my father I couldn't understand why you wouldn't join me on the funeral pyre."

"That's horrible," she said.

"I always get horrible when I'm hungry," I said. "Is that like him too?"

"Exactly," she said, getting to her feet. "And I'm going to deal with you exactly as I did with him. I'm going to make you the biggest breakfast you ever ate."

"That's enough," I said. "I won't have to eat for a week now."

She smiled. "That was the idea." She put the empty plates in the sink and refilled the coffee cups. "Do you know where you're going?"

I shook my head. "Not really. South first, then maybe west. But it all depends which way the traffic is going."

"You will be careful?"

I nodded.

"There are all kinds of people on the road."

"I'll be okay."

"Will you write and let me know how you are?"

"Sure. But don't worry."

"I will," she said. "If there's any trouble, you'll call me?"

"Collect."

"Collect." She smiled. "That makes me feel better."

I glanced at the kitchen clock. It was a quarter to seven. "I'd better get going."

She looked up at me as I got up. "I'm too young. I've always been too young."

"What do you mean?"

"First I was too young to be a bride, then too young to be a mother. Now I'm too young to be a widow and alone."

"Everybody has to grow up sometime," I said. "Maybe this is your time."

"That's your father speaking. He had that same cold, clinical way of separating himself from his feelings." A strange look came over her face. "Are you really my son, Jonathan? Or are you just an extension of him that he implanted in me, as he said?"

"I'm me. I'm your son. And his. Nothing else."

"Do you love me?"

I was silent for a moment. Then I took her hand and kissed it. "Yes, Mother."

"Do you have enough money?"

I laughed. I had almost one hundred dollars. At ten dollars a week, I had no sweat. "Yes, Mother."

I slung the backpack over my shoulders and went down the driveway. When I hit the still-sleeping street, I looked back. Mother was standing in the doorway. She waved to me. I waved back and went down the street.

The morning already held the promise of the day's heat. The chippies were all over the lawn grabbing the early worms, and their chatter was mixed with the occasional trill of a robin. The air smelled green. U.S. 1 was a mile and a half away, just the other side of the bridge over Schuylkill Creek.

The Dairihome Milk truck turned the corner just as I did. Pete stopped the truck when he saw me. "Jonathan!"

I turned and waited while he climbed down. He had a container of orange juice in one hand, a can of beer in the other. "Traveler's choice," he said.

I took the beer. It was a good morning for it. Already the heat was reaching into me. He put the O.J. back into the truck and took another can of beer for himself. We pulled the tabs at the same time, and the sound of their popping was the only one on the street.

He took a deep draft, then wiped his mouth with the back of his hand. "Sorry for your trouble," he said. Pete was Irish.

I nodded.

"Where you off to?"

"Don't exactly know. Just off."

He nodded. "Good thing to get away. Your mother all right?"

"Fine," I answered. "She's a tough lady."

He studied me for a moment while he thought that over. Pete had known us for a long time. Fifteen years. Finally he answered. "Yes."

I finished the beer and crumpled the can. He took it from my hand. "How long will you be gone?"

"Seven weeks."

"Shit!" He grinned. "That's eighty-four quarts. There goes my milk bonus."

I laughed. "Leave the two quarts anyway. My mother will never notice."

"She might not. But I'll bet that Mamie has a note in the bottle before I get there." He went back into the truck. He fished around for a moment, then came out with a six-pack. "Better take this with you. It's gonna be a hot day."

"Thanks."

He looked at me. "We're gonna miss your father." He touched the union button on his white coveralls. "He made this mean a lot. I only hope your brother does half as well."

"He'll do better than that," I said.

Again he looked at me for a moment. "We'll see. But he's not your father."

"Who is?"

"You are," he said.

I stared at him. "But I'm not old enough."

"Someday you will be," he said. "And we'll be waiting."

He put the truck into Drive, and I watched it go out of sight around the corner. Then I crossed the street.

"Now do you believe me?"

"No. That's what you wanted people to think. So you put the idea in their heads."

"Why would I do a thing like that?"

"Because you're a prick. And because you were jealous of D.J. You know he'll turn out better than you ever were."

"Suddenly you love your brother."

"No way. But I can see what he is. He cares."

"I cared."

"When? How many years ago? Before I was born, before you fell in love with power and money?"

"You still won't allow yourself to understand."

"I understand. Too well."

"You only think you do. But you'll find out. In time."

"Go away. You're just as boring dead as alive."

32

"I'm alive just as long as you and your children will be alive. I'm in your genes, your cells, your mind. Give yourself the time. You'll remember."

"Remember what?"

"Me."

"I don't want to remember you."

"You will. In a thousand different ways. You can't help it."

"But not just now, Father. It's vacation time."

She was sitting on the concrete abutment at the entrance to the bridge, a backpack beside her, her legs hanging over the side facing the river. She was staring down into the water, the gray pungent smoke curling like a cloud from her lips. "Good morning, Jonathan," she said, without turning around.

I stopped but did not answer.

"I was waiting for you," she said, still without turning around. "Don't be angry with me."

"I'm not angry," I said.

She swung her feet around to face me. She smiled. "Then you'll take me with you?"

I knew that look in her eyes. "You're stoned."

"Just a little." She held the joint toward me. "Want a drag? This is real good shit."

"No, thanks," I said. "U.S. Number One is no road to stand out in the middle of with your head in the clouds."

"You are angry with me." There was hurt in her voice.

"I said I wasn't."

"But you didn't mean it."

"I meant it."

"Then why can't I come with you?"

"Because I want to be alone. Don't you understand that?"

"I won't bother you. I'll keep out of your way."

"Go home," I said. "It won't work." I started up the steps to the bridge.

"Then why did you tell me to meet you here?" She called after me.

I turned halfway up the steps and looked down at her. "When did I do that?"

"Yesterday afternoon," she said, a strange intensity shining through clouds in her eyes. "Just after you finished talking with your father."

"My father's dead," I said.

"I know that."

"Then how could I have been talking with him? I think the shit you're smoking has made you cuckoo."

"I saw you talking to him," she said stubbornly. "Then you got up and went to the screen door and turned to look at me. I heard you say, 'Meet me at the bridge in the morning.' I nodded to you and went inside."

I was silent.

"Your voice sounded exactly like your father's," she said.

I looked at her. The heat of the morning had already drawn fine beads of sweat across her face, making it shine in the bright sunlight. I could see the tracings of moisture gathering in the cleft of her blouse between her breasts and the damp shadows gathering under her arms. "Did I say anything else?"

"Yes. But it was fuzzy. I didn't quite get it. It was something like 'I'm not finished with you yet.' All I know is that it made me very horny. I went upstairs, took off all my clothes and lay on the bed naked and without doing anything to myself, just came and came until I was exhausted."

I held out my hand. "Give me the joint."

Anne placed it in my fingers. Her touch was hot and dry. I flipped it out into the river. "Got any more shit?"

She dug into her pack and came out with the Bulldog pouch. I took it. "That's it?"

She nodded.

I threw it into the river. She turned to watch it float a moment on the surface of the water, then sink slowly as it moved with the current under the bridge. "You just can't get shit like that anymore," she said sorrowfully. "Why did you do that?"

"I'm not lookin' to get busted and spend the next seven weeks in some tank-town jail."

Suddenly her eyes began to fill with tears. "Touch me," she said.

I took her hand and she guided me to her breast. She closed

34

her eyes, squeezing the tears from the corners of them. "God, that feels good," she whispered.

Anne came down from the abutment. We went down around the corner and under the bridge. We made it there, with the sound of the trucks roaring against the pavement over our heads drowning her moaning cries. Afterward she was very quiet and lay there looking up at me as I pulled my jeans up around my hips and snapped the buttons. She reached over for her pack, pulled out some Kleenex and stuffed it into her cunt. Then she got up and pulled up her own jeans.

"It feels so good in there, I don't want to lose any of it," she said. "Better than anything I can do in my head."

I didn't answer.

She reached for my hand. "Jonathan. Do you think maybe I'm in love with you?"

I looked into her eyes. There was a bright and shining contentment in them. "No," I said shortly. "You're not in love with me. You're in love with my father."

U.S. 1 was already hot and dusty, and a gray-blue pall of exhaust fumes hung heavy in the air over the road. We waited for a break in the traffic, then made it to the southbound side. We stood there watching the traffic roar by.

She pushed long, damp hair back from her face. "It's got to be over eighty already."

I nodded.

"Maybe we can find some shade and cool off a bit first?"

I led her over to a clump of trees and we plunked ourselves down on the ground under them. I broke out the six-pack Pete had given me. "This will help."

She took a long swallow. "Grass dehydrates me. So does fucking."

I laughed. "You'll have to pace yourself."

She smiled at me. I pulled at my beer and looked out at the road. The early trucks had already gone, and the highway was filled with commuter traffic to New York. The big cars, air-conditioned against the heat and smell, had their windows rolled up tight. The little cars had their windows wide open, their occupants hoping to escape the heat with the speed, although in the morning crush it seemed a futile thought.

"Where are we heading?" she asked.

"West Virginia," I said, without thinking.

"Why West Virginia?"

"Good a place as any," I said. "Besides, I've never been there."

I didn't tell her that that was where my father had come from. Near a town named Fitchville, which I had once found on an A.A.A. map. I wondered what it was like, because he never spoke about it at all. Now, suddenly, I knew I had to go there, even though I hadn't realized it when I left the house this morning.

I finished off my beer in a long swallow and got to my feet. I slung the pack behind my shoulders and looked down at her. "Ready?"

She reached into her pack and pulled out a floppy-brimmed felt hat, which she stuck on her head. "How does it look?"

"Beautiful."

She got to her feet. "Let's go."

An hour later we were still hanging our thumbs on the doors of the cars going by. By now she was sitting on her pack, her face flushed and warm. I lit a cigarette and gave it to her.

"It's not as easy as it looks in the movies," she said.

I grinned as I lit another cigarette for myself. "It never is."

"I've got to pee," she said.

"Over there." I gestured to the clump of trees.

She looked at me questioningly.

"Might as well get used to it," I said.

She fished some Kleenex from her pack and disappeared behind the trees. I turned to watch the road. Traffic was lighter now that the morning rush was over. Fewer passenger cars, more trucks. The road began to shimmer in the heat haze.

I heard her come up behind me as I squinted into the sun.

A giant Fruehauf trailer crested the hill and came down the hill toward us. Automatically I raised my hand in the familiar signal. Then I heard the hiss of its powerful air brakes as it slowly came to a stop, its giant shadow shielding us from the sun.

I watched the door open silently outward from the cab three feet off the ground. The voice came from a man I could not see. "You kids want a ride into town?"

I felt her restraining hand on my arm, but the voice I heard was not her voice. *"Daniel. Paw tol' us to walk."*

I shook her hand angrily off my arm. "We suah do, mistuh," I said.

Book One

Another
Day

Chapter 1

THE SMALL field on the side of the hill was bare except for a few sparse clumps of bushes that resisted the drought and the heat of summer. The earth was beginning to cool with the first fading of the afternoon sun when the rabbit cautiously stuck his nose out of the small hole behind one of the bushes and sniffed at the still air. A second later he emerged on the ground. With tiny jerking movements he turned his head. He saw nothing. The world was safe.

Still he moved cautiously. Ears back, flat against his head, he kept his body close to the ground so that his white-flecked sandy-gray fur did not stand out against the bare, sun-bleached earth. In short quick hops he jumped from bush to bush, pausing at each to reconnoiter, before moving down the hill toward the small green wooded forest near the banks of the almost dried-out brook.

He covered the last hundred yards in an extraordinary burst of speed, coming to a stop in the dark shadows of the small trees, his heart pounding with the fear of his exposure. But the hunger had been too great. And the smell of the fresh wild fennel growing near the roots of the acacias had finally overwhelmed his caution.

But now his sense of caution had returned. He kept very low to the ground, his fur blending into the shadows. The bouquet of the fennel was stronger now, but since it was within reach, he was able to contain his hunger until he was sure of safety. He waited until the wild pounding of his heart returned to normal, then moved very slowly into the acacias.

He found the cluster of fennel a few yards from the slowly trickling brook. Quickly he began to scratch at the earth to loosen the juicier, more tender shoots. A moment later he had a long stalk in his front paws and sat up on his haunches, holding it front of his nose. Tentatively, almost delicately, he nibbled at the shoot. It was the most delicious thing he had ever tasted. It was also the last. For just at that moment, he saw the boy standing almost fifteen yards away. Their eyes met for a brief second; then, before he could react to the explosion of fear within him, the .22 bullet ripped into the cortex at the base of his neck, shattering his spine. He flipped backward into the air, dead before he touched the ground.

Daniel Boone Huggins let the echo of the gunshot and the faint wisp of smoke from the rifle fade before moving forward to pick up the dead rabbit. He lifted it by the ears. Already the eyes were glazed and empty. Carefully he tied it to a leather loop around his waist; then he knelt carefully and studied the creature's tracks.

Quickly he grabbed a handful of the fennel shoots and began to retrace the rabbit's trail. A few minutes later he was in the field on the side of the hill opposite the clump of bushes from which the rabbit had come. He found the small hole in the ground. Carefully, soundlessly, he loosened the thong and placed the rabbit in front of the hole with the fennel shoots around him.

A moment later he was on his haunches about twenty yards away, waiting. It would be only a question of time before the smell of the fennel and the rabbit would bring his mate up from the ground to investigate.

Jeb Stuart Huggins sat on the rickety wooden front steps of his house, his jug of evening squeezin's beside him, watching his eldest son come toward him. "Any luck?" His voice was rusty from lack of use.

"Two rabbits," Daniel answered.

"Let's see 'em," his father commanded.

Daniel loosened the thong around his waist and held them out to his father. The older man hefted them for a moment, then returned them.

"A mite scrawny," he said. "Fittin' only for stew."

"The drought ain't been much good for the game either," Daniel said defensively.

"I'm not complainin'," his father said. "We take what the Good Lord sees fittin' to give us."

Daniel nodded. It would be the first meat they would have had in more than a week.

"Take it roun' to your maw an' tell her to make it ready fer the pot."

Daniel nodded and started to walk away.

"How many bullets did you use?" his father asked.

Daniel stopped. "Two."

Jeb nodded approvingly. "Don't fergit to clean the gun real good, now."

"I won't, Paw."

Jeb watched his son walk around the corner of the house. Daniel was getting to be a big boy now. Almost fourteen and as tall as he was, and beginning to swell out his britches. It was time to move him out of the room he shared with his brother and sisters. It wouldn't do at all to have the young ones seeing things like that. It put wrong thoughts in their heads, and he had enough trouble with Molly Ann as it was.

Molly Ann was his oldest child, a little more than a year older than Daniel and a full woman already, bleeding for more than two years now. Time to be thinking of getting her married. But there were no young men around. All the young ones had gone down from the hills to work in the glass and textile mills in town.

He sighed and picked up the jug and took a sip. The white-hot liquor burned its way into his stomach and warmed him. Problems; there were always problems with seven children. And there would have been ten if three hadn't been stillborn. The Good Lord had known what he was doing. He'd figured out that Jeb Stuart Huggins would have a hard enough job providing for those he had. But still, it wasn't fair. Especially since Maw had crossed her legs and closed him out. No more children. It wasn't easy on a man. Especially a man like himself who was used to getting it. And now with Molly Ann walking around with those ripe young titties and chunky fat ass, he was getting all kinds of sinful thoughts. He took another sip of the squeezin's and wondered when the circuit preacher would come by. A good old-fashioned revival meeting would do a lot to dispel the sinful sacrilegious notions the Devil was planting in his mind. He sighed again. It wasn't easy being a family man in these hard times.

Marylou Huggins stared into the fire-blackened iron pot sitting on the ancient wood-burning stove. The water was simmering and bubbling, and there were great yellow fat blobs swelling and breaking on its surface. With a long-handled fork she rescued the square of fatback from its watery grave. She studied it, dripping from the edge of the fork. With satisfaction she placed it on a plate. It should be good for at least two more cookings before it was used up. Quickly she dumped a heap of scrubbed potatoes, turnips and greens into the boiling stock and began stirring. She sensed rather than heard Daniel come through the kitchen door. She did not turn around.

"Maw." As always, she felt a shock at the boy's deepening voice. It seemed only yesterday that he had been a baby.

"Yes, Dan'l."

"I got me two rabbits, Maw. Paw says fer you to fix 'em fer the pot."

She turned to face him. She was only thirty-four, but she was thin and gaunt, and the lines on her face made her seem much older. She took the rabbits from his outstretched hand. "Make a nice change from squir'ls," she said.

"But we ain't had no squir'ls for more'n a month," he protested.

Her lined face relaxed into a smile. Daniel was altogether too serious for a boy his age. "I was jes' funnin', son."

His eyes lightened. "Yes, Maw."

"Go tell Molly Ann to come an' he'p me clean the rabbits. You'll find her out back mindin' the kids."

"Yes, Maw." He hesitated a moment, sniffing the air. "That suah smells good."

" 'Tain't nothin' but fatback and greens," she said. "You hungry?"

He nodded.

She took a piece of hard bread from the board next to the stove and wiped it with the salt pork so that all its grease was absorbed, then handed it to him.

He took a massive bite, chewed and swallowed. "That is good. Thank you, Maw."

She smiled. "Now go git your sister."

She watched him leave, then turned and took out the cleaning knife and began to hone it gently against the sharpening stone.

Daniel walked slowly toward the back of the house. He waited a moment before turning the corner so that he could finish his piece of bread. He didn't want the other kids to see him or they would all start hollering for some of it. When he had swallowed the last bite, he went around the corner.

The blast of noise hit him as two of the kids charged past him toward the open field. Mase, the baby, sixteen months, began squalling from his sling, which hung suspended from the bare old pine tree near the woodpile. Molly Ann straightened up, the kindling hatchet gleaming in her hand. "Richard, Jane, you come back heah this minute. If Paw hears you, you'll get a tannin' fer sure."

The children ignored her warning. Molly Ann turned to Rachel, her ten-year-old sister, who was sitting on a block of wood, looking at a picture book. "Rachel, you go git 'em and bring 'em back here."

Rachel, the studious one of the family, got to her feet, after marking the place in her book, and ran after the two younger children, who were now lost in the tall grass in the field.

Molly Ann pushed her long brown hair back from her flushed face, then picked up a twig from the cut kindling and pushed it into the baby's mouth. Immediately Mase was quiet, gumming the small piece of wood.

"These kids'll drive me crazy," Molly Ann said. She stared at her brother. "Where at you been all day?"

"Huntin'."

"Git anythin'?"

"Two rabbits. Maw says fer you to come an' he'p her clean 'em."

She suddenly became aware that he was staring at the top of her dress. She had opened the top buttons across her breasts so that she could swing the kindling hatchet, and she was almost completely exposed. "What you starin' at?" she said, although she made no move to cover herself up.

"Nothin'." He looked away guiltily, feeling the flush creep up into his face.

"You were starin' at my titties," she said accusingly. She began to fasten the buttons. "I could tell from the look on your face."

"I was not," he muttered, still looking at the ground.

"You was too." She finished with her buttons and came toward him. "You'll have to finish the kindlin' if'n I go to he'p Maw."

"All right." He still did not meet her gaze.

"Your pants is all swole," she said.

Daniel felt his face grow even hotter. He couldn't answer.

She laughed. "You're jes' like Paw."

Now he looked at her. "What do you mean?"

She laughed again. "I was down at the brook this afternoon washin' myself when I saw Paw outta the corner of my eye watchin' me from behin' a tree."

He couldn't keep the wonder out of his voice. "Did he know you saw him?"

"No." She shook her head. "I made believe I didn't know he was there, but I kep' watchin' outta the corner o' my eye. He was jackin' hisself off jes' like you do. On'y he's bigger. His pole looked like it was a yard long."

He stared at her, open-mouthed. "Sweet Jesus!"

"Don' you go blasphemin'!" she said sharply.

He didn't answer.

"Maw was right," she said. "All you men are alike. You're on'y thinkin' o' one thing. It's the Devil in you, Maw says."

46

Rachel came back, followed by the two smaller children. "You git them two kids cleaned up," Molly Ann commanded. "Then go find Alice out in the vegetable garden an' tell 'em to come in an' finish their lessons."

Obediently, the children went off to the house. Molly Ann reached up and took Mase from his sling. He gurgled happily, pieces of bark sticking to his lips. Molly Ann brushed them off with her hand, then wiped her hand on her skirt.

"Better git that wood cut," she warned. "Mr. Fitch is comin' this evenin' and Maw wants a nice fire goin'. Paw is fixin' to sell him some 'shine."

Daniel watched his sister go to the house, holding the baby easily in one arm, her body full and strong under the cotton dress, then turned to the woodpile and picked up the axe.

After a moment there was nothing but the sound of the striking blade and crack of the splitting wooden logs.

Chapter 2

THEY WERE just about to sit down at the table when they heard the sound of creaking wagon wheels in the front yard. Jeb held up a hand. "Set another place at the table, Maw," he said, getting to his feet and going to the door.

He was already down the front steps and in the yard when the mule came to a halt. "Evenin', Mr. Fitch," he called. "You're jest in time to jine us fer supper."

"Evenin', Jeb," Mr. Fitch replied. "Don't want to bother you folks none."

"No bother 'tall. Miz Huggins made a fine rabbit stew. 'Twould be a shame fer you to miss it."

"Rabbit stew," Fitch said thoughtfully. He had expected fatback and greens. "I do favor a good rabbit stew." He climbed down from the wagon, breathing heavily. Mr. Fitch was extremely large around the middle. "Be with you jes' as soon as I water an' feed my mule."

"Dan'l'll take care o' that fer you," Jeb said. He called to his son, who came out of the house. "You know Mr. Fitch here."

Daniel nodded. "Evenin', Mr. Fitch."

The big man smiled. "Evenin', Dan'l."

"Take care o' Mr. Fitch's mule, son."

"You'll find the feed bag in the back of the wagon," Mr. Fitch said. "Don't let him drink too much water, though. It makes him fart somethin' awful, an' I still got to ride twenty miles behind 'im tonight."

Jeb picked up the jug of evening squeezin's. "You jes' have a taste o' this, Mr. Fitch. It'll wash away some of the travel dust from yer mouth."

"Why, that's right kind of you, Jeb," Fitch said. He wiped the rim of the jug with his hand and took a long pull. He smacked his lips and smiled as he lowered the jug. "Looks lak you don't put much water in this mule either, Jeb."

Ten minutes later they were seated around the table, and Marylou placed the big iron pot of stew in front of her husband. Right behind her came Molly Ann with a platter heaped with freshly baked hot corn bread.

Jeb clasped his hands before him and looked down. They all followed suit. "We ask Thy blessin's, Lord, on this table, on this house, on those who dwell in it and on our guest, Mr. Fitch. And for Thy bounty and the food we are about to receive, we thank Thee, Lord. Amen."

The chorus of "Amen's" rose from the table, and the children looked up hungrily. Quickly Jeb spooned Mr. Fitch's plate full, then his own. He nodded to Marylou. She took the spoon and began to fill the children's plates. By the time she got to her own there wasn't much meat left, but she didn't care. She never ate much anyway.

Besides, it just made her feel good knowing that Mr. Fitch would be telling all the neighbors that the Hugginses had served him rabbit stew for supper and that they didn't eat fatback and greens all the time the way some of the others did.

They ate silently, quickly, with no conversation, wiping their plates clean of even the last drop of gravy with the smoking-hot corn bread.

Mr. Fitch pushed his chair away from the table and patted his stomach contentedly. "That's the best rabbit stew I ever tasted, Miz Huggins."

Marylou blushed. "Thank you, Mr. Fitch."

The big man picked at his teeth. Ceremoniously, he took

out his pocket watch and looked at it. "It's nigh on to six thirty, Jeb," he said. "Shall we go outside an' git down to business?"

Jeb nodded. He rose from the table. "Come, Dan'l."

Daniel followed the older men down the steps into the yard. His father led the way around the back of the house and up the small hill to the still. They walked single file on the narrow path.

"How much you got fer me, Jeb?" Mr. Fitch asked.

" 'Bout twenty gallons. Right prime 'shine."

Mr. Fitch was silent until they came to the still. "That's not very much."

"The drought is burnin' up all the corn, Mr. Fitch," Jeb explained apologetically.

"Scarcely wu'th my haulin' all the way up here." This was no longer Mr. Fitch the nice man, who had sat down to the dinner table; this was Mr. Fitch the trader, who kept half the sharecroppers in the valley in his debt with the credit he ran for them at his general store and the prices he paid them for their moonshine and whatever else they had to sell.

The big copper kettles and tubing were camouflaged by leafy, interlocking branches. To one side lay a pile of cut wood.

"Git out a jug, Dan'l," his father commanded.

Daniel began to lift wood from the pile. A moment later the brown clay jugs lay uncovered. Jeb picked one up and pulled the cork with his teeth.

"Jes' you smell the 'shine, Mr. Fitch," he said.

Fitch took the jug and sniffed at it.

"Taste it," Jeb urged.

The big man tilted the jug. He took a swallow.

"That's quality, Mr. Fitch," Jeb said. "Right smart bead. No carbides, no lye. Smooth an' natural. You can give it to a baby."

"Not bad," Mr. Fitch admitted. He squinted. "How much you want fer it?"

Jeb didn't look at him. "I figgered at least a dollar a gallon."

Fitch didn't answer.

Jeb lost his nerve. "Six bits?"

"Four bits," Mr. Fitch said.

"Mr. Fitch, four bits for that 'shine jes' ain't right. That's what they been gettin' for quick 'shine, not the real slow, natural 'shine like this," Jeb protested.

"Business is bad," Mr. Fitch said. "People jest ain't buyin' things no more. They's a war on in Europe an' ever'thing's upset."

"Fifty cents a gallon ain't much." Jeb was almost pleading now. "At least meet me halfway, Mr. Fitch."

Mr. Fitch looked at him steadily. "How much do you owe me, Jeb?"

Jeb's eyes fell. " 'Bout four dollars, I reckon."

"Four dollars an' fifty-five cents," Mr. Fitch said.

"I guess that's 'bout right," Jeb admitted. He still did not look up.

Daniel didn't dare look at his father. He was too ashamed. It wasn't right for a man to be humbled so just because he was poor. He looked off into the fields.

"Tell you what, Jeb," Mr. Fitch said. "I'm in a good mood. A generous mood, you might say. An' you can thank Miz Huggins' fine rabbit stew fer puttin' me in it. I always say that a full stomach dulls a man's sharpness in business. I'll give you sixty cents a gallon."

Jeb looked up. "You cain't do better?"

" 'Generous,' I said. Not 'foolish.' " Mr. Fitch's voice held a tone of finality.

Jeb felt the bitter taste of defeat. Three months' work, day and night, rain and shine, tending the still, taking the 'shine off drip by drip as it slowly condensed along the tubes so that every drop was crystal clear and perfect. He forced himself to smile. "Thank you, Mr. Fitch," he said. He turned to his son. "Fetch the jugs down to Mr. Fitch's wagon."

Daniel nodded. He didn't trust himself to speak. There was an anger inside him that he had never felt before. An anger that left the inside of his stomach tied like a knot on a hangman's noose.

Jeb looked at the big man. "Come down to the house, Mr. Fitch," he said. "Miz Huggins must have the coffee ready by now."

"Don't know what the country's comin' to," Mr. Fitch said, the steaming mug of chicoried coffee in his hand. "Business the way it is, people movin' off the land because they cain't pay their rent. You don't know how lucky you are, Jeb, ownin' your land free an' clear the way you do."

Jeb nodded. "We kin thank the Good Lord fer that. But I don' know. Nine mouths to feed. With the drought an' poor crops, it ain't easy."

"Ever think of comin' down to town to work?" Mr. Fitch asked.

Jeb shook his head. "I'm not a city man. Never will be. If'n I cain't git up in the mornin' an' look out over my land, I'd rather be dead. Besides, what kin I do there? All I know is farmin'."

Marylou came into the room and touched a match to the kindling in the fireplace. "There's a chill comin' to the air."

"Miz Huggins." Fitch smiled. "You suah do know how to make a man feel good."

Marylou blushed and smiled. She looked down at the floor. "Thank you, Mr. Fitch," she said, and left the room. But she stayed near the doorway, just inside the kitchen, so that she could hear every word that was said.

Fitch took a sip of the hot coffee. "Ever think of sendin' the two oldest kids down to work?"

Jeb was surprised. "Dan'l and Molly Ann?"

Fitch nodded. "The boy's fourteen and his sister's older, if I recollect rightly."

"Fifteen."

"I'm good friends with the men who run the mills and glass factories. They're always lookin' for good young kids to work. I kin put in a word for them."

"I don' know." Jeb was doubtful. "They seem mighty young to be outta the house to me."

"They kin make four, mebbe five dollars a week. Room and board at a respectable house will cost 'em on'y a dollar and a half. That leaves five, maybe seven dollars a week they kin send home. It could go a long way to feedin' the others." Fitch looked at him. "You could even make some improvements to the house here. I understand the electric company will put in lights if you kin guarantee them five dollars a month."

"I don' like them electric lights," Jeb said. "It ain' natural. It's too bright. It ain' soft like the oil lamps." But at the same time, he wondered. His would be the first house on the mountain to have electric lights.

Daniel came into the room. "All finished, Paw."

Mr. Fitch stuck his hand in his pocket and came out with a shiny new nickel. "You're a good boy, Daniel. Here's a little somethin' fer you."

Daniel shook his head. "No, thank you, Mr. Fitch. Ain't no cause for you to do that." He hurried from the room.

"That's a good boy you have there, Jeb," Fitch said.

"Thank you, Mr. Fitch."

Fitch started for the door. "Better be on my way. Ol' mule don't see too good in the dark on these country roads."

"Still got another hour of daylight at least," Jeb said. "Be in the valley by that time. Won't be so bad."

Fitch nodded. He raised his voice, knowing full well that Marylou was just inside the kitchen door and could hear him. "Please express my appreciation to Miz Huggins for that delicious rabbit stew an' her gracious hospitality."

"I'll do that, Mr. Fitch."

Fitch went down the steps and climbed back up into his wagon. He bent over the side and spoke to Jeb still in a loud enough voice for Marylou to hear. "An' keep in mind what I said. Four, five dollars a week for each kid ain't chicken feed. Anytime you want, jes' send 'em on down to me an' I'll find a place for 'em."

Jeb nodded again. "Thank you, Mr. Fitch. Evenin', Mr. Fitch."

"Evenin', Jeb." Mr. Fitch clucked to his mule as he snapped the reins sharply. Slowly the mule began to pick his way out of the yard. Mr. Fitch began to hum to himself in satisfaction. Jeb was right. It was the best 'shine he had ever tasted. He ought to be able to get a dollar a quart for it. That was sixty-eight dollars' profit right there.

And he also had a feeling that the Huggins kids would

soon show up on his doorstep. That would mean money too. There was no reason for him to tell Jeb that the companies paid him a twenty-dollar recruiting fee for every kid he sent them.

Chapter 3

THE FLICKERING yellow light of the oil lamp cast a wavering glow over the table, and the silver coins heaped in front of Jeb seemed to turn to a dull gold. Slowly, laboriously, he counted them. After a moment, Marylou came in and sat down silently opposite him. She didn't speak until after he had finished his count.

"How much is there?"

"Seven dollars and forty-five cents."

"That's not much," she said. There was no complaint in her voice, only a sad acceptance.

"We owed him four fifty-five," Jeb said defensively. "An' prices is down. Times is bad, Mr. Fitch says. There is a war in Europe."

"I don' rightly see how a war that fur off kin be o' bother to us."

"I don't either," Jeb confessed. "But if a man like Mr. Fitch says so, I guess it's so. I reckon all we kin do is hope that Mr. President Wilson kin git things straight. He should be able to do it 'f anybody can. He's an eddicated college perfessor, y'know."

"I know," she said. "But things ain't been gittin' better

in the time he's been President. It's 1914 an' it's worse'n ever."

"Things take time," Jeb said. "Women don't have the patience or the understandin' that men have fer those things."

Marylou was silent, accepting the rebuke without comment. Sometimes she wondered why the Good Lord had given women a brain if they were not supposed to use it. But that was a thought she kept only in her own head; it was a Devil-inspired thought and not a proper one.

"Scarce enough money here to buy seed fer another plantin'," he said.

She nodded. It had always been like this. Each year they seemed to fall deeper into debt. "I need some cloth to make the children some clothes. They growin' so fast, I cain't keep up with 'em. An' soon it will be fall an' they'll need shoes fer school. It'll be too cold for 'em to go barefoot. An' besides, it don't look proper."

"I didn' have no shoes until I was goin' on sixteen," Jeb said. "An' it didn' hurt me none."

"You didn' go to school, neither," she said. "Things is different now. Kids have to be eddicated."

"I learned ever'thing I had to know from my paw," he said. "I don' see where readin' he'ps Dan'l any to be a better farmer. Now that he finish school, he ain't no better off 'n I was."

Again she was silent.

"An' goin' to school didn' he'p Molly Ann none. She ain't foun' a husband yet, an' by the time you was sixteen we was already married."

"It ain't her fault," Marylou said. "She's more'n ready to git married, on'y all the young men have gone down to the towns to work."

He looked at her. "Mr. Fitch says he can git 'em good jobs if'n we want him to."

She didn't speak. She had heard Mr. Fitch's offer, but it wasn't her place to acknowledge it.

"He says they can get mebbe four, five dollars a week."

"That's good money," she said.

He nodded. "An' mebbe Molly kin fin' herself a man down there. That girl's ripenin' so fast I cain't believe my eyes."

Marylou nodded. She saw the way Jeb's eyes followed his daughter as she moved. She knew her husband. Jeb was a good man, but he was human and he had a lot of the Devil's earthy lusts in him. She also knew that sometimes the lusts could get too much for a man. There were enough incidents in the hills around them to prove it. Many the girl was sent off to live with relatives because her paw had given in to the Devil. And it had been a long time before the preacher had come and purified them. "It mought be a good thing fer 'em," she said.

"I don't have much fer Dan'l to do 'roun' here," he said. "What with the drought an' the earth doin' so poorly. The north field's 'bout wasted."

"Rachel could he'p me with the little ones when she comes home from school," Marylou added.

He looked down at the coins on the table. "We mought even be able to git electricity up here."

She stared at his hands as he touched the money. "Mebbe we could git some chickens, a sow or two, mebbe even a cow. The little ones could sure do with some fresh milk."

"Callendar, over the hill, is willin' to let me have his other mule fer five dollars," Jeb said thoughtfully. "It would suah he'p with the plowin', an' on Sundays we could hitch 'im up an' go visitin' kinfolk."

They fell silent, separately thinking their own thoughts. After a moment, he began gathering up the coins and putting them in a soft leather pouch drawn together by thongs. "Mebbe we ought to do it," he said tentatively.

"Mebbe," she said, not meeting his eyes.

He got to his feet, and he placed the money on a top shelf high over the fireplace. He turned and looked down at her. "You kin use two dollars o' that there money fer what you need," he said.

"Thank you, Jeb," she said. It wasn't near enough, but it was better than nothing. "I think I'll have a look in on the children before I go to bed."

She went to the door. "Will you be comin' to bed soon?"

He didn't meet her eyes. "I think I'll jes' set a spell an' smoke my pipe."

"Don' be too late," she said. "'Specially since you 'n' Dan'l are plannin' to clear the west field tomorrow."

He sat down heavily and began to fill his pipe with tobacco from the jar on the table. They both knew why he was coming to bed late. This way she could pretend to be asleep and he didn't have to ask and she didn't have to refuse.

Daniel lay quietly in the bed he shared with his brother Richard. Richard slept on the inside against the wall, curled in a tight ball on top of the rough cotton sheet. From across the room, he could hear the soft sounds of his sisters' sleep. Molly Ann shared her bed with the youngest girl, Alice, and Rachel shared her bed with Jane. The baby, Mase, still slept in a crib in their parents' room.

He closed his eyes, but sleep still would not come. There was a vague discontent within him. Unformed, unshaped, the source unknown to him, but it was still there and still disturbing.

It wasn't that they were poor. He had always known that, and they were no worse off than any of the other families he knew. But somehow, today made it seem bad. Mr. Fitch was so sure and confident. And his father's hidden fear had suddenly been so plain to him. It just wasn't right.

The white mountain moon stared in the window, and Daniel turned to look at it. It had to be about nine o'clock, he reckoned, from where it hung in the sky. He heard the sound of footsteps through the thin walls separating his parents' room from their own. Those were his father's footsteps. He heard the clump of the boots dropping to the floor, then the creak of the bed as his father lay down. Again there was silence. A strange silence.

It hadn't used to be like that. Only since Mase was born. Before that there were always rustling night sounds. Warm and loving sounds, sometimes cries of pleasure and laughter. Now there was always the silence. It was almost as if no one lived in the room next to his.

Molly Ann had once explained it to him. His father and mother didn't want no more babies. But that didn't make much sense to him either. Did that mean they weren't going to have any more pleasure with each other? Why couldn't they? Sex was no mystery to him. It was always around him. Farmyard animals were always at it. He just assumed his parents were too. There was something not natural about them stopping just like that.

He turned on the bed so that he was head to toe with his brother, and lying on his stomach so he could look out at the moon. On the night wind he could hear the faint sound of distant, running dogs. Vaguely he wondered who would be out hunting coons when everyone knew that the coons had gone farther north to be near the water.

Quietly he crept out of bed and went to the window. The sound of the baying hounds seemed to be coming from the hill west of the house. He thought he recognized one of the dogs. The big yaller dog that belonged to Mr. Callendar, down in the valley.

He heard the soft rustle of clothing behind him. He turned.

"Cain't you sleep neither?" Molly Ann asked.

"No," he whispered.

She stood next to him at the window and looked out.

"I been thinkin'," she said. "You heered what Mr. Fitch said to Paw?"

He nodded.

"I allus wondered whut it would be like to live in town," she whispered. "I heered said—"

There was a creaking sound from one of the beds. "Shh," he hissed. "You'll wake the kids."

"Want to go outside?"

He nodded, and silently they went out into the yard, closing the door softly behind them. The bright moon made it seem almost like day.

"The night smells so sweet," she said.

"It do smell good," he agreed.

"An' quiet, too," she added. "The night is very different than the day. Ever'thing seems so calm an' restful."

He led the way to the well and filled the dipper with water and sipped at it. He held it toward her. She shook her head, and he put it down. The baying of the hounds faded into a thin yapping.

"Think they treed somethin'?" she asked.

"Fool hounds," he said scornfully. "Mebbe a hoot owl, nothin' more."

"You heered Maw talkin'," she said. "If'n we go down to town, they kin git some chickens and mebbe even a cow. Paw says he kin git Callendar's ol' mule fer five dollars."

Daniel didn't answer.

"What you thinkin'?" she asked.

His words came slowly, almost reluctantly. "I don' like that Mr. Fitch. They somethin' about him I don' cotton to."

"That mean you won't go if'n Paw sends you?"

"I didn' say that," he replied. "I jes' don' lak that man."

"He seems nice enough to me," she said.

"Don' let his fancy ways and highfalutin manners fool you," he said. "He's a very hard man."

"Do you think Paw will send us?"

He turned to look at her. After a moment he nodded. "I think so," he said. "Paw ain't got no choice. We need the money, and they ain't no other way to git it."

A note of excitement crept into her voice. "I hear tell they have dances ever' Satiddy night in town after they git th'u work."

He looked at her for a moment. "That's the Devil's thoughts you're thinkin'."

She laughed and pointed a finger down at him. "You're a fine one to be talkin', standin' there with a hard pokin' out the front o' your union suit."

The hot flush crept into his face. He had hoped she wouldn't notice in the night. "It gits lak that when I got to take a pee in the night," he said defensively.

"Go take a pee, then," she said, flouncing her head and starting back to the house. "On'y don' be too long about it, or I'll know what you're doin'."

"Molly Ann."

She turned and looked back at him.

"Why are you so anxious to leave here?" he asked.

She stared at him. "Don' you really know, Dan'l?"

He shook his head.

"There's nothin' here fer me," she said quietly. "On'y to grow up to be an ol' maid. Down there, in town, mebbe I got a chance. Mebbe I won' feel so empty an' useless."

60

He didn't speak.

"It's different fer boys," she said. "They kin do what they want. They don' have to git married if'n they don' want to." She came back toward him. "Dan'l, I'm not a bad girl, really I'm not. But I'm not a girl anymore, I'm a grown woman, goin' on sixteen, an' they's things inside me, things I feel I should be doin', lak havin' a family o' my own afore I git too old."

She reached for his hand and took it. Her hand was cold to his touch. "I love Maw and Paw an' you an' the kids, but I got my own life to live. Do you understan' that, Dan'l?"

He looked at her for a long moment. "I guess so," he said hesitantly.

She dropped his hand. "You better come to bed soon," she said. "You gotta be up early to he'p Paw clear the west field."

"I will," he said. He watched her go into the house and then went over behind the woodpile to take his pee. By the time he was back in their room, there was only the soft sound of the sleeping night.

He could smell the fried grits as he went into the kitchen. "I was out in the west field," he said. "But Paw didn' come."

Marylou turned to look at him. "Yer paw left early this mornin' to see if'n he could borrow the Callendars' mule to he'p out. Should be back any minute now." She handed him a plate. "Set yourse'f down an' have a mite o' breakfast."

He pulled a chair up to the table and began spooning the mushy food into his mouth.

"Yer paw an' I been thinkin' 'bout mebbe you 'n' Molly goin' down into town to work," his mother said. "Would you like that?"

He shrugged. "Never give it much thought."

"Mr. Fitch says you kin make four, mebbe five dollars a week."

He looked at her. "What does he git out of it?"

She was puzzled. "Who?"

"Mr. Fitch."

Marylou was shocked. "Nothin'. How kin you think a thing

like that? Mr. Fitch's a fine man. He jes' sees how bad things is an' wants to he'p out."

" 'N'en why don't he give Paw a fair price fer his corn?" Daniel asked.

"That's different," his mother answered. "That's business."

"It's the same thing to me," he said. He finished his food and stood up. "Seems to me a man cain't be one way in one thing and another in another."

Marylou was angry. "You have no right to talk like that about a fine man like Mr. Fitch. He's always been good to us. Don' he give us credit at his store when we ain't got no cash?"

"He gits it back when he comes to git the squeezin's. He ain't takin' much risk."

"You hush your mouth, Dan'l," she said sharply. "Your paw won't like it if'n I tell him what you said. Mr. Fitch's he'ped many a family out here. He also foun' good jobs fer many of the young 'uns. So you jes' min' your tongue an' your manners."

Still without speaking, Daniel went outside. He crossed to the front steps and sat down. He stared down the road along which his father would come. Maybe it would be a good thing if he went down to town.

Molly Ann could be right after all. There really wasn't very much here for him either.

Chapter 4

"If y'all don't dawdle along the road, you should reach Mr. Fitch's store afore sundown." Jeb squinted up at the morning sun. "Shouldn' be too hot today, so 'twon't be too bad."

Daniel looked up at his father. "Won't be."

"Got yer extry pair of pants an' shirt nice 'n' clean," his mother said. "Now, remember to wash yer drawers ever' day."

"I'll remember," Daniel said.

"We don' want people to think we live like pigs jes' because we's mountain people. We got a good name, old an' proud as any, an' I don' want them to fergit it."

Daniel shifted uncomfortably. The shoes he was wearing were already beginning to feel tight. Usually he didn't wear shoes until the first frost of winter.

Molly Ann answered her mother. "I'll keep after him, Maw. Don't you fret none."

Marylou turned to her daughter. "You be a good girl. Remember what I taught you. Don't you go listenin' to sweet talk from those no-'count fellers, now."

"I know how to act, Maw," Molly Ann said. "I'm not a baby."

Marylou looked at her daughter. She didn't speak.

Molly Ann flushed. She knew what her mother was thinking. "I'll be good, Maw," she said.

Jeb reached into his pocket and came up with some coins. "I'm givin' y'all a dollar between you. That's jes' so's you kin pay fer yer food an' board until you begin to work. You don't accep' nothin' from nobody. I don' want to hear that the Hugginses took charity from anyone."

Silently Daniel took the coins from his father and slipped them into his pocket.

"That there's a lot of money," Jeb said. "Don't go fritterin' it away on foolishment."

"I won't, Paw," Daniel said.

Jeb looked up at the sky again. "I think you better git goin'."

Daniel nodded. He looked at his parents, then at his brothers and sisters all gathered in the yard around them. "I guess so."

The children stared silently back at them. This was a solemn moment, but there was nothing for them to say.

Daniel half-waved his hand, then picked up his small cotton sack with his other shirt, pants and union suit. He pushed the small stick through the knot and placed it over his shoulder. "C'mon, Molly Ann."

The girl looked at him for a moment, then ran to her mother. For a long minute Marylou held her eldest daughter, then let her go. Quickly Molly Ann pecked each of the children on the cheek, then rejoined Daniel. Slowly they started toward the road.

"Dan'l!" Jeb's voice was hoarse.

They stopped. "Yes, Paw?"

He came toward them. "If'n it don' work out," he said awkwardly, "fer whatever the reason, y'all come home. Don' fergit you have a family that loves you an' is proud of you."

Daniel felt a tightness in his throat. His father's face was stiff and controlled, but his pale eyes were watering. "We know that, Paw," he answered, with an unaccustomed feeling of gentle understanding. "But don' worry. We'll be all right."

Jeb looked at him silently for a moment, then nodded. "I know you will," he said finally. He blinked his eyes. "Look after your sister, son."

"I will, Paw."

Jeb reached out a rough hand and took Daniel's in his grasp and pressed it. Then abruptly he let it drop and turned and walked away.

Daniel watched his father walk around the corner of the house until he was hidden from view, then turned back to his sister. "C'mon, Molly Ann," he said. "We got a long walk in front of us.

It was thirty-four miles, to be exact.

The day had turned warm, much warmer than Jeb had predicted. The sun hung high over their heads, its white rays beating down unmercifully on the dirt road.

" 'Bout how fur d'you think we've come?" Molly Ann asked.

Daniel pushed his wide-brimmed hat back on his head and wiped at his face with his forearm. It came away wet and salty. "Mebbe eleven, twelve miles."

"My feet hurt," she complained. "Kin we take a few minutes an' rest?"

He thought for a moment, then nodded. "I guess so."

She followed him off the road into a field and they sat down beneath a tree. They quickly took off their shoes and, lying back, let their toes wiggle in joyous freedom. "The on'y thing I don' like 'bout goin' to town is shoes," she said.

"I don' like 'em neither," he agreed. He rubbed his feet. "But I guess we'll have to git used to 'em."

"My mouth is dry," she said. "I wish we had some water."

"There's a brook 'bout three miles fu'ther on," he said. "We kin get a drink then an' have our san'wiches."

"An' wash our feet too?"

He laughed. "That too." He got to his feet. "Let's go."

She stared at his feet. "You didn' put your shoes on."

"I reckon we ought to save 'em," he said. "Otherwise by the time we git to town they'll be all wore out."

She smiled. "That's good thinkin'."

Carrying their shoes, they began once again walking down the hill. After a few minutes, she spoke. "Dan'l."

"Yes?"

"D'you think Mr. Fitch really meant what he tol' Paw?"

"I reckon he did."

"You don' like him, do you?"

Daniel didn't answer.

"Well, it don' matter, if'n he really kin git us the jobs he said."

Daniel thought for a moment. "I reckon it don't."

"Dan'l." A strained note came into her voice. "Dan'l, I don't feel too good."

He looked at her quickly. She had suddenly gone pale, and there were beads of perspiration standing on her forehead. Quickly he pulled off his hat and put it on her head. Her long light brown hair was hot to his fingers. He took her arm. "Come over here 'n' set," he said. "You have a tetch o' the sun."

She let him lead her slowly to the shade of another tree. He put her down gently. "You rest a mite."

She shook her head weakly. "No. We have to keep on or we won' git there."

A note of command crept into his voice. "You set. We ain' goin' to git there if'n you git sunstroke neither. You lay there while I see if'n I can fin' us some water."

She leaned back, closing her eyes. "All right, Dan'l," she said meekly.

Nimbly he untied the knot that bound his sack and found the tin mug that he had placed among his clothes. He ran down the hill toward a larger group of trees. Generally, where there were that many trees there would be water. He knelt and scooped a handful of earth and sniffed at it. It was damp.

Dropping to his hands and knees, he crept along, tracking the moisture. When his fingers came up wet with the earth, he began to scratch away the surface with his hands. The water began to trickle through when he was about a foot deep into the ground.

Quickly he scooped out a round hole in the ground, then patted the earth hard around its sides. Spreading his fingers, he pressed the heel and palm of one hand down against the bottom of the hole and threw his weight against the earth. A moment later the water began to gather around his fingers.

He kept up the pressure until it had almost reached his wrist and was beginning to drain away into the sides; then with his other hand he held the cup until it was filled with water.

Holding the cup carefully, he ran back to his sister. Molly Ann was lying quietly, her eyes closed. She didn't seem as pale as she had been. She opened her eyes wearily and tried to sit up.

"Be still," he said, kneeling beside her. He pulled a small kerchief from his pack. Moistening it, he pressed it to her forehead and gently wiped her face.

"That do feel good," she whispered.

He wrung out the kerchief and moistened it again. This time he squeezed the drops out against her parched lips. Her lips moved, and her tongue licked at them. "Better?" he asked.

She nodded. "I'm so thirsty. Kin I have a drink?"

"Jes' a little." He put an arm under her shoulders and raised her. He held the cup to her lips. "Not much, now," he warned. "Jes' a taste."

She took a small sip, then sighed. She looked up at him. "I jes' don' know what come over me."

"You should've wore a hat," he said. "That there sun's powerful strong."

"Kin I jes' rest a bit?" she asked. "Then I'll be all right an' we kin go."

"No hurry," he said. "Mr. Fitch'll be there when we git there."

She leaned back and closed her eyes. A moment later, she was asleep. Slowly he wiped her face again with the kerchief and then let her rest. A little sleep would do no harm.

Daniel sat back and squinted up at the sun, then down at the road shimmering in the heat. It had to be about noon. No sense getting back on the road now. For the next few hours it would be like the inside of an oven. It would be best to wait until after two o'clock. By that time the sun would be over the hills to the west and the road would begin to cool. He lay back, putting his arms behind his head, and closed his eyes. A moment later, he too was asleep.

A warbler, sitting on a branch over his head, woke him up. Peering through the leafy branches at the clear blue sky, he stared up at the singing bird for a moment. Then he sat up. The bird, startled by the movement, flew away.

He looked at his sister. Her eyes were open. "How're you feelin'?" he asked.

"Better," she said.

He pushed himself to his feet. "Mought as well go, then."

She sat up. "That never happened to me afore."

He smiled. "You never been out in the sun fer four hours with your head uncovered afore neither."

"I s'pose." She rose and stood there for a moment, then looked at him. "I'm all right now."

He nodded and began to tie up his clothing again. "We'll git you a real drink when we reach the brook." This time he picked up her sack as well as his own, and they started down the road.

She made a gesture to return his hat. "No, you keep it," he said. "I'm more used to it 'n' you are."

They walked along silently for about a half-hour before they came to the brook. They left the road and joyously washed their faces and drank their fill.

"That there's good water," he said.

She smiled in agreement. "Tas'e' lak sugar."

"We got to keep movin'," he said.

"I'm ready," she said.

He led the way back to the road just as a mule and wagon came around from behind the curve hidden by the trees. He stopped at the edge of the narrow road to let it pass. She halted behind him.

A lanky young man, his face half hidden by his wide-brimmed mountain man's hat, sat in the driver's seat, the reins dangling loosely from his fingers. "Git a move on, there!" he called to the reluctant animal, who was dragging in the heat.

The mule never changed his pace, but just kept plodding along. The young man swore good-humoredly. "Goldanged critter!"

The wagon drew opposite to where they were standing,

and the young man looked over the side of the wagon at them. "You kids want a ride into town?"

Molly Ann put a restraining hand on her brother's arm. "Dan'l. Paw tol' us to walk."

Almost angrily, he shook her hand away. Dumb girl. Didn't she know she was in no condition to make it? He looked up at the lanky young man. "We suah do, mistuh," he said.

Chapter 5

JIMMY SIMPSON had sandy blond hair, blue eyes and a bright, flashing smile. He had never held a job in all the twenty years of his life and never needed one. Money was not a problem. He could get it in many different ways—from playing klab with the Polish miners, seven-card stud with the mountain men or pool with the city slickers. And there was always a little bootleg when things were tough. Like today.

He had spent the whole day in the hills. That hadn't been easy. Old Man Fitch had made his rounds just the day before and had skimmed the cream. If it were not for the fact that Jimmy paid twice as much as Fitch, he would be returning now with an empty wagon. But his price was good. And it brought out the good corn, the corn they had tucked away for their own.

He watched the boy place the two sacks he was carrying into the wagon, then help his sister to the bench and climb up beside her. He pushed his hat back on his head, and an unruly lock of blond hair fell across his forehead. "I'm Jimmy Simpson."

The boy had grave eyes. "Honored." His voice was deeper

than Jimmy had expected. "I'm Dan'l Boone Huggins, an' this yere's my sister Molly Ann."

"Pleased to meet ya," he said, smiling. He looked at the girl. From what he could see of her face, hidden by the wide-brimmed hat that was obviously her brother's, she was very pretty. "Been walkin' fur?"

Daniel nodded. "'Bout fifteen miles since early mornin'. But the heat made it slow goin'."

"How fur you goin'?"

"Fitchville."

Jimmy smiled again. "That's where I'm headin' too. Visitin'?"

Daniel shook his head. "No. We're goin' to work."

"You got jobs already?"

"Not yet. But Mr. Fitch tol' my paw he would see to it."

"Fer both of you?"

"Yes."

Jimmy fell silent. The old bastard had the country by the balls. There wasn't anything that went into or came out of the hills that he didn't have his long greedy fingers into, even people. But there was no way the son of a bitch could lose with a whole town named after his great-great-grandfather.

Daniel glanced into the wagon. He recognized the jugs, even though they were covered by old sugar bags. He turned back to the road. It was none of his business.

Jimmy looked at the girl. She was leaning against her brother, her body swaying gently with the rolling wagon, her eyes closed. She seemed to be dozing. "If'n your sister is tired," he said, "we kin fix up a place in the wagon fer her to lie down."

Molly Ann straightened up. "I don' want to be no trouble," she said quickly.

He stopped the mule. "No trouble 'tall. 'Specially fer such a pretty girl." He climbed over the seat into the wagon and moved a row of jugs to the side. Quickly he made a mattress of the cotton sugar bags, then rigged a small cover over part of the pallet to shield her from the sun. "It's not bad," he said, straightening up. "Slep' there myse'f las' night." He held out a hand to her.

Molly Ann looked at her brother for approval. He nodded. She took Jimmy's hand and stepped back across the seat. She looked up into his face. "You're very kin', Mr. Simpson."

He grinned. "Jimmy. Ever'body calls me Jimmy."

"Jimmy," she said.

Suddenly he became aware that he was still holding her hand. He dropped it. "Make yerse'f comfortable," he said awkwardly.

She felt her heart beating wildly inside her breast and a flush beginning to rise into her face. She didn't trust herself to speak. She must have taken more sun than she realized. She only nodded.

He climbed back into his seat and picked up the reins. A quick glance over his shoulder confirmed that she was already lying down. He snapped the reins. "Giddap, danged critter!" he swore, in a voice that was almost a whisper so that he would not disturb the girl.

Molly Ann awakened suddenly, feeling the evening chill in the air. As she started to sit up, she became aware that she had been covered with a coarse blanket. She pushed it down and drew a deep breath. She was better now.

She turned and saw her brother and the young man sitting, their backs toward her, silhouetted against the evening sky. Idly she wondered how long she had slept. The young man shook the reins. Again she felt a warmth in her face. He was nice.

"You're awake?" Daniel had heard her.

"Yes."

Jimmy turned toward her. "Want to come up here?"

She nodded. He stopped the mule and held out his hand. She took it. Again she felt her heart begin to beat wildly. In confusion, she let it go. "How fur we have to go?"

"'Nother couple hours," Jimmy said. "I cain't git this critter to move. He's the lazies' mule in the county."

She looked at Daniel. "It'll be late when we git there. What if Mr. Fitch's store is closed?"

"We'll git him in the mornin', then," Daniel replied.

"Got a place to stay?" Jimmy asked. "Any kinfolk?"

"No," Daniel answered.

"I kin fix you up at my place," Jimmy said. "The Widdy Carroll runs a fine boardin'house."

They looked at each other hesitantly.

"She won' charge you nothin' fer the night," Jimmy said quickly. "Y'all are my guests."

"We kin pay," Daniel said as quickly. "We got money. It's jes' that we wanted to git to work as soon as we could."

"Where you goin' to work?" Jimmy asked. "At the mill?"

Again Molly Ann looked at her brother. "We don' rightly know," Daniel admitted. "He jes' tol' our paw fer us to come down an' he would take care of it."

"Fitch didn' say what kin' o' work you'd be doin'?"

"Nope. Jes' said we'd git good money. Four, mebbe five dollars a week."

Jimmy laughed, but there was humor in it. "That Fitch, he sure is a smooth talker."

"You mean there's no jobs?" Molly Ann's voice was anxious.

"I don' mean that. There's jobs, all right. But at seven cents an hour, you gotta work at leas' twelve hours a day to git that kind of money."

"We don' min' workin'," Molly Ann said.

He looked at her. "You ever work in a mill?"

"No."

"You stan' on your feet all day changin' bobbins on a speedin' machine fer twelve hours an' yer body feels lak it's about to break into a hunnert pieces. It ain't easy."

"Nothin' is," she said. "If'n the pay is good, we don' expect it to be easy."

"Good pay!" He laughed again. "You call that good pay? Why do you think they use kids? Because they kin pay you seven cents an hour when they have to pay grown people fifteen cents an hour, an' they keep the difference in profits."

"It's none of our concern what others do," Daniel said. "On'y that we do an honest day's work."

Jimmy wanted to laugh again, but something in the boy's expression stopped him. This was no ordinary hillbilly.

73

Somewhere behind those eyes lurked an earth-born maturity, an awareness of people that went far beyond his years. After a moment, he spoke. "People must do what they mus' do."

But in his heart, Jimmy knew better.

Out here, people did not do what they must; they danced like puppets on a string, maneuvered by other men for their own profit and purpose.

It was after nine o'clock when they came down Main Street and the wagon stopped in front of Mr. Fitch's store. The door was closed and the windows were dark. They sat there a few minutes in silence.

Jimmy felt he had to apologize. "I'm sorry. If this ol' mule didn' have such a min' of his own, we would've been here an hour earlier."

" 'Tain't your fault," Daniel said. He looked at his sister. "Mebbe we getter git off here."

"No sense in that atall," Jimmy said quickly. "Y'all come over to the Widdy's with me. You'll git some supper an' a bed, an' you kin be here fust thing in the mornin'."

Daniel met his eyes. "We don' want to put nobody out. We're already obliged to you fer your favor."

"You'll put nobody out," Jimmy said. "Room 'n' board is the Widdy's business."

The Widow Carroll was an angular woman with a sharp face and an equally sharp tongue, which she used to keep her boarders in line. A rough, strange mixture of men who worked in the mills and factories and mines, they came from near and distant portions of the world. Slavs from Central Europe were thrown together with thin-lipped, taciturn mountain men, who were working in an environment as alien to them as it was to the immigrants. Despite everything, the Widow kept them in tow. No fighting on the premises, no drunkenness, no blasphemy. What the men did outside was none of her concern, but when they came to her table, they had better come with clean hands and washed faces or she would not let them be seated. And every one of them lived in

holy terror of her, speaking in strangely hushed tones whenever she was around, because none of them wanted to lose his
place in her boardinghouse. The meals were not fancy, but
she set the best table in the area.

"Yer too late fer supper," she snapped at Jimmy. "You well
know that supper's at six thirty."

"It's that ol' mule." Jimmy turned on the charm. "I jes'
couldn' git him to move nohow. Then I foun' these kids
walkin' on the road in all that heat, an' I couldn' let 'em do
that, could I?"

The Widow Carroll looked at Daniel and Molly Ann and
sniffed without speaking. They fidgeted under her baleful
gaze.

"They was comin' down to Mr. Fitch's to git theirselves
placed," he said. "But the store is closed."

"No women," she snapped. She turned to Jimmy. "You
know the rules of my house."

Daniel took his sister's hand. "Come, Molly Ann," he said.
"We don' want to make you no trouble, Mr. Simpson. Thank
you fer your kindness."

Something in the tone of his voice reached into the Widow
Carroll's memory. Her husband had been a mountain man,
and many years ago, when they had both been young, he had
sounded like this boy—strong and filled with a sense of pride.
But that was long ago, before the mines used up his lungs and
the white mule had rotted his gut, and he'd died spitting up
black blood all over her clean white sheets. "Besides, I on'y
got one room vacant," she said.

Daniel met her eyes steadily. "That's all right, ma'am. My
sister an' I been sleepin' in the same room all our lives, together with our brother an' sisters."

"I don't care what you been doin'," she said sharply. "No
man an' woman shares a room in this house even if they is
brother an' sister."

"I kin sleep on the porch, with your permission, ma'am,"
Daniel said. "Molly Ann kin have the room."

"I don't know," the Widow said doubtfully. "It ain' proper
to have someone sleepin' on the porch."

"He kin use the cot in my room," Jimmy said quickly.

The Widow Carroll made up her mind. They looked like

nice, respectable children from a good family. "All right," she said. "But the on'y thing left to eat is some cold pork and bread."

"That will be mighty kind o' you, ma'am," Daniel said.

She looked at him. "That'll be ten cents for each of you," she said. She hesitated a moment, then added, "Including breakfast, which is at five thirty prompt."

Silently Daniel took some coins from his pocket. He put two nickels and a dime in her hand. "Thank you, ma'am. We appreciate yer bother."

She nodded and turned to Molly Ann. "Now you come with me, miss, an' I'll show you yer room."

Molly Ann lay on the bed in the small dark room and listened to the quiet. It was strange. There was not a sound. It was the first time she had ever slept alone in a room, without the familiar nighttime noises of her brothers and sisters. It took getting used to.

She wondered about them at home and if they missed her. Unaccountably, the tears began to roll down her cheeks. A soft knock came at the door. She slipped out of bed and crossed the room. "Yes?" she whispered.

"It's Dan'l." The soft voice filtered through the door. "Are you all right?"

"I'm fine," she replied.

He hesitated a moment. "Well . . . good night, then."

"Good night."

She heard his soft steps move away from the door, and she crept back to her bed. In just one short day, so many things had changed. Everything had changed.

Until now, Daniel had been her younger brother. But now, today, suddenly he was different. There was a strength in him she had never known before. As if in one flashing moment he had grown past her into manhood.

A curiously warm feeling of comfort and security came over her, the tears stopped and she fell into a deep, dreamless sleep.

Chapter 6

DANIEL AND Molly Ann were waiting in front of the store on Main Street a little after six o'clock in the morning when the door opened and an old Negro came out, a broom in his hands. He glanced at them curiously but didn't speak and began to sweep the wooden walk in front of the entrance. Daniel walked to the door and looked into the store.

"Ain' nobody in yet," the Negro said. "If'n yo' wants to buy somethin', Mistuh Harry will be here any minute."

"We're waitin' fer Mr. Fitch," Daniel said.

"He doan come until eight o'clock," the Negro said.

"We'll wait." Daniel walked back to his sister. There was a small bench in front of one of the windows. They sat down.

A few minutes later, a small, nervous-looking man in a shiny jacket, starched collar and tie came bustling up to the store. "Any customers yet, Jackson?" he asked in a high-pitched, officious voice.

The Negro stepped aside politely to let the little man pass. "No, suh, Mistuh Harry."

The man stopped and looked at Daniel and Molly Ann, but he didn't speak to them. "What do they want?"

"They lookin' fo' Mistuh Fitch."

"You kids lookin' for jobs?" The little man spoke to them now.

Daniel got to his feet. "Yes, suh."

"Well you can't sit there," he said abruptly. "That there bench is reserved for customers."

"I'm sorry," Daniel began to say, but the little man had already disappeared into the store. He turned to Molly Ann, who had already risen to her feet. They stood there uncertainly.

"They's a bench 'roun' the side of the sto' y'all kin use," the old Negro said.

"Thank you," Daniel said. He led the way around the corner of the building and they sat down again.

Slowly the small town began to come to life around them. Stores were opened, people started to appear on the street; then there were a few wagons, then more, and by a few minutes after seven the day was in full swing.

They watched curiously, silently. People walking by seemed to pay no attention to them. They all seemed caught up in their own thoughts. Men going to work, women to their marketing, children playing. All seemed preoccupied.

"How much longer?" Molly Ann asked.

Daniel squinted at the sun. "Half-hour, mebbe."

"Did you see Mr. Simpson this morning?" she asked.

"He was still asleep when I lef' the room," Daniel replied.

"He didn' come down fer breakfast," she said.

"He tol' me afore we went to sleep, he never eats breakfast," Daniel said. "An' that lady serves a real good breakfast, too. Aigs 'n' grits, corn bread 'n' butter 'n' real coffee. It don' make sense to me that he should miss a good meal like that."

"I wanted to thank him for his kindness," Molly Ann said.

"You don' have to fret about it," Daniel said. "I thanked him fer both of us."

"He was real nice," she said softly.

Daniel glanced at his sister. He grinned. "Reckon yer a little sweet on him?" he teased.

She blushed. "Don' be silly. Cain't a girl say a feller's nice 'thout it bein' misunderstood?"

78

Daniel smiled. He could have told her that Jimmy had wanted to know all about her—but if she knew that, it might turn her head.

The old Negro came around the corner to them. "Mistuh Fitch jes' came in, if'n yo' wants to see him."

They followed him into the store. The darkness took some getting used to after the bright sunlight, but in a moment their eyes adjusted, and they saw the barrels and sacks piled around them and the shelves stacked high with all kinds of articles from canned food to bolts of cloth. He led them down around the long counter, past the officious little man, into a small glass-enclosed office.

Mr. Fitch was seated behind his desk, his broad-brimmed hat still on his head. There was no recognition on his face. "What do you kids want?" he asked gruffly.

"Paw tol' us to come down here," Daniel said. "He said you tol' him you would git us jobs."

Mr. Fitch's face was still blank. "Yer paw?"

"Yes," Daniel said. "Jeb Huggins."

The big man's voice suddenly changed. It became more jovial. He rose from behind the desk. "You're the Huggins kids. Danged if'n I recognized y'all in them fine clothes. Sure thing. That's what I tol' yer daddy."

A sense of relief came over Daniel. For a moment he'd thought there had been a misunderstanding. "That's right, Mr. Fitch."

Fitch looked at him. "You're Dan'l?"

Daniel nodded.

He turned to Molly Ann. "And you're Molly Ann?"

Molly Ann smiled. "Yes, Mr. Fitch."

"That was a delicious rabbit stew yer mother served fer supper," he said. "I'll never fergit it."

They didn't answer.

He sat down and began to shuffle some papers on his desk. "Now, let me see. . . . Ah, here they are." He held them toward Daniel. "Now, you git youah daddy to sign these papers an' we kin git you a job."

Daniel stared at him. "Paw didn' tell us there was no papers to be signed."

"They's always papers to be signed," Mr. Fitch said. "You kids is still minors under the law, an' until yer twenty-one yer parents have to sign fer you."

"But Mr. Fitch," Daniel protested. "That's more'n a thirty-mile walk each way. It would take us two days to git 'em signed."

"Cain't he'p that," Mr. Fitch said. "The law's the law."

Daniel felt an anger rising in him. "Why didn' you tell that to my paw afore you tol' him to send us down here?"

Fitch looked across the desk at the boy. Daniel's eyes had suddenly turned dark. The kid had a temper. He didn't have the disposition to work in the mills and glass factories around there. The best place for him would be about twenty miles farther south, in the coal mines at Grafton. He let out a deep breath. "I plumb fergot," he admitted. "But since it's my fault, I'll git you to work right away an' see to it m'self that your daddy gits the papers to sign."

Daniel relaxed. He nodded silently.

"How tall are you, son?" Fitch's voice was more friendly now.

"Almos' five ten, I reckon," Daniel answered. "Paw says I got my growth early."

"You are tall," Fitch agreed. He thought for a moment. "You're too tall fer work in the glass factories. They lookin' fer shorter boys because all the pipes they have to duck under. You objec' to workin' a tipple?"

"A tipple?" Daniel asked. "What's that?"

"Coal mine," Fitch answered. "You kin start by pickin' slate; later you kin git right into the mines."

"I don' objec'," Daniel said.

"Good." Fitch nodded. "There's a good openin' in a new mine near Grafton. I'll give you a note an' send you down there right away."

"But Grafton's twenty miles away," Daniel protested.

Fitch fixed him with a glance. "You want to work, don't you, boy?"

Daniel nodded.

"Yer daddy trusted me enough to sen' you down here; now you jes' got to trust me to git you the bes' job I kin."

"But Molly Ann an' me, we figgered on bein' able to stay together."

"You kin stay aroun' if'n you want, but there's no jobs aroun' here fer you. Grafton's the only place."

"What about Molly Ann, then?" Daniel asked.

Fitch looked at the girl. "I kin git her a good job in the mill right here."

Daniel looked at his sister. "I don' know." He hesitated.

"Don' worry, Dan'l," Molly Ann said quickly. "I'll be all right."

"I'll look after her m'self, boy," Fitch said. "Miz Fitch'll see to it that she had a decent place to stay."

Daniel looked at the heavyset man behind the desk, then at his sister. He didn't like it. But he didn't have much choice. Paw had sent them down here to work. He couldn't go back and tell him he didn't like it. At that moment, he made up his mind to go back to the Widow Carroll's house and ask Jimmy to keep an eye on his sister. There was something about the young man that Daniel felt could be trusted. It was very different from the feeling he had about Mr. Fitch.

"All right," he said reluctantly.

"That's better." Fitch smiled. He rose. "I got a wagon goin' down to Grafton this afternoon. You kin ketch a ride on it." He walked to the door of the small office. "Now you kids wait right here while I make some arrangements."

They looked at each other when he had gone. "I don' lak him," Daniel said simply.

Molly Ann reached for his hand. "Yer growin' up too fast, Dan'l," she said. "But don't fergit, I'm growin up too."

It was slightly past ten o'clock when Daniel and Molly Ann were back at the boardinghouse. The Widow Carroll came to the door in answer to their knock. "Is Mr. Simpson still in, Miz Carroll?" Daniel asked.

"He's roun' back in the barn fussin' with his mule," she said shortly. She shot a glance at him. "You plannin' to stay the night?"

"No, ma'am," he answered. "I'm goin' on to Grafton this afternoon."

"Yer sister too?"

"No, ma'am. She got a job heah in the mill."

"Well, she cain't stay here," she said sharply. "Las' night was an exception, but I don' allow girls to stay here. Sooner or later there is always trouble."

Daniel looked into the woman's eyes. "We thank you fer your hospitality, ma'am," he said quietly. "An' we have no intention of abusin' it."

Her eyes fell before his gaze. She felt oddly confused. "Of course, if she—"

He interrupted her: "I trust it won't be necessary, ma'am. Thank you kindly."

She watched them walk down the porch steps and around the corner of the house before she closed the door and went back to her cleaning. She was right. She knew she was right. Girls were always trouble. Sooner or later the men would begin to fight over her. But this was a nice girl from a good family. Not like the cheap trash that usually worked in the mills. Maybe she had spoken too quickly. She cursed her tongue silently. It had always been her worst fault. Angrily, she began making the dust fly with her broom.

Daniel and Molly Ann found Jimmy in the barn, but he wasn't fussing with his mule—at least, not that mule. The animal was contentedly munching on some hay in his stall. Jimmy was bottling the squeezin's.

He was standing in front of a wooden bench which was covered with clear glass pint bottles. Under one arm he held a jug, in the other hand a funnel. Quickly, efficiently, with a motion born of years of practice, he slipped the nozzle of the funnel into the bottle, tipped the jug and let the clear white liquid flow into the bottle. When it was full, he moved on to the next.

Daniel was fascinated. Not so much by the rebottling, but by the fact that when he poured the clear 'shine into the bottles, it immediately turned smoky brown in color. He had never seen anything like that before. They stood there silently until Jimmy had emptied one jug and reached for another. "Mr. Simpson," he said.

Jimmy turned and smiled. He put down the empty jug. "Ever'thing okay?"

Daniel nodded. "I guess so." He glanced at the bench. "We don' mean to be interruptin'."

Jimmy laughed. "They waited this long fer Simpson's whiskey, they kin wait a bit longer."

"Whiskey?" Daniel was puzzled.

Jimmy nodded. "That's what I'm makin'. A few drops of sarsaparilla and flavorin' an' you cain't tell the difference between mine an' store-bought. Gits a better price'n clear 'shine, too."

Daniel hesitated. "Got a favor to ask, but you already been so kin'—"

"Go ahead an' ask," Jimmy said quickly. "Anythin' I kin do."

"Mr. Fitch says I'm too tall to work in the glass factory heah, an' he got me a job in a mine down Grafton way."

Jimmy made no comment. "An' your sister?"

"She's goin' to the mill heah." Daniel looked at Molly Ann. "It's not 'zactly the way we thought. We thought we would be together. Mr. Fitch says he'll look after her." He fell silent.

Jimmy looked at Molly Ann. Her gaze dropped demurely. He saw the faint blush come into her cheeks. "What d'you think?" he asked her.

She didn't answer.

He turned back to Daniel. "You don' lak Mr. Fitch." It was more a statement than a question.

"I don' rightly cotton to that man," Daniel admitted. "I'd feel much better in my own mind if'n I knew that you was keepin' an eye out for her rather than Mr. Fitch."

Jimmy nodded. "I know the feelin'." He spoke again to Molly Ann. "How do you feel about that, Miz Molly Ann?"

Her voice was very soft, but she did not look up at him. "I would feel right comforted by your kindness."

He smiled. "Then I'll be glad to he'p. Fust thing to do is fin' you a proper place to live. I have some friends, a good family. Their oldes' girl jes' married an' they have an empty room, an' they kin use the boardin' money. Let's us go over there an' fin' out if they're agreeable." He put the funnel on the bench and started toward them.

"But what about your whiskey makin'?" Daniel asked.

Jimmy laughed. "Let it set there. Haven't you heard that agin' whiskey is the best thing fer it?"

Chapter 7

IN HIS sleep Daniel heard the distant shriek of the mine whistle, signaling the first changeover of shifts. He rolled over on his narrow cot and opened his eyes. The three other boys with whom he shared the small room were still huddled under their coarse blankets.

Quietly he pulled himself out of bed and made his way barefoot to the washstand. He put the stopper in the bowl and poured some water from the giant pitcher into it. The water was cold on his face and helped awaken him. He stared into the faded, cracked mirror over the basin.

The face that was reflected there was a different face from the one he'd first seen in this mirror almost three months before. All traces of color from the sun had long since gone. His skin was now a peculiar blue-tinged white, and it was drawn tight across his cheeks. Large black hollows held the eyes, which looked like the pieces of anthracite he worked with all day long.

He rubbed at his cheeks. There was a faint stubble of blue-black beard. Without feeling it, he never could be sure whether it was a beard or merely coal dust that had penetrated his pores and become a permanent part of his complexion. He dug his fingers into the can of Gresolvent and rubbed the gritty paste into a lather on his face. But even after he had rinsed it away and dried himself with the rough towel, there was no change except that his face hurt from the rough sandy grains in the soap. Coal dust had a way of implanting itself into the skin the way a weed clung to the earth. No matter what you did, you couldn't get it out.

After wetting his hair and combing it flat against his scalp, he went back to his cot and began to dress. The blue work shirt and overalls were stiff with coal dust, as were his heavy work boots. He picked up the denim miner's cap and checked the lamp fastened to its peak. The wick was soft, and there was enough oil in the can to last through the day. Softly he walked to the door. He took a last look at the other, sleeping boys before he went out, but made no move to awaken them. They were breaker boys, and they didn't have to be on the job until a half-hour after him, at seven o'clock.

He closed the door behind him and went down the narrow staircase to the main floor of the boardinghouse. He walked through the hallway to the kitchen. The heavyset cook, her black face already shining with the heat from the ovens, looked at him. She smiled. "Mawnin', Mistuh Daniel."

"Mornin', Carrie."

"Usual this mawnin', Mistuh Daniel?"

"Yes, please. An' don't fergit—."

She grinned. "No, suh. Aigs fried hard with lots o' salt an' pepper."

He sat down at the table and poured himself a steaming mug of coffee from the big iron pot on the table. He added cream and three heaping spoonfuls of sugar and stirred the coffee.

"Ah got some good cally ah kin fry up with the aigs if you lak," she said.

"That's right kind o' you, Carrie," he said. "I sure would fancy that." He spread butter thickly on the still-warm home-baked bread and took a bite. "I declare, Carrie, next to my maw, you bake the best bread in West Virginia."

"Aw, go on, now, Mistuh Daniel." But her face broke into a pleased smile as she brought the eggs and pork butt over to

86

the table. He reached for the salt. "Hold on a minute," she warned him. "I got lots of salt in there already."

He tasted the eggs and nodded. "It's fine." But as soon as her back was turned, he added more salt.

He ate quickly and carefully, wiping the yolks of the eggs from the plate with his bread. He finished his coffee and got to his feet.

She brought him his black metal lunch box. "Ah slipped in a extra apple an' orange fo' you," she said. "Ah knows how much yo' laks fresh fruit."

"Thank you, Carrie." He took the lunch pail from her hand and walked to the door. "See you tonight."

"Yo' be caihful, now, Mistuh Daniel," she said. "Doan' yo' go too near them dynamite charges."

"I won't," he said, and smiled as he went out the door, knowing that it was his job as shot man to place the fuse and light it. It got him an extra dollar a week, and he was not about to let that get away from him. Seven dollars a week was almost as much as a grown man was paid.

Silently he trudged down the rain-dampened mud street past the rows of company houses, all gray-and-black with mine dust, and turned on the street that led to the mine entrance. The road was beginning to fill with men going to work and men coming from work. Some would be going to the beds that had just been vacated by the day shift. Beds were at a premium, and many boardinghouses accommodated two shifts. On Sundays, when the mines were closed, confusion was rampant, and often there were fights about which shift had first claim on the beds. The house rules said that they were to alternate on Sundays, but that didn't really help, because everybody was too tired and short-tempered. Daniel felt that he was lucky to have found a sharing room. But the grown men didn't seem to want to share.

Daniel reached the front of the mine. As usual, he was the first of his work gang to arrive. He sat down on a wooden box and watched the men coming out.

Their faces were black, their clothing even dustier than his own, and their eyes squinted painfully as they adjusted to the morning daylight. They moved slowly, almost painfully, as they accustomed their bodies to walking erect instead of half hunched over, as they did in the low-ceilinged corridors of the mines.

One of the men stopped in front of him. He was a heavyset, barrel-chested man, and his blond-white hair was covered with coal dust. "Andy here yet?" he asked.

"No, sir." Daniel shook his head. Andy was his shift foreman. The man who spoke to him was the night-shift foreman.

The foreman looked around for a moment. "You tell him the west tunnel needs shoring before you do any more blasting. The walls are getting thin."

Daniel nodded. "I'll tell him."

"Don't forget, now," the man warned. "Or you may all find yourselves eatin' dirt."

"I won' fergit," Daniel promised. "Thank you."

The man shook his head and lumbered wearily away. Daniel fished in his pocket and pulled out a piece of chewing tobacco. He bit off a corner and began to work up a wad in the corner of his mouth. A good spit helped keep the dust out of a man's lungs. Expertly he shot a gob of tobacco juice at a water bug crawling near his feet. The bug drowned in a brown stream of poison.

Daniel looked after the night foreman. He wasn't particularly concerned. The warning was an old story to him. Each shift tried to unload the shoring on the other because the time it took decreased the mining tonnage. You couldn't bring out the coal while you were boarding up the walls.

The air in the mine was heavy with humidity, and the walls were soaked with moisture. The earth underfoot was soft and spongy, and as their heavy boots sank into it, water rushed in to fill the footprints.

"Damn!" the foreman swore. "We better git some pumps down here or we'll be in water up to our ass before we know it."

"All the pumps is in use in the East Tunnel," one of the men told him.

The foreman turned to Daniel. "You git up to the superintendent's shack an' tell him we gotta git some pumps 'cause our mules are up to their bellies an' cain't haul the coal."

Daniel nodded and turned away. He walked back up the tunnel toward the main entrance, passing a gang of workmen who were laying track for the coal trucks.

"What's it lak down there?" one of the men called.

"Wet," Daniel answered. "I'm goin' fer some pumps."

"Bring back a bird while you're at it," the man said. "I don' like the smell down yere."

Daniel grinned. He had been sent on those errands before. Canaries were supposed to be used to detect leaking gas or oxygen shortages, but in all the time he had been working in the mine, he had never seen one. "I think I kin ketch an eagle if'n y'all kin git me the afternoon off," he replied.

The shout of laughter followed him until he turned the corner. The entrance was up the inclined corridor about twenty yards in front of him. He stared through it toward the dark blue sky in which thousands of stars twinkled. A sense of wonder filled him. Outside it was daylight, but seeing the sky through the long narrow tunnel made it night. The stars were always there behind the sun. They faded and began to disappear as he approached the entrance.

The timekeeper stopped him at the entrance. "Where at you goin', boy?"

"Andy sent me to git some pumps from the super's office." he replied.

"Yer wastin' yer time," the timekeeper said. "Git back down there on the job."

"Andy says the mules is up to their bellies an' cain't haul the coal."

The timekeeper looked at him. After a moment, he shrugged his shoulders. "Go ahead," he said truculently. "But it won't do you no good."

Daniel walked over to the office. He knocked on the door and went in. The clerk looked over his desk at him. "What do you want?"

"Andy says we need pumps in the West Tunnel," he replied. "We cain't git the coal out."

"Why not?"

Daniel stared at him. Already he had the ingrained dislike of office workers that every miner felt. "Ever'body knows mules cain't swim an' haul coal at the same time," he said.

The clerk stared back. "Wise kid." He looked down at his desk. "Go back and tell Andy there ain't no pumps."

Daniel was stubborn. "He tol' me to see the super."

"The super ain't in."

"I'll wait." Daniel looked around for a chair.

"No, you won't," the clerk said. "You go back to work or you git docked."

"Okay," Daniel said purposefully. "I'll go back an' tell him. But you know Andy. He don' mess aroun'. He's goin' to come up here hisself."

The clerk backed down. Everyone knew Andy's reputation. He had been in the mines all his life and had a very short temper. Nobody got into an argument with him unless he was prepared to fight. "Okay," he said. "Tell him I'll git some pumps down there."

Daniel nodded. He turned to leave. The clerk called him back. "You new aroun' here?"

"Not 'zactly."

"What's your name?"

"Dan'l Boone Huggins."

The clerk made a note on the sheet of paper in front of him. "Okay," he said. "I'll remember that."

"You took yer own sweet time about it," the timekeeper said sourly as Daniel went past him.

Daniel didn't answer. He went down into the blackness. Andy came over to him. "What about the pumps?"

"The super wasn't there," Daniel replied. "The clerk says he'll git 'em down to us."

Andy nodded grimly. He kicked the ground beneath his foot. The water sprayed. "They better git here damn soon," he said. "I got a feelin' we're comin' into an undergroun' spring." He looked up at Daniel. "You start bringin' over shorin' planks."

"Okay," Daniel said. He walked along the tunnel until he reached the stack of shoring timber. Then, one by one, he laboriously dragged the ten-foot planks through the thick mud back to the end of the tunnel.

Nearly an hour had passed, and he had moved almost thirty of the two-by-eight planks, when he heard the pickman yell, "Hey, foreman! I hit water!"

For a moment they all froze, looking at Andy. The foreman was calm, his eyes appraising the situation. A stream of water was gushing from the far wall, washing the earth away.

"Don't stand there lookin' at it, you donkeys!" Andy shouted. "Start packin' it."

Immediately a dozen shovels began to fly, throwing the earth back against the wall in an effort to seal off the water. "Git the shorin' planks up there!" Andy yelled. "I want a two-foot wall." He turned to another man. "Dig a drain trench."

They all worked frantically, but it took more than an hour before the water was sealed off, and by that time they were all heaving and sweating with the exertion. One by one they dropped to the ground in exhaustion.

Andy leaned against the shoring planks and looked down at them. He ran his arm across his forehead, wiping away the dripping sweat. He took a deep breath. "On yer feet," he said. "Move that coal. We're more'n twenty ton behind already."

Daniel struggled to his feet. His clothing was soaked through to his skin. "What about the pumps?" he asked.

Andy stared at him. "Fuck 'em," he said. "We're okay now. Let the night shift git 'em, like they should've in the first place."

"But—" Daniel said.

The foreman fixed him with a baleful eye. "You start loading coal in them trucks," he said. "Or I'll have your ass outta here."

Daniel stood there hesitantly.

"Git a move on!" Andy snapped. "It ain't our affair to worry any more about 'em than they worry about us."

Silently Daniel went to work. The foreman was right. Each man had to look out for himself.

That was the way it seemed until about three o'clock in the morning, when the weird, wailing shriek of the mine whistle pierced his sleep.

He sat up in bed rubbing his eyes. The other boys in the room were already awake. "I wonder what that's fer," one of the boys said.

Outside, there was a sound of people running. He went over to the window and looked out. Already men were pouring from their homes into the night street. He pulled up the window and leaned out. "What happened?" he yelled down.

A man stopped and looked up at him, his face white and pale in the night. "Cave-in at the mine!" the man shouted back. "The West Tunnel fell in!"

Chapter 8

"You, boy! Get me another torch over here!" The superintendent's voice echoed in the mouth of the tunnel.

Daniel scrambled back through the wet muck, grabbed a torch from a wall bracket and made his way back to the wall of earth where the cave-in had come to a stop. He looked at the superintendent.

"Get up on those shoring planks an' hold the light steady," the super commanded.

Daniel clambered up on the wooden planks until his face was within inches of the wall of wet earth. He put out one hand to balance himself.

The superintendent gestured to Andy, and the two men climbed up beside Daniel and stared down at the moist earth. Below them they saw a steady flow of water coming up from under the dirt, and they heard the hissing, suckling sound of the pumps. The two men fell silent, studying the earth beneath them.

Daniel watched them in fascination. They were very different. Andy was large and powerful and gruff; his work clothes were layered with mud and coal. The super, on the other hand, was prim, small, neat; his tie and white shirt with starched collar and gray suit seemed untouched by the mud and dirt around him. His eyes glistened behind the wire-framed pince-nez. Daniel followed the man's gaze. In the few minutes they had been standing there, the mud line on the shoring planks had risen almost an inch.

"It's still comin' in." The superintendent's voice was expressionless.

"Yes, sir." Andy's customarily booming voice was hushed.

"Why didn't you get pumps in here?" the super asked.

"I sent Daniel for 'em," Andy answered. "He came back without 'em."

The super turned to Daniel. "Why didn't you bring them back with you?"

Daniel cleared his throat. "The clerk said he would send them down."

The super turned back to Andy. "I think we'd better get up to the office." He started to leave, then stopped. "Bring the boy with you." He stepped down from the shoring; then, walking carefully on the wooden planks so that his shoes would not get wet, he made his way out of the tunnel.

Andy stared after him for a moment, then spat some tobacco juice onto the ground. He looked at Daniel. "You sure you spoke to the clerk, Daniel?"

"I'm not in the habit o' lyin', Mr. Androjewicz," Daniel said quietly.

Andy didn't answer. He climbed down from the planks and waited as Daniel followed him. He turned to the work gang. "Keep pumpin' an' see if you kin move some of that dirt some more."

The men nodded and went back to work. But as fast as they could empty each shovelful into the barrel, the wet earth moved to fill up the gap. Andy stood there for a moment watching them, then started off. "C'mon, Daniel," he flung back over his shoulder.

The daylight outside the mine hurt Daniel's eyes and the strange silence of the waiting crowd of people pressed heavily on him. When his eyes cleared, he could see the women, their heads covered with worn shawls, their mouths tightly pressed with fear. He saw children with wide, dark, silent eyes, and men whose patient faces reflected their familiarity with death in the mines.

One of the older men spoke to Andy as he walked by. "What's it like down there?"

Andy shook his head without answering. A hushed sigh of pain escaped from the crowd. Then the quiet again, the terrible quiet of resignation.

"It's been two days," another man said. "You git any closer to em?"

"No," Andy answered. "The groun's too wet an' still movin'."

A woman began to cry. Immediately her neighbors gathered around to shield her tears. A moment later they were taking her away. There was an old rule. No tears at the mine shaft. You must never show that hope is lost.

Daniel followed Andy into the office. The clerk looked up from behind his desk. He gestured to the door behind him. "Mr. Smathers says for you to go right in."

There were two other men in the office with the superintendent. They were seated in chairs next to Mr. Smathers, who was behind the desk. An open drawing of the mine was on the desk in front of them. Smathers made the introductions. "This is Mr. Androjewicz, foreman of the day shift in the West Tunnel. Andy, Mr. Carter and Mr. Riordan—government safety engineers."

The men nodded. They did not offer to shake hands. Andy made no move either.

"These gentlemen are trying to establish the reason for the cave-in," Mr. Smathers said.

Andy nodded. He didn't speak. Any damn fool ought to know why the cave-in happened. Too much water. The pumps might have prevented it, but there weren't any pumps, so there was nothing anyone could do about it now.

Mr. Carter was the first to speak. "I understand you tapped a spring on your shift and that you packed and shored it. Why didn't you also put pumps on?"

"I asked for pumps, but they never sent 'em down," Andy said.

"You, personally?"

"No, sir. I sent Daniel here."

The two men looked at Daniel. "Who did you ask?"

Daniel stared at them. "That clerk out there."

The two men glanced at each other silently.

"If'n you don' believe me," Daniel said quickly, "why don' you jes' call 'im in an' ask 'im?"

Mr. Smathers spoke quietly. "We already did, boy. He says you never came up here. Now, why don't you just tell us the truth? We'll go easy on you."

Daniel began to feel an anger rising inside him. "I *am* tellin' the truth, Mr. Smathers. Twenty-seven men are dead down there. I knew some of 'em. Do you think I would lie if I was guilty of their death?"

"He insists no one came up here to ask for pumps," Mr. Smathers repeated.

"I was up here," Daniel said hotly. "The timekeeper even checked me out."

"There's nothing on his report," the super said. "We looked at it."

Daniel felt the color leave his face. They were all in on this together. They were going to hang it on him to save their own necks. He thought quickly, looking from one to the next. "Mr. Smathers, did you ask him about me by name?"

"How could I, boy?" the superintendent asked testily. "I don't even know your name."

"Do you think your clerk might?"

"What for? He's got nothing to do with personnel."

"He wrote my name down in a book on his desk," Daniel said. "He was mad when I tol' him Andy would come after him if'n he didn' send us the pumps an' he made a point of askin' my name."

"Even if he knows your name," Smathers said, "it won't prove anything."

"It'll prove I was up here like I said," Daniel answered.

Andy spoke suddenly. "I'll vouch fer Daniel here. He's not a liar."

"I'm afraid you're wrong," Smathers said smoothly. "No matter what the boy says."

"It don' cost you nothin' to check the book on his desk," Andy said. His face began to flush.

Smathers stared at him silently for a moment, then rose. "Come with me, gentlemen."

They followed him into the outer office. The clerk looked up at them. "Hatch," the super asked. "Do you know this boy here?"

Hatch answered. "No, sir."

"Did you ever see him before?"

"No, sir."

Smathers glanced at the two men. "Satisfied?"

They nodded.

Smathers started back into his office. At the door, he turned and looked back at the clerk. "Hatch, get me the boy's personnel record from the file."

They followed him into his office and he closed the door behind him. He walked behind his desk and sat down. Daniel stared at him. "If'n he don' know my name, how's he gonna git my record?"

Smathers looked at Daniel, a sudden respect coming into his eyes. "You *think*, boy," he said.

A moment later the clerk entered the room. He held a paper in his hand. He placed it on the desk in front of Mr. Smathers and started to leave.

"Hatch." Mr. Smathers picked up the paper and was looking at it. "You brought me the wrong file."

Hatch turned, a look of confusion coming into his face. "Oh, no, sir. That's the right file. Daniel Boone Huggins. It's marked right on . . ." His voice suddenly trailed off as he became aware they were all staring at him.

"What they goin' to do with 'im?" Daniel asked.

Andy shifted uncomfortably on the log outside the superintendent's office on which they were sitting, his narrowed eyes watching the mine entrance. "Nothin'."

Daniel was shocked. "But it was his fault—"

"Shut your mouth!" Andy's voice was sharp. "You fergit about that, now. The company ain't about to take the blame for what happened. Jes' be thankful they didn't lay it on you."

"But they got to give some reason," Daniel protested.

"They will," Andy answered. "Mark my words, they will."

The door to the building opened. Smathers stood there. "Come back inside."

They went into the building. Hatch was sitting at his desk, his head bent over an open ledger. He didn't look up as they walked past him into the superintendent's office.

Smathers closed the door behind him and went back to his desk and sat down. The two government engineers stood casually against the wall. Smathers looked up at Andy. "We've established the reason for the cave-in and we would like to know if you agree with us."

Andy was silent.

Smathers cleared his throat. "We found out that the day shift fired some shots to loosen up the coal without first checking the shoring. It was their fault. They shouldn't have been so damn careless."

Andy met the superintendent's eye steadily. "Damn careless," he said.

Smathers relaxed. "That's what will go in the report these gentlemen will write."

Andy glanced at them, then back at Smathers. "They ought to know," he said drily. "They're experts."

There was an uncomfortable silence. Smathers broke it. "But the company is going to be generous. In spite of the fact that the accident was the fault of the men, we're goin' to give each of the miners' families a hundred dollars death compensation and six months' free rent at the company's houses."

Andy didn't speak.

Smathers got to his feet. "Now we have to get the mine back in operation. There's no money for any of us if we don't start bringin' out the coal."

"It'll take a month to clear out that West Tunnel again," Andy said.

"I know that." Smathers' voice was matter-of-fact. "We're not going to clear it. We're going to seal it off. We'll begin a new tunnel on the South Vein."

"But what about the men in there?" Andy asked.

"What men?" Smathers' voice was unemotional. "Their bodies, you mean? They're dead and buried already. We can't afford to risk more lives just to get them out and bury them over again."

98

Andy was silent. He looked at Daniel. Daniel could see the anger and despair in his foreman's eyes. After a moment he turned back to Smathers. "I guess you're right, Mr. Smathers."

Smathers smiled. "You can also tell your men that the company won't dock them for the time lost during the past two days, even if we didn't bring out any coal. The company looks out for its own people."

Andy nodded. "Yes, Mr. Smathers."

Smathers turned to Daniel. "How old are you, boy?"

"Sixteen," Daniel answered, remembering the lie on his application.

"Can you read and write?"

"Yes, sir. I got me six years o' rural school."

"Mr. Hatch will be leaving here today," Smathers said. "I'd like you to come in here tomorrow an' be my clerk."

Daniel's surprise showed in his face. He looked at Andy, undecided. The foreman's hooded eyes lowered in a half-nod. Daniel turned back to Smathers. "I'd be right grateful fer the chance, Mr. Smathers."

The atmosphere in the office relaxed. Even the two government engineers were smiling. This time, they shook hands all around.

Daniel looked at Andy as they walked back to the mine. The foreman seemed lost in thought. Finally he spoke. "Got a chaw?"

Daniel fished the plug of tobacco out of his pocket and handed it to him. Andy took a massive bite from the plug, chewed a moment, then spat. "Son of a bitch!" he exclaimed.

"What do you mean?" Daniel asked.

"That Smathers is smart. He got ever'body off the hook. Even the company. An' he got us so tied in that there's nothin' we can say about it. An' even the families of those poor dead bastards down there have got to be grateful to him."

Chapter 9

THE SIX-O'CLOCK whistle was a piercing shriek that signaled the end of the day. Molly Ann stepped back on the narrow platform, away from the rapidly winding spindles. Carefully she calculated the thread speeding to the end of the reel, then, just at the right moment, raised her hand and pressed the switch, turning off the machine. She watched the reel wind down and nodded to herself with satisfaction as it came to a stop just when it was full. Quickly she lifted the coil of thread from the spindle and placed it in the shipping basket. With a last look, she stepped down from the platform. The air was filled with a hissing whisper as the great steam engines that supplied the power ceased their pounding. It was Saturday, the one night of the week the mill would be silent.

She fell into the throng of girls who walked through the mill, past the silent giant machines, on their way to the pay-master's window near the gates. There was a holiday air about them. Payday. Saturday night. Their voices, still shrill from trying to rise above the noise of the day, were filled with the excitement of their plans for the evening and the next day.

100

"Goin' to the Baptist Church dance tonight, Molly Ann?" one of the girls asked.

"There's a picnic tomorrow at the Fairgrounds," another girl said.

"The Holiness Church has a revival goin' on tomorrow," a third girl said. "Heered they got a whole passel of new copperheads and rattlers an' several of the Saints is already preparin' to partake of the Spirit."

Molly Ann smiled but didn't answer. In the six months she had been there, there had been many changes. The slight traces of baby fat had gone from her face, giving her an oddly exotic look. The high cheekbones accentuated her country green eyes, and her full lips blended into a strong chin. Her body too had changed. Her breasts were fuller, her waist narrower, and her hips flared into long straight legs.

"Molly Ann never knows what she's goin' to do," the first girl said. "She's waitin' fer Jimmy to tell her."

"Go on," Molly Ann said smiling.

"Yer sweet on 'im," the girl teased.

Again Molly Ann didn't answer. They were only children. What could they know about how she felt about Jimmy? Or for that matter, how he felt about her? All they knew was dances and good times Saturday night and Sunday, then the long waiting until the next weekend.

She took up her place in the line in front of the paymaster's window. It moved rapidly, and soon it was her turn.

The old clerk peered through the window at her. "Evenin', Molly Ann," he said, pushing the voucher through the grilled window for her to sign.

"Evenin', Mr. Thatcher," she replied, signing the slip and giving it back to him.

He took the voucher, checked it, then went through a box of envelopes on the counter next to him until he found one with her name. He took it out and gave it to her. "Better count it," he advised. "You have a big pay there with your overtime. You put in eighty hours last week."

She nodded and silently opened the envelope. The money tumbled out into her hand. Quickly she counted it. "Six dollars and forty cents," she said, looking at him.

"That's right." He nodded. "Eight cents an hour. Now, you be careful with all that money. Don't spend it all in one place."

"I won't, Mr. Thatcher," she promised. She put the money back into the envelope and started toward the gates. The usual crowd of men and boys who waited for the girls to come from work were lined up along the street. Fathers waiting for daughters, husbands for wives, young men for their girl-friends. All with the same thought. Today was payday.

The chill evening air raced through her sweat-dampened cotton dress, making it cling closely to her figure. She shivered and pulled her shawl closer around her. She walked past the first row of young men. They called and whistled. She averted her face and quickened her steps.

One of them called after her. "What you doin' tonight, Molly Ann? I don' see Jimmy aroun'."

She didn't answer. She hadn't expected Jimmy to be waiting for her. He had gone up into the hills to collect some squeezin's and would not be back until later.

The sound of a girl crying made her turn around. She was just in time to see the man strike the child. He was a large man and already half drunk. The girl tumbled backward into the mud of the streets, staring up at the man with frightened eyes.

He stood there weaving, her yellow pay envelope clutched in his hand. "That'll teach you who yer pay belongs to!" he shouted. "I'm yer father an' you'll do as I tell you. Go an' tell yer mother I'll give her whatever I danged feel like."

After a moment, he turned and walked away unsteadily. The other men just stood there silently, not moving. Molly Ann walked back to the girl and helped her up.

The child seemed to be no more than eleven years old, and she was whimpering with fear. "There, now," Molly Ann soothed. "It'll be all right."

"No," the girl cried. "My mother said she'd whup me if'n I didn' bring home the envelope."

"You jes' tell her what happened," Molly Ann said.

"It won't do no good," the child said. She began brushing the street mud from her dress. She looked up at Molly Ann,

102

the tears still in her eyes. "I cain't wait till I'm growed up like you are. Then I kin do whatever I want with my money." She finished brushing at her dress. "Thank you kin'ly."

Molly Ann watched the child walk forlornly down the street. She took a deep breath. There were many things wrong in this town. What right did parents have to treat their own blood as if they were slaves? She thanked God for her own good parents.

A boy fell into step beside her. "Want to come to the dance with me tonight, Molly Ann?"

She looked up at him. He was tall, and his hair was slicked back in the latest fashion. She could smell the beer on his breath. She shook her head. "No."

He put his hand on her arm. "Come on, Molly Ann," he said. "Don't be so snooty. Jimmy's not the only man in town. You're a pretty girl. You should git out more an' have some fun."

Her voice was quiet. "You take yer hand off'n my arm or Jimmy'll hear about it."

His hand dropped quickly. "You're a fool," he said. "You think you're the only girl Jimmy's got, but you're not. Jimmy's got more girls than anybody in town."

"You're a liar," she said. "Now go away."

He stopped, and she continued walking. "Wait, Molly Ann," he shouted after her. "You'll find out."

She reached the corner and turned down toward Main Street and Mr. Fitch's store.

"This is a good town, Mr. Cahill." Fitch's voice was filled with warm sincerity. "Good people—simple, hardworking, God-fearing, honest. Plenty of labor available. Large families hereabouts. Nothin' atall to have eight or ten kids aroun' the house. Sooner or later they all have to git jobs. Kids are no trouble. They do their work an' don' ask fer much. It ain't like back East or up North. No unions down here. People don' want 'em, people don' need 'em. They're much too independent. Mountain people. They don' trust outsiders."

"But they do trust you?" Mr. Cahill asked.

Fitch laughed. "Why shouldn't they? I'm one of 'em. Born and bred. My great-great-gran'pappy founded this town. Ever'body knows Sam Fitch is their friend.

"You kin take this message back to your associates in Phillydelphia. Sam Fitch assures them if they bring another mill down here, they'll have all the labor they want at the price they want to pay an' that there'll be no city taxes in Fitchville fer at least twenty-five years."

"You make Fitchville sound like a mighty attractive place, Mr. Fitch." Mr. Cahill was smiling now.

"It is," Fitch said. "It is. You people have no complaints with the first mill. Build another an' it'll be even better."

"Same arrangement as with the first?" Cahill asked.

"Same arrangement. Sam Fitch ain't greedy. All he wants is to do good fer his town."

Mr. Cahill nodded. "Very well, Mr. Fitch. I'll discuss this with my colleagues and I'm sure they'll be very impressed. You can be sure that you have my support."

"Thank you, Mr. Cahill, thank you." Fitch rose behind his desk, his tremendous girth filling the small office. He squeezed around the desk and walked with Mr. Cahill through the store and out into the street. They shook hands and Mr. Cahill climbed up into his carriage.

Fitch stood there as the carriage drove away, then turned and went back into the store. His face was thoughtful. A new mill meant another two hundred jobs at the very least. No matter how he looked at it, it meant a lot of money to him.

"Mr. Fitch." Her voice was soft.

He turned in surprise. He hadn't noticed her come into the store. He had been too occupied with Mr. Cahill. "Why, Molly Ann."

"It's Satiddy night, Mr. Fitch," she said.

He recovered quickly. "So it is." A broad smile came to his face. "Come into my office."

He sat down heavily behind the desk and looked at her appraisingly. Molly Ann had turned into a fine figure of a woman. He felt his mouth watering as he mentally compared her with his wife. "How're you gittin' on, my dear?" he asked.

"Fine, thank you, Mr. Fitch," she answered. She opened her pay envelope and counted out three dollars. "I would like fer you to put that in my paw's account."

"Nothin' would give me greater pleasure," he said. He picked up the money and put it in a desk drawer. "How are your folks?"

"They're not much fer writin', Mr. Fitch," she said. "But I did see them last month an' they was all well. Paw's happy with his new mule. He figgers on at least four times the crops come plantin' time."

"They should be right proud of you an' your brother," Fitch said. "Mr. Smathers tells me Dan'l is the best clerk he ever had."

Molly Ann nodded. "Thank you, Mr. Fitch."

He rose to his feet again. "You ought to come down here more often, Molly Ann. Not jes' once a week on Saturday night fer business. You know I like to see you."

"You're a busy man, Mr. Fitch," she said. "I don' like to be a bother to you."

He came around the desk and took her hand. "A pretty girl like you, Molly Ann, is never a bother."

Awkwardly she withdrew her hand. She didn't know what to say.

"Do you know that man who jes' left here?" he asked suddenly.

She shook her head. "No."

"That's Mr. J. R. Cahill. He came here to talk to ol' Sam Fitch about buildin' another mill here. You know what that means?"

She shook her head again.

"It means that if'n you treat me right, I kin see to it you get a forelady's job in the new mill."

She smiled suddenly. Now she understood him. She looked up into his face. "That's right kin' of you, Mr. Fitch."

He took her hand again. "You're a right pert girl, Molly Ann. There's no need for you to be wastin' your time on no-'counts like Jimmy Simpson when all you have to do is say the word an' you got a real friend."

"I 'preciate that, Mr. Fitch. I really do." She smiled. "An' when the new mill opens, don' be surprised if'n I come knockin' at your door."

He looked at her for a long moment, then let go of her hand. "You do that," he said heavily. "You jes' do that."

She was at the door of his office. "Evenin', Mr. Fitch."

He nodded, his heavy-lidded eyes veiling his thoughts. "Evenin', Molly Ann." He kept staring at the door long after she had gone. He picked up a cheroot and chewed on it. After a moment he lit it. Young girls were so stupid. He sucked in a lungful of the heavy gray smoke deep, then blew it out slowly. He watched the smoke drift idly toward the ceiling. Ah, well, it really didn't matter. Sooner or later he would get her. He was a very patient man.

She sat in the portable iron bathtub in the middle of the kitchen floor. Her landlady took a big kettle from the hot coal stove and came toward her. "More hot water?"

Molly Ann nodded. "Yes, thank you, Miz Wagner." She inched forward so that the water could spill behind her without scalding her. The clouds of steam came up around her face. After a moment she leaned back, her eyes closed. She could feel the aching weariness of the long day at the machine seeping out of her. "Miz Wagner," she said.

"Yes, Molly Ann?"

"Is bathtubs like this very expensive?"

"'Bout three, four dollars, I reckon."

Molly Ann sighed. "Someday if'n I ever git some extry money, I'd like to git one fer my maw. I bet she would love it."

Chapter 10

SUNDAY WAS bright and sunny, and the gentle March wind held the first hints of spring. Buds were forming on the trees, their yellow-green shoots casting a golden glow on the naked branches. Molly Ann came down the porch steps to where Jimmy waited for her next to his mule and wagon.

He turned toward her, his eyes taking in her white flowing dress, the yellow ribbons at her waist and around her hat. He whistled. "That really you, Molly Ann?"

She blushed, smiling. "Do you like it?"

He grinned. "You're beautiful. It's beautiful."

"I made it," she said. "I got the material at the French store. It's a genuine Paris, France, patent."

He took her hand. "I don't know," he said doubtfully.

"What?"

"This ol' wagon, this ol' mule. Almos' seems a shame to dirty up a nice new dress lak that."

"You jes' put a blanket up on that ol' seat," she said. "An' don' gimme none o' yer sass."

He laughed and helped her up. He stood there looking up at her. "You sure do look pretty, Molly Ann."

"Thank you," she said. "Now go back to the kitchen. I fixed us a picnic basket."

"You did? How'd you know it would be a nice day?"

She laughed. "I looked out the window, silly. Hurry up, now. The day's gittin' shorter."

A few minutes later, he was on the seat beside her and the mule was pulling them down the road. "You got yer druthers," he said. "There's a picnic at the Fairgrounds, a Holiness Church revival an' the party at Woodfield Brook."

"The party at Woodfield Brook?" she asked. "I didn' hear 'bout that one. What's goin' on?"

"Nothin'," he said. "Only us."

She slipped her arm through his and smiled. "That's my druthers."

He finished off the last piece of apple pie and leaned back on one elbow and looked at her. "That was the best victuals I ever et," he said.

She smiled. "Go on, now. 'Twas nothin. Jes' some ol' fried chicken and corn bread and apple pie."

"You fergot the pink lemonade," he said. "You shouldn' ought to spend all that money. You work too hard fer it."

She looked at him. "How else you goin' to know I kin cook?"

He laughed. "Maybe you're right."

"Did you git up to see my paw?" she asked.

"Yes," he answered. "They was all fine, an' they send you their best."

"Li'l Mase mus' be gittin' pretty big now," she said.

"He is. You should see him runnin' aroun' on his fat li'l legs."

Her voice was wistful. "I wisht I could see 'em. But it's so far."

"Maybe your forelady kin give you next Satiddy off. We kin go up there an' come back on Sunday," he said.

She brightened. "That would be nice." Then the brightness was gone. "But she wouldn' do it. They runnin' behin' and we're all workin' extra hours."

They were silent for a moment. Then she spoke again. "Maybe when the new mill opens things'll be easier."

"New mill?" he asked. "What new mill?"

"The one Mr. Fitch was talkin' 'bout. I was in his store yestiddy to put some into my paw's account an' he mentioned that mebbe he could get me a forelady's job when the new mill opened."

"He did?" Jimmy's voice had a strange hard edge that had not been there before. "Was there anything special you had to do to get the job?"

She looked at him. She knew full well what he meant, but she thought it better not to mention that part of the conversation. "No. He jes' said that when the time came I should see him."

Jimmy was silent. He stared down at the blanket thoughtfully. A new mill. He wondered where it would be built. Probably Old Man Fitch had already bought up the property from some poor broken-down farmer. He was silent for so long that she spoke again.

"Is there anything wrong, Jimmy?"

He shook his head. "No." Then his voice turned bitter. "When are the people o' this town goin' to git wise to that man? Cain't they see he's bleedin' their life away and suckin' their blood?"

"Jimmy!" She was horrified. "How kin you say turrible things like that?"

"Because it's true!" he answered hotly. "Look, you give him money ever' week for your pappy's account, don't you?"

She nodded.

"You ever ask him what your balance is?"

"No. That's not my affair. That's my paw's."

"If'n you put that money in a bank, they'd pay you interest," he said. "He don' give you nothin', an' I bet he steals the money. I bet if'n yer paw should ask him the balance, there wouldn' be none."

She didn't speak.

"How many people do you think he's got doin' what you're doin'? Maybe more'n a hundred. That's a lot of money ol' Sam Fitch's got without doin' anythin' fer it." He laughed harshly. "An' all you hillbillies are grateful to 'im fer gittin' you jobs so that you kin starve to death bein' in debt to him. But jes' you step out of line an' you'll fin' out how much of a friend Sam Fitch is. No money. No credit. No nothin'. Along comes the sheriff with a writ, an' then no more house an' lan' or place to live. Jes' like happened to the Craigs on the bend of the river. Forty acres one day. The next, nothin'." He stopped suddenly as he realized what he was saying. "Damn!" he exploded. "That's it!"

"Don't blaspheme," she said sharply.

He stared at her. "That's jes' what happened. Don't you see? He's been plannin' this fer more than a year. Fer no reason at all, the Craig kids lost their jobs in the mill an' the glass factory. As if in one week they'd all turned bad. A few months later, ol' Fitch came in an' bought their property fer a li'l more'n they owed him an' they moved away."

"I don't understand," she said.

"The new mill," he said. "That's where it's goin' to be. On the old Craig place. It's got ever'thing. Water. Power. An' room. Lots o' room."

"What're you gittin' all het up about?" she asked. "It's got nothin' to do with us."

He looked at her. "Maybe it hasn't. Not now. But in time it will. He jes' gits more 'n' more power an' pretty soon he'll own everything in the valley, includin' the people."

She stared at him for a moment, then reached for the pitcher. "Here. Have some more lemonade. You're gittin' all riled up fer nothin'."

He took the glass from her hand. His face relaxed, the grim angry lines softening into a smile. He held up the glass of lemonade and looked through it at the sun. "You're a lovely, innocent child, Molly Ann," he said. "And someday you're goin' to make some man a fine wife."

The glass shot from his hand; the pink lemonade sprayed over his shirt. She scrambled angrily to her feet. "I'm not a child! I'm past sixteen an' I'm a woman!" she snapped. "An' you better be man enough to ask me or else you kin take me home!"

He stared up at her in surprise. Hurt and anger made her even more beautiful. He felt his heart well up inside him almost as if it would burst his sides. His own voice sounded strange in his ears. "I'm askin', Molly Ann."

It was her turn to be surprised. She was speechless.

"I'm askin', Molly Ann," he repeated. "What is your answer?"

"Oh, Jimmy!" she said, flinging herself down on him, the tears coming to her eyes. "Yes, yes, yes!"

They were married a little over a month later on the first of May, 1915, at the First Baptist Church of Fitchville. All her family was there, down from the hills, dressed in their Sunday best. All except Daniel. He could not get time off from his job.

It was the same day they began clearing the land on the old Craig farm to build the new mill.

Molly Ann came into the bedroom, her face flushed with excitement. "Wake up!" she said, shaking his shoulder. "Wake up!"

Jimmy threw one arm over his head. "Let me be, woman," he mumbled. "It's Sunday morning."

"Mr. Fitch is here to see you," she said.

"Ol' Man Fitch?" He was awake now. "To see me?"

She nodded.

"I wonder what he wants."

"I don' know," she said. "Theah was a knock on the door. I opened it an' theah he was. It's very important, he said."

"Very important?" He moved suddenly, pulling her down on him. "This is Sunday morning an' I didn' git my morninger yet."

Her arms pushed against his chest. "You were too busy sleepin'." His mouth covered her lips. "Please, Jimmy, what will he think?" she murmured.

"I don' give a damn," he said.

She pushed herself away. "Don't blaspheme!" she said sharply. "Now you git yerself dressed an' come downstairs." She walked to the door. "I've made some fresh coffee."

Mr. Fitch was seated at the table in the kitchen when he

came into the room. In front of him were a plate of ham and eggs, a steaming mug of coffee and hot rolls and butter. He was shoveling food into his mouth as if years had passed since he had eaten his last meal.

"Mornin', Mr. Fitch," he said.

Mr. Fitch swallowed a mouthful of food before he replied. "Mornin', Jimmy. I declare, yer li'l wife heah is as fine a cook as her mother. Yer a very lucky man."

Jimmy nodded. He walked to the table and sat down. Molly Ann placed a mug of coffee in front of him and went back to the stove. Jimmy picked up the mug. The coffee was steaming and fragrant. "I know that," he said.

Mr. Fitch wiped the last bit of yolk from his plate with his roll. He swallowed it whole, washing it down with the coffee. He leaned back, patting his stomach gently. "That's a mighty fine breakfast, Miz Simpson."

Molly Ann blushed much like her mother. She didn't miss the fact that he'd promoted her from Molly Ann to Mrs. Simpson. "Thank you, Mr. Fitch." She looked at Jimmy. "Ready for your breakfast now?"

"Not yet," Jimmy said. "I'll just have some coffee fer now."

"Then I'll leave you gentlemen to your business," she said politely, and went into the next room. But also like her mother, she stayed near the doorway so that she could hear what was being said.

"What brings you out on a Sunday mornin'?" Jimmy asked, not waiting for Fitch to lead off.

Fitch smiled. "I missed seein' you in church the las' few Sundays."

Jimmy didn't answer. He realized Fitch knew that he was not much for Sunday churchgoing.

"But I figgered," Fitch continued smoothly, "young man, newly married, beautiful young wife. What would he be doin' in church of a Sunday mornin' anyhow?"

Jimmy picked up his coffee mug and studied it. "Molly Ann told me you said it was important."

"It is," Mr. Fitch said seriously. "Very important." He paused for effect. "I've been keepin' an eye on you fer a long time, young man. An' I've liked what I've seen. You remin' me very much of myself when I was your age. Full of git-up-an'-go."

Jimmy nodded silently.

"An' I been thinkin'," Mr. Fitch said. "I'm not gittin' any younger, an' a young man like you can go a long way in business with me. I got nobody I can depend on an' too much to do."

"Are you offerin' me a job, Mr. Fitch?" Jimmy was incredulous.

"In a sort of way," Mr. Fitch replied. "But more'n that. I want you to take over some things fer me so that I can pay attention to others."

"What sort of things, Mr. Fitch?"

"You call me Sam," Fitch said.

"All right, Sam. What things?"

"The folk hereabouts know you an' like you," Fitch said. "You can he'p out at the store, buy the squeezin's, handle things with the good folk. You know what I mean."

"I don't know," Jimmy said.

"In business there are always problems," Fitch said. "Sometimes people don' understand what yer doin' is fer their own good."

Jimmy nodded without speaking. He could appreciate that without any trouble. It wasn't always easy to make people understand you were cheating them for their own good.

Fitch interpreted Jimmy's nod as approval. "I've always done my bes' fer this town. But now there's beginnin' to be some talk that I'm doin' it jes' to butter my own bread. Like the new mill. That's two hunnert jobs fer the good folk hereabouts. Still there's talk that I'm jes' doin' it fer my own interest."

"You're not benefitin' from it?" Jimmy asked with pretended naiveté.

"Of course I'm benefitin'," Fitch said. "That's only good business. But so is the town. I'm bringin' more industry an' work to it, an' still all I hear is that the Craigs say I squeezed them off'n their land in order to sell it to the mill. Now they claim they still own seven acres along the river that was deeded separate in their gran'pappy's name an' he's still alive."

113

"But they're already clearin' on the riverfront," Jimmy said. "How can they do that if'n they don' own the land?"

"That's jest it," Fitch said. "The Craigs are wrong. But it would take a long time to win the case in court. Meanwhile, the mill would not open an' the townfolk would lose all that work an' pay. So bein' generous, I made 'em an offer, but they refused."

"How much did you offer?" Jimmy asked.

"Ten times what the land is worth. Fifty dollars an acre. Three hundred and fifty for the parcel. An' that's fer land they don' even have clear title to."

"But neither does the mill, if'n they press their claim," Jimmy said.

"Ain't no court in the lan' that will hold up the Craigs' claim against the mill. I already spoke to Jedge Hanley an' that's what he tells me."

"Then what're you worried about?" Jimmy asked.

"I jes' don' want no unpleasantness. I want the folks to see that what I'm doin' is fer their own good."

"I still don' see how I kin he'p you there," Jimmy said.

"The Craigs know you an' like you," Fitch said. "They would listen to you."

Jimmy nodded. "They might." He rose and refilled his mug. "An' what do I get out of it?"

Fitch looked up at him. "You'll be with me, boy. I'll make you rich. I'll start you out with a salary of twenty-five a week."

That was at least five dollars a week more than any man in town was paid. Jimmy knew that. It was also ten dollars more a week than he averaged even in the best of times. "I don' know," he said cautiously. "That's jest a job, an' I kind of like the idea of bein' in business fer myself."

"You don' make nowhere near that kind of money."

"But then, I don' have to go to work every day neither," Jimmy said.

"That was all right when you were alone, but now you're married an' settled down. An' pretty soon there'll be a family. You got to be thinkin' of them now."

Jimmy sat down at the table. "I don' know," he said.

Fitch smiled. He felt he had him. "You talk it over with

your wife." He got to his feet. "She'll agree with me. She's a good sensible girl. You can let me know tomorrow."

After he had gone, Molly Ann came rushing back into the kitchen. "Isn't it wonderful?"

He looked at her. "You don't understand, do you?"

"What?" She was bewildered.

"That he wants me to be a crook like him. To cheat an' steal from folk like your family an' the Craigs."

She was silent for a moment. "Then what are you goin' to do?"

"Same as I been doin'," he said. "Mindin' my own business an' sellin' my whiskey."

But that was not the way it was to be. For two days after Jimmy refused Mr. Fitch's offer, someone fired a rifle through the open window of the ramshackle wooden house about eleven miles from town where the Craigs now lived and killed Grandfather Craig.

Mr. Fitch was as indignant as the rest of the townspeople at the senseless murder of the old man and put up a fifty-dollar reward of his own money for the arrest and capture of the killer. And despite the fact that the Craigs' claim to the river acreage was even further obfuscated by the old man's death, he raised his offer for the land to five hundred dollars in order to help out the poor family. He also promised to intercede in their behalf and see to it that the Craig children got their jobs back in the mill and the glass factory.

It was a very generous offer, he thought. There was only one thing wrong with it. The Craigs turned it down. And a few days after the funeral, a shot fired from the woods adjoining the Craig land killed the mill construction foreman as he was issuing orders to his work gang to resume clearing along the river edge.

All work came to a stop. There was no way for the men to tell which one of them would be next, and they would not return to work until armed guards were brought in to patrol the perimeters of the property. The first day after the guards arrived, one of them was found dead on his post by his relief man. He had been shot through the back of the head at close range with a Smith & Wesson .44-caliber revolver.

When Sam Fitch got the news of the killing late that afternoon, his lips tightened grimly and all his geniality disappeared. For the first time in his life, his rule was being threatened. His reply was the inevitable reply of power. That same night, nineteen-year-old John, the Craigs' eldest son, was shot to death as he went to water his mule.

And that was how the war that would become known as Craigs' War began in Fitchville. It would not end for almost two years and not until many more people were killed, among them women and children. It would be remembered as the bloodiest mountain feud in the history of West Virginia.

Chapter 11

DANIEL FELT the rumbling in his stomach and looked up at the clock on the wall. It was twelve thirty, and Mr. Smathers and his visitors had not yet left for lunch. It had to be a very important meeting, because Mr. Smathers was a prompt twelve-o'clock man when it came to lunch. Maybe there was something to the rumors that had been flying around for the last few months that the mine was about to be sold.

The door to the inner office opened and Mr. Smathers stood there. "You still here, Daniel?" There was a note of surprise in his voice.

"Yes, sir." Daniel was polite. "I was waitin' until you left for lunch."

"It's all right, Daniel. There's no need for you to wait. You can go to lunch now."

Daniel closed the posting ledger and got to his feet. "Thank you, Mr. Smathers." He bent down and took the lunch box from under his desk. Mr. Smathers went back into the inner office as Daniel went out the front door.

Daniel sat down on the bench just outside the building and opened the lunch box. He smiled to himself. Carrie had been extra good to him. He had a fresh banana as well as the usual apple, and the liverwurst-and-potato-salad sandwich on the fresh home-baked bread smelled real good.

He leaned back against the building, his eyes half closed in contentment as he chewed his sandwich. His collar was beginning to feel tight. He loosened his tie and opened the collar. Many things had changed in the year he had been working as a clerk.

Perhaps the most important was being able to afford a room all to himself. The other was that his eyes no longer hurt in the daylight. It more than made up for having to wear a collar and tie every day. He unscrewed the cap of the thermos bottle and took a sip of the hot, sweet coffee. That Carrie was a gem. She was worth every penny of the extra half-dollar he slipped her each week.

He heard footsteps approaching and turned his head in the direction of the sound. His former foreman, Andy, came around the corner of the building and stopped in front of him. "I want to talk to you, Daniel," he said abruptly.

"Go ahead and talk, Andy. I'm listenin'." He wondered what was so important that Andy had come up out of the mine to talk about it. Usually Andy took his lunch in the shaft with the rest of the men.

"Not here," Andy said. "Too many people around."

Daniel didn't see anyone, but got to his feet anyway. "Okay," he said. "Where?"

"Behind the toolshed," Andy said, walking away. "I'll wait for you."

Daniel nodded. He finished his sandwich and then slowly made his way to the toolshed. Andy was leaning against the back wall, his mouth working on a chaw. He let fly as Daniel came up. The spit sounded like a shot as it hit a rock ten feet away.

Daniel looked at him. Andy was acting strangely. He had never seen him this way before.

Andy looked both ways before talking. "Anybody see you coming over?"

"I don't think so." Daniel was puzzled. "What difference would it make if'n they did?"

Andy didn't answer his question. Instead, he asked one of his own. "Is the mine being sold?"

118

"I don't know," Daniel answered honestly.

"There's talk that it is," Andy said. "I thought you might know."

"I heered the rumors, too, but I don't know any more'n anybody else."

"Those men with Smathers. They're from Detroit."

"I don' know," Daniel said. "Nobody tol' me."

"They say the mine's goin' to be taken over by an automobile company an' that the fust thing they're goin' to do is change over to scrip pay like they did over at the Parlee."

"You're talkin' to the wrong man," Daniel said. "Mr. Smathers' the man you should ask them questions, not me. I'm jest a clerk."

"I thought you might have heard somethin'," Andy said.

"Why should I?" Daniel asked. "I don' go listenin' at keyholes."

"I'm not sayin' you do," Andy said quickly.

"I don' know what you're so het up about," Daniel said. "What difference does it make who owns the mine as long as we git paid?"

"Big difference," Andy said dourly. "They pay you in scrip instead of money an' they got you by the short hairs. You got to git everything at their stores an' next thing you know you're in hock up to your ears an' you never git out."

"Still, if'n they sell the mine, they ain't much you kin do about it excep' if'n you don' like the job you kin quit."

"They would like that," Andy said. "Then they could replace us with cheaper men. No, there's another way. A better way."

"What's that?" Daniel asked curiously.

Andy's face took on a guarded look. "I can't talk about it right now. I don't know whose side you're on."

Daniel was bewildered. "What sides?"

"Management or ours."

"Ours?"

"The miners'," Andy said. "It's different when you're not workin' down there."

"I don' see that makes no difference," Daniel said. "I'm workin' for my keep, the same as you."

Andy stared at him for a moment. "You're a strange one."

Daniel was silent.

"Would you tell me if you hear anything?" Andy asked.

"No." Daniel's voice was flat. "I don't believe in spyin'. Fer anybody."

"Even for a good cause?"

"I'd have to see the cause real clear," Daniel said. "Then I'd make up my mind."

Andy grinned suddenly and was once again the man whom Daniel knew. "What're you doin' with your nights, boy?"

"Nothin' much."

"I hear tell that you're spendin' a lot of evenin's with Miss Andrews, the new teacher down at the school."

Daniel felt the flush rising over his collar. There were no secrets in a mining town. "She's bringin' me on with my schoolin'."

"Sure that's all she's bringin' you on with?" Andy asked shrewdly.

Daniel felt the flush grow deeper. "I got a lot to learn."

"I'll bet you have," Andy laughed. Abruptly he grew serious. "I may be callin' on you again in a few days."

"You know where to find me," Daniel said. "I ain't goin' no place."

He watched the foreman walk off, then turned and went back to his bench outside the building. He sat down and took the banana out of the lunch box and carefully peeled it down. He ate it slowly, savoring the ripe sugary sweetness of it. That Carrie was a real love.

He washed down the last piece of his apple with the remainder of his coffee. Carefully he closed his lunch box and went back into the office. Mr. Smathers' door was still closed. He glanced up at the clock as he put his lunch box under the desk. There was time enough for him to stroll over to the breaker room and see what was going on.

The breaker room was located at the other end of the track from the mine shaft. It was there that the coal hauled from the mine was dumped onto a conveyor belt. From there it traveled down a chute, where the boys would pick out the slag by hand and send the coal itself on to one truck while the slag was carted away to be dumped on the other side of the mountain.

Daniel walked into the shed that was built over the breaker room, which was cut on a sharp incline into the side of the mountain, and out onto the platform that overlooked the breaker boys. The room was getting back into full operation after the lunch hour. It never really stopped completely, because while half the boys had their lunch, the other half were working. Now they were all back at work and the coal was tumbling down the chute, sending clouds of gray-black dust into the air and partly obscuring the view from the platform. After a moment his eyes adjusted and he could see the boys below.

They sat, in rows, on either side of the chute. Cramped together on their tiny benches, they huddled over the breaker boxes, their hands flying over the coal, separating out the slag more by touch than by sight. The speed of their work was controlled by the supervisors, who forced the pace by increasing the flow of coal into the chute. If a boy should fall behind, he would soon find his arms buried in a pile of coal.

Over the rumbling sound of the coal falling down the chute, Daniel could hear the voices of the supervisors as they walked up and down the narrow steps beside the chute shouting at the boys to speed up and empty their boxes. They were young, their ages running from nine to thirteen or fourteen, but with their drawn, blackened faces and permanently curved backs, they looked like miniature old men.

One of the supervisors climbed up onto the platform beside him. He glanced at Daniel and nodded as he went to the bucket and held a dipper of water to his mouth. He drank his fill before he spoke. "Lazy little bastards!"

Daniel didn't answer him. The supervisor came over and stood beside him, looking down at the boys. "I wonder if the office knows how hard we have to work to get the boys to move that coal."

Daniel turned to him. "They seem to be workin' all right."

"You don't know 'em," the supervisor said. "Half the time they're fakin'. They jes' look busy. Not like when I was young. The boys really picked slag then."

Daniel shrugged.

"The mine bein' sold?" the supervisor asked.

"I don' know," Daniel answered shortly.

"You kin tell me," the supervisor said in a confidential voice.

"I said I don' know." Daniel's voice took on a hard edge.

"Okay, okay," the supervisor said quickly. "Don't git tetchy jes' because you work in the office now. You're no better than the rest of us."

Daniel looked at him, his eyes suddenly cold. "What do you mean by that?"

"You think we don' know why you come down here? Not jes' to pass the time of day you don't."

Daniel's mouth tightened as the anger rose inside him. He took a step toward the man, but was stopped by a shriek from below. It was the scream of a boy in pain.

"Stop the coal!" A supervisor shouted.

The supervisor on the platform next to Daniel reached up and pulled the trap. The flow of coal to the chute stopped immediately. "Damn! What now?" he said, coming back to the rail and peering down into the breaker.

They could hear the boy screaming, but couldn't see him until the clouds of dust cleared a little. A small boy near the bottom of the chute had his hand trapped between the conveyor and his sorting box.

"Stupid little bastard!" the supervisor swore, heading for the steps. He went down the steps three at a time. By the time he reached the boy there was a cluster of other children around him. The boy himself had fainted.

"Git back to your boxes!" he shouted. Another supervisor joined him, and quickly and expertly they extricated the boy's hand from the chute. He lifted the boy, not too gently, in his arms and started up the steps with him. As he reached the platform with the unconscious boy, he freed one hand to start the coal down the chute again.

Daniel looked at the boy. He seemed to be no more than ten years old, his face pinched white, his mangled hand dripping blood as he hung limply in the supervisor's arms.

The supervisor caught Daniel's glance. "You kin tell the office 'twarn't our fault. Damn kid couldn't keep up."

Daniel didn't answer.

"'Twarn't our fault," the supervisor repeated.

"Better go git the kid's hand tended to," Daniel said.

He watched the supervisor hurry out of the shed with the boy. There was no infirmary, but the old man in charge of the toolshed knew what to do about accidents. The boy would be taken there, his hand would be bandaged and then he would be sent home. Of course, his pay would stop until such time as he could return. That is, if he could ever return to work as a breaker boy. There was no such thing as a one-handed breaker boy.

Daniel looked down into the shed. Coal was tumbling down the chute; the dust was flying, the supervisors shouting; the boys were sorting coal. It was as if nothing had happened.

He was suddenly aware that his hands were gripping the platform railing tightly. He stared down at them. He imagined his own hand torn and bleeding. Something had to be wrong. A pair of hands had to be worth more than the three dollars a week they paid the breaker boys.

Chapter 12

WHEN HE hadn't appeared by nine o'clock, Sarah Andrews decided that he was not coming that night and made ready to go to bed. Usually he was there by seven thirty, right after supper. She locked and bolted the front door of the little house adjoining the school where she taught, and left the small living room for the even smaller bedroom.

Slowly she began to undress. Strange that he hadn't said anything yesterday. Usually when he was not coming he would tell her the night before. Maybe something had happened to him. She had heard there was an accident at the mine today. A flash of fear leaped through her for a brief moment—but then she reminded herself that he didn't work in the mine, he worked in the office.

She hung her dress neatly, stepped out of her petticoat and pulled the pins from her hair. Long and dark brown, it came tumbling around her shoulders. She caught a glimpse of her face in the mirror, with the dark hollows of her eyes set deep. She stopped and looked at herself. Her mother had been right. But then, her mother had always been right.

"Sarah Andrews," her mother had said. "You with your nose buried in books all day and night will be an old maid."

And that was what she was. Thirty years old. Unmarried. No prospect in sight. An old maid. Just as her mother had predicted.

She took off her camisole, and her breasts seemed to fill the mirror. She stared at them in fascination. As she watched, the nipples seemed to grow larger and the breasts began to ache. She cupped them in her hands and held them tightly. It seemed to ease the hurt. She closed her eyes. They were his hands.

But they were not. It had been five years since he had touched her and then gone away. Her mother said that he had never intended to marry her. But never was too strong a word. He was just not the kind of man to get married. Responsibility frightened him. She had realized that when it was too late.

Still, she had never regretted knowing him and loving him. For the first time she'd been aware that she was a woman, and she had learned to take joy in her own femaleness. Her mother had said that she was a hussy, that all the neighbors were talking and that she could no longer hold up her head in the community. From that point on it had been just a question of time until she could get away. And after that it had been a different school in a different town almost every year. Not once in the five years had she ever gone home.

There had been other men. Brief, quick affairs, brought on by the desperate physical clawing deep inside her. But when her body was satisfied, a deep disgust replaced the longing. Each time she would promise herself that it would not happen again. But it did. And in the end, it had driven her from town to town, changing schools as she sensed the growing awareness of the townspeople. Especially the men. The way they looked at her, like hounds after a bitch in heat. There were no secrets in a small town.

It was seven months since she had come to this small mining town just outside of Grafton. When she saw the little house next to the school, she had known it would be different this time. Here she would be alone—not in the usual boarding-house, subject to the temptations and the smells of men around her. Alone, she would have nothing to stir her longing. She would be content in her work. This time she would not let herself be frustrated by trying to get some knowledge into the heads of children who knew that they were there only until work was found for them in the mines or in the mills. Silently she accepted the fact that the boys would disappear by the time they were ten or eleven years old. The girls would stay a little longer, but they too would be gone by the time they were twelve, thirteen or fourteen. Still, there was never a shortage of children in the school. Good year or bad, it was the only crop that never failed.

That was why she had been surprised when she had looked up from her desk one day during lunch hour and seen him at the other end of the room. At first she had thought he might be the father of one of the children, coming to withdraw his child from the school to put him to work. He filled the doorway. He was big, almost six feet, wide-shouldered and deep-chested. A few locks from the mass of unruly black hair fell toward the thick eyebrows over the deep-set startlingly blue eyes. And the shaven blue-black beard outlined a wide mouth and strong chin. As he came into the classroom, she knew that he was not as old as she had first thought.

"Miss Andrews?" His voice was deep but gentle.

"Yes?"

He took a few hesitant steps toward her. "I'm sorry to disturb you, ma'am. I'm Dan'l Boone Huggins."

She almost smiled, his awe of her was so visible. "You're not disturbing me, Mr. Huggins. What can I do for you?"

He didn't come any closer. "I'm the clerk in Mr. Smathers' office at the mine."

She nodded without speaking.

"I been workin' fer him fer about a year now, an' I'm beginnin' to re'lize jes' how stupid I am. I need more learnin'."

She stared at him in real surprise. This was the first time in all the years she had been teaching that anyone had ever admitted that to her. Book learnin', as they called it, was considered a waste of time. "Exactly what is it you would like to learn, Mr. Huggins?" she asked.

"I don' know," he said. Then, after a moment, "Ever'thing, I reckon."

She smiled. "That's a pretty large order."

His face was serious. "There's so many things I don't know

nothin' 'bout. Since I been workin' in the office I heered people talkin'. Politics, business, eeconomics. I don't know nothin' 'bout them things. I kin read 'n' write 'n' figger some, but there are words I don' know the meanin' of, an' when it comes to multiplyin' an' dividin' I git real mixed up."

"Have you had any schooling?"

"Yes, ma'am," he nodded. "Six years in a rural school. But it stopped when I was fourteen, an' that's all there was."

She looked at him thoughtfully. "Did you ever think of going to the library?"

"Yes, ma'am. But the nearest one is in Grafton, an' I work six days an' it's closed on Sunday."

She nodded. Grafton was almost sixteen miles away, so there would be no chance of his being able to get there during the week. "I don't know what I can do," she said.

"Anything you kin do, ma'am, I would truly appreciate," he said earnestly. "It's more'n what I kin do myself."

She thought for a moment. The children began drifting back into the classroom. Lunchtime was over. They looked at Daniel, curiosity on their normally unexpressive faces. She looked up at him. "There is very little we can do now," she said. "Class is starting again. Can you come back later?"

"I work until six, ma'am," he answered. "I kin be here right after."

She nodded. "That will be all right, Mr. Huggins."

"Thank you kindly, ma'am."

She watched him close the door behind him, then turned back to the class. The children's eyes swiveled from the doorway back to her. She heard a snicker from some of the larger children toward the back of the room. She rapped the pointer sharply on her desk. "You in the back," she snapped. "Open your books to page thirty, geography lesson number two."

It wasn't until the last of the children had left the classroom after four o'clock that she thought about him again. She puzzled over what she could do for him. Perhaps the best thing would be to find out how much he had actually learned. At least, that would be a beginning. She went to the cupboard and took out a set of six-year final-examination papers and spread them on the desk in front of her.

That had been six months ago. Since then, much to her

surprise and excitement, she had found that this big, quiet boy had a bright, inquisitive mind that soaked up knowledge as fertile ground soaked up rain. They spent three evenings a week and Sunday afternoons together. Daniel read voraciously and questioned endlessly. Finally she had written to her mother and asked her to send her college books. For the first time she had been filled with the pure joy of teaching. Somwhere in the back of her head she knew this was the way it should be.

Gratefully, he had offered to pay her for the lessons. She had refused. She was glad to have something to do with her spare time. But he still wanted to do something. Finally she agreed that he could reciprocate by cutting a week's supply of cordwood for both the school and her little house every Sunday.

She had begun to look forward to Sunday mornings, when she would be awakened by the ringing sound of the axe in back of her house. There was something strangely reassuring and comforting about it. A touch of home. An echo from her childhood when her older brother used to perform the same chore. Somehow she no longer felt strange here. No longer alone.

For her, the simple warm feeling had lasted throughout the winter and into the beginning of spring. Then, one sunny morning, she had risen from her bed and gone to the window.

He had stripped to his waist. The sweat streaming down his body shone redly in the sunlight. The muscles rippled as the axe rose and fell. Transfixed, she watched the light tan cloth of his trousers darken with sweat across his buttocks and around his crotch.

The sudden surge of heat and the rush of wetness to her groin took her by surprise. She felt her legs begin to give away under her, and she held on to the windowsill to keep from slipping to the floor. Angrily she shook her head to clear it. This was not the way it was supposed to be. She closed her eyes tightly and kept them closed until she regained her self-control.

From that day on she was more consciously circumspect, more careful not to sit too close to him, more careful in her dress, more formal in her language. If he was aware of how or why she was acting the way she did, he gave no sign. Occasionally when her glance took him by surprise, his face would flush, but she attributed that to his normal shyness.

That was the way it had been last evening when she had looked across the kitchen table and caught him watching her. Immediately the redness had begun to creep up into his face.

"Daniel," she asked, without thinking, "how old are you?"

The flush grew deeper. He hesitated. "Eighteen, ma'am," he lied.

She was silent for a moment. "You look older." She lied too. "I'm twenty-five."

He nodded.

"Don't you have any friends?" she asked.

"Some," he answered.

"Girlfriends, I mean."

"No, ma'am."

"Not even back home? A special girl?"

He shook his head.

"What do you do in your time off? Don't you go to the socials and the Saturday-night dances?"

"I was never much one fer dancin', ma'am."

"It doesn't seem right," she said. "You're young and handsome and—"

"Miss Andrews," he interrupted.

She stared at him in surprise. It was the first time he had ever done anything like that.

His face was scarlet. "I'm not one fer games neither. Girls is allus lookin' fer to git married, an' I'm not about to. I got family dependin' on me."

"I'm sorry," she apologized, accepting the rebuke. "I didn't mean to pry."

He rose from the chair. "It's late. Time fer me to go."

She rose with him. She reached over and closed the book he had left on the table. "We'll finish this lesson tomorrow night."

But it was now nine o'clock and he still hadn't appeared. Slowly she made ready for bed. The last thought she had before she turned out the light was that she had lost him. He would never come again.

Chapter 13

THE TINY parlor of Andy's house was crowded and filled with the smoke from the black, ropelike cigars most miners used. Daniel looked around the room from the corner in which he had placed himself. There was an air of tense expectancy, and the miners spoke among themselves in hushed, almost secret tones as if they were afraid that the man they were speaking to would hear them.

Andy had appeared at his boardinghouse just as Daniel was preparing to leave for his lesson with Miss Andrews. "You come with me," the foreman said shortly.

Daniel looked at him. "What fer?"

"You'll find out," Andy said tightly. He started down the steps of the porch and then looked back up at Daniel. "Well?"

Daniel nodded and descended the steps. He fell in beside the foreman. They had walked almost a block before Andy spoke.

"I'm takin' a big chance bringin' you," he said. "Most of the men think you gone over. They think you're with the bosses."

"Then why you goin' to this trouble?" Daniel asked.

The stocky foreman stopped and looked at him, his shock

of white hair gleaming in the light of the gas lamp. "I been asked to make sure you were there."

"By who?"

"You'll find out," Andy said mysteriously. He began to walk again. "Besides, I think you're with us. I worked in the mines beside you, and once you work in the mines you never stop bein' a miner, no matter what else you do."

The rest of the walk to his home was made in silence. Shortly after they got there, the other men began to arrive. They glanced at Daniel but didn't say anything to him. Gradually Daniel drifted into the corner, where he leaned against the wall and smoked his cigar. There were more than a dozen men clustered together in small groups.

There was a sound of an approaching automobile. One of the men near the window looked out. He turned back to the room. "They're here!"

There was a general movement to the door. Andy opened it. Daniel could see the black Model T roll to a stop. The men spilled out onto the porch. Daniel didn't move.

A moment later Andy came into the house with a big, stocky man walking beside him. Daniel looked at the man with curiosity. He wasn't a tall man, but he looked big. Broad-shouldered and barrel-chested, with the beginning of a big belly, he had a shock of thick, unruly black hair that fell over bushy eyebrows and deep-set, penetrating blue eyes. He moved with an aura of importance and assurance through the men who clustered around him, shaking hands firmly and looking each of the men directly in the eyes. His teeth were amazingly small behind his thick, fleshy lips. They came over to Daniel.

"This is Daniel," Andy said as if that explained everything. The man reached for Daniel's hand. "John L. Lewis, the executive vice president of the United Mine Workers."

Mr. Lewis' hand was soft but amazingly strong. He looked at Daniel. "You're Jimmy Simpson's brother-in-law," he said. "Jimmy told me a great deal about you."

Daniel kept the surprise out of his voice. "You know Jimmy?"

Mr. Lewis nodded. "And your sister, Molly Ann. A fine

girl. Jimmy's doing a fine job for us up Fitchville way. Let's all hope that we make the same kind of progress down here."

Before Daniel could answer, he turned and made his way to the front of the room. He wasted no time. He held up a hand, and the men fell silent.

"First of all, I have to correct Andy's introduction," he said. "My good friend keeps introducing me as executive vice president of the union. I thank him for the promotion, but that job still belongs to Frank Hayes."

A chorus of voices interrupted him. "Not for long, John." "You're our man."

Lewis smiled. He held up a hand, and they were silent again. "That's for the future to decide. I have no ambitions; all I want now is to do a good job for you men. That's the reward I'm looking for. To see your jobs secure, your work made safe and your pay equal to the highest standards in the industry."

The men began to cheer. Lewis waited for their shouts to die down. After a moment, he began again. "As you know, the U.M.W. is already one of the largest unions in the country. As of the beginning of this year we have over a quarter of a million dues-paying members. That we are accepted by the government of the United States is evidenced by the fact that President Wilson appointed as the first Secretary of Labor one of our own U.M.W. leaders and founders, Mr. William B. Wallace."

Again the men cheered. This time Lewis overrode their cheers. "For the past year, I represented Sam Gompers as legislative assistant in Washington. This year I returned to my old U.M.W. local in Indianapolis to once more devote myself to the people I love, the miners. Two months ago, after much consideration, we decided that it was time for the U.M.W. to move into the last remaining nonunion section of the country. The West Virginia–Kentucky mining sector. I won't go into the history of why we have not come here before. A number of times we have tried to unionize, but we have always been defeated. It was not your fault. You men wanted the union. But the owners' corruption and terror tactics proved too much for us, so in order to protect your lives and health, we backed away. I do not plan to argue now whether our decision was right or wrong. It was made eight years ago, and perhaps it was right then in order to prevent bloodshed. But since that time, conditions have not improved; instead they have worsened. Today, you miners in this area are getting less for your labor than you were then, you are more in debt and you are working longer hours under more dangerous and hazardous conditions. And now that the Detroit automobile companies have put together a consortium of the twenty biggest mines in this area, it don't look to get better. It looks to get worse."

The men were silent. Lewis glanced around the room. "Now it is time for decision. A few months from now may be too late. Once the consortium takes control, it may be too late. By then you will truly be in their power. By then we might not be able to help you.

"To meet this emergency, the executive board of the U.M.W. has created a new district local for this area. It will be known as District 100. We are pledging five thousand dollars for immediate organizing expenses, and the first thing you men have to do is go out and sign up every one of your brothers into the union. If you can do this before the mines are officially taken over, we'll be in a good bargaining position. Already men are at work all over the district. Now is the time for each of you to demonstrate his solidarity with his brothers. Each of you here must become an organizer. Our success, your own success depends on your own individual efforts."

Now there were no cheers. The men were silent. They looked at each other dubiously. It was one thing to join up; it was another to put themselves in the forefront of a battle which, if they lost it, would cost them their jobs and futures.

"Are you sure the mines are bein' taken over?" one of the men asked.

Lewis nodded. "As sure as I'm standing here. We have information which leads us to believe that once it's done, the owners will launch the biggest campaign in history to bring down the union and further enslave the workers."

"We never had no trouble at this mine," another man said.

"Thirty-four men dead and over a hundred men permanently injured in the last two years in this mine and you say you don't have trouble? The worst safety record in the country, and all for the lowest pay scale in the industry, and you say you don't have trouble? If you don't consider that trouble, then I must say that you people don't know what trouble is. Is there a man among you who owns his own home, is there a man among you who does not owe his next month's wages to the stores for food and necessities, is there a man among you who if he should be injured and not able to work could continue to live in the house the company overcharges him for? Now to make it worse, when the mines are taken over you won't even get paid in United States dollars. They're goin' to turn back the clock an' pay you in company scrip. Then you'll see how much further into the hole the mining bosses will shove you. You'll be in so deep that you'll never get out, because the only way out will be the grave."

Lewis waited for a moment before he spoke again. "Your only hope is speed. To organize quickly before the bosses become aware of what you're doing. Next week may be too late. Tomorrow each of you men must go out and sign up every one of his brother workers before word has a chance to get back. Because once it gets back, all hell will break loose. Your only chance is for all of us to be together in the union."

Lewis opened the briefcase he had brought with him and took out a document. "I have here in my hand the articles of incorporation and the constitution approved by the general council of U.M.W., organizing you in this mine as Local 77 of District 100. Andy Androjewicz will be provisional president until you have a membership quota, at which time you will elect your own board and officers." He took out another sheaf of papers. "Here are membership applications. I expect every man in this room to sign one before he leaves and afterward to sign up every other miner he contacts. The executive board has waived application and membership fees for the first three months, which gives you a chance to benefit before you pay and will place no hardship on the members. You show us you want us here by signing up one hundred men and we'll send in an organizer from our own headquarters to help you. The rest is up to you. Support your brothers of the U.M.W. and your brothers will support you."

He gave the membership applications to Andy, who began to pass them out. He went through the room quickly, followed by his thirteen-year-old son, a worker in the breaker shed, who handed out pencils. Almost without a word the men began to fill out and sign the forms.

Daniel took the form that Andy gave him and looked at it. He didn't speak. Andy went to the front of the room and joined Mr. Lewis. He held up a hand. "If any of you men have any questions, Mr. Lewis will answer them."

Daniel was the only one who held up his hand. Mr. Lewis nodded. "Yes, Daniel?"

"I'm a clerk in the mine superintendent's office. I don't work in the mines. I don't know if it's proper fer me to sign this."

Lewis looked at Andy. Andy nodded. The big man turned back to Daniel. "You work for the mine?"

"Yes, sir."

"I don't see any problem. The same things can happen to you that can happen to any of them. You need the same job protection as the rest."

"Mebbe that's true, Mr. Lewis. But I'm privy to many things that concern the miners. I don' see how I kin rightly do an honest job fer Mr. Smathers an' at the same time be a member of the union when doin' my job fer Mr. Smathers might be the contrary of what the union wants."

Lewis was silent for a moment. "You pose a delicate problem in ethics," he said, "I'm afraid you have to decide on the basis of your own conscience what is right."

Daniel looked up at him. "I agree with what you said about workin' in the mines, but the on'y way I see I kin join up is if'n I quit my job in the office. I cain't serve two masters an' be honest with both, an' I won't be a spy an' a carrytale. My paw allus tol' me that a man's honor is all he got between hisself an' his fellowman."

"What you're saying, then, is that you won't sign the application?"

"That's right, sir. I don't honestly feel I could."

A low, angry murmur swept through the room. A few of the men moved threateningly toward Daniel. Lewis stopped them by holding up a hand. "Daniel!" he said sharply. "I respect your honesty. If you leave this meeting, do I have your word that nothing that transpired here will be told to management?"

Daniel met his scowling gaze. "I already said that I was no carrytale and no spy. If they hear anything, it won't be from me."

Lewis looked around the room. "I, for one, am willing to take Daniel's word. I know his brother-in-law, Jimmy Simpson, up Fitchville way, who is now representing the textile workers there and is helping us to organize the mines. Jimmy says that Daniel is the straightest lad he ever met. I say we should permit Daniel to withdraw from this meeting and hope that the future will give us the opportunity to work and be together. Anybody second that?"

There was a moment's silence. Then Andy spoke up. "I'll second that, Mr. Lewis. It's my fault Daniel is here. When I spoke to him this afternoon he tol' me exactly what he said right now. I should have taken him at his word then. But I trust him. I worked side by side with Daniel in the mine, an' I know in his heart he's with us an' will do nothin' to hurt us. I say let him go."

The men looked at each other for a moment, then murmured a reluctant assent. Daniel put down the application blank on a table and slowly walked to the door. He could feel the weight of their eyes on his back. He closed the door behind him and through it could hear the sound of voices begin again. He went out toward the street. For a moment he shivered; the night had turned cold. He looked up at the sky. The moon was high. It was nine o'clock.

He hesitated a moment, then began walking rapidly, his mind made up. If the lights were still on in Miss Andrews' house, he would explain to her why he hadn't shown up this evening.

Chapter 14

SILENTLY, MOLLY ANN watched him break open the revolver and check the cylinder carefully to see that each chamber was loaded. Satisfied, he snapped the cylinder shut and stuck it in his belt. He turned to her and saw the expression on her face. "Don't worry," he said.

"I cain't he'p it," she said. "Guns is fer killin'. Somehow the idee you carryin' a gun lak that ever' day, it gives me the shivers."

"They shot at me twice already," he said. "What am I s'posed to do? Jes' stand there an' let 'em kill me?"

She didn't answer.

"They killed more'n ten men. Men who had nothin' to shoot back with."

"What's goin' to happen today?"

"You know well as me. They're goin' to try to open the mills today. Fitch got hisself an army of Pinkertons to march the scabs into the mills. If we let 'em git in there, it's all over. They'll never come out. He'll send in food, supplies, ever'thing they need until we're starved out an' beaten."

"The miners comin' out to he'p you?" she asked.

He shook his head. "No. The miners fell right into the trap.

They took the ten-percent raise the owners offered 'em without even figgerin' that changin' to scrip instead of money took it all back with interest. If the U.M.W.'s got more'n ten members left in the whole valley, I'd be surprised."

Her voice was bitter. "I tol' you not to trust that man Lewis."

"It's not his fault. There's that ol' sayin'. 'You can lead a horse to water, but you cain't make him drink.' "

"Dan'l was smarter'n all of you," she said. "He stayed out of it."

He didn't answer, but she knew he had been deeply hurt when he heard that Daniel had not followed his lead.

"Oh, Jimmy. I'm scairt!" she said, running into his arms and placing her head against his chest. "We was so happy, an' you was doin' so good with yer bootleggin' an' all. Why did you have to go an' git yourse'f caught up in all this?"

He held her tightly. His voice was somber. "Comes a time when a man has to stop talkin' an' start doin'. These people —the farmers, the mill workers—they all my friends. I grew up with 'em. What was I goin' to do? Stan' by an' let Sam Fitch turn 'em all into slaves fer his own benefit?"

She began to cry. Softly he stroked her head. "Stop frettin'," he said. "It's not good fer a pregnant woman to carry on so."

She looked up into his face. "You'll be careful? I couldn't stand it if'n somethin' happened to you."

"I'll be careful," he promised. "I don' want nothin' to happen to me neither."

It was not yet daylight when he arrived at the store on Front Street that served as union headquarters. Several men were already there, waiting in the street for him. He took the keys from his pocket and opened the front door. They followed him inside. It was damp and dark. Quickly they lit a few oil lamps. The electric company had refused to give them power. The flickering golden light shone on the picket signs and boards lining the walls. He walked behind the battered table that served as his desk and sat down.

"Okay, Roscoe," he said. "You first. What's goin' on out at the new mill?"

Roscoe Craig shifted the wad of tobacco in his mouth. "They got about fifty Pinkertons out there an' maybe about a hundred scabs."

Jimmy nodded and turned to another man. "What about the city mill?"

The man cleared his throat. "They got a reg'lar army there. More'n a hundred Pinkertons an' maybe three hundred scabs. They been comin' in by truck all night."

Jimmy was silent for a moment. They were hopelessly outnumbered. He could count on perhaps seventy men at the very most. There were several hundred women and girls who could be used for picket duty, but on a day like this he was reluctant to put them out there where they could be hurt. And hurt they would be. The Pinkertons were armed and under orders to let nothing keep them from getting into the mill. He drew a deep breath. He dreaded the coming of daylight.

"What time will our men get here?" he asked.

"Any minute now," Roscoe answered. "They'll all be here by six o'clock."

"They ready?"

Roscoe nodded. "They comin' with shotguns an' rifles. The Pinkertons ain't goin' to jes' walk in."

"We're goin' to have to make up our minds," Jimmy said. "We cain't beat 'em in both places. We got to decide which one we want to keep 'em out of."

The men were silent.

"I vote we make up our minds to let 'em have the new mill. Ain't but ten percent of the machinery hooked up. They cain't produce beans once they in there."

"I don' lak it," Roscoe said flatly. "Two people in my family died to keep 'em off our lan'. The idee of 'em jes' walkin' in—"

"They won't jes' walk in," Jimmy said. "We put ten sharpshooters in the forest an' the hills aroun' the entrance, an' they'll git mighty cautious about walkin' up that road." He paused for a moment. "But the city mill, that's another story.

If'n they git in there, they kin produce full blast. Then we're finished. If that mill begins rollin', it's all over but the shoutin'."

Jimmy stood on the corner looking at the mill on the other side of the street. Already the pickets, most of them women, were walking four abreast in front of the closed gates. From inside the gates and along the wire fence that ran along the sidewalk in front of the mill, the guards stared silently at the signs carried by the chanting pickets.

"Lincoln freed the slaves. How come we're still here?"

They shouted back their own answer: "Nobody tol' the textile mill!"

Then another shout: "Freedom!"

A man came running down the street toward Jimmy just as the seven-o'clock whistle blew. At the same moment, the rain began to fall. "Three truckloads of scabs!" he shouted. "Just turnin' down High Street!"

Jimmy looked across the street. The pickets were still marching. The Pinkertons inside the fence began to move toward the gate. There was a scraping sound of an iron chain being pulled, and the gate began to swing open.

Jimmy felt the pain knot his stomach, as real as any pain he had ever felt. He turned to the man around him.

Suddenly it all came home. It was him they were watching. It was him they were waiting for. It was him they looked to for leadership in the midst of this madness. He felt old, so very old. Molly Ann was right. What was he doing here? He was no hero.

Then the feeling was gone. He held up his hand and started toward the picket lines. Silently the men followed him. He stopped in front of the line. "All right, you ladies," he said in a strong voice. "Time fer you to go home."

They stood watching him, not moving.

He spoke again, his voice more urgent this time. "You heard me, ladies. It's time to go home!"

There was a moment's silence. Then one of them called out, "We'll stay right here, Jimmy. Its our fight too!"

"But ladies," he shouted, "there might be shooting!"

"They'll have to shoot us too, then!" one of them shouted back. "We're not goin' home!"

The women began to lock arms, and in a moment they formed a living chain in front of the open gates. They began chanting again. "Freedom. Bread and butter, not chains!"

The trucks rounded the far corner and headed down the street toward the mill. They were halfway down the block and the lead truck showed no sign of slowing up. Jimmy moved out in front of the picket line and faced them. Suddenly there was silence behind him. The trucks kept moving toward them.

"Out of the way!" a guard yelled from behind the wire fence. "You'll all get killed!"

No one moved.

The lead truck jammed on its brakes and rolled to a stop just a few yards short of the picket lines. Men began to jump out of the backs of the trucks. Pinkertons, big, ugly and menacing. They formed a line facing the pickets, each of them holding a club or an iron pipe in his hand, their bowlers sitting squarely on their heads. At a signal, they began to move forward.

Jimmy held up a hand. "I warn you, men. There are women here. I won't be responsible for your lives if even one of them gits hurt!"

The Pinkertons stopped uncertainly. "Hiding behind their skirts won't save you!" one of them shouted. "Come out an' fight like men!"

"We're here to stay whether you scabs like it or not!" a woman shouted from the picket lines.

The other women picked it up. "Scabs! Scabs! Scabs!" they chanted.

An iron pipe came hurtling through the air. Jimmy heard a woman's scream behind him. He glanced back quickly and saw a woman falling, blood streaming from her head. He swung back to face the Pinkertons. "I'll kill the next man who does that!" he yelled, pulling the gun from his belt.

Jimmy saw the man with the rifle on the top of the truck almost before he heard the bullet hiss past his ear. There was another scream. This time Jimmy didn't turn to see who was hurt. He fired. The man fell crazily from the top of the truck into the street. He lay there, blood oozing into the round hole in his bowler, which somehow still clung to his head.

"Let's git 'im!" one of the Pinkertons shouted. He pulled a gun and fired at Jimmy.

Jimmy's shot caught him in the chest, blasting him backward, just as another Pinkerton fired with both barrels of a shotgun. Jimmy heard the screams and fired again. The shotgun fell from the man's hands as he clutched at his throat. He started for Jimmy, the blood welling through his fingers, a horrible growling sound coming from inside him. Then he fell forward, rolled over and lay face up in the street, the blood leaping up from his severed jugular like a pulsing red fountain.

The strikers and the Pinkertons stared at each other without a word. Jimmy motioned with his hand. Quietly, the men came from behind him and placed themselves on either side, forming a long line in front of the women. Shotguns and rifles suddenly appeared in their hands. These men, with their grim faces, were mountain men and farmers, and it was their women who had been fired upon and hurt.

Slowly Jimmy unlatched his revolver and replaced the three bullets that had been fired. He snapped the chamber shut and turned back to the Pinkertons. His voice was low, but they could hear him clearly through the lightly falling rain. "Pinkerton pay y'all a bonus for dyin'?"

Without answering, the Pinkertons slowly began to move away. A few minutes later, the trucks started back down the street. Except for the three dead men lying on the cobblestones, the street was empty when they heard the big iron gate creak closed.

A cheer came up from the strikers. "We beat 'em!" "We won! We won!"

Jimmy's face was somber. He glanced at the bodies in the street, then back at the triumphant strikers. "No," he said, a strange foreboding knowledge within him. "We lost."

And he was right. Two days later, the National Guard marched into Fitchville and all they could do was watch silently as the scabs entered the mill under the protection of the government.

142

Chapter 15

SAM FITCH's tiny office in the rear of his store was crowded, although there were only three men in there besides himself. Mr. Cahill, the millowners' representative, his associate from Philadelphia and Jason Carter, the county sheriff. Cahill's voice was angry as he stood in front of the desk staring down at Fitch, who overflowed the tiny chair in which he sat.

"It's one month since we opened the mills," Cahill said. "And look what's happened. The new Craig mill shut down, its machinery rotting; the city mill functioning at only ten percent of capacity. All because the workers didn't come back the way you said they would if we opened the mills. Besides that, the employees we brought in have left in droves. There's maybe ninety left when we need four hundred."

Sam Fitch nodded. "I know," he said with as much sympathy he could get into his gravelly voice.

"You know?" Cahill was sarcastic. "I know you know. What we want to know is what are you going to do about it?"

"The sher'f an' me are doin' the best we kin," Fitch said. "But you jes' don' know these people here. It ain't a strike no more, it's a feud. It's them against the company. I tol' you not to bring in the Pinkertons, to let the sher'f an' me handle it. Might have taken longer, but we'd have gotten 'em back in. Now they got themselves some help from the Textile Union up North, an' they're lookin' up to Jimmy Simpson like he was a god or somethin'."

"But he's a murderer!" Cahill's voice was shocked. "He killed three men."

"Pinkertons, you mean," Fitch corrected. "An' only after they fired on their women. We mountain folk don't take kindly to havin' our women shot at."

"Now you're defending him," Cahill accused. "Whose side are you on?"

"I'm on your side, Mr. Cahill," Fitch said smoothly. "Don' think I ain't been hurt by all this. Business in my store has fallen away to nothin'."

"Then act like it," Cahill snapped. "You do somethin' to get that Simpson out of our hair and the people back to work or we're through here. The company has been losing forty thousand dollars a month, and they've given me exactly one month to get the mills back in operation or we're closing up here and moving the plants somewhere else."

Fitch was silent for a moment. He looked up at the Philadelphian. "Jimmy's goin' into court fer the killin's week after next. Maybe they'll take care of him. We got Jedge Harlan on our side."

Cahill laughed derisively. "But the jury will all be locals. Simpson will walk out of the court not only a free man but more of a hero than ever. Whatever you're going to do, you'd better do it before he walks into that courthouse. Because the day he walks out of it, the mills close down and we begin to move out."

When Cahill and his friend left, Sam Fitch lit up one of his cigars. He looked across the small office at the sheriff, who hadn't said a word all through the meeting. "What d'ya think, Jase?"

"That Mr. Cahill's a hard man," the sheriff said.

Fitch nodded. "City folk'll never understand us."

"Never," the sheriff agreed.

"What about Jimmy? Your boys keepin' an eye on him?"

"We cain't git near him," the sheriff said. "He don' go nowhere 'thout six or seven men all armed with him. An' that Jew lawyer from New York don' make life any easier. Ever' time we bust one of their men, he's at the courthouse with a habeas corpus almos' 'fore we got the cell door closed on him, and he gits the man out."

"Ah, sheeit," Fitch swore. "I allus knew that Jimmy Simpson was goin' to turn out to be a bad one."

The afternoon sun streamed through the dusty store windows, cutting patches of light in the gloom. The bell over the door jangled harshly as it opened. Jimmy looked up. So did all the other men in the store, their hands unconsciously dropping closer to their guns. When they saw who it was, they relaxed and resumed their conversation.

Morris Bernstein hulked into the store. He didn't walk, he clumped, his size eleven city shoes pounding under his six-foot-three and two-hundred-and-ten-pound frame. One wouldn't think to look at his broken nose, the scar tissue under his eyes and the cauliflower ears that he was an attorney. But he'd gotten that face working his way through college as a semipro club fighter. He made his way directly to the table behind which Jimmy sat.

"Well?" Jimmy asked.

"They said no," he answered flatly.

Jimmy masked his disappointment. "Did you explain to 'em it was jes' fer another month?"

"I did everything except whistle 'Dixie,' " Morris said. "They still refused."

"They give a reason?"

Morris looked at him. "I want to talk to you privately."

Jimmy didn't answer for a moment. Then he got to his feet. "We'll go out in the alley in the back."

He started for the door, but one of the men blocked his path. "Wait a minute. We'll check it out for you first."

Jimmy stood there while two of the men went out the back door. "You're bein' too careful," he said.

"Cain't be too careful," the man who was blocking his path

said. "They tried to git you four times already. I'm not about to let 'em git lucky with a fifth."

The two men came back into the store. "It's okay," one of them said.

The man in front of Jimmy stepped aside. Jimmy took a step, then stopped. "Thank you, Roscoe," he said.

Roscoe Craig smiled through thin lips. "They got my gran'pappy an' my brother that way. They ain't goin' to git any more of us."

Bernstein followed Jimmy out into the alley. The sun's rays were bright after the dark of the store. They stood there a moment; then Jimmy turned to him.

"Okay," Jimmy said. "Let me have it."

Bernstein stared into his eyes. "The strike is finished."

Jimmy didn't answer.

"They're pulling me out. They're not sending down any more money." His voice was flat. "The executive board says they have no money for lost causes, they have to place it where it counts."

"What makes 'em say that?" Jimmy asked.

"They learned in Philadelphia yesterday the company's getting ready to move the mills farther south. They gave Cahill his orders. The mills open in one month or they move."

Jimmy was silent.

Morris looked at him. "I'm sorry, Jimmy."

Jimmy's voice took on a bitter edge. "So that's how it is. We break our ass fer a year. We git ourselves killed, chased out of our houses, starved an' shit on, an' some men who never been to this town, sittin' in some city in front of their comfortable tables, decide it's all over with us."

"It's the realities, Jimmy," Morris said. "We can't win 'em all."

"I don' care about all of 'em!" Jimmy said hotly. "Jes' this one. This is my friends, my town, my people." He looked at the lawyer. "What do I tell 'em now?"

The lawyer saw the anguish in his eyes. "You tell them to go back to work." His voice softened. "Tell them there will come another time. Losing a battle doesn't mean the war is lost. Someday the union will be here."

Jimmy looked at him. "The union don' mean shit to these people. They began the strike without the union, they'll carry it on without the union." He started back into the building.

"Jimmy!" the attorney called him back. "I got their permission to stay down here for your trial."

Jimmy nodded wearily. "Thank you, Morris." He hesitated, then added, "I know you did the best you could. I appreciate that."

"What are you going to do, Jimmy?" the attorney asked.

"I don't have much choice, do I? I got to tell 'em what you said. This is their strike. It's still up to them to decide what they want to do with it."

"And you, Jimmy?" the attorney asked. "What are you going to do after it's all over?"

Jimmy grinned. "I was doin' all right in the whiskey business before this started. I kin allus go back to it."

"We can use men like you in the union," Morris said. "You can come up to New York with me. They said they would find a place for you."

Jimmy shook his head. "That's not fer me. I'm a small-town boy. I belong here with my own kind. But I'm grateful fer the consideration."

He went back into the building. The attorney followed him. A moment later, Roscoe Craig came out into the alley. He looked up at the rooftops across the alley and waved his hand.

The guards he had posted up there to protect Jimmy waved back at him, then slung their rifles under their arms and started down to the street.

At the general meeting that night, the vote was unanimous to continue the strike. Even if it meant that the mills would move out and that they would all lose their jobs forever.

The day of the trial dawned bright and clear. The early-May breeze brought a fresh spring fragrance to the air that came softly through the open windows of the kitchen, where they were having breakfast.

Morris Bernstein took out his watch and looked at it. "Time to go," he said. "Court begins at ten o'clock."

"I'm ready," Jimmy said, getting to his feet. Roscoe Craig and Morris rose with him.

"I'll git yer jacket an' tie," Molly Ann said.

Jimmy looked at Morris while she was out of the room. "How long do you reckon the trial should take?"

"A few days," Morris answered. "One or two days to pick the jury, another couple of days for the trial and then you'll be a free man."

"I hope so," Molly Ann said, coming back into the room.

"Can't go any other way," Morris said confidently. "We have a hundred witnesses to prove it was self-defense."

"They'll have witnesses too," Molly Ann said.

"Pinkertons," Roscoe said contemptuously. "Ain't nobody down here goin' to believe 'em."

Jimmy finished knotting his tie and slipped into his jacket. He walked over to the mirror in the hallway and inspected himself. "Don't look bad in my store-brought clothes," he said.

"You look real handsome, honey," Molly Ann said.

He came back into the kitchen and, opening a drawer, took out his revolver. He started to put it in his belt.

"No," Morris said. "Put that back."

Jimmy looked at him. "I don' feel comfortable 'thout my piece."

"You can't go into court packing a gun," Morris said. "It's not respectful. Besides, they're not going to try anything in front of all those people. The whole town is going to be there."

Jimmy looked at Roscoe doubtfully. "What do you think?"

"Mebbe he's right," Roscoe answered, but he didn't seem sure.

"I am right," Morris said. "Do you know the judge can hold you in contempt if you take a gun in there?"

"Do I have to leave my gun too?" Roscoe asked.

"What you do is your own affair," Morris answered. "I have to worry about my client, that's all."

"Leave it, then," Roscoe said. "Me an' the boys'll be there. Ain't nothin' goin' to happen."

Jimmy put the gun back into the drawer. Molly Ann took off her apron and folded it neatly across the back of a kitchen chair. "I'm ready," she said.

Jimmy looked at her. She was in her sixth month and noticeably pregnant. "Don' you think it would be better if'n you stayed home?" he asked. "Mebbe too much excitement won't be good fer the baby."

"I'm goin'," she said firmly. "A wife's place is by her husband's side."

"Let's go, then," Morris said. "It's getting late."

Courthouse Square was in the exact center of the town. By the time Jimmy and Molly Ann got there, it was filled with people all in their Sunday best. There was almost a picnic air about it. Children were running around yelling and playing; the adults were talking excitedly. They clustered around Jimmy and Molly Ann as they made their way to the courthouse. All eager to touch Jimmy, to slap him on the back and wish him well. It was easy to see whose side they were on.

Sam Fitch and the sheriff stood in the doorway of his store and watched the crowd across the street. The sheriff shook his head. "I don' know," he said, "I don' like it."

Fitch looked at him. "I don' like it neither, but you got a better idee?"

The sheriff took a deep breath. "Too many people. Could turn into a riot."

"We got no choice," Fitch said. "You heard the man with your own ears. Or would you ruther be sher'f of a ghost town?"

The sheriff looked back across the square. "I still don' like it," he said. "Lookit there. He's got Roscoe Craig an' some of his boys aroun' him an' the people aroun' them. Ain't no way we goin' to be able to git to him."

Fitch followed the sheriff's gaze. "Sooner or later he's got to be standin' alone. Even if it's only fer a moment. Jes' hope yer boys are ready fer it."

"If'n that happens," the sheriff said grimly. "My boys'll be ready."

With the backslapping, handshaking and good-wishing, it took them almost twenty minutes to make their way across the square to the courthouse steps. The doors of the building opened just as they reached the foot of the steps. The mad rush of people who jammed up in front of the doors was slowed by the four deputy sheriffs who checked each man entering the building for arms.

The large wooden boxes on either side of the doorway slowly began to fill with guns. The deputies were polite but firm. "No guns in the courthouse," they explained. "You kin pick 'em up at the sher'f's office after court."

Some of the men grumbled, but if they wanted to get into the courthouse they had to give up their guns. Roscoe stared up the steps. "I don' like that," he said.

Morris looked at him. "Nothing's going to happen once we're inside."

"I'm not worried about inside," Roscoe said. "I'm worried about when we come out."

"We'll wait inside until you go pick up your guns an' come back fer us," Jimmy said.

"That makes me feel better," Roscoe replied.

Jimmy looked at the crowd pushing their way into the courthouse. "You an' the boys better git on in, else'n they won't be any room fer you all."

Roscoe glanced around the square. "You come up the steps with us," he said. "I'll feel better if we git off the street."

Roscoe and his men had already passed through when the deputies stopped Jimmy. "You don' go in this way, Jimmy," one of them said. "You're s'posed to go in th'u the court clerk's office on the side portico."

Jimmy stared at him. "Why?"

"Got somethin' to do with yer pickin' up yer bail receipt. You don' wanna lose five hunnert dollars, do you?" the deputy answered.

Roscoe overheard them. "I'll go with you," he said, starting back.

"Never mind," Jimmy said. "I'll see you inside." Molly

Ann had entered the courthouse just ahead of him. Now she turned back. "You git Molly Ann an' follow me," Jimmy said to Morris, and started off.

"Wait a minute," Morris said, and turned to reach for Molly Ann. By the time they cleared the doorway, Jimmy was twenty steps ahead of them, almost at the corner of the portico.

It was then they came at him from around the corner. There were three of them, two Pinkertons and Clinton Richfield, one of the sheriff's deputies. He was not in uniform.

Jimmy never saw them, because they came with guns blazing. Seven bullets tore into him and slammed him, already dead, against a corner post, from which he fell, face downward, half on the porch, half on the steps.

The three men fired again. Jimmy's body jumped with the impact of the bullets and slipped farther down the steps. The men stood there waiting for Jimmy to move.

"Jimmy!" Molly Ann screamed. She broke from Morris' grasp and ran toward him, throwing herself across his body. She pulled him toward her, his blood staining her dress. She stared up at the men, her eyes filled with horror and streaming tears. "Please!" she begged. "Please, don't shoot my Jimmy no more."

Jimmy's body shook in a last convulsive spasm. Automatically the men opened fire again. They tore Molly Ann from her husband and sent her rolling, dead, down the white concrete steps to the street. Her own blood mixed with that from her husband's body, staining red the simple white dress she had freshly washed and pressed just hours before.

"My God! What have you done?" Morris shouted, staring at them.

"He came at us with a gun," Richfield said.

"What gun?" Morris shouted. "He had no gun. I made him leave it home."

Richfield raised his pistol and pointed it at Morris. "Jew boy, you callin' me a liar?"

"Yes, goddamn you!" Morris shouted, his anger and revulsion overcoming the fear that was knotting his stomach. "You're a liar and a murderer!"

The bullet from the deputy's .38 tore into Morris' shoulder, throwing him backward on the stone floor. Through eyes hazy with pain, Morris saw the deputy raise his gun again and take careful aim. It was over. There was nothing more he had to lose. "Liar! Murderer!" he screamed defiantly.

But the shot never came. Suddenly the sheriff was there and there were deputies all over the place, keeping the crowds away. The sheriff came over and looked down at him. "Jew boy," he said in a cold voice, "there's a train leavin' here in an hour. Because we're good Christian folk, I'm gonna have a doctor patch you up afore we put you on it. An' you take this warnin' back No'th with you. If you or any other No'the'n Jew agitator an' anarchist shows up here, we're goin' to kill you on sight."

He turned to a deputy. "You an' Mike git him over to Dr. Johns, then put him on the train."

Morris almost fainted with the pain as the deputies unceremoniously hauled him to his feet. They started down the steps, the crowd staring at him with curiosity but making a path for them.

Behind him, he heard the sheriff's voice. "Now all you good folk clear the square an' go home. Leave the law to take its rightful course."

Chapter 16

JEB HAD just hitched his mule to the plow on the west field when he saw the wagon coming out of the forest down the road. There were two men sitting up front as the mule pulled wearily at the wagon behind it. They were still too far away for Jeb to recognize them. He clucked to the mule and began to plow the first furrow. It would take them another half-hour at least to reach him.

It was almost an hour, and Jeb had started his third long furrow, by the time they got there. He halted his mule, dropped the reins and walked over to the road to greet them. He recognized one of the men by the heavy broad-brimmed black hat he wore. It was Preacher Dan, the circuit-riding minister who covered the countryside around Fitchville. Idly he wondered what the minister was doing up this way. Usually he showed up only for weddings, christenings and funerals.

As the wagon drew opposite him, he recognized the other man. Roscoe Craig. He took off his hat and wiped his forehead with his bare arm. It was warm in the morning sun. The wagon stopped. He started toward it, smiling. "Preacher Dan," he began, then stopped abruptly, the smile fading.

The minister, a tall, heavyset man, climbed down from the wagon and came toward him. "I got bad news fer you, Jeb."

Jeb looked at him, then up at Roscoe. Roscoe's face was gray and weary. Without speaking, Jeb walked around to the back of the open wagon and looked in. The two coffins, covered by a tarpaulin, lay side by side.

He heard the minister's heavy footsteps as he came to his side. Without looking at him, he asked, "Molly Ann an' Jimmy?" He didn't need an affirmative answer. He already knew.

Still staring at the cheap pine coffins, he asked in a dull voice, "What happened?"

The minister didn't answer. It was Roscoe who turned to him from the front of the wagon. "They were shot in front of the courthouse, the day before yesterday." His voice was bitter. "We would've brung 'em before, but the coroner wouldn' release us the bodies. We figgered you'd want 'em buried t'home ruther than in town."

Jeb nodded. "That's right. Thank 'e kindly." He looked up at Roscoe. "Who done it?"

"Clinton Richfield and two Pinkertons," Roscoe said. "They was layin' fer him, aroun' the corner of the porch. He didn' stan' a chance. He didn' even have no gun on him. Molly Ann ran to he'p him an' they shot her too."

The lines of Jeb's face were stonelike. He climbed into the wagon and lifted the tarpaulin from the coffins. He raised the lid of each coffin in turn and looked inside. He took a deep breath, his mouth suddenly dry. Slowly, his hands trembling, he lowered the lids. He looked up at Roscoe again. "The sheriff that done this in jail?"

Roscoe shook his head. "It was self-defense, they claimed. He got off."

"But you said Jimmy had no gun," Jeb said.

"He didn't. I was there when he put it in the drawer in his kitchen," Roscoe said quickly. "They lied."

Jeb's pale eyes were cold. "Where are they now?"

"The Pinkertons lef' town," Roscoe said. "On'y one around is Clint."

154

Jeb nodded. He turned and looked down at Preacher Dan, standing in the road behind the wagon. "You come with me up to the house to tell Miz Huggins. Then while you're comfortin' her, Roscoe an' me'll prepare the graves."

Preacher Dan returned his gaze. "I don't want you to be thinkin' evil thoughts, Jeb. There's been too much killin' already. Remember, 'Vengeance is mine,' saith the Lord."

Jeb climbed down from the wagon without answering. "I'll fetch my mule an' we'll go up to the house," he said, going toward the west field. He paused at the edge of the field and looked back. "Nail the coffins shut," he said. "I don' want fer Miz Huggins to see Molly Ann all shot up like that." His voice broke. "She was sech a purty girl."

The last shovel of dirt fell on the graves. Slowly, Jeb picked up the two small wooden crosses and pressed them into the earth, one at the head of each grave. He stepped back and looked at them.

The language burned into the wooden crosses with a hot iron poker was simple. One read, MOLLY ANN SIMPSON, OUR DAUGHTER; the other, next to it, said simply, JIMMY SIMPSON, HER HUSBAND.

He looked at Marylou, standing at the foot of the graves, the children around her. Her face was lined and filled with pain. Unconsciously her arms had spread out, seeming to draw the children to her. She raised her eyes and met his gaze. "I'll fix Mr. Craig and the minister some lunch before they start back."

Jeb nodded.

"Come, children," she said. The children began to follow her. All through the service they had been very quiet. Jeb wondered if they really understood what had happened. Now they all began to chatter almost at the same time.

Only one question stood out in Jeb's mind. It came from Alice, the youngest girl, who was now eight. "Does it mean now that Molly Ann's in Heaven, she cain't no longer come to visit us?"

Richard, with the superiority of his eleven years, answered,

"When they're dead, nobody comes back, 'cept if'n they're a ghost."

"Will she be a good ghost or a bad ghost?" Alice wanted to know.

Rachel, now the oldest daughter, answered in an annoyed tone of voice, "There is no sech things as ghosts. Besides, Molly Ann is now an angel in Heaven at God's side. An' he ain't about to let her come back."

By that time Marylou and the children were down the hill out of earshot. Jeb turned to the two men. "I think a bit of squeezin's mought be of he'p."

Preacher Dan nodded. "Cain't hurt none. I'm bone-dry."

"Foller me up to the still," Jeb said. "I'll lead the way."

After lunch, Jeb and Roscoe went out front, while Preacher Dan remained in the kitchen to speak to Marylou. The men sat down on the steps and lit up small black cigars. "I don' unnerstan'," Jeb said.

Roscoe looked down at the ground. "It was the on'y way they could break the strike. Ever'body trusted Jimmy. Now that he's gone, they's nobody. Already some of 'em are goin' back to the mill."

"I don' know 'bout that," Jeb said. "The Richfields allus been good friends. Why'd Clint do a thing like that?"

"His pappy's a mill foreman. The whole family's scabbed through the strike."

"That's no cause fer killin'," Jeb said. "We never done nothin' to them."

Roscoe glanced at Jeb. The mountain man had no conception of the differences between the workers and the mill-owners. To Jeb, everything was translated into very personal terms. Feuds were one thing—he had grown up with that; the strike was something else. He would never understand it. But then again, he couldn't blame Jeb. He himself had not understood until after his father and his eldest son had been killed. At first, he too had been fighting a very personal war. But then he had come to understand just what it really was. It was obvious to him now that it was power and money feeding on the labor of people to create more power and money for itself.

"I know how you feel, Jeb," he said awkwardly. "I los' my paw and my oldest to them."

Jeb looked at him. "And what did you do?"

"You know what I did," Roscoe answered. "I fought back. But now I don' know."

"Don't know what?"

"We been talkin', my woman an' me," Roscoe said. "We don' see no chance here now. Mebbe we'll go up Detroit way. We hear the auto companies are hirin'."

Jeb was silent. After a moment he spoke. "I don' know as you'd be content up there. Yer farmin' people, not city folk."

"What other choice we got?" Roscoe questioned. "It's between workin' an' starvin'. My woman got letters from her kinfolk. They makin' good money up there. Three dollars a day, sometimes more."

They fell silent for a long while. Finally, Jeb spoke. "I'll be comin' down to town."

Roscoe looked at him. Jeb's face was impassive. "When?" he said.

"Tomorrow mornin'." Jeb looked at Roscoe. "Kin I count on you?"

Roscoe didn't say anything for a moment, then nodded slowly. "You know you kin."

She heard him stirring in the night. Then she felt him leave the bed and walk silently from the room. She lay there until she couldn't stand it any longer. She got out of bed and went into the kitchen. It was empty.

She opened the door and looked out into the yard. He wasn't there either. She went out into the chill night air and looked up the hill to the small cemetery. He was standing in the pale moonlight, looking down at the graves. The night chill ran through her.

Quickly she went back into the house and wrapped a warm shawl around her, then went up the hill to him. He heard her footsteps but did not look up. The small wooden crosses shone silver with the dew of night.

After a moment he spoke. "There was no reason fer Clint

157

Richfield to shoot her. She was on'y a girl an' no part of their fight."

"You musn't dwell on it," she said. "I'm tryin' not to."

"The Richfields 'n' us'n has allus been friends. It don' make sense."

"The Lord's will be done," she said. "We got to count our blessin's. We got the other children, an' Dan'l's doin' us proud. We got to be thankful fer that."

He turned to her. "Yer soundin' like Preacher Dan."

She looked up into his face. "He makes sense. Look to the future, not the past, he says."

"It's easy fer him to say." Jeb's voice was flat. "It's not his daughter layin' in that grave." Abruptly he started back down the hill to the house.

She watched him walking down the hill, then turned to look at the grave for a moment before starting down the hill after him. By the time she entered the kitchen, he was sitting at the table with the shiny black Winchester rifle in his hand and was slipping shells into the magazine. A cold dread came over her. "No, Jeb," she said. "Don' do it."

He looked at her with the distant eyes of a stranger. He didn't answer.

"No more killin', Jeb," she said. "It won' bring 'er back."

"You don't unnerstan'," he said. "It's a matter of honor. How would it look if'n I let Clint git away with it?"

"I don' care how it would look!" she said passionately. "You prove nothin' startin' a blood feud with the Richfields. They'll come right back fer us an' then we'll go after them an' soon there'll be none of us lef' to matter."

"I didn't start it by killin' one of them," he said stubbornly.

"It don' matter who started it. On'y that you don' continue it! We got other children to think about. I don' want 'em to be growin' up 'thout a father."

"Nobody goin' to kill me," he said.

"How can you be sure?" she cried.

He didn't answer for a moment. Then he got to his feet. "Better I'd be dead an' layin' in a grave up there beside my daughter then to have the worl' lookin' down on me fer a coward."

158

She moved toward him, pressing herself against him, her hands gripping his shirt. "We kin have another baby, Jeb," she whispered. "Another Molly Ann."

He took a deep breath and slowly unfastened her hands and placed them back at her sides. "No, Marylou," he said gently. "That's not the answer neither, an' you know it."

Through a blur of tears, she watched him walk to the door. He stopped and looked back at her. "I'll be back by nightfall tomorrow," he said.

Somehow she found her voice. "Better wear somethin' warm," she said. "The night air is cold."

He nodded. "I'm takin' my sheepskin coat."

Then he was gone, and she sank numbly into a chair. After a moment, she heard him clucking softly to the mule, then the rattle of the wagon as they went out of the yeard onto the dark night road.

Chapter 17

Sheriff Jason Carter stomped angrily around the office in the rear of the courthouse. Through the open door at the back of the room he could hear a deputy giving coffee to the occupants of the small detention cellblock. Only four of the cells were occupied this morning. The usual haul of nighttime drunks and fights. Nothing special about them. For the first time in more than a year, the town was really quiet. There had been no demonstrations by the strikers. Already some of them were drifting back to work. There was no reason for him to feel the way he did. Still, he had a sense of danger that was making him nervous and jumpy as a skittish mule.

The deputy returned from the cellblock. "They all fed, Jase," he said. "What ya want done with 'em?"

Carter looked at them dourly. "They got any money on 'em?"

The deputy shrugged his shoulders.

"If they have, grab a dollar fine off'n each of 'em an' throw 'em out," the sheriff said.

"An' if they haven't?" the deputy asked.

"Throw 'em out anyway. No reason fer us to buy 'em lunch." He turned to the cabinet as the deputy left the office and pulled out a sheaf of papers. Swearing softly to himself, he went back to his desk and sat down, spreading the papers in front of him. He picked up a pencil and began scribbling laboriously on the sheets. This was the worst part of the job. Too many forms to fill out. Damn nosy state government. What business was it of theirs what went on in his county anyway?

Concentrating on his paperwork, he almost jumped out of his skin when the outside door burst open and Clint Richfield came in.

Clint was pale and sweating. "I think Jeb Huggins is in town!"

The sheriff's anger erupted. "God damn you, Clint!" he roared. "Why didn't you git outta town lak I tol' you?"

"I couldn' see no reason to run," Clint said. "I was jes' performin' my sworn duty."

"Your sworn duty didn' include killin' the girl," the sheriff said sarcastically.

"I tol' you I saw him goin' fer a gun," Clint said.

The sheriff stared at him. "Dead men don't reach fer guns."

"How'd I know he was dead?"

"Christ!" the sheriff swore. He looked down at his desk. Clint had been so well drilled in the story that he believed it himself. He pushed the papers on his desk back into a pile and looked up. "How d'ya know Jeb's in town?" He got to his feet heavily. "Anybody see him?"

"My kid brother saw a strange mule 'n' wagon out front of the Craig house on his way to school this mornin'. He came back to tell me."

"Mought be somebody else's," the sheriff said. Inside himself he knew better. He drew a deep breath and took his gun belt from the peg on the wall behind him and strapped it on. He took out his big Ingersoll and looked at it. "The eight-fifteen'll be through here in about a half an hour. I'm goin' to put you on it."

Clint stared at him. "I gotta git home an' git my clothes."

"We'll send you your clothes," the sheriff said. "I got 'nough to fret about 'thout havin' another blood feud on my han's."

The deputy returned from the cellblock. "They gone," he said, placing three crumpled dollar bills on the desk. "They all paid up 'cept Tut. He didn' have no money."

"Tut never has no money," the sheriff said, picking up the bills and putting them in his pocket. "The cells clean?"

The deputy nodded. "I made 'em sweep an' clean up afore I let 'em go."

"Good." The sheriff nodded. "Now you take over here. Clint an' me's goin' out fer a bit."

"Ain't you goin' to git some deputies?" Clint asked nervously.

The sheriff shook his head. "Don' want to attract no attention. I know Jeb Huggins, we was kids together. An army wouldn' keep him off'n yer back. The way I figger it, we mosey along nice 'n' quiet down the back streets an' come up on the railroad station from the far side of town."

The sweat ran down Clint's cheeks. "But what if he finds us?"

The sheriff's voice was grim. "Then you better start prayin' that I kin talk him out of it. Jeb's won every shootin' contest 'roun' here fer the past twenty years." He paused for a moment, then, seeing Clint's fear, added, "But don' worry—he won' fin' us."

Clint nodded, his Adam's apple working tightly.

The sheriff reached for his hat. "Okay, let's go." Clint started for the door. The sheriff stopped him. "Not that way," he said. "We'll go out through the jail door back of the building."

They came out back of the signal tower on the far side of the station. In the distance they heard the faint hoot of the train whistle. "You wait here," the sheriff said, "whilst I go down to the station and have a look-see. Don't you come out less'n I signal you."

"Yes, Jase."

"Stay outta sight, now," the sheriff cautioned. "I don' want anybody spotting you."

"I will, Jase," Clint said, stepping back against the shadowed wall of the signal shack.

The sheriff glanced at him, then crossed the tracks toward the station. From what he could see, there was no one there except the usual station crowd. Pokey, the stationmaster, was trying to look important, even though he had nothing to do. A few old men and George, the porter, were waiting for the train.

Pokey was the first to see him as he stepped up onto the wooden platform in front of the station. "Howdy, Sheriff," he called out in his singsong trainman's voice. "What brings you down our way this mornin'? Plannin' to leave town?" He broke into a laugh at his own joke.

The sheriff didn't laugh. "Not 'zactly."

The voice came from the station doorway behind him. " 'Zactly what brung you down here, Jase?"

The sheriff spun around. Jeb was standing in the doorway, his Winchester .30-30 resting lightly in the crook of his arm. "Howdy, Jeb," he said.

Jeb didn't reply to the greeting. His voice was cold. "You didn' answer my question, Jase."

The sheriff eyed him warily. "I was jest moseyin' about this mornin'. Happened to come down here."

"Wouldn' have happened to run across Clint Richfield in your moseyin' about, would you?"

"Now, c'mon, Jeb. You don' want no part o' that business. That strike got nothin' to do with you."

"It had nothin' to do with Molly Ann neither," Jeb said. "Still, he killed 'er."

"It was an accident," the sheriff said. "They thought Jimmy was goin' fer a gun."

"Jimmy didn' have no gun," Roscoe said, appearing in the doorway behind Jeb. "Besides, ever'body knowed he was already dead."

"No way they could have," the sheriff said. He looked at Jeb. "You got to believe that, Jeb. Nobody wanted to hurt your Molly Ann. Besides, they found a gun on the steps near Jimmy's hand."

"They put it there after he was dead," Roscoe said.

"If'n they did, I didn' now nothin' 'bout it," the sheriff said quickly. "You know me since we was boys together, Jeb. You know I wouldn' have no part of a thing like that."

163

Jeb came out onto the platform, his eyes searching the area. The sheriff watched him cautiously. The train whistle hooted again, closer this time. Pokey and his station cronies were silent, their eyes on them. Silently, the sheriff prayed that Clint would stay in back of the signal shack and not try anything stupid. It was almost too much to hope that he would be smart enough to hide behind the train as it pulled into the station and board it from the far side.

The whistle was louder this time. Jeb crossed to the edge of the platform, looking up the tracks to where the train would appear beyond the signal shack. He began to shift the rifle from one hand to the other, and by instinct the sheriff started to step away. He had no intention of being caught in the line of fire, and he knew that if Jeb moved his rifle, Clint would think he had been spotted.

The sheriff was right. But not fast enough. Clint's first shot caught him in the leg, and he tumbled to the platform.

Jeb was across the tracks and running toward the shack before the sheriff hit the wooden planks. Roscoe jumped across the sheriff's prostrate figure, following Jeb. "He's behind the signal shack!" he yelled after him.

The sheriff turned and pulled himself onto his hands. "God damn it, Jeb!" he yelled. "Don' do it. It'll on'y start another feud. They'll come after you, then Dan'l—" The rest of his words were lost in the noise of the train as it pulled into the station, hiding their view.

He turned and saw the stationmaster and George staring at him. The Negro was the first to move. "Yo' huht, Sher'f?"

"The son of a bitch shot me in the laig!" he yelled. "Of course I'm hurt."

"Le'me he'p you, Sher'f," George said, coming toward him.

"Pokey kin help me!" the sheriff shouted. "You git your black ass up to my office an' bring back all the deputies you kin fin' there!"

George hesitated a moment, then jumped from the platform and began running up the street as the train pulled to a stop. As usual, the two mailbags tumbled to the platform, but no passengers got on or off. "Pokey, git over here an' he'p me," the sheriff yelled at the stationmaster.

Pokey looked at him, then at the train, then back at him. "But I got to git the train movin' again," he said in his thin, reedy voice.

"Fuck the train!" the sheriff swore. "I'm bleedin' to death!" The sound of gunfire came from the signal shack. Then silence.

"Oh, Jesus!" the sheriff swore. He reached up and grabbed a loose slat in the side of the station and pulled himself to his feet. With one hand he pulled off his pants belt and tried to tighten it around his leg to stop the bleeding.

The train began to move again. Slowly it went out of the station. A yell came from across the tracks. "Sher'f!"

He looked up. Clint was standing there, his shirt covered with blood. "Y'all right, Clint?" he shouted, forgetting his own wound for a moment.

Clint stood there for an instant as if making up his mind how to answer. "They kilt me, Sher'f!" he cried, and tumbled face downward across the tracks.

"Oh, Jesus! Take it easy, there, Doc," the sheriff groaned, writhing on the table in Dr. John's treatment room.

"Stop wrigglin' 'roun' lak a baby," the doctor said. "Else how you expec' me to git that bullet out?"

"It hurts, Doc," the sheriff complained, staring up at the forceps in the doctor's hand.

"Of course it hurts," Dr. John said in a reassuring tone. "But you're lucky the bullet's in the flesh part o' your thigh, that it didn' smash up your bone." He turned to the table behind him and picked up the bottle of whiskey. "Here, take another pull of this."

The sheriff swallowed a big mouthful.

"Now grab aholt o' the edge of the table," the doctor said.

The sheriff did as he was told. The doctor moved too fast for the sheriff to realize what he was doing. A white-hot flash of fire ran through his leg. Involuntarily, he yelled.

"You kin stop hollerin' now," the doctor said. "Its all over."

He raised the forceps so that the sheriff could see the bullet held in its small prongs. "That's the li'l bugger that done it."

The sheriff leaned back on the table, his face white and sweating. "Oh, man," he said.

The doctor put down the forceps. "Now we'll git you bandaged up, an' in a few days you'll be good as new." He picked up a roll of bandage and began to work.

Sam Fitch and Clint's father, Mike Richfield, came over to the table and looked down at him. They had been waiting at the far end of the room until the doctor finished. "You swearin' in a posse to go after them that kilt my boy, Sher'f?" Richfield asked.

The sheriff looked up at him. "No."

Richfield stared at him. "They kilt my boy, Sher'f."

"Clint was a horse's ass," the sheriff said flatly. "I tol' him not to start nothin', but he knew better, he had to start shootin'. Ain't a jury in the world'll convict 'em. It was a clear case of self-defense, an' I got the bullet from outta my laig to prove it."

"But they was comin' after him."

"They didn' even know he was there until he fired that shot. All he had to do was sneak on that train an' there wouldn'a' been no trouble."

"You got to go after 'em, Sher'f," Sam Fitch said. "It's your sworn duty."

The sheriff met Fitch's gaze. "My sworn duty holds as fur as the county line," he said. "The Huggins place is ten miles past it."

"It don't matter," Fitch said. "You let 'em git away with it an' they got new heroes. The strike kin start up all over again."

"That ain't my problem," the sheriff said. "I done enough already that's goin' against my conscience. They's a passel of children up there at the Huggins place. I ain't gonna be responsible fer no more killin'."

"My son's blood is cryin' out fer vengeance," Richfield said.

The sheriff looked at him. "Then maybe you kin understan'

166

how Jeb felt when he looked at the body of his daughter," he said. He raised himself on his elbows. "You take my advice an' leave it alone."

"What are you goin' to do, then?" Fitch asked.

"Notify the state police," the sheriff said. "Let 'em do somethin' else besides sendin' back forms to me because I writ 'em up wrong."

"You know they won't do nothin'," Fitch said.

The sheriff didn't answer.

"That's it," the doctor said. "You kin swing yer laigs off'n the table now." He helped the sheriff into a sitting position and then to his feet. "How does it feel?"

"It hurts," the sheriff said.

"It'll do that fer a while," the doctor agreed. "Jes' don't put too much strain on it."

"We cain't let the strike start up again," Fitch said.

The sheriff didn't answer him. One of his deputies, who had been leaning against the wall, came over to help. He began hobbling to the door.

"Yer forcin' me to go to the Pinkertons ag'in," Fitch said. "Yer th'owin' away a good job, Jase. Yer makin' a big mistake."

The sheriff stopped at the doorway. He put his weight on the deputy's shoulder. "It's not me who's makin' the mistake, Sam," he said coldly. "You do that an' you'll be makin' the biggest mistake o' yer life."

In silence, they watched him hobble out of the treatment room. They heard him swearing as he tried to maneuver his way down the stairs.

Sam Fitch turned to Richfield. "I kin have the Pinkertons here on the noon train."

Richfield was silent.

"One bullet an' the sheriff's turned yeller," Fitch said. "We'll meet at my store at one o'clock."

Richfield didn't meet his eyes. "I won't be goin' with you, Mr. Fitch. The sher'f's right. Enough blood has been shed. Makes no sense to begin another feud."

Fitch's voice filled with contempt. "Yer all yeller. But I kin manage 'thout yer help. Jes' don' come suckin' ass when it's all over. 'Cause you'll git nothin' from me." He angrily stomped out.

For a moment there was silence in the room. Then Richfield turned to the doctor. "You'll take care of my boy?"

The doctor, who was also the coroner and the local undertaker, nodded. "I'll fix him up real good."

"Thank you, Dr. John," Richfield said.

Chapter 18

Sarah Andrews opened her eyes when she felt him leave the bed. It was barely daylight, and his naked body gleamed whitely as he padded on bare feet across the room to the chair where his neatly folded pants hung. She saw the muscles moving under the pale skin as he picked up his trousers and felt the stirring within her. She caught her breath. She had never felt anything like this. It had been like that from the very first time, the night Mr. Lewis had come down to organize the miners into the union, over three months ago.

She had been half asleep when she'd heard the knocking. Quickly she had gotten out of bed, put on a robe and gone to the door. "Who is it?" she asked without opening it.

His voice came through it, oddly softened by the thick wooden planks. "It's me, Miss Andrews."

"But I've already gone to bed," she said.

"I'm sorry, Miss Andrews, I didn' mean to bother you none. I jes' came to explain why I was late." There was a moment's silence. Then his voice came through the door again. "I'll see you in the morning."

With surprise she had suddenly realized that the next day was Sunday. And on Sundays he came to cut the wood.

169

There was no school on Sundays, so it didn't matter if she stayed awake a bit later. "Just a minute," she said quickly. "I'm awake now. You might as well come in. I still have some coffee made."

She pulled the bolt on the door and opened it. He stood there hesitantly. "Sure it's no trouble, now?" he asked.

"No," she said. "Come in."

He stepped into the house and she closed the door behind him. "You wait right here. I'll light the lamp."

The soft glow of the lamp on the table spilled through the room. She turned back to him. "I was wondering what had happened to you."

"I had to go to a meetin'," he said.

"A meeting? What about?"

He hesitated. "I don' know if I kin tell," he said. "I promised not to talk about it."

"It wasn't anything illegal, was it?" she asked, a sudden concern in her voice.

"No, ma'am, it wasn't anything like that."

"Then you don't have to tell me about it," she said. "You sit down. I'll go put a fire under the coffee.'

When she came back into the room, he was still standing. She placed the coffeepot and the cups on the table. "Why didn't you sit down?" she asked.

"I jes' looked at your clock over there," he said. "It's after ten. I didn't realize it was so late. Mebbe I'd better go."

"Don't be silly," she said, filling a cup. She held it toward him, her loose robe parting with her gesture. She saw the sudden flush in his face as he took the cup with averted eyes. It took her a moment before she was aware of what had happened. She glanced down at herself. The thin cotton night-dress she wore was almost transparent. Suddenly a wave of heat ran through her and her nipples sprang into life, thrusting themselves against the sheer fabric.

Her legs felt weak and she put a hand on the table to support herself, but she made no move to close the robe. His eyes were still averted when she spoke. "Daniel."

He looked at his coffee cup. "Yes, Miss Andrews?"

She felt her heart hammering inside her breast. "Why aren't you looking at me?"

170

He didn't answer for a moment. "Your robe . . ." He didn't finish.

"I want you to look," she said, her voice sounding strange in her ears.

He raised his eyes slowly. She could see the sudden bulge in his tight-fitting pants. The coffee cup trembled in his hand.

She moved toward him, took the cup from his hand and placed it on the table. "Have you ever been with a girl?"

His eyes fell again. "No, ma'am," he whispered.

"Then what do you do when you get excited?" she asked.

He didn't answer.

"You must do something," she said. "You can't walk around like that."

He still didn't look at her. "I jack off."

"Often?"

He shook his head, his face suffused with red. "In the morning an' at night. Sometimes at lunchtime, when it gits too bad."

She felt the flood of moisture running against her thighs. "What do you think of when you do it?"

He raised his eyes suddenly and looked at her. "You."

"I want to see you," she said.

He didn't move.

She placed a hand on his crotch. Her fingers felt the hard throbbing through the cloth. Quickly she unbuttoned his fly. The rigid phallus, freed from its prison, sprang moistly into her hand. She pressed back the foreskin gently and looked down.

The blood-filled glans seemed to be on the point of bursting. As she looked down, the orgasm shuddered through his body and the heavy white semen came shooting from him.

"My God!" she whispered, her legs no longer able to support her. She sank to her knees before him, her own orgasms wracking her loins. Frantically, she pulled at her gown with her free hand, exposing her breasts. The semen spattered against her flesh. "Oh, my God!"

Half an hour later, they lay naked on her bed, her loins choked with him. She drifted in memory and sensation. It had never been like this. Somehow, before, she had always felt used; now she felt giving. She felt him moving again inside her, and a beginning tremble signaled the coming of his orgasm. Quickly she slipped her hand down between them, cupping his large, round, stonelike testicles, and with her other hand moved his face down to her breast. "Not yet, Daniel," she whispered. "Slowly. Ever so slowly."

He held himself still for a long moment. When he began to move again, it was with the long gentle strokes she loved.

"That's better," she whispered, her body's rhythms matching his own.

She felt his lips moving against her breast. "You jes' tell me what to do, Miss Andrews," he murmured. "I'll learn."

Daniel had proved to be an indefatigable lover. A born eroticist, strong, uninhibited once set free, he seemed never to tire. It seemed to take no effort for him to have four or five and sometimes more orgasms in the course of a night's lovemaking. More than once she had been surprised at his readiness. One time she had touched him by accident and found him hard. She laughed. "My God, Daniel, do you walk around like that all the time?"

He still hadn't lost the ability to blush. His face turned red, and he smiled. "Does seem like that at times, Miss Andrews. Don't it?"

The one habit she hadn't been able to break him of was his addressing her as Miss Andrews. Not even in their most intimate moments, when he was roaring like a bull and she was screaming at the top of her lungs in mutual orgasm, had she been able to make him call her Sarah. After a while she gave up. Somewhere in the back of his mind she would always be his teacher.

Outside the bedroom he had never crossed the line. He read, studied the books and lessons she gave him. His increasing ability to learn and comprehend what she taught had surprised her almost as much as his lovemaking. The speed with which he absorbed ideas had begun to make her wonder just how well equipped she was to educate a mind such as his. Already they were working with the schoolbooks from her junior year in college. Soon he would have gone as far as she would be able to take him.

But the months they had been lovers had seemed to fly by

like so many days, and she had stopped thinking about what would happen with the lessons. It was getting toward the end of May, and in a little while school would be closing and she would go home, perhaps never to return to the school. Or him. That too she would not let herself think about.

She closed her eyes when he slipped into his trousers and went outside. A few minutes later she heard the ringing sound of the axe, and she drifted off into a warm sleep.

It wasn't the sunlight coming through the open window that awakened her. It was the silence. She lay still for a moment until she realized she no longer heard the sound of the axe. She glanced at the clock near the bed. It was only a few minutes after eight. Usually he didn't finish before ten o'clock.

She rose from the bed and looked out the window. Daniel, the axe still in his hands, was talking to a stranger. The man's back was to her, so she could not see what he looked like, but his clothes were torn and covered with dirt. While she was watching, Daniel put down the axe and started toward the house. The man followed. Quickly she grabbed for a robe, then went into the other room to meet them.

The door opened just as she got there. Daniel entered, the man right behind him. Daniel looked at her for a moment, his eyes strangely veiled, a grayish pallor under his skin. It was almost as if he hadn't seen her.

"Daniel," she said, suddenly aware of an unknown dread.

He blinked rapidly a few times. "Miss Andrews." His voice seemed empty of life. "Miss Andrews, this is my friend Roscoe Craig."

She looked at the man. He was almost as tall as Daniel, but much thinner. Two or three days' growth of beard stippled his face, and there were dark hollows under his eyes. His shirt and pants were torn and dusty, and his shoes were covered with mud. He took off his sweat-stained mountain man's hat, revealing thin dark hair on a balding head. "Ma'am," he said.

"Mr. Craig," she replied. She turned back to Daniel. "Daniel, is there anything wrong?"

He didn't answer her question. "Mr. Craig's been travelin'

fer three days an' two nights. Would it be all right if'n we fix 'im somethin' to eat?"

"Of course," she said quickly. "Let me do it."

"Thank you, Miss Andrews," he said, still in the same empty voice. Then, abruptly, he was gone through the open door.

"Daniel!" she called, starting after him.

The stranger's outstretched arm stopped her. "Leave him be, ma'am," he said quietly. "He'll be back."

She stared at him in bewilderment. "What happened?"

"His whole family is dead, ma'am," Roscoe answered in his quiet voice. "Murdered!"

It had been past midnight when Roscoe, sleeping in the barn, heard the voices. He slowly raised his head and listened. He heard the harsh sibilants of men more used to shouting than to speaking. He pulled on his shoes and got to his feet. In an unconscious movement, his hand searched his belt for his gun. He swore to himself when he realized he had left it inside on the Hugginses' kitchen table.

The voices were coming nearer now. Frantically, he looked for a place to hide. The only thing he could find was a pile of hay behind the mule in the stall. Quickly he slithered under it. Annoyed, the mule nudged the hay with his nose.

"Damn mule!" he swore, crawling even deeper into the hay. Footsteps entered the barn. Peeking out, he saw the shoes of several men. He held his breath.

The men stood there for a moment; then a pair of shoes walked toward him. He froze. The man stopped just short of the mule, then went back to the others. He could hear the man's hoarse whisper. "Nothin' there but the mule."

"Go tell Fitch," another voice said. "We'll go up on the little hill in back of the house like he said."

The men left the barn. Roscoe let his breath out slowly and crawled out from under the hay. He crawled along the dirt floor until he was in a position to see out of the barn.

There were two men standing there—Pinkertons, with their hard derby hats sitting squarely on their heads. Each man had a rifle in his hands. Roscoe looked beyond them toward the house.

More men were there—at least nine that he counted, and maybe more on the other side of the house. While he watched, the men seemed to be taking up positions. After a few minutes, one of them raised his hand in a signal.

Sam Fitch came out of the shadows, moving silently for all his big girth. "All the men in position?" His hoarse whisper carried back to the barn.

One of the Pinkertons, the one who had signaled, nodded.

"Get the torches up near the porch steps and light 'em," Fitch said.

Two men ran silently up to the house and jammed the wooden torches into the ground next to the steps. Then he set a match to the oil-soaked rags and ran back just as they roared into a bright yellow flame.

Sam Fitch turned to the house. "Jeb!" he shouted. "You 'n' Roscoe got jes' one minute to come out of the house with your han's up or we're comin' in after you!"

There was a moment's silence. Then the door opened a crack.

"Roscoe ain't here," Jeb yelled back. "I'll come out, but I don' want no shootin'. I got Miz Huggins an' the children in the house."

"Jes' come out slow with your han's high an' there won't be no shootin'." Fitch said.

Slowly the door swung open, revealing Jeb standing with nothing but his pants on, his pale body gleaming in the flickering yellow torchlight. His hands were over his head. He blinked, trying to see past the torches in front of him. Slowly, he walked onto the porch and started down the steps.

Roscoe saw Sam Fitch bring his arm down, giving the signal. "Now!"

"Go back, Jeb!" he began to yell. But his voice was lost in roaring of the rifle fire.

The bullets spun Jeb around, and he tumbled from the top step sideways onto one of the torches, knocking it to the ground beneath the wooden porch. A second later, the dry wood was ablaze, the fire racing up the walls of the house.

The fire leaped through the open doorway into the house and became a searing wall of flame.

The mule, frightened by the smell of smoke, broke from his stall and ran past Roscoe into the yard. He charged into the middle of the Pinkertons, who scattered in front of him, then galloped crazily down the road.

The Pinkertons regathered in a cluster. "We gotta try to get 'em out!" one of them said.

"Don't be a damn fool!" another replied. "Ain't nobody left alive in there no more!"

"Then what are we goin' to do?" the first asked.

"We're gettin' outta here," the second man said. "I don't want to be in this neighborhood when they find out what happened." He walked over to Sam Fitch, who seemed to be transfixed by the fire. "Mr. Fitch."

"Yes?" Fitch's voice was dull. He didn't take his eyes from the fire.

"I think we better go, Mr. Fitch," the Pinkerton said.

Fitch turned to him. "It was an accident. You saw it. It was an accident."

"Ain't nobody goin' to believe that when they find that man's body filled with bullets," the Pinkerton said.

Suddenly Fitch seemed to regain his strength. "We'll fix that. You men come help me. We'll throw his body into the fire."

The Pinkertons didn't move.

Fitch looked at them. "You're all as guilty as I am. Do you want to leave the evidence around to hang you?"

Silently, several of the men went with him. They picked up Jeb's body by the hands and feet and threw it into the center of the burning building.

Fitch looked after it for a moment, then turned away. "Now let's git outta here."

A few minutes later they were gone, and Roscoe climbed wearily to his feet. He walked toward the still-burning ruin that had once been the Hugginses' home. After a moment, he fell to his knees and, tears streaming down his cheeks, began to pray. "Oh, God," he wept. "Why did you have to let it happen to all those beautiful children?"

176

Chapter 19

"WHEN THE sun come up, I went down in the valley to the Callendar place," Roscoe said. "Ol' Man Callendar an' his boy drove me back up in their wagon, an' we give 'em a Christian burial. Callendar had his Bible with him, an' he read from it an' all."

Daniel's face was impassive. "I'm grateful to you an' to him fer that."

Sarah looked at him. It had been almost five hours before he had came back. In the time he had been gone, he had seemed to age ten years. The lines that had appeared on his face had suddenly seemed to destroy his youth. Instead, a man was there. And something else, too. Something strange and implacable. Strong and yet distant, as if a part of him had gone, never to return.

"I done all I could," Roscoe said. "It took me the better part o' three days to git here. I kep' off the roads durin' the day an' took a wide berth aroun' Fitchville. I was of no min' to let Sam Fitch git aholt of me."

"What are you goin' to do now, Mr. Craig?" Daniel asked.

"My missus an' me has been talkin' about Detroit. They's

work up there. I think I'll head up that way. I got kinfolk who'll take me in. Soon's I git a job I'll sen' fer the fam'ly."

Daniel was silent.

"I don' see there's anthin' more I kin do aroun' home," Roscoe said. "Ever'thin's gone now since the courts went against us an' give the mill our lan'."

"I'm not blamin' you, Mr. Craig," Daniel said. "You done the bes' you could, an' that's all a man could do. I was jes' thinkin' it's a mighty long way."

"I'll git there," Roscoe said.

"Do you have any money?" Daniel asked.

"I have enough," Roscoe said. "I kin manage."

"How much?" Daniel was persistent.

Roscoe didn't look at him. " 'Bout a dollar 'n' six bits."

"You'll need more'n that," Daniel said "I have twenty dollars I won't be needin'. I'd been plannin' to send it up to my folks. I think my paw would be right pleased if'n you'd let me lend it to you."

"I couldn't do that," Roscoe said quickly.

Sarah kept silent. The pride of the mountain people was sometimes beyond her understanding. If it seemed like charity, they would not accept it.

"You could pay me back when you git a job," Daniel said.

Roscoe thought for a moment, then nodded. "Put that way, Dan'l," he said. "I don' see how I kin rightly refuse."

"When do you plan to leave, Mr. Craig?" she asked.

He looked at her. "I'd like to git back on the road by nightfall, ma'am," he replied.

"Then let me fix a hot bath for you," she said quickly. "Then you rest a bit, and while you're sleeping I'll brush and clean your clothes."

"That's right kind of you, ma'am," Roscoe said. His eyes followed her as she left the room. He turned back to Daniel. "She's a right fine woman. One would never think she was a schoolmarm. She's like folks."

Daniel nodded. His thoughts were somewhere else. He pulled himself back to the present. "There's a coal train leavin' the mine at midnight," he said. "It goes to Detroit, an' the trainman's a friend of mine. Maybe he'll let you ride back there in the caboose."

178

"That would be mighty he'pful," Roscoe said.

"We'll go down there about eleven, when the train gits in," Daniel said.

Roscoe looked at him. "An' you, Dan'l—what are you gonna do?"

Daniel met his gaze steadily. "I don't know, Mr. Craig," he said slowly. "First thing, I'm goin' home to tend to the graves an' pay my respec's. After that—I jes' don' know."

But Roscoe, looking into the boy's eyes, knew better. They were the same eyes he had seen in Jeb's face just a few days ago.

Daniel spent the rest of the afternoon at the woodpile, the axe ringing rhythmically as it rose and fell. After a while he began to stack the cut cordwood against the side of the schoolhouse. When he had finished, almost the entire side of the building was hidden. Dark was approaching when he came in.

"Hungry?" she asked.

He shook his head.

"You have to eat something," she said. "You didn't have your supper."

"I'm not hungry," he said. Then he saw the expression on her face. "I'm sorry, Miss Andrews. I don't mean to cause you any upset."

"It's all right," she said. "Join me in a cup of coffee?"

He nodded.

She came back into the room with the coffee. He put three spoonfuls of sugar in his cup and stirred it slowly. "He's still asleep," she said.

He sipped at the coffee. "He walked more'n seventy miles to git here."

"Have you known him a long time?" she asked.

"Since I was little. Him an' my paw knowed each other real good when they was boys, but we didn' see much of each other. They had a farm along the river outside Fitchville, an' we lived in the hills. Before the mills came, it seemed like ever'body knowed every'body else. Then things changed. Farmin' went bad along with land, an' the mills started takin' over. People began leavin'. Like he's plannin' to do."

What happened to his farm?" she asked.

"They foreclosed on him, an' they built a mill on the land. They was seven acres of riverfront that belonged to his pappy an' they got into a dispute over it. The mill an' him."

"Then what happened?"

There was coldness in his eyes as he looked at her. "They kilt his pappy an' his eldest son an' had the courts take the land away from 'em. Now he's got no place to go. Except Deetroit."

"You're fortunate," she said. "You have a place to go."

"I have?" he questioned.

"Yes," she said. "You have a good job here. And a future. You can take care of yourself."

His voice was expressionless. "A good job? Forty a month. Is that a good job?"

"There are men who don't make that much," she said.

"That's right," he said. "It all comes down to a question of how much hunger a person kin tolerate. The miner 'n' the farmer 'n' the mill hand is all in the same boat. The on'y choice they got is how hungry they want to be."

She was silent.

He looked at her. "I don't rightly understand it, Miss Andrews. I seen my paw sweatin' because Mr. Fitch wouldn' give 'im a few pennies more fer a jug o' corn. I seen miners dyin' in the shafts fer a dollar 'n' a half a day. I heered stories 'bout girls in the mills gettin' their arms tore out in the machinery fer a nickel 'n' hour 'n' breaker boys manglin' their han's fer the same wages. I don' unnerstand why the people who decide these things cain't jes' give a little more so that them as works fer 'em kin git along."

It was the longest speech she ever heard him make and the first time she had ever been allowed into his thoughts. She had no answer for him. For the first time she felt her own inadequacy. "It's always been like that," she said.

"It doesn' have to be," he said quietly. "And someday it won't be."

She said nothing.

"I been thinkin'," he said. "There had to be a reason. A reason fer all o' this. What happened to my folks. Jimmy understood it. I didn't. There's jes' two kinds of people in this

180

world. Them that owns it 'n' them that works fer it. Now I know where I am."

She looked at him. "Daniel, have you ever thought of continuing with school? Going to college, making something of yourself?"

"When I figgered out how little I knew, I thought about it," he said. "But that takes money."

"Maybe not as much as you think," she said quickly. "I have friends at the university. I'm sure you can get a partial scholarship at the very least."

"It still takes money," he repeated.

"Maybe you can sell your father's farm?" she suggested.

"There'll be nobody to buy it," he said flatly. "The land's used up, wu'thless. The on'y reason my paw was able to live on it was because Molly Ann 'n' me went to work 'n' sent our money home. If we didn' do that, we'd all of starved."

Her hand reached across the table and touched his. "Daniel," she said softly. "I know how you must feel. I'm sorry."

He looked down at her hand, then up at her face. "I thank you fer your sympathy, Miss Andrews." He got to his feet. "I'm goin' down to the boardin'house 'n' git the money fer Mr. Craig. I'll be back in a little while."

Roscoe came out of the bedroom about eight o'clock rubbing the sleep from his eyes, wearing the faded bathrobe that Daniel used when he stayed over. "It's dark already," he said in a faintly surprised voice. "Where's Dan'l?"

"He went to his boardinghouse for a few things," she said. "He should be back soon." She crossed the room to the kitchen and returned with his clothing. "I did the best I could, Mr. Craig," she said, giving it to him.

"They jes' fine, ma'am," he said, noting the neatly pressed shirt and trousers and the freshly shined boots.

"I'll get supper ready while you're dressing," she said. "And I'll fix some sandwiches for your journey."

"You don' have to go to all that bother, ma'am."

"It's no trouble, Mr. Craig," she said. She started for the

181

kitchen, then turned back to him. "Mr. Craig, what's going to happen to Daniel now?"

He looked at her thoughtfully. "I don' rightly know," he answered. "He's a man alone now, an' he'll be makin' his own mind."

Daniel returned while she was still preparing supper. It was a Daniel she had never seen before. Gone were the white shirt and tie, the pressed store-bought trousers, the shiny black shoes. In their place were worn and faded denim overalls held up by crossed straps over a clean but tired-looking blue cotton shirt, and on his feet were heavy farmer's boots. A broad-brimmed, faded black mountain man's hat sat squarely on his head. Suddenly he seemed no longer a boy but a man. A man worn, hurt, embittered by life. She felt a pain inside her. It was then that she finally accepted what she had known ever since the morning. That he was leaving.

They ate supper in silence. After it was over, she gathered up the dishes and took them into the kitchen. She placed the dishes in the sink and went back into the parlor without washing them. There would be time enough for that later.

Daniel rose from the table when she came into the room. "It's almost ten o'clock," he said. "We'll have to be leavin'."

She looked at him for a moment. "I fixed some sandwiches," she said. She went back into the kitchen and returned with a large paper bag and gave it to Roscoe.

The farmer took it gratefully. "Thank you very kin'ly, ma'am."

But she wasn't looking at him. Her eyes were on Daniel.

"I'll be waiting outside, Daniel," Roscoe said with a gentle understanding, and went out the front door.

They stood there silently for a long while just looking at each other. Finally she let out a deep breath. "Are you going to Detroit with him?"

He shook his head. "I'm goin' home. The train kin leave me off at Turner's Pass. That's on'y eight miles from our place."

"And after that?"

"I don' know," he said.

"Will you be coming back?" Her heart was aching.

He looked into her eyes. "I don' think so, Miss Andrews."

Her eyes began to fill with tears. "Just for now, Daniel, for this time, please call me Sarah."

He hesitated a moment, then nodded. "Yes—Sarah."

She went into his arms and placed her head against his chest. "Will I ever see you again?" she whispered.

He held her gently without answering.

She looked up into his face. "Daniel, do you love me? Just a little?"

He looked down into her eyes. "Yes," he answered. "Jes' how much I don' know. It's the fus' time I ever loved a girl."

"Don't forget me, Daniel," she wept. "Don't forget me."

"How can I?" he answered. "I'll never forget you. I owe you so much."

She held him tightly; and later, when he was gone and she was alone in her bed and she heard the train whistle at midnight, she turned her face into the pillow and could still feel his arms around her.

"I loved you, Daniel," she wept, saying the words she had never never been able to bring herself to say to him. "Oh, God, you'll never know how much I loved you."

Chapter 20

THE LOCOMOTIVE dragging the twenty-two coal cars laboriously puffed its way up the grade toward Turner's Pass shortly after eight o'clock in the morning. There had been only eight coal cars when Daniel and Roscoe had boarded, but stops had been made at three more mines along the way. The small caboose swayed gently at the rear of the train.

The brakeman stuck his head out the window, then pulled it back inside. "We're comin' up on Turner's Pass, Daniel."

Daniel got to his feet. "Thank you for the courtesy, Mr. Small."

"Anytime, Daniel," the trainman said, smiling.

Daniel turned to Roscoe. "Good luck, Mr. Craig. I hope ever'thin' works out fer you."

Roscoe held out his hand. "Good luck to you, Dan'l."

Daniel nodded. He started for the door at the rear of the caboose. Roscoe called him. Daniel turned.

The older man spoke awkwardly. "You're the on'y one left, Dan'l. I don' think yer father would want anything to happen to you."

Daniel looked at him silently.

184

"What I mean," Roscoe added, "if anythin' happens to you, then all your father's life would of meant nothin'."

Daniel nodded. "I'll think on it, Mr. Craig."

"She's slowin' down," the brakeman said. "You better git movin', Dan'l."

Daniel went out onto the tiny platform and waited on the bottom step as the train slowed to a crawl. Roscoe and the brakeman came out onto the platform. Daniel jumped, ran a few steps, slid down the embankment beside the tracks, then scrambled to his feet, waving his hand to let them know he was all right. They waved back, and the train began to pick up momentum again. A few minutes later it disappeared into the curve, and Daniel began walking through the hills toward home.

He found the old paths as if he had never been away. This was where he had grown up, and he knew the land like the back of his hand. He remembered when he was little and his father had taken him hunting for the first time. How proud he had been when he brought home a rabbit for the pot.

Engrossed as he was with memories, the two hours it took to walk the eight miles to his house seemed only as many minutes, so he wasn't prepared for the shock when he came out onto the road where the house had once stood.

He froze. It was reduced to a charred shell, only the frame and the chimney still intact. In the morning sun, the air seemed to shiver over the remains of the house. Behind it the barn stood, untouched, empty of life. He drew a deep breath and forced himself to walk into what had been the front yard.

There was a heavy sound behind him. He whirled quickly. The mule came out of the brush on the other side of the road. His big round eyes looked at Daniel questioningly.

The mule was the first to move. He came across the road to Daniel and nudged at him with his nose. Daniel stepped to one side, and the mule continued through the yard into the barn.

Daniel followed him. The mule had his nose buried in the hay. Daniel looked into the trough. It was dry. He went back into the yard to the well. The big water bucket still hung there on the pump nozzle. He began pushing the pump handle. It took some moments for the water to come gushing up and fill the pail. Daniel carried it back to the trough.

The mule raised his head and watched him. Slowly, Daniel emptied the water into the trough. Still munching bits of hay, the mule approached the trough. He looked down at it for a moment, then up at Daniel.

Daniel nodded. "Yes, stupid mule, that's how water gits there. Drink up."

The mule seemed almost to be smiling as he cleaned his teeth of the hay. Then he put his muzzle delicately into the water and began to drink. Daniel turned away.

Without looking at the house again, he walked up the side of the small hill to the cemetery. He looked down at the graves, the earth still black and new over them. He took off his hat and stood bareheaded in the sun. He had never been to a funeral, so he did not know the right prayer to say. The only one he could remember was the one his mother had taught him when he was a little child. His lips moved softly.

> "Now I lay me down to sleep.
> I pray the Lord my soul to keep.
> If I should die before I wake,
> I pray the Lord my soul to take.
> God bless Maw; God bless Paw;
> God bless my sisters and brothers . . ."

His voice faded away, and for the first time the tears came to his eyes, blurring the graves. He stood without moving, the tears running down his cheeks. After a while the tears stopped, but he remained, the graves and the small wooden crosses burning their way into his brain, the loss and hurt and emptiness draining his soul. Then suddenly it was over. The pain stopped. He closed his eyes for a long moment. He knew what he had to do.

Without looking back, he left the small cemetery and went up the path to the hill. He came around the small turn and there it was, as it always had been. His father's still—the small shed, the copper tubing, the stone jugs. It was if nothing had happened.

186

He opened the door of the shed and went inside. It was dark, and very little light came in through the door. He reached up to the top shelf and found what he had come for. He searched again with his fingers and found the small box that he knew would be next to it. He took the tarpaulin-wrapped double-barreled 20-gauge shotgun and the box of shells into the sunlight. Quickly, he stripped away the tarpaulin. The gun was clean and shining. He cocked both hammers and pulled the triggers. They clicked in cleanly, the hammers snapping into the firing pin sharply. His father had always insisted on keeping his guns clean and in working order. He opened the box of shells. It was almost full.

He laid them down on a wooden bench and went back into the shed. This time he came out with a steel cutting saw and a file. Carefully he locked the shotgun into the vise on the workbench and slowly began to cut the barrel of the shotgun down to about a quarter of its length. When that was done, he filed the edges smooth, then wiped it clean with a lightly oiled rag. With another rag he removed the remaining traces of oil, and took the gun from the vise. He hefted the gun and looked at it. The whole gun, including the wooden stock, was now less than two feet long.

He put the gun down on the bench, picked up two stone jugs and set them up on the fence in the sunlight. He continued until he had ten jugs sitting about two feet apart on the fence. He picked up the shotgun and placed a shell in each chamber.

He turned and measured the distance from the fence with his eye. About five feet. Just right. Holding the shotgun waist high, braced against his hip, he pulled both triggers. The kick spun him halfway around, and the noise seemed to shatter his ears. He turned back to check his target. He had missed completely. The jug at which he had been aiming was still untouched.

He went over to the fence, his eyes searching the tree behind it for traces of the buckshot. He found it. High and to the left and widely scattered. The tree was a few feet behind the target, which meant that he would have to move in closer for the gun to be effective. He moved deliberately. There was no rush. He had all afternoon.

By the time he was satisfied, he had used all the cartridges but four. Of these two went into the gun and two went into his pocket.

The sun was beginning its descent into the west as he went down the path. He went by the cemetery without stopping and right to the barn. The mule was standing contentedly in his stall.

He took a bridle and reins from a peg on the barn wall and approached the mule. The animal watched him warily.

"C'mon, mule," Daniel said. "It's time you earned your keep."

Jackson began sweeping the wooden walk in front of Fitch's store at seven o'clock that morning. He paid no attention to the man who was sitting on the bench in the square across the street. He seemed just another farmer, catching a snooze, his hat pulled down over his eyes to keep out the morning light. Even the old mule tied to a nearby tree was not worth a second glance.

A little while later, Harry, the fussy chief clerk, came to the store and began setting up the doorway displays. He had just finished his work when Mr. Fitch arrived. Harry stole a glance at the big clock in the back of the store. Eight o'clock. Exactly on time.

Mr. Fitch was in a good mood. "Everything all right, Harry?"

The little clerk bobbed up and down. "Yes, Mr. Fitch. Everything's just fine."

Mr. Fitch chuckled and went past him into the store. Harry followed him. "We have those new canned beans, Mr. Fitch. Do you want me to put them on sale?"

Fitch stopped for a moment, then nodded.

"How much, Mr. Fitch?"

"Three fer a dime, Harry. That's cheap enough an' still a good profit. They on'y cost us two cents apiece."

"I'll take care of it right away, Mr. Fitch," Harry said. Fitch continued on to his office in the back of the store as Harry yelled for Jackson to bring the canned beans up from the cellar.

188

Across the street, the man rose from the bench. He looked up and down the street for a moment. There weren't too many people about. Slowly he crossed the street to the store, his arms hugging his jacket close around him, his hat still low over his eyes. He entered the store.

Harry popped up from behind the counter. "Anything I can do for you, sir?"

The farmer didn't look at him. "Mr. Fitch aroun'?"

"He's in his office in the back."

"Thank you," the man said politely. He was already moving away as he spoke. He disappeared behind a stack of wooden crates near the office door.

Sam Fitch, seated behind his desk, looked up as the man came in. "Mornin', frien'," he said in his customer voice. "Kin I be of he'p?"

The man stopped in front of the desk. He pushed the hat up from his face to the back of his head. His voice was emotionless. "I guess you kin."

Sam Fitch's face paled. "Dan'l!"

Daniel was silent.

"I di'n' recognize you, boy. You growed so big," Fitch said.

Daniel looked at him steadily. "Why did you do it, Mr. Fitch?"

"Do what?" Fitch tried to act bewildered. "I don' know what you're talkin' 'bout."

Daniel's eyes were cold. "I think you do, Mr. Fitch. What did we ever do to you to make you kill all of 'em?"

"I still don' know what you're talkin' 'bout," Fitch insisted.

"Roscoe Craig was there, hidin' in the barn, 'n' he saw all of it. He tol' me." Daniel's voice was still emotionless.

Fitch stared at him. He abandoned pretense but not lies. "It was an accident, Dan'l. You got to believe me. We never intended to start no fire."

"You never intended to kill my paw neither, did you? You on'y give the signal to shoot when he come outta the house."

"I was tryin' to stop 'em. That's what I was tryin' to do. Stop 'em." Fitch's eyes widened as Daniel's coat swung open and the sawed-off shotgun came into view. He kept on talking as he slid open a drawer of his desk and reached for the gun inside. "I tried to stop 'em. But they wouldn' listen to me. They was crazy."

"You're lyin', Mr. Fitch." Daniel's voice was flat and final.

Fitch had his hand on the gun now. Moving quickly for a man his size, he pulled out the gun and jumped sideways from his chair in front of the glass windows separating his office from the store. But he didn't move quickly enough.

The roar of both barrels was like a thunderclap in the tiny office. Fitch's body was torn apart from chest to belly as the shot propelled him backward through the glass partition. His blood and insides spattered the wooden crates as they fell around him.

Slowly Daniel walked over and looked down at the broken body of Sam Fitch. He was still standing like that when the sheriff, followed by a deputy, came rushing into the store.

The sheriff took one quick look at Sam Fitch, then moved his eyes up to Daniel. He put his own gun back in its holster. He held out a hand to Daniel. "I think you better give me that there gun, Dan'l," he said.

Daniel raised his eyes from Sam Fitch's body. "Sher'f," he said. "he kilt my whole fam'ly."

"Give me the gun, Daniel," the sheriff repeated gently.

Daniel nodded slowly. "Yes, sir."

The sheriff took the gun and handed it to his deputy. "Come, Dan'l."

Daniel came out of the office and stopped to look down at Sam Fitch once again. When he raised his head to look at the sheriff, there was a strange agony in his eyes. "Sher'f," he asked in a hurt voice. "Wasn't there nobody in this whole town to stop 'im?"

The judge looked down from his bench. Daniel stood silently before him in the almost empty courtroom. "Daniel Boone Huggins," the judge said solemnly. "In view of the extenuating circumstances, the death of your family and your extreme youth, and in the hope that the death and violence which have plagued this county the past year have finally come to an end, it is the considered judgment of this court that you be sent to the State Correctional Institute for Boys for a period of two years or until you reach the age of eighteen, whichever is sooner. It is the further hope of this court that you will apply yourself diligently to learning a trade and taking advantage of the many opportunities you will find there to become a useful member of society."

He rapped his gavel twice on the bench and rose to his feet. "The court is now closed." He started down from the platform as the sheriff came toward Daniel.

The sheriff took a pair of handcuffs from his pocket. "I'm sorry, Dan'l," the sheriff said. "The law says I got to use these on sentenced prisoners."

Daniel looked at him, then silently held out his hands. The handcuffs clicked and locked around his wrists.

The sheriff looked at him. "You ain't angry, are you, Dan'l?"

Daniel shook his head. "No, Sher'f. Why should I be? It's over. Now, mebbe, I kin fergit it."

But he never did.

Now

THE AIR brakes hissed as the big trailer truck pulled to the side of the highway. The door swung open and the driver stared at us as I got out of the cab. I held up my hand to help Anne down.

"You kids are crazy," the driver said. "Gittin' off in the middle o' nowhere. It's thirty-five miles down the road to Fitchville an' fifty miles back to the next town. An' nothin' in between except maybe some sharecroppers."

Anne swung out of the cab. I picked up the backpacks. "Thanks for the lift," I said.

He stared at me. "Okay. But be careful. These people ain't exactly friendly toward strangers. Sometimes they shoot before they ask question."

"We'll be all right," I said.

He nodded and closed the door. We watched the truck pick up speed, and in a moment it was lost in the highway traffic. I turned to Anne. She hadn't spoken until now.

"Do you know where we're going?" she asked.

I nodded.

Her voice turned sarcastic. "Mind telling me?"

I let my eyes scan the countryside, then pointed at a small hill rising above the trees about a mile from the road. "There."

She looked at the hill, then back at me. "Why?"

"I'll know when I get there," I said. I scrambled down the side of the embankment from the highway. When I looked back she was still standing there, staring down at me. "Coming?"

She nodded and started down after me. About halfway, she slipped. I caught her and she came to a stop, her head against my chest. She was trembling. After a moment, she looked up into my face. "I'm frightened."

I looked into her eyes. "Don't be," I said. "You're with me."

It took us almost two hours to reach the crest of the hill, another half-hour to the knoll about a quarter of the way down the other side. I dropped my backpack and sat on the ground. I took a deep breath, then, on my knees, began to feel the earth under the tall wild grass.

"What are you doing?" she asked.

"Looking for something," I said, and at the same moment my hand hit a stone. Carefully I felt it. Rectangular in shape, the upper surface slanting slightly toward me. Quickly I pulled the grass and weeds from around it. It was a block of stone no more than two feet long and a foot wide. With my hand I brushed away the earth and dirt covering it until the letters etched into the stone were clear and sharp.

HUGGINS.

Her voice was soft behind me. "What have you found?"

I looked once more at the stone, then up at her.

"My grandfather's grave."

"You knew where it was?" she asked.

I shook my head. "No."

"Then, how?"

"I don't know," I said.

"Tell her, son. I told you."

"You're dead. You never told me anything even while you were alive."

"I told you everything. You weren't listening."

"What makes you think I'm listening now?"

His laugh was the deep, heavy chuckle I had heard all my life. "You haven't any choice now. I'm inside your head."

"Let go, Father. You're dead. And I have my own life to lead."

"You're young yet. You have time. First you have to lead mine. Then you'll be able to lead your own."

"Shit."

"Exactly." The deep, heavy chuckle again. "But you'll have to learn how to walk before you can run."

"And you're going to teach me?"

"That's right."

"How are you going to do that with seven feet of dirt sitting on your head up there in Scarsdale?"

"I told you. I'm in every cell of your body. I am you and you are me. And as long as you live I'll be there."

"But someday I'll be dead too. Then where will you be?"

"With you. In your child."

The man's voice came from behind us. "Turn aroun' slow and don't make any sudden moves."

I got to my feet. Anne put her hand in mine, and slowly we turned toward the man. He was tall and thin, faded overalls and work shirt, sun-squint lines etched around his eyes, a wide-brimmed straw hat on his head and a double-barreled shotgun pointing at us across the crook in his elbow. "Didn't you see the No Trespass signs along the path?"

"We didn't come along a path. We came up the side of the hill from the highway."

"Turn aroun' and go back the way you came. Whatever you was lookin' fer, you won' fin' it here."

"I already found what I was looking for," I said, pointing to the headstone on the ground.

He stepped to one side and looked down at it. "Huggins," he said softly, pronouncing it with a soft G. "What's that got to do with you?"

"He was my grandfather."

He was silent for a moment. His eyes searched my face. "What's your name?"

"Jonathan Huggins."

"Big Dan's son?"

I nodded.

The muzzle of his gun dropped toward the ground. His voice seemed gentler. "You kids foller me down to the house. My wife has some nice cool lemonade hangin' in the well."

We followed him down a path through the trees on the far side of the hill. We came out on a small knoll just above a cornfield. Beyond the cornfield was the house. If that was what it could be called. More a lean-to shack—odd pieces of wood nailed together, the crevices sealed with construction paper and tar, the roof more boards nailed together over plastic. In front of the house was a battered old pickup, dusty in the afternoon sun, whatever paint was left on it a faded, indistinguishable color. He led us past the cornfield, past the pickup, to the door.

He opened it and called in. "Betty May, we got visitin' folk."

A moment later, a girl appeared in the doorway. She couldn't have been more than sixteen, round face, round blue eyes, long blond hair and pregnant. She looked at us carefully, a hint of fear in her eyes.

"It's okay," he said reassuringly. "They f'om up No'th."

"How do?" Her voice ws a child's voice.

"Hello," I said.

He turned to me, holding out his hand. "I'm Jeb Stuart Randall. My woman, Betty May."

"Pleased to meet you, Jeb Stuart." I took his hand. "This is Anne."

He made a half old-fashioned bow. "Honored, ma'am."

"Not ma'am, Ms."

"I beg your pardon, miz," he said, not picking up on the word.

She smiled at him. "Nice to meet you Mr. Randall, Mrs. Randall."

"Git the lemonade f'om the well, Betty May. Our visitors must be parched f'om the afternoon sun."

Betty May seemed to slip by us as we followed him into the shack. The interior was dark and cool after the bright heat outside. We sat down around a small table in the only room.

On one wall were an old-fashioned coal cooking stove and a sink with cupboards over it; the other wall had one old wooden closet, a chest of drawers and a bed, over which was thrown a patchwork quilt. A small oil lamp was in the center of the table.

Jeb Stuart took a half-smoked cigarette from his pocket, placed it in his mouth without lighting it. Betty May came back into the house with a pitcher of lemonade. Silently she filled three glasses and placed them in front of us. She took none for herself, neither did she sit at the table with us. Instead she went to the stove and stood next to it, watching us.

I tasted the lemonade. It was thin and watery and very sweet. But it was cool. "Very good, ma'am,"

"Thank you," she said in her pleased child's voice.

"I heard on the news about your pappy passing away," Jeb Stuart said. "My sympathy."

I nodded.

"I seen your pappy once," he said. "He cut a fine figger, an' man, could he talk! I 'member listenin' to him an' thinkin', That man could charm the angels f'om the trees."

I laughed. "That's probably what he's doin' right now. Either that or getting the Devil to change the working hours down there."

He didn't know whether to smile or not. "Your pappy was a God-fearin' man. He's prob'ly up there with the angels."

I nodded. I had to remember that we didn't speak the same language.

"Yer pappy was one of us. Born right yere. He made a name for hisself that the whole country could respec'." He fished in his pocket and came up with the familiar blue-four-leaf-clover-on-white union button, the letters C.A.L.L., one to each leaf, shining white. "When he started up the Confederation, we was among the first unions to jine up with 'im."

"What union was that?"

"The S.F.W.U."

That made sense. Southern Farm Workers Union. The shit end of the union stick. Neither the C.I.O. nor the A.F.L. had ever bothered more than to collect dues from them. There wasn't any real money there. But my father knew better. He

199

knew he had to begin somewhere. What he was looking for first was members, not money, and the South was ripe for picking. That was why he insisted on the word "Confederation" rather than "International." He was right. Within one year he had every union in the South with him, and with that as his his base he moved rapidly, north, east and west. Three years later he could call on a national affiliation of seven hundred unions, with a membership of more than twenty million workers.

Jeb Stuart gestured to his wife, and without a word she refilled his empty glass. "I kin still remember his ever' word.

" 'I'm one a you,' yer pappy said. 'I was born in these yere mountains. I he'ped my paw with the plowin' an' 'shinin'. My first job, when I was fourteen year ol', was in a coal mine. I punched cattle in Texas, worked oil rigs in Oklahoma, loaded river barges in Natchez, drove a dump truck in Georgia, crated oranges in Florida. I been fired f'om more jobs than any o' you fellers ever dreamed existed.'

"He looked aroun' the meetin' hall at us f'om under them big, bushy eyebrows. We was all laughin'. He had us. He knew it an' we knew it. He didn't smile, though. He was all business.

" 'I'm not askin' you to leave the C. of I.O. to come and jine with us. The C. of I.O. is doin' a good job fer you. Even though ol' John L. is gittin' on up there in years an' sot in his ways an' them Reuther boys up No'th in Detroit is a mite young an' needs some seasonin', they still doin' a good job. But they cain't do it all. Not even when they git back together with the A.F. of L.—an' min' you, they will git back together —will they be able to do it all.

" 'I'm not askin' you people to saddle yerselves with more dues an' assessments. Heaven knows you fellers are payin' enough right now. I'm askin' you fellers to jine a confederation. Now, everyone in the South knows from their history books exactly what a confederation is. It is a group of people jinin' together of their own free will to preserve their rights as individ'ls. Jes' like our great-gran'parents did years ago in the War between the States.

" 'The purpose o' the Confederated Alliance of Livin' Labor

is to he'p each individual union to maintain its independent status and to achieve the best results fer its members. We give you services. Consultation, plannin', management. So that you can decide to do what is best for yerselves, jes' like the big unions and big businesses call in specialists fer their problems. You pay no dues, nothin' at all less'n you call us in to work fer you. Then you only pay us while we're workin'; when the job is finished, you stop payin'.' "

He picked up his lemonade and took a sip. "I didn' know what he was talkin' 'bout, an' I don't think anyone else in the hall did neither, but it didn' matter. He had us all wrapped up."

I laughed inside. I knew the speech by heart, having heard it a million times. My father made it sound like a call to the Confederacy: the South would rise again. Once a union was signed up, that was only a beginning; then the sales program would go into action. I don't think there was ever a union that realized they needed so much assistance. Where they thought they had only one problem, C.A.L.L. would show them they had ten. Then it was all over but the shouting. And the beauty of it was, there was nothing the A.F.L. or the C.I.O. could do about it, because after all, C.A.L.L. was there to help them too.

"What happened then?" I asked.

"Later that summer, there was a great deal o' talk about goin' out on strike because there was a bumper harvest comin'. C.A.L.L. showed us we'd be hurtin' ourselves more than the big farmer, because there was a good chance of ever'body workin' for the first time in three years. An' if we lost that big harvest, it would take us more'n six years at increased wages to make up that loss. The predictions were all for a poor harvest the following year. That was the time to nail the farmer, when he needed it more than we did because half the membership would be out o' work anyway. An' it worked. The strike was over in two weeks. The farmers caved in. they couldn' afford a total loss."

I looked at him. "And after that there was always someone from C.A.L.L. down at the union office working on some important project."

He stared at me. "How did you know?"

I smiled. "That's where I grew up. I knew my father."

"He was a great man," he said reverently.

"Do you still think so now that you're farming on your own?"

He seemed puzzled. "I don' understan'."

"I saw a field of corn out there," I said.

"That's nothin'," he said. "On'y three acres. I kin handle that myself."

"What if the union comes in an' says that you have to have a couple men to help?"

"They ain't comin' up here. Ain't nobody comes up here no more. Not fer a long time. Nobody even knows I'm farmin' up here. The land all aroun' is wasted."

I remembered the words he quoted from my father's speech many years ago. "I he'ped my paw with the plowin' and 'shinin'."

Suddenly I knew. "My grandfather's still."

There was a sudden pale under his tan. "What did you say?"

"My grandfather's still," I repeated. "Did you find it?"

He hesitated a moment, then nodded.

Now it all began to make sense. Three acres of corn in moonshine was a small fortune. "I want to see it."

"Now?" he asked.

"Now."

Silently he rose from the chair, picked up his shotgun and started for the door. I rose to follow him.

Betty May's voice suddenly wasn't a child's voice anymore. "No, Jeb Stuart, no. Don't do it."

I looked at him, then back at her. "Don't worry, ma'am. He's not going to do anything."

Jeb Stuart nodded and went out the door. I looked at Anne. "You wait here until I get back."

Anne nodded.

"I'll have supper fixed by the time you get back," Betty May said.

"Thank you," I said, and went out the door after Jeb Stuart.

He walked ahead of me rapidly, not once looking back. He

didn't say a word as we threaded our way through the small forest on the side of the hill on a path almost completely obliterated by weeds. Suddenly he stopped. "It's there."

I looked at what seemed an almost solid wall of forest brush. "Yes," I said.

"How did you know?" he asked.

"You told me," I said.

"I don't understan'."

"It doesn't matter," I said.

He walked a few steps farther on and pulled a clump of bushes aside and went through them. I followed, and the bushes sprang closed behind us. The still was in a small clearing partly cut into the side of the hill behind it, a log roof covered with forest brush over it. The black iron smoke pot seemed clean and untouched by time, and the copper tubing shone like new. Ten forty-gallon charred oak barrels were lined up next to the still, and on the other side was a long pile of neatly cut and stacked fire logs. I heard the thin trickle of a small stream and walked behind the still. It was there, sparkling in the thin light as it ran down over the stones and rocks. I put my hands in the water and held it up to my lips. It was sweet and fresh.

"That water runs into our well below," he said.

"How did you find it?" I asked.

"Huntin'. Two years ago. My dog treed a coon. I took the coon, then tracked the stream down to where the ol' house used to be. Right away I knew what I had to do. Three good years an' I'd be rich. No more chicken-shit farmin'. I could live like a human bein'."

I walked back to the still. He followed me. I looked at the shining copper tubing. "The pipes are new?"

He nodded. "I had to fix ever'thing up. Betty May an' I worked fer a whole year. Clearin' the land fer the corn, buildin' the shack. Took all our savin's to buy the supplies an' the materials. More'n six hundred dollars. 'Twarn't till we got the corn in las' spring that we really believed it was all happenin'. Ever'thing was jes' comin' along fine. Nobody even knowed we was here. We never went down to Fitchville to buy anythin'. Once a week we drive down to Grafton, fifty-some miles down the highway, to git our stuff. It was jes' fine. 'N'en you come along."

I looked at him without speaking.

He put the shotgun down on the ground and looked around thoughtfully while he fished in a shirt pocket for a cigarette. It was wrinkled and crooked, as if it had been in there for a long time. Carefully he straightened it, then lit it. He let the smoke out slowly, and it swirled up around his face as he turned to me. "I guess Betty May an' me knowed in our hearts it was too good to be true. That it would never happen." He paused for a moment. His voice seemed strained. "We ain't got much here. We can be off the place by tomorrow mornin'."

"What makes you think I would want you to do that?"

"It's your propitty, ain't it?" He met my eyes. "I saw that in the county records when I went to check on the owners. I saw your name there big as all git-out. Yer father put it in yer name three years ago. But ever'one down there in the record office said ain't nobody been around the place in more'n thirty years 'cept fer the lawyer who come down to register the transfer."

I turned away from him. I didn't want him to see the rush of tears I was suddenly fighting. Just another thing my father had never told me. Among others. "Go back down to the house and tell Betty May that I said you're not moving. I'll be down there in a little while."

I heard him get to his feet behind me. "Sure you kin fin' your way back?"

"I'm sure."

I heard the rustle of the brush, and when I turned around he was gone. I could still hear the sound of his steps crackling down the path. Then that was gone too and there was nothing but silence and the sound of a soft wind in the trees. I sat down on the ground. It was cool and damp to my fingers. I dug my hand into it and came up with a handful of earth. I looked at it. It was black and wet. I pressed it to my face and let my tears run into it. For the first time since my father's death, I began to cry.

It was still daylight when we finished eating. [ ]
butt, black-eyed peas and greens in a thin brown [ ]
home-baked corn bread and mugs of steaming co[ ]
Betty May watching me out of the corner of my eye[ ]
good," I said, wiping up the gravy in my plate with t[ ]

She smiled, pleased. " 'Tain't much, but it's rea[ ]
home cookin'."

"That's the best kind, Betty May," I said.

"That's what I allus say," Jeb Stuart said quickly. '
May, she's always readin' them highfalutin recipes in the
azines, but they ain't fer real eatin'—jes' readin' about."

Anne laughed. "Betty May doesn't have anything to wo[ ]
about. I have the feeling she can cook just about anything s[ ]
sets her mind to."

"Thank you, Anne," Betty May said, a faint blush rising i[ ]
her cheeks.

Jeb Stuart pushed his plate away from the table. "As you
kin see, we ain't got much room in here, but you all kin
have the bed. Betty May an' I 'll sleep in the back of the pickup."

"You don't have to do that," I said quickly. "Anne and I
have our sleeping bags. Besides, we like to sleep outside."

"Then the best place is the cornfield. The skeeters won't git
you there. I keep it sprayed real good." He rose from the
table. "Come, I'll fin' you a good place where you'll be shel-
tered from the night wind."

I rose to follow him. Anne got up too. "Let me help with
the dishes," she said.

Betty May shook her head. "They ain't much. You jes' set
and enjoy yerself."

Darkness fell quickly, and ten minutes later, when Jeb
Stuart and I came back from the cornfield, there was an old
glass-enclosed oil lamp burning on the table, its yellow light
dancing on the walls.

I glanced at my wristwatch. It was almost eight o'clock.
"Do you have a radio?" I asked.

Jeb Stuart shook his head. "We don' have much time to
listen if we did. We usu'lly turn in right after supper."

"I wanted to get the news," I said. "My brother was sup-posed to become acting president of C.A.L.L. this afternoon."

"Sorry," he said.

"It's okay." I turned to Anne. "Come, I'll show you where I put the sleeping bags." We went to the door. "Thank you for dinner, Betty May. We'll see you in the morning."

We walked silently to the sleeping bags. By the time we reached them it was really dark, and the last bit of light faded from the sky as we wriggled into them.

"They don't have any electricity," Anne said.

"They don't want any."

"She misses television. She told me so."

I didn't say anything.

"Are you going to let them stay here, Jonathan?" she asked.

"Yes."

"I'm glad. She was afraid you would order them off."

"She told you?"

"Yes. They found your name on the records. Did you know that your father gave you this land?"

"No."

"Then why did you come here?"

"I don't know," I said. "And don't ask me any more. I don't know anything. Why we're here today. Or where we'll be tomorrow."

Her hand searched out mine and held it tightly. I turned to her. The moon had come up now, and I could see her face. "You're strange, Jonathan," she said. "You're becoming more and more like your father with every passing minute. Even the sound of your voice."

"Shit," I said. We were silent for a moment. "I'm sorry now I made you throw away all that grass. I could go for a few good tokes myself."

She giggled. "You mean that?"

"I mean it."

She wriggled out of her bag and sat up. A moment later she came up with a small pouch and papers. "My emergency stash," she said. "I'm never without it."

I didn't say anything while I watched her deftly roll a joint and seal it with a quick taste of her tongue. She reached for a match.

206

"Better let me do it," I said. "Let's not start any fires." I struck the match and sucked in a long toke, then gave it to her while I buried the match in the ground. She hit it twice, then leaned back on her elbow with a contented sigh. I did it again, gave her another turn, then pinched it out and put it into my shirt pocket.

"Did you ever see so many stars?" she asked.

I looked up at the sky. "No." I sensed rather than felt a movement in her sleeping blanket and turned toward her.

Her face had that peculiar look of concentration I recognized. Suddenly her breath rushed out through her tight lips. "Oh, Jesus!" she sighed. She became aware that I was watching her. "I couldn't help it. I suddenly got very horny."

She reached for me, her hands pulling my face down to her. I could feel her lips moving under mine. "Daniel!" she whispered.

Angrily I pushed her away. "I'm not the one who's strange, you are," I said. "You're trying to fuck a ghost."

Suddenly she was crying. "I'm sorry, Jonathan."

Then I was angry with myself. "Don't be sorry." I pulled her head over to my shoulder. "It's not your fault."

She turned her face up to me. "You've been talking to him, haven't you, Jonathan?" she whispered."

"It's not real," I said. "It's all taking place inside my head."

"You're talking to him," she said. "I feel it. I know about those things."

"I don't."

She laughed. Her lips brushed against mine. Soft and light. "Jonathan Huggins."

"That's my name."

"Someday you'll learn."

"Learn what?"

"That you're just like your father."

"No. I'm me."

Her eyes looked up into mine. "Jonathan Huggins." She raised her mouth to mine. "I want you to make love to me. Please."

"And who will you be making love to? Me, or my father?"

"You, Jonathan." Her eyes were still looking into mine. "There's no way you can fuck a ghost."

I stood in the glass telephone booth on the edge of the parking lot and waited for my call to travel home. The sign over the supermarket at the far end of the parking lot was simple. Big red letters on a white circle. FITCH'S. And on the line underneath the name, SINCE 1868.

The telephone clicked in my ear as my mother's voice came on the line. I started to speak, but the operator cut me off the line. I could hear her voice. "I have a collect call for Mrs. Huggins from her son, Jonathan." I couldn't hear my mother's reply, but the operator came back on. "You can speak now."

"Hello, Mother," I said.

I heard the tightness in her voice. "Jonathan! Where are you?"

"In West Virginia, a little town called Fitchville. Ever hear of it?"

"No." Her voice was still tight. "I was going out of my mind. It's been four days since you left."

"I'm okay."

"You could have called. Anne's parents were wild. She didn't leave a note. We figured she went with you."

"You figured right."

"Her mother wants her to call."

"I'll tell her."

"I hope you two aren't doing anything foolish," she said.

I laughed. "Nothing to worry about, Mother. She's on the pill."

"That's not what I'm talking about." Her voice grew annoyed.

"Tell them she's not doping either. I made her throw the grass away." I changed the subject. "I haven't caught the news. What happened with Dan?"

"They made him president. It all worked out just like your father said it would."

"I'm glad," I said. "Give him my congratulations when you see him."

She was silent.

"Mother."

The phone was still silent.

"Mother, what's wrong?"

Her voice broke. "The house is empty. So silent. Nobody comes here anymore."

"The King is dead," I said.

She was crying now. "Jonathan, please come home. I feel so alone."

"Even if I were there, Mother, I couldn't help that."

"There were always people here. Something was always going on. Now Mamie and I just stare at each other all day. Or watch television."

"Where's Jack?" I asked.

She hesitated before she answered. She still had to get used to the fact that I knew about them. "He won't be able to come up until next weekend. Dan wants him to stay in Washington with him."

"Why don't you go down there? There's still the apartment."

"Its not ours anymore. It's the Confederation president's apartment."

"I'm sure Dan wouldn't mind."

"It wouldn't look right. People would talk."

"Marry him, then, if that's what you're worried about."

"I don't want to." She paused for a moment. "I was married to your father. I'm not ready yet to settle for less of a man."

"I believe you, Mother. But you have to start putting your life together again. He's dead. You don't have to wear black the rest of your life."

Her voice was suddenly hushed. "Jonathan, are you my son? Or your father's? You're saying exactly what he would say."

"I'm your son. And his. Think about it, Mother. We all have to grow up sometime. We never had to while he was around. He made all the decisions for us. Now we have to find our own way."

"Is that what you're doing, Jonathan?"

"I'm trying, Mother. And I will. If he lets me."

"He never let go easy," she said.

"I know."

"So do I." There was a brief pause. "Where are you staying? Is there any way I can reach you?"

"No, Mother. I'm moving around. I don't know exactly where I'll be."

"Will you call me again? Soon."

"About the middle of next week," I said.

"Do you need any money?"

"I'm okay. But if I run short, I know where to call."

"Take care of yourself, Jonathan," she said. "I love you."

"I love you too, Mother," I said, and hung up the telephone. I heard my dime tinkle down into the return tray. I fished it out and left the phone booth.

Anne was waiting for me outside the market door. She opened a paper bag. "These seeds okay?"

I looked at the labels. Violets, pansies, roses. "Looks okay to me. I don't know anything about flowers."

"Neither do I. But I thought they'd look nice around the cemetery plot. The man said they grow practically by themselves."

"That's good enough for me."

"Jeb Stuart said he would wait for us just past the Exxon station at the edge of town."

"Okay," I said. "Your mother wants you to call her."

She looked at me. "You tell your mother I was okay?"

I nodded.

"That's good enough," she said.

"Let's go, then," I said.

"Wait a minute. I got two big bags of groceries on the cart just inside the door. I had a feeling you weren't all that crazy about black-eyed peas and collard greens."

I laughed. "You did it all just for me?"

She smiled. "Betty May's baby won't be hurting for a change either."

"There's twelve graves here," Jeb Stuart said.

I stared down at the freshly turned earth. It was black and moist. "No," I said. "Only eleven."

"How do you know?" he asked. "There's no stones—no markers."

"I know," I said. "There's a place for my father. But he's somewhere else." I pulled the hoe along the ground and cut a rectangle near the corner of the plot. "This was to be his place."

Jeb Stuart looked up at the sky. "It's gittin' late. We can finish tomorra."

"Yes," I said.

He leaned his rake against a tree. "I'll let Betty May know we're comin' down."

I nodded and turned to Anne, who was sitting with her back against a tree. "Do you have a cigarette?"

She nodded, lit one and gave it to me. We didn't speak until Jeb Stuart left us. "I'm afraid." she said.

"Of what?"

"Death."

I didn't answer. Just dragged on the cigarette.

"Death is here," she said. "On this place. Whoever lives here will die."

"Everybody dies," I said.

"You know what I'm talking about," she said. She got to her feet and came toward me. "Jonathan, let's leave. Now. Tonight."

"No," I said. "Tomorrow. When I'm finished with this."

"Promise?"

"I promise."

"Okay," she said. "I'm going down to see if Betty May needs some help."

"Just don't let her burn the steaks," I said.

"I won't." She laughed and started down the path.

I turned back to the plot and with the corner of the hoe, carved my father's name into the earth over his empty grave.

"Thank you, my son."

"What were their names, Father?"

"Their names no longer matter. They were your aunts and uncles, my brothers and sisters. But they're gone now and no longer exist."

"But you do?"

"Yes. You see, I have you. They have no one."

"It doesn't make sense."

"It doesn't have to. Nothing is supposed to. Like your girl."

"What about her?"

"She's pregnant." I heard his silent laughter. "Last night she opened up for you. She took your seed into her and kept it."

"Shit."

"It will only be for a short while. Then she will reject it. It is not time yet. For either of you."

"You know a lot for a dead man."

"Only the dead know the truth."

I heard music coming from the shack when I came down from the knoll. Jeb Stuart was sitting on the running board of the pickup. "I didn't know you had a radio," I said.

He looked up at me. "I thought you knowed. Anne bought it. Betty May is pleased to death with it."

"I'll need some help with the planting of the seeds. I don't know anything about it."

"Betty May will help. She loves flowers and has a right good sense of 'em."

"I'll be grateful," I said.

He looked past me at the cornfield. "Five, six weeks. 'N'en we begin the harvestin'."

"Need help?"

He shook his head. "We kin manage."

"When is Betty May expecting?"

"Two more months, we reckon. 'Bout the time we begin to draw the bead off'n the 'shine."

"Are you going to sell it then?"

"No. It's too raw. I'll barrel it over the winter. It'll be good then. I'll git top dollar. Raw whiskey ain't wu'th nothin'."

The door to the shack opened. Anne came out. "Supper's ready."

Jeb Stuart got to his feet. "We're acomin'."

The steaks were not too bad, but Anne was disappointed. Betty May and Jeb didn't seem to care too much for them. They looked aghast at blood pouring from our steaks and put their own back on the fire, leaving them to cook until they were burned almost into pure coal. Then they seemed to be satisfied. We were having our coffee when we first heard the roaring rhythmic sound coming near.

Betty May paused, her coffee cup in hand. "What's that?"

I didn't look up. "A chopper." I knew the sound well. My father had had one which he used for quick trips. Then I saw the puzzled expression on Jeb's face. "A helicopter," I explained.

The roaring sound came closer. "She's pretty low over us," I said.

"Mebbe I better take a look-see." Jeb got to his feet, picked up his shotgun from where it leaned against the wall and opened the door.

We followed him out. The helicopter was coming in low over the cornfield, heading for a small clearing not far from the shack. We could see the black painted letters on its side as it hovered for a moment, then settled to the ground. POLICE.

The side port opened and two men dressed in khaki uniforms, wearing troopers' hats, got out. The pilot sat in the cabin behind the controls. He too wore a uniform, but no hat. The late sun glinted from the silver stars pinned to their shirts as they turned toward us.

Jeb was the first to speak. "Howdy, Sher'f."

A note of surprise came into the bigger man's voice. "That you, Jeb Stuart?"

"None other."

The sheriff smiled and came toward Jeb, hand outstretched. The other policeman stayed near the chopper. "Right glad to see you, Jeb."

Jeb nodded as he shook hands with the sheriff. "We was jes' finishin' supper. Yer in time to jine us fer coffee."

"Thank you. I sure would appreciate that." He turned to the policeman behind him. "Ever'thing's okay. I'll be back in a bit."

He followed us into the cabin. This time Betty May did not join us at the table. Quickly she put a mug of steaming coffee in front of the sheriff.

The sheriff took a sip. "Fine coffee, Betty May."

She smiled without answering.

"I'm suah glad to fin' you up here," the sheriff said. "We

213

got reports that they was squatters up heah fo' more'n a year now, but until we got us the new helicopter las' week we didn' have time to check it out. We was all set to roust some nigguhs off'n the place."

Jeb nodded without speaking.

"We all kind of wondered where you disappeared to," the sheriff said. "It's more'n a year an' a half since anyone in town saw you."

"I been wu'kin' the place," Jeb said.

"I kin see that. You got about three acres o' corn out there." He shot a shrewd glance at Jeb. "O' course, you got a proper leasehold on the place."

Jeb hesitated, glancing at me. I nodded. "Yes," he answered.

"From the lawful owners?"

I spoke for the first time. "That's right."

The sheriff looked questioningly at Jeb. "This yere's Jonathan Huggins," Jeb said. "Big Dan's son. Jonathan, Sher'f Clay, Fitch County."

We shook hands. "Sheriff Clay."

The sheriff nodded. "Yer daddy was one of us. We all had great respec' fer 'im. My condolences."

"Thank you, Sheriff," I said.

"You're the legal owner?" he asked.

"Yes. You should know." Then, suddenly, I knew. There was no way he could know. "The papers are in the county office."

He looked uncomfortable. "Of course."

"In Sentryville," I said. "This property is in Sentry County."

The sheriff nodded.

"That's sixty miles from here," I said. "You're just helping out the sheriff up there since we're close by. That right?"

"That's right," the sheriff said quickly.

I leaned from my chair, picked up Jeb's shotgun from against the wall, laid it across the table, the muzzle against the sheriff's belly, and released the safety. "You're trespassing, Sheriff," I said. "I could squeeze this trigger and blow you in half and there isn't a court in the land that wouldn't uphold

214

my right to do it. You have no authority and no business here."

He stared down at the gun, his face suddenly white. The others seemed frozen in their chairs. Jeb began to rise.

"Don't move, Jeb!" I snapped. I looked at the sheriff. "Now, suppose you tell us why you came up here."

He gulped. "Jeb's wife has a warrant out fer him an' Betty May fer unlawful fornication."

"Not good enough to make you jump county lines," I said. "Try again."

He was silent.

"Couldn't be three acres of corn," I said. "A green patch in the middle of wasted land that you saw from over the highway. Could it?"

He was still silent.

"And maybe there would be black people you could roust. Three acres of corn could be worth a lot of money. You're the sheriff. You know the people who could handle it."

A grudging respect came into the sheriff's face. "You're right," he admitted. " 'Tain't none o' my business what goes on up here."

I took the gun from the table and put it back against the wall. "That's where you're wrong," I said. "You and Jeb have important business to talk about." I rose to my feet. "Anne and I will go outside and leave you gentlemen to talk it."

The sheriff looked up at me. "F'om what I heered about yer daddy, you got to be the spit an' image of him."

"I'm nothing like him at all," I said, and went outside.

Anne followed me, and I leaned against the pickup and lit a cigarette, passed it to her and lit one for myself. "We'll be leaving tomorrow," I said. "After we get the flower seeds planted."

"Where are we going?" she asked.

I closed my eyes and stared through time. "Farther south."

She was silent for a long moment. "Will you be coming back here again?"

"Yes. On my way back home."

"I'm going home tomorrow," she said.

Time dropped out. I opened my eyes and saw the helicopter. The pilot had gotten out and was talking to the deputy, and they were staring at us. I turned to look at her.

"I'd like to come back here with you someday. May I?" There were tears in her eyes.

"You know you can," I said.

Her hand reached for mine and held it tightly. "The sheriff. He was right. You are your father."

"That's not what the sheriff said."

"It's what I said."

I did not tell her that it was what my father had said also.

"I've seen so much of him just since we came here. That's why I want to go home. I don't want to see any more. I'm frightened. I think it would blow my mind."

I raised her hand to my lips and kissed it.

"You're not angry with me?" she asked.

"No." I looked at her. "It's okay."

The door behind us opened, and Jeb and the sheriff came out. They walked around the pickup to where we were standing. Jeb was smiling. "The sher'f 'n' me come to 'n agreement."

"Good," I said.

"There'll be no trouble now," he said.

I turned to the sheriff. He spoke quickly. "No way could Jeb do it alone. The nigguhs and the Eyties already had him pegged. They was jes' waitin' fer him to do the work afore they moved in."

I nodded.

"Goin' to stay around, son?" the sheriff asked.

"I'm leaving tomorrow."

He squinted up at the sky. The sun was beginning to fall into the west. "Better be gittin' back. Still don' trust them things in the night." He turned to Jeb. "Y'll kin come on into town on Satiddy. I'll have that warrant quashed fer you."

"Thank you, Sher'f."

The sheriff looked at me again. "How old are you, son?"

"Seventeen."

He nodded. "That's what I kep' thinkin' all the time you had that shotgun in my belly. Seventeen. That an' the expression on yer face. That's the way yer daddy must of looked

216

when he blew Old Man Fitch in half in the back of the general store close on to fifty yeahs ago. He was seventeen then. They sent him up to reform school until he was eighteen. But he didn' stay. They was a war, an' he enlisted in the army an' went to Europe. He never come back to Fitchville until twenty years atter the war. Then, one day, he showed up at the railroad station in a wheelchair. He was all broke up. Couldn't walk. There was a woman with him. 'Twarn't 'is wife. They heered somewhere out West he had a baby son. The woman bought a car from the Dodge dealer fer cash an' they drove up yere into the hills. After that, nobody saw 'im, on'y the woman when she come into town to do the shoppin'. Then 'bout six months atter that, he shows up at the railroad station, kisses the woman goodbye, gits on the New York train an' that was the las' time anyone in town ever seen him theah."

"And the woman?" I asked.

"She waited till the train pulled out of the station; then she drove off an' nobody ever seen her again either."

"Did you ever see my father?" I asked.

"No. But I heered the story f'om my father. He was the sher'f's depitty in '17 an' the sher'f in '37. An' I must of heered the story myse'f a thousand times, 'cause ever' time yer father's name came up, my father used to tell the story." He looked at me. "He used to be very proud o' yer father. One of our boys becomin' one o' the most important men in the country." He squinted up at the sky again, stuck out his hand. "If you wanna read about it, the library in town has all the back issues of the *Fitchville Journal* back to the War Between the States." We shook hands. "If you need anythin', jes' call me."

"Thank you, Sheriff," I said.

We watched the helicopter lift off and race into the setting sun. When its noise stopped bouncing around in the hills, we went back into the shack.

I picked up my sleeping bag and Anne's. "It's been a long day," I said. "I think we'll let you two get to bed early."

The sky was still gold when we sat down in the cornfield. "I didn't know they weren't married," Anne said.

"Neither did I."

Silently she rolled a joint, lit it, then handed it to me. I took a couple of tokes and leaned back on one elbow. I could feel its tranquillity moving through me. I gave the joint back to her.

"Jonathan," she said, the smoke curling from her nostrils.

"Yes?"

"Come home with me."

I looked at her. "I can't. Not just yet."

"Why?"

"You keep asking me that and I keep giving you the same answer. I don't know why."

She passed me the joint. I took a few more tokes, then lay back and watch the dark cover the sky like a blanket. She finished the joint and pinched it out carefully, burying it in the ground. She moved over and put her head on my shoulder. "I'll miss you."

I didn't answer.

"You know where to find me. I'll be sitting on the back porch, looking over at your house."

"I know," I said.

"Don't be too long," she said. "I'd like to be young with you just a little while longer. We all grow up too fast."

I stood in front of the shack and watched the pickup make its way down the dirt road. I saw Anne's face in the rear window, looking back at me. She held up her hand in a gesture of farewell. I held up mine. Then they were gone, and I picked up my backpack and slipped it over my shoulders. It was almost eleven o'clock, and the sun was already hot. The twelve-thirty bus would put her in New York at five; if she could catch the five-fifty out of Grand Central, she could be home by seven.

I started up the hill. The path to the highway led me past the cemetery knoll. I paused there for a moment, looking down at the freshly turned earth, the neat rows of seeds planted around the graves.

"Don' you worry, Jonathan," Betty May promised. "I'll see to it they git water ever' day. There'll be flowers there almost afore you kin turn aroun'."

I looked down at the shack and wondered if I ever really would come back. Maybe I would be somewhere else.

"Don't wonder, my son. You will come back."

"Are you sure, Father? You never came back."

"I did once, Jonathan. The sheriff told you about that."

"But you didn't stay."

"Neither will you."

"Then what is the purpose? I might as well not come back."

"You'll have to. For the same reason that I came back. To make yourself whole again."

"I don't understand, Father."

"You will, Jonathan. When the time comes. You will come back for your child."

"My child, Father?"

"Yes, my son. The child you never made."

Book Two

Another
Day

Chapter 1

It was two o'clock in the morning, and the last spring snow had melted in the warmth of the day, then turned the highway into a sheet of glazed ice with the night wind. Clouds scudded across the face of the moon, obscuring even the edges of the road, and there was no light to keep him from slipping and sliding on the precarious footing. Silently he swore to himself, clutching his thin jacket against him as he walked along.

Ten miles west of St. Louis. Highway 66. Walk far enough and he would wind up in California. He grinned bitterly to himself. That is, if he didn't freeze to death along the way. He peered through the dark in front of him. He had been walking almost an hour. There should be a truck stop up there somewhere. At least, that was what they had told him when they had thrown him out of the car. Two miles west along the road. A truck stop.

He paused suddenly. What if they had been lying to him and there was nothing? He was beginning to freeze through. Five hours like this and there would be nothing to worry about. He would be dead, stiff as cardboard in the ditch at the side of the road. Then everybody would be happy. John L. at U.M.W., Big Bill at the Carpenters, Murray and Green at

A.F.L. headquarters. Even Hillman and Dubinsky, who hated each other, would be just as happy if he did not exist.

"You go out to K.C.," they had said. "If anyone could get the meat packers together, you're the man to do it."

Like going to Siberia. Of the last four organizers they'd sent out there, according to his count, he was the only one still alive. And for how long was a matter of conjecture. No truck stop, four out of four. They could just as well have hung him on a meat hook in a freezer locker the way they had poor Sam Masters.

Three days in a car with the Eyeties. Three of them with accents as big as the guns and knives they packed. Three days eating garlic-sausage sandwiches until the stink could have run the car better than the gas they put in it. Three days shitting at the side of the road with your ass freezing in the wind, wondering whether they were going to come up behind you and put a bullet through your head or up your ass. Three days of waiting outside phone booths while they telephoned back for instructions. Then, last night, when they got back into the car, he had known the waiting was over. They suddenly stopped talking. Even to each other. The car began to go west along 66. At midnight they slipped through St. Louis. Twenty minutes later they stopped the car on an empty stretch of highway.

The door opened, a heavy shoe kicked him in the side and he went flying out onto the icy road. He landed on his back, flat on the ground, his hands outstretched. He saw the man lean out the door over him, the pistol looming like a cannon in his hand. Reflexively he curled himself into a ball, trying to become as small a target as possible. He heard the roar of the gun as the automatic emptied. He could almost feel the bullets tearing through him. Then the gun was silent. Nothing. He couldn't believe it. He turned, staring up at the gunman.

The Italian was grinning broadly. "You shit in your pants. I can smell it."

"Yeah," he said.

"You lucky," the gunman said. "Don't come back to Kansas City or the next-a time you won't smell your own shit. You'll be dead."

The car door slammed, the motor roared and the car made

a U-turn and sped back on the road toward Kansas City. Suddenly it stopped, reversed abruptly and backed up toward him. By now, he was standing up.

The driver stopped opposite him. He reached out, pointing his hand in the opposite direction from the one in which the car was going. "You go that-a way. Two miles. There's a truck stop." Then the car took off again and its rear lights vanished down the highway.

He moved off the side of the road and cleaned himself as best as he could with snow he melted in his hand, dried himself on pieces of cold, brittle newspaper the wind had blown there, then began to walk. Two hours. Then he saw the lights. It took him another half-hour of running and walking to get there.

The white and red bulbs shone like the sign over the gateway to heaven. TRUCK STOP. GAS. EATS. BUNKS. BATHS. Six big trucks were parked on the far side of the station, their tarpaulins tied down in gray-shrouded silence against the elements. Carefully he walked around behind the trucks before he entered the building. There were no cars parked. No point in taking any chances in case the Eyeties changed their minds and doubled back on him. Then again, it might have been a setup. Someone could be waiting there for him.

Quietly he went to a side window and peered in. The restaurant was empty except for one waitress, busy setting up the tables for breakfast, and a counterman, leaning his heavy belly against the cash register while reading the newspaper. After a last glance around to reassure himself, he went to the front door and opened it.

He did not go inside. Stood in the open doorway. The wind blew into the restaurant, and they looked up at him.

"Shut the fuckin' door," the counterman said. "It's freezin'."

"Come in," called the waitress.

"I need a bath first," he said. In spite of himself, his teeth began to chatter.

The waitress looked at him. "You need something hot inside you more. I'll get a cup of coffee."

"Where's the bath?" he asked. "Bring the coffee there." He

looked at the counterman. "Got an extra pair of pants to sell me?"

The counterman stared at him. "You all right?"

"Some Wops beat the shit out of me and dumped me up the road a piece," he said. "And I'm toting a couple of lumps of ice around with me."

The counterman was silent for a moment. "I got a pair of work pants that might do you. It'll cost you two dollars, though. They're almost new."

The man struck his hand in his jacket pocket and came up with a bill. He held it out toward the waitress. "There's five dollars. Bring the coffee and the pants over to the bath. And a razor too, if you can spare it."

The waitress took the bill from his hand. "The bath is over in the building on your left, next to the bunkhouse."

"Thank you, ma'am," he said politely.

The door closed behind him, and they saw him walk past the windows around the side of the building. The waitress took the five-dollar bill over to the register and gave it to the counterman.

"Those pants ain't wu'th more'n a dollar an' you know it," she said reproachfully."

"Mebbe to you an' mebbe to me. But to him, it's wu'th two dollars." The counterman rang up twenty-five cents on the register, took out the change, pocketed two dollars and gave her the rest. "I took out fer the bath and razor."

"Okay."

"The pants are hangin' in the locker behind the door."

"I know where they are," she said, walking around him into the kitchen.

He slapped her full buttocks as she passed. "If'n yer smart," he laughed, "you kin make it so he gits no change at all."

She shot him a baleful look. "He's not you, stupid." she said sarcastically. "He kin have it for free."

He was soaking in the hot tub when she came into the bathhouse, his head leaning against the back, his eyes closed. The first think she noticed was the black-and-blue bruises on his body. Then she remarked the puffed, swollen eye, cheek-bone and jaw.

"They really worked you over," she said in a hushed voice.

He opened his eyes. "I'm lucky they didn't kill me," he said matter-of-factly. He gestured to the floor near the tub. His pants lay there crumpled up. His jacket and shirt were hung neatly across the back of a chair in front of the heater, drying out. "Throw the pants into the garbage. I already washed the shirt."

"Okay," she said, bending to pick them up."

"Better get some newspaper first," he said. "I wasn't kidding."

She went into the other room and came back with paper. Carefully she picked up the pants without touching them and wrapped the paper around them. She put the razor and his change on the chair where his jacket was hanging. "I'll git rid of this. Then I'll come back and he'p you."

"Thank you, ma'am, but I think I can manage."

"Don't be a fool," she said sharply. "I been brought up with five brothers an' I been married twice an' I know when a man needs help an' when he don't."

He turned to look at her. Despite the swollen eye and cheek, she felt the strength in his face. "And you think I need help?"

"I know," she said.

He nodded. "Then I thank you kindly, ma'am, and I'm grateful to accept your offer."

When she came back, she pulled a chair over to the tub and with a small towel soaked in water and soaped began to wash him gently. There were bruises all over his body, and despite himself he winced whenever she touched him. She changed the water in the tub twice, finally washing his face and his hair, then carefully shaving him. Blood had begun to flow from a cut over his heavy eyebrow. "That's a bad 'un," she said. "We better git the doctor in the mornin' to come an' stitch it up. Otherwise there'll be a big scar." She tore a strip from a clean cloth and pressed it to the cut. "You hol' that while I git some adhesive to keep it together."

She was back in a moment with a wide roll of Johnson &

227

Johnson. Expertly she tore it down the middle and made a neat cross patch over his eye. "Okay, you kin git up now an' dry yourse'f."

Wincing, he got to his feet, taking the towel she held out to him and wrapping it around himself. She held out a hand to steady him as he stepped out of the tub.

"You okay?" she asked.

He nodded.

"Mebbe you ought to lie down fer a while. I kin bring you something to eat."

"I'll be all right," he said, drying himself. "Is there a telephone in the restaurant?"

She nodded.

"I have to make a phone call first." He ran his finger over his cheek, looked in a mirror, then turned to her. "You know," he said, almost shyly, "that's the first time a lady ever gave me a shave."

"Is it all right?"

He smiled at her, and suddenly he seemed almost young. "Real good. A guy can get spoiled by something like that."

She laughed. "I'll go back an' git yer breakfast ready. Wheat cakes, sausages and eggs all right?"

"Right perfect," he said. "Just give me ten minutes to get there."

Chapter 2

THE COUNTERMAN'S pants were two sizes too big for him, and his belt held it around his waist in gathers. After he had demolished his second stack of wheats, eggs and sausages and was working on his second pot of coffee, he leaned back in his chair with a contented sigh. "That was good," he said.

The waitress smiled at him. "Fer a bit there I thought you were goin' to eat your way into them pants."

He smiled ruefully. "I didn't know how hungry I was. You got any cigars?"

"Sure do. Tampa Specials. Real Havana. A nickel each."

He grinned. "Just what the country needs. A good nickel cigar. I'll take two."

She went behind the counter and came back with the box. He picked out two cigars, stuck one in his mouth. She struck a match and held it for him while he puffed deeply. He peered up at her from under his bushy eyebrows through a cloud of smoke. "Thank you. Now where's the telephone?"

She pointed to the pay phone against the far wall. He took another sip of his coffee, then went to the telephone. She cleared the table and went behind the counter, where the counterman was leaning against the register. She placed the dishes in the wash rack. Another half-hour and the pearl diver would come in. He could clean them.

She came back to the counterman. "I'm whupped," she said. "I cain't wait to git home."

"I don' know what fer," he replied. "You didn' do nothin'. There was no business tonight."

"Those are the worst nights of all. At least if you're busy the time doesn't drag."

"Another half-hour, that's all." They heard the coin tinkle down into the telephone box and looked up.

His voice was low, but it carried. "Long distance, please. Station collect to Washington, D.C. The number is Capitol 2437."

The coin jingled back into the return chute. He fished it out and stood there, puffing at his cigar, waiting. After a moment, he spoke again. "Just keep on ringing, Operator. There's someone there. They'll answer."

He puffed patiently on the cigar. The operator came on again. A sudden authority came into his voice. "You just keep ringing, young lady. The phone is downstairs in the hall and they're upstairs sleeping. Ring long enough and they'll hear it.

A moment later someone answered. His voice lowered. "Moses, it's Daniel B. . . . No, I ain't dead. They don't make phone calls from Hell. . . . Yeah, they went back to work in K.C. I know that. Tell John L. and Phil that we went in there like a bunch of amateurs. The packers had everything set up. The cops and the Wops. We didn't have a chance. I spent the last three days riding around in a car with a bunch of garlic eaters. I knew the minute they dumped me the strike was over. I wouldn't be alive now if it was still on. They dumped me outside St. Louis on 66. I'm calling from a truck stop. The office owes me a new suit."

He was silent, puffing on the cigar, while the voice on the other end of the line spoke. His voice was slightly hoarse when he began to speak again. "I'm okay. Just banged up a little; I've had worse. . . . No, I'm not coming back for a while. I've been four years without a vacation or a rest. It's

230

time I took one. I want to do some thinking on my own. I'm tired of doing everybody else's bidding."

Again the voice on the other end of the line spoke while he listened. This time his voice was definite. "No more. . . . I don't give a damn what they got lined up for me. Probably another suicide job. . . . California, I guess. I'm halfway there now. Maybe I can pick a few oranges off the trees an' eat them fresh and sweet from the sun. . . . Yeah, I'll keep in touch. . . . No, I got money. . . . I ain't hangin' around here for John L. to call me back. For all I know the garlic eaters might have changed their minds. I'm moving on while the gettin' is still good. . . . Yeah. I know. Things'll get better—but I don't know what good that will do us. John L. is pushing for Landon, and Roosevelt won't take him too kindly for that. . . . You can bet your ass that F.D.R. is gonna win a second term. . . . Okay. I'll call you when I get to California."

He put down the telephone and went back to his table. He held up his hand, and the waitress brought him another cup of coffee. "Is there any hotel around here where I can rent a room?" he asked.

"The nearest is back in St. Louis," she said.

He shook his head. "Wrong direction. I'm going west, not east." He took a sip of his coffee. "Think I can get a hitch on one of those trucks out there going west?"

"You kin ask," she said. "They'll be gittin' up soon."

"I will, thank you."

She started back to the counter. Halfway, she turned and came back to him. "You mean what you said? Goin' to California?"

He nodded.

"I never been there either," she said. "I hear it's real pretty out there. The sun shines all the time an' it's never cold."

He looked up at her without speaking.

"I got a car," she said. "It's not much. An ol' Jewett. But it runs. We can split the drivin' an' the expenses."

He puffed on the cigar for a moment. "But what about your job?"

"I kin git a job like this anywhere. They don' pay me no salary, jes' tips."

"Family?"

"None. My las' husband took off in a cloud of smoke the minute he found out he didn' like payin' bills. I divorced him las' year."

"What about those brothers you told me about?"

"Nobody left. They're all scattered. Ain't much work aroun' here."

He nodded thoughtfully. "Got any money?"

" 'Bout two hundred cash. Got a man wants to buy my house. Give me four hundred cash if'n I th'ow in the furnishin's."

He was silent again. His eyes peered at her. "How old are you?"

"Twenty-six."

"You ain't gonna be no movie star," he said.

She smiled. "I don' expec' to be one. I jes' want to fin' a place where I kin live decent."

He leaned back in his chair. "How soon can you leave?"

"Today," she said. "I kin pack my things, see the man, git my money an' we kin be on the road this afternoon."

He smiled suddenly, his whole face lightening. He held out his hand. "Okay. California, here we come."

She laughed. Then the touch of his hand ran up through her arm, and suddenly she found herself blushing. "California, here we come."

Still holding her hand, he looked up at her. "I don't even know your name."

"Tess Rollins."

"Pleased to meet you, Tess. My name's Daniel. Daniel B. Huggins."

The doctor straightened up and snipped off the end of the suture. "As fine a job of sewing as my missus ever laid down on her Singer. Take a look."

Daniel peered into the mirror the doctor held for him. What had been a wide gash was now a pencil-thin line with tiny black dots over and under where the sutures surfaced. The only thing that seemed different was that the eyebrow below seemed slightly raised. He touched it. "Will the eyebrow stay like that?"

"It'll come down a bit when the stitches come out. After about a year it will be like the other."

Daniel got out of the chair.

"Wait a minute," the doctor said. "I want to put a bandage over it." He worked quickly. "Important to keep it clean. Change the bandage every day. Come back in six days and we'll take the stitches out."

"I won't be here," Daniel said.

The doctor finished the bandage and fastened it neatly into place with thin strips of Johnson & Johnson. "You can get it done at any hospital or clinic. Just make sure you keep it clean until then."

Daniel reached into his pocket. "How much do I owe you, Doc?"

"Two dollars too much?" the doctor asked hesitantly.

"Two dollars is fine," Daniel said. He took out a roll of bills from his pocket and counted out the two bills. "Thank you, Doc." He saw the doctor looking at the bills. "Anything wrong, Doc?"

The doctor smiled, shaking his head. "No. I was just thinking that you were the first cash patient I've had in two months."

Daniel laughed. "Well, don't go gittin' nigger-rich with it."

The doctor laughed. "Don't worry. Might just frame it to remind myself what money really looks like."

He followed Daniel into the waiting room, where Tess was seated. She got to her feet. "Was it bad, Doc?"

The doctor smiled. "I've seen lot worse. Just make sure he keeps it clean."

She nodded. "I'll do that."

Daniel went out to her car. It was a Jewett touring car with the winter celluloid shields fastened. He got into the car. She walked around to the driver's side.

"Now where?" he asked when she got behind the wheel.

"Down to the bank so I kin sign the papers an' transfer the mortgage. Then we go out to the house an' give the new owner the keys."

He stuck a cigar in his mouth. "Sure you want to do it?" he asked. "You can still change your mind. After the papers is signed you got no druthers."

"My mind's made up," she said.

At the bank, the lawyer advised her to leave the money in the bank and send for it when she reached California. She looked at Daniel.

"It's a good idea," he said. "No telling what might happen on the road when you have all that money with you."

"How much cash do you think I might need?"

"Maybe a hundred. Probably less. But that should do us. Besides, if we have any problems, I have money with me. We can straighten up after."

"Okay," she said to the lawyer.

They started after lunch and drove all afternoon and into the late evening. When they pulled off the road to find a room for the night, they were three hundred and thirty miles from St. Louis.

They stopped in front of an old house that had a sign, ROOMS FOR RENT, lighted by a single electric bulb. They got out of the car, knocked on the door and went inside.

An old man, smoking a pipe, looked up at them. "Howdy, folks. What kin I do fer you?"

"A room for the night," Daniel said.

"Including breakfast?"

Daniel nodded.

"Got a right nice one fer you. Big double bed. One dollar fifty with breakfast," he said, adding, "in advance."

"Okay," Daniel said, reaching into his pocket. "Any place around here we can get supper?"

"If yer not lookin' fer anythin' fancy, my missus kin fix somethin' fer you. That'll be an extra fifty cents each."

Daniel counted out the money. The old man got to his feet. "Need any help with yer bags?"

"I can manage," Daniel said.

The old man took a key from a bureau drawer and gave it to him. "It's the first room at the top o' the stairs," he said. "Meanwhile I'll go tell the missus to fix yer supper. It'll be ready by the time you wash up an' come down."

Dinner was simple. Pan-fried chicken and potatoes. Canned

green beans and corn. Hot bread and coffee. "Breakfast is at seven sharp," the old man said as they went up the stairs.

They went into the room. Daniel looked around the room, then took off his jacket and hung it over the back of a chair. "Next town we come to," he said. "I got to buy me some shirts, socks, underwear, a suit and another pair of shoes."

"Okay," she said.

He began to unbutton his shirt, then stopped and looked at her. "You undressing?"

She nodded. "Thought I'd wait until you went to the bathroom. I'll go after you. It takes me more time. You know, take off my makeup an' things."

"Okay," he said. He walked out of the room, the tops of his B.V.D.'s sticking up white over his pants, and down the hall to the open bathroom. He was back in less than ten minutes.

She had undressed and wore a white bathrobe. "Why don't you stretch out a bit an' rest? I'll try not to be too long."

He nodded and took off his pants and stretched out on the bed in his underwear. He looked up at the ceiling. Life had a way of dealing the cards from the bottom of the deck. A week ago in Kansas City, he had had a fine suite in the best hotel in town. All he'd had to do was pick up the phone and he had anything he wanted. The finest whiskey, the best cunt. And breakfast was served whenever he wanted it.

Twenty minutes later, she came back into the room. "I didn't mean to take so long," she said. He didn't answer. Then she noticed he was fast asleep. "Daniel," she said.

He didn't move.

Silently she took off her robe and placed it on the foot of the bed. She looked down at herself. Damn! she swore silently. She had put on her sexiest nightgown.

She pressed the wall switch and the room went dark. She walked around the bed to the other side and slid between the sheets. Tentatively, she reached across the bed and touched him.

He still didn't move.

She drew back her hand and peered at him through the dark. His face was relaxed. He looked much younger when he was sleeping. Much more vulnerable.

Suddenly she smiled to herself. With all the guys at the

stop trying to get into her pants, the first guy she went for since her husband left her fell asleep on their first night together.

Impulsively, she leaned across the bed and kissed his cheek. "I hope it takes us a long time to git to California," she whispered. Then she drew back to her side of the bed and closed her eyes. Before she knew it, she was asleep.

Chapter 3

THEY ARRIVED in Tulsa about one o'clock the next afternoon in the midst of a driving rain-and-sleet storm. The wipers could no longer clear the windshield because of the ice forming on the glass, and the weather shields did very little to keep the cold from blasting through the car. He reached up again and tried to clear the windshield by the manual knob. It didn't help, the wiper blades just skimming over the ice.

"We'd better pull in here," he said. "No use going any farther till the storm clears."

She nodded, her teeth chattering despite the heavy sweater she wore beneath her cloth coat.

"Keep your eyes open," he said. "Look for a hotel that seems reasonable."

They moved slowly down what seemed to be a main thoroughfare and into a commercial section of the city. The streets were almost empty, the storm keeping most pedestrians away. The stores, their windows lighted at midday, seemed strangely forlorn.

"There's a sign over there," she said. "Brown's Tourist Hotel. Just up ahead."

A sign in front of the hotel indicated the parking lot adjacent. He pulled the car into it and as near to the side entrance of the hotel as possible. He cut the engine. "Doesn't look bad," he said.

"Let's git inside," she said. "I'm freezin'."

They dashed from the car into the doorway. The lobby was small and plain but looked clean and neat. The clerk stood behind the desk as they approached. The sign over the key rack on the wall behind him was very simple: NO NIGGERS OR INDIANS ALLOWED. "Yes, sir?" the clerk said.

"Got a double?" Daniel asked.

The clerk looked down at his room chart. "Do you have a reservation, sir?"

Daniel just looked at him.

The clerk was suddenly flustered. "Yes, sir. Would you like a deluxe double with bath in the room for one dollar or a regular double with bath in the hall for six bits?"

"We'll take the deluxe," Daniel said.

"Thank you, sir," the clerk said, pushing the register toward him. "Please sign the register." He punched the bell for the bellman. "That'll be one dollar, payable in advance."

Daniel glanced at Tess, then signed the register, *Mr. and Mrs. D. B. Huggins, Washington, D.C.*, as the bellman came up. The clerk gave the bellman the key. "Room 405, sir," he said politely, glancing down at the register. "I'm sure you'll like it, Mr. Huggins. It's a nice corner room. The boy will help you with your luggage."

Daniel turned to the bellman. "Show us up to the room first; then you can get our bag from the car. It's the Jewett just outside the door."

They followed the bellman to the elevator and then to the room. The room clerk was not wrong. Tess made for the bathroom as soon as they entered. Daniel turned to the bellman. "After you get the bag, what's chances to get a big pot of coffee and a bottle of whiskey?"

The bellman's face was impassive. "This is a dry county, sir."

Daniel pulled a dollar bill from his pocket. He held it up. "Still dry?"

The bellman nodded. "Yes, sir."

Daniel added another dollar. "Still dry now?"

The bellman grinned, taking the two dollars. "We'll see what we can do. I'll be right back. Thank you, sir."

The door closed behind him as Tess came out of the bathroom. "Jesus," she said. "Fer a minute there I thought the dam was about to bust."

He laughed. "I know just what you mean. I'm right behind you."

The bellman was back in less than ten minutes with everything. The valise, the pot of coffee, a pint bottle of whiskey, glasses, ice water and cups and saucers. "Anything else, sir?"

"Good restaurant around here?" Daniel asked.

"Right next door. You get a complete three-course luncheon for thirty-five cents until two thirty."

Daniel tossed him a quarter. He picked up the bottle of whiskey and broke the seal, then pulled the cork from the bottle with his teeth. He looked at Tess. "It'll warm the gizzards."

"Jest a taste," she said. "I git tipsy real quick."

He poured a little into her glass, then a good shot for himself. "Down the hatch." He swallowed the whiskey in one gulp, then another shot while she finished her first. He put down his glass and poured the coffee. They sipped slowly.

"Feel better now?" he asked.

She nodded.

He glanced around the room. "Not bad."

"It's real nice," she said. She looked at him. "You know, I never stayed in a real fancy hotel like this before."

He laughed and got to his feet. "Come on. Let's go down and get some food. Then I've got some shopping to do."

He stood in front of the long mirror and looked at himself. The suit looked well on him, dark gray with a thin pin stripe. He turned to Tess. "What do you think?"

Before she could answer, the clerk spoke eagerly. "The latest New York style, sir. Notice the reverse pleats on the trousers. Genuine real wool with silk lining. Only fourteen ninety-five with one pair of pants, seventeen fifty with two."

"Mighty handsome," Tess said.

"I'll take it," Daniel said. "With two pairs of pants. How long will it take to put on the cuffs?"

"Ten minutes, sir?"

"Good. While I'm waiting, I want three shirts, Arrows, two white, one blue, three pairs of black socks, three pairs B.V.D.'s and a pair of black shoes and a dark tie with a gray or red slant stripe."

A broad smile split the clerk's face. "Yes, sir. And we'd be pleased if you'd accept the tie as our gift. We like to take care of our good customers."

Fifteen minutes later, Daniel was knotting the tie in front of the mirror. The clerk held the jacket while he slipped into it.

"If I may make a suggestion, sir?" the clerk said tentatively.

"Yes?"

"Just one thing missing. A hat. We're direct agents for Adam Hats of New York and have a special on the new snap-brim style. One ninety-five."

When Daniel left the store, the hat sat squarely on his head. They walked carefully under the overhang of the buildings. He didn't want to get too much rain on it the first time he wore it. Tess hung proudly on one arm. He was a real good-looking man.

A few doors down was a sporting-goods store. Daniel stopped abruptly and looked into the window. It was filled with rifles and shotguns. "Let's go in here," he said.

She followed him into the store. He went to the man behind the counter in the rear of the store. "Howdy," the man said. "What can I do for you?"

"I'm interested in a handgun. Nothing too big."

"Twenty-two caliber, .38, .45?"

"I'd prefer a .38, but it depends on the size."

The man nodded. He took a ring of keys from his pocket and unlocked a drawer beneath the counter. He placed a long-barreled Colt Police Positive on the counter. "What do you think of that?"

Daniel shook his head. "Too big."

The man exchanged it for a Smith & Wesson Military and

Police Model. He looked at Dan. Again Dan shook his head. "How about a Colt Government Automatic?"

"Don't like them," Daniel said. "Used them in the army. They don't shoot where you point 'em. Kick's too hard, anyway."

"Only got one other, then, in .38. If that don't do you, you'll have to go to a .22."

"Let me see it."

This time the man came up with a small leather case. Respectfully he opened it. The gun was silver-blue shining metal, and the grips mother-of-pearl. "Smith and Wesson Snub-nose .38 Terrier," he said reverently. "Comes complete with real leather shoulder holster. It's expensive, though."

Daniel looked at it. "How much?"

"Thirty-nine fifty."

"That is expensive," Daniel said. He picked it up and hefted it. "Doesn't feel like much."

"It's a fooler. It can do anything the big one can do. An' better."

Daniel broke the gun and spun the cylinder with his thumb. Then he snapped it closed and held it up. "Give me a price."

The man hesitated a moment. "Thirty-five."

"You can do better."

"Thirty-two fifty. That's the bottom."

"Got a test range?"

"Down in the cellar." He pressed a button under the counter. A young man in grease-stained work clothes came out of the back room. He gave the gun to the young man, together with a handful of cartridges. "Take the gentleman downstairs. He wants to try the gun."

They followed the young man down a flight of steps at the back of the store. At the bottom of the landing he switched on a light. There was a brightly lit shooting range at the far end, a white paper mounted circle target on a stand resting against sandbags. The young man gave the gun and six cartridges to Daniel.

Quickly Daniel loaded the gun. He spun the cylinder, tested the trigger for tension, then cocked the hammer. Satisfied that it was smooth, he held the gun with both hands outstretched, aiming at the target.

"Hold the nose down," the young man says. "It spins up about one foot in every twenty. The range is thirty feet."

"That's not so good," Daniel said.

"Snub nose," the workman said. "Got to give up something to get the size. It's okay, though. You get used to it real quick."

Daniel squinted down the barrel and squeezed off one shot. The gun kicked slightly. He checked the target. He had missed it completely.

"Hold it down," the workman said. "Aim with the hammer, not the muzzle."

Again Daniel squeezed off one shot. This time he hit the outer rim of the target. He nodded and fired off the remaining shots in rapid succession. Three were dead center, one just slightly off. He gave the gun back to the workman. "Okay," he said.

He turned to Tess. She was staring at him, her face pale. He reached out and took her arm. She was trembling. "You all right?" he asked.

She took a deep breath. "Yeah."

He held her arm while they went back upstairs. "I'll take it if you throw in a box of cartridges," he told the man behind the counter.

"Can't do that," the man said. "But I'll throw in the cleaning rag and rod and a bottle of oil."

"Deal," Daniel said. "And I'll take a box of cartridges."

"Okay." The man pulled out a form. "Regulations," he said apologetically. "Got to fill out this form with your name, address and identification."

"No problem." Daniel took out his wallet and placed his driver's license on the counter. "That do?"

The man nodded. "Give me one minute to fill it out; then I'll clean the gun out for you."

While he waited for the man to finish the form, Daniel took off his jacket and put on the shoulder holster and cinched the cross strap tight. By the time he had it comfortable, the man had the form filled out and the gun clean.

"That'll be thirty-seven fifty with a box of fifty cartridges."

Daniel counted out the money and took the gun from the man's hand. Quickly he loaded it and slipped it into the holster, then put on his jacket. He patted the jacket. It fell smoothly across the gun as if there were nothing there at all.

They went back into the street. He looked at his wristwatch. "It's early yet. Want to take in a movie before we go back to the hotel?"

She shook her head. "No," she said in a strained voice. "Let's go back to the hotel right away."

There was surprise in his voice. "You sure you're all right?"

A hint of annoyance came into her voice. "I'm jes' fine, stupid. But jest how long do you think you kin keep a lady waitin'?"

Chapter 4

SHE AWOKE slowly, first becoming aware of a delicious hurting between her legs, a heavy feeling of being full and swollen. It was good. She opened her eyes.

He was standing, naked, his back to her, peering out through the curtains in front of the window. In one hand he held a cigar, in the other a glass of whiskey. He was big, his shoulders and body square to his hips, resting on thick, strong legs. He was strong. She knew that. She could still feel the strength of him. She knew she was not small and weighed about one hundred and fifty pounds, but he had held her and moved her as if she were a paper doll. But paper dolls never could feel the way he made her feel.

"What time is it?" she asked. "I fell asleep."

"Nigh on to six o'clock," he said. He turned to look at her. "The rain just stopped."

"Good." She sat up in the bed, pulling the sheet over her full naked breasts. A sudden warm wetness came out of her and ran down the inner softness of her thighs. Surprise echoed faintly in her voice. "You're still coming out o' me."

He didn't speak.

"Better git me a towel from the bathroom," she said.

"What for?"

"It don't look nice to have your come all over the sheets."

"Hotels expect that," he said. "Even married folks fuck more when they go to a hotel than when they're at home."

"You sound like you know. You ever been married?"

He shook his head. "Never."

"How come?"

"Never been in one place long enough to feel settled down, I reckon."

"Didn't you never want to git married?"

"I thought about it. Maybe, someday."

"I was married twice."

"I know," he said. "You told me."

She felt her nipples harden and a flush came up into her cheeks as she remembered what they had done. "And in none of them times did I ever do the things I did with you."

"What *did* you do?"

"You know. Just fuck. Stick it in. Sometimes from the front, sometimes from the back—that's all. I never frenched a man before."

He laughed. "It wasn't so bad, was it?"

She laughed with him. "No." She looked up into his eyes. "Was I all right?" she asked shyly.

"You were just fine," he said. "If you hadn't told me, I would have thought you'd been doing it all your life."

"I have," she said suddenly. "Inside my head. But I was always afraid to do it to my husbands because they might think I was a whore."

"Too bad you didn't," he said. "You might have still been married."

"I'm glad I didn't," she said quickly. "Neither of them was a lovin' man like you are. They was jes' fuckers."

He took a sip of whiskey from his glass. "Want a drink?"

"No, thanks." She picked up her robe from the floor where it had fallen and put it on as she slipped out of bed. She started past him for the bathroom. "I'm goin' to take a bath."

He put his hand on his arm and stopped her. "Don't take a bath."

"Why?"

245

"I like the smell of your cunt all over you."

"Oh, Jesus!" She saw the appetite in his eyes. "You're makin' me all wet ag'in."

He laughed and reached for her hand. "Look what you're doing to me."

Her hand closed around his growing hardness. A weakness came into her legs, and she didn't need his hands on her shoulders pushing her down to her knees on the carpet before him. He guided himself into her open mouth. He kept one hand on the back of her head. "Cup my balls and squeeze them," he said.

She felt them turn into heavy rocks in her hands, then suddenly contract. His semen spattered into her mouth and down her throat. She felt herself choking, almost gagging as she tried to swallow the flooding from him. Then, when she thought she couldn't take any more, it was over.

Still gasping for breath, the corners of her mouth and chin covered with him, she looked up. "I never knew a man like you."

He looked down at her without answering. He reached for the whiskey and tossed the rest of the drink down his throat, then reached down to raise her to her feet.

"No." She shook her head. "Hit me first. Slap my face."

"Why?"

"Because I want you to make me feel like a whore. Because if'n I don't feel like a whore with you, I'm goin' to fall in love with you."

His open hand caught her on the cheek and she sprawled on the floor on her side, one heavy breast falling from her open robe, crushed against the floor by her heaving chest. Slowly her fingers reached up to touch her cheek. The white imprint of his hand was still there and slowly turning red and flushed. She stared up at him almost angrily. "Every time," she said.

He didn't speak.

"Every time you fuck me, you do that," she said. "So I don't fergit where I'm at."

For a moment he didn't move. Then he reached down and helped her to her feet. "Get dressed," he said almost gently.

"We better have dinner if we want to get an early start in the morning."

He had just finished putting on the shoulder holster when she came from the bathroom. She stood there watching him while he checked the cylinder and put the gun into the holster. He looked up into the mirror over the dresser in front of which he was standing and saw her. He nodded approvingly. "That's a right pretty dress you have on."

"Thank you." She felt pleased that he had noticed. It was her very favorite. Beige and black. Made her look slimmer, her breasts and hips not as large. He finished knotting his tie. "You don't look too bad yerself."

He touched the bandage on his forehead. "Except for this."

"On'y a few more days. Then we'll find a clinic and it'll be gone." She crossed the room for her coat while he put on his jacket. "Daniel."

He turned. "Yes?"

"Maybe I oughtn't to ask, but what are you runnin' away from?" She tried to keep the nervousness she felt from her voice.

"I'm not running away from anything."

"But you bought a gun."

He turned away from her without answering. He buttoned his jacket and reached for his hat. She came close to him.

"You don't have to tell me if'n you don't want. But if yer in trouble, mebbe I kin help."

He reached for her hand and pressed it gently. "I'm not in trouble. Not with the law, not with anybody. And I'm not running away. I just wanted time for myself to go off and think."

"An' a gun helps you think better?"

"No." He laughed. "But I'm in a rough business. Just a few days ago some men in a car took me as I came out of my office. For three days they drove me around while they decided what to do with me. They could have killed me at any time and there would have been nothing I could do about it. Finally, they threw me out of the car and emptied a pistol into the ground around me. I thought they'd killed me, and I was so scared I shit in my pants. That's something that never happened to me, even during the war—and I was in Sergeant York's squad in France and saw lots of death there. I made up my mind right then and there that nobody would ever again take me without a fight."

"I don't understand. What kind of a business are you in anyway that people would want to do a thing like that to you? Only gangsters have things like that happen to them."

"I'm a union organizer," he said.

"I don't know what that is," she said.

"I'm on assignment from the U.M.W. to the C.I.O to help in the organization of new unions in different industries."

"Are you one o' them Communists I been readin' about in the papers, then?"

He laughed again and shook his head. "Nothing like that. Most of the men I work for are Republicans, though I myself lean toward the Democrats."

"I never heard of nothin' like that before," she said.

"Come," he said, taking her arm and steering her toward the door. "I'll try to explain it to you over dinner."

Chapter 5

By the time they reached Los Angeles, Tess was certain of only one thing. She was in love with him. She had never known a man like him before. Half the time she did not know what he was talking about; most of the time she never knew what he was thinking. He came from a world she had never known existed. Organized labor, politics were foreign to her. All she knew was that you got a job, went to work and got paid for it. Sometimes more, sometimes less, but whatever it was, you managed on what you got and were grateful for it.

It was late afternoon and pouring rain when they drove onto Hollywood Boulevard. The theater and store lights were already on, throwing a dancing glare onto the wet pavement.

"Did you ever see so many lights?" she asked in an awed voice as they drove past Grauman's Chinese Theatre.

He grunted. "New York has more."

She looked at him. "You don't sound happy."

"I'm tired," he said shortly. "We better find us a place to stay the night."

"That's a nice hotel over there." She gestured at the Hollywood Roosevelt.

249

"Looks too expensive," he said. "We'd do better off the main streets."

They found a small hotel off La Brea on Fountain. The charge was a dollar a night with bath included. It was a new kind of hotel. Motel, they called it. You parked your car right in front of your room.

The first thing she noticed when they entered the room was a small kitchenette complete with stove, sink, refrigerator and dishes. "How would you like me to make us a couple of steaks tonight?"

He opened his valise and took out a bottle of whiskey. He pulled the cork with his teeth, then took a long swig. He put down the bottle without speaking.

"You must be as tired of eating in restaurants as I am," she said quickly. "Besides, I'm a really good cook an' I'd like to make dinner for you."

He took another pull at the bottle, still without speaking.

"I saw a market on the next block," she said. "I kin run over there and git the fixin's. You git into a hot bath an' rest yourself from all the drivin'."

"Sure you want to?" he asked.

She nodded.

He reached into his pocket and gave her a ten-dollar bill together with the car keys. "Get me another bottle of whiskey an' some cigars while you're at it."

She gave him back the bill. "This is my treat. You paid fer enough already."

Quickly she went out the door. He stood there for a moment listening to the sound of the motor starting up, then the car pulling away. He took another drink, then wearily began to undress. He threw his clothes over a chair and naked went into the bathroom and turned on the water in the tub. He went back into the other room and took a cigar from his pocket and lit it. He rubbed his cheek reflectively. He needed another shave. He took his razor and shaving soap from his suitcase. He saw her valise near the window. He went over to it, picked it up and put it on a luggage rack, then stared out the window. The rain was really coming down; it made the afternoon seem like night. He watched it for a moment, then went

250

back, picked up the bottle of whiskey and went into the bath-room.

The tub was almost full. He pulled a chair close to the tub, put an ashtray and the bottle of whiskey on it and got into the tub. The water was hot and it seeped into his bones. He took another drink, then put the cigar in his mouth and leaned his head back against the rim of the tub, staring up at the ceiling.

California. He had to be crazy. What was he doing here, anyway? There was nothing for him to do out here. All the action was back East. He had read in yesterday's paper that Lewis and Murray were setting up a Steelworkers Organizing Committee. That was where he should be. If he were there, he would be right in the middle of it.

He reached for the bottle of whiskey and took a long pull, then put the bottle back on the chair and leaned back with a sigh. He had to be crazy, all right. For even thinking about being back East. He'd probably draw the shit end of the stick as usual and wind up getting his ass kicked off in the field. He had had twenty years of that, and that was enough. From the very first time he had met Phil Murray and Bill Foster back in 1919.

He'd just been discharged from the army and gotten a job as a guard at the big U.S. Steel plant in Pittsburgh. They'd fixed him up with an army-type uniform, a gun and a billy club swung from the belt around his waist. He was one of a squad of twenty men under the command of a former army sergeant who was tough as nails and ran his squad on strict army discipline.

The first two months were easy. He had nothing to do but stand at the gate eight hours a day and watch the workers come in and go out as the shifts changed. They were mostly Hunkies and Polacks from Central Europe and spoke little or no English. They seemed all right—minding their own busi-ness, never making any trouble, even if they didn't seem to smile very much. Then, subtly, the atmosphere seemed to change.

Now they never smiled at all, and when they looked at him

there was an expression of sullen resentment on their faces. Even in the bar he used to go to after his shift was over, they would fall silent when he came in for his drink and quietly move away from him until he was alone in a small open space.

One day the owner of the bar called him to one side. He was a small Italian who spoke with an accent that could be cut with a knife. "You a good-a boy, Danny," he said. "I know that. But do-a me a favor. Don't come-a in the bar no more."

"Hey, Tony," he said, astonished. "Why not?"

"There's a big-a trouble comin'. And the men, they're gettin' nervous. They think you come-a to spy on them."

"Shit," he said. "How can I spy on them when I don't even understand what they're sayin'?"

"Do-a me a favor, Danny. Don't come-a no more." The little man walked away from him.

That night the sergeant called a meeting of his squad. "You fellers have been leadin' the easy life up to now. But pretty soon you're goin' to have to earn your keep.

"Any day now, the Reds an' I.W.W.'s are goin' to call the Hunkies out on strike. They're goin' to try to close down the mills. An' it's our job to see that they don't do it."

"How we goin' to do that, Sergeant?" one of the guards called out. "We don't know nothin' about workin' the foundry."

"Don't be stupid," the sergeant said sarcastically. "They walk out, there'll be other men to take their place. The strikers'll try to keep 'em out. It's up to us to see that them that wants to work gets in."

"That means we'll be helpin' the strikebreakers," Daniel said.

The sergeant fixed him with a baleful glare. "It means you'll be doin' your job. What do you think you're gettin' paid fifteen dollars a week, room and board for? Those Hunkies work twelve hours a day in the foundry fer less'n ten dollars a week. Now they think they're entitled to as much money as you're makin' an' more. An' most of 'em can't even speak, read or write English."

Daniel met his glare. "How are we expected to get the strikebreakers through the picket lines when we're inside the gates?"

"You'll have help. Lots of it. There are over two hundred men deputized by the sheriff who'll be outside the gates keeping an open passage."

"An' what if that's not enough?"

The sergeant smiled. "Then we go out an' help 'em." He pulled his billy club from his belt and held it up. "It's amazin' how persuadin' this little friend of ours can be."

Daniel was silent.

The sergeant continued to stare at him. "Any further questions?"

Daniel shook his head. "No, sir. But . . ."

"But what?"

"I don't like it. I seen what happens in a strike. Back home we had trouble. In the mills, in the mines. Lots o' people got hurt. Even some who had nothin' to do with it."

"Nobody gets hurt if they mind their own business."

Daniel thought of his sister. Of Jimmy. He took a deep breath. "I don' like it. I was hired as a guard to protect the mills. Not to beat up on people. Not to be a strikebreaker."

The sergeant exploded. "If'n you don't like it, git your ass out of here!"

Daniel stood there silently for a moment, then nodded slowly. He turned and started, still silent, from the room. The sergeant's voice turned him around.

"Leave your gun and club here."

Silently Daniel unbuckled his belt, placing the gun and club on a table. Then he turned and started again from the door. The sergeant's voice followed him.

"I expect you out of the barracks in fifteen minutes. If I find you there when we get back, you're goin' to git the livin' shit kicked outta you."

Daniel opened the door and stepped out. Before the door closed, he heard the sergeant's voice speaking to the others.

"I never trusted the bastard. We got word that he's a secret Red. Now, if there are any more of you Commie yellowbellies in here, speak up now an' git out while you can."

Daniel walked down the hall to the barracks-type room he shared with five other men. Quickly he stripped off his uniform, folded it neatly and placed it on his bunk. From his locker he took his old army pants and blouse and put them on.

Quickly he gathered up his few other belongings, put them in a duffel bag, slung them over his shoulder and walked out.

He went down the hall and out of the building. Silently he walked to the front gate. The guards on duty let him out without a word. They had already got the word.

He set the duffel bag squarely on his shoulder, crossed the street and turned the corner. They came out of a doorway behind him. He heard the footsteps and began to turn, but it was too late. A club caught him across the side of his head, and he stumbled forward to his knees.

Desperately trying to get to his feet, he heard the sergeant's voice. "Git the son of a bitch good."

He lashed out in the direction of the voice, but his fist reached nothing but air. His body turned into a sheet of pain under the rain of blows coming from clubs and fists. He went back to his knees, curling into a ball to protect himself as much as possible. Heavy boots began to kick him in the sides, and he rolled off into the gutter. He tried to move, but it was impossible. Everything was hurting inside him. There was no strength left, not even to fight back.

Finally the blows stopped. He lay there half conscious, his head swirling. From a long distance, he heard the sergeant's voice again.

"That'll teach the Commie bastard not to try any of his shit again."

A voice came from one of the other men. There was a note of fear in it. "I think he's dead, Sergeant."

He felt the sergeant's foot in his side, rolling him over onto his back. He squinted his eyes, trying to see up. He could feel the sergeant's breath on his face, but he couldn't focus on him.

"He ain't dead," the sergeant said. "But if he comes anywhere near us again, he'll wish he was."

There was a sudden sharp, stinging blow on the side of his head as the sergeant kicked. Then everything went black. It was quiet for a long time.

Slowly he began to come to. Bit by bit his body began to send him signals of pain. After a few moments he tried to move. An involuntary groan escaped him. He tried to force himself to clear his head. He made it to his knees, then, by holding on to a lamppost, managed to pull himself to his feet.

In the light he looked down at himself. His shirt was torn and covered with blood, his pants ripped down one leg. Slowly he moved his head. His things were scattered all over the street, the duffel bag opened and emptied.

He took a deep breath, then began to move slowly, every step and motion sending exquisite pain shooting through him. In spite of it, he set about gathering up his things and stuffing them back into the duffel bag. Then he paused to catch his breath.

He looked up at the sky. The moon was high. It had to be about midnight. It had been eight o'clock when he walked out of the gates. The windows in the houses were all dark. He moved slowly back to the corner and stared at the gates.

The guards were still there in their small cabin. Through the open window he could see them talking. They had known the sergeant was waiting out there for him when he came through, but they had said nothing. For a moment he thought of going back and taking them. But then the thought was gone. He was in no condition to take anything. He would be lucky if he made it to someplace where he could get himself taken care of. He tried to pick up the duffel bag and sling it over his shoulder. But it was too much for him. He had to be content with dragging it along behind him.

He made his way through the dark streets to Tony's Bar. The lights in the windows were out and the door was locked, but through it he could see the little Italian cleaning up behind the bar. He knocked on the door.

Without looking up, Tony waved his hand indicating that he was closed for the night. Daniel knocked at the door again, more heavily this time.

Tony looked up. He could not see who was standing there. He came out from behind the bar and peered through the glass window in the door. "We-a closed," he began to say. Then his voice stopped in shock. Quickly he took the chain from the door and opened it. "Danny! Wha' happen?"

Daniel stumbled through the door. Tony put out a hand to help him. Daniel dragged his duffel bag behind him and slumped into a chair. He leaned forward and put his head on his arms on the table.

Quickly Tony went behind the bar and came back with a

bottle of whiskey and a glass. He filled the glass. "Drink," he said. "You'll feel-a betta."

Daniel had to hold the glass with both hands. The whiskey burned its way down his throat. He felt its heat running through him. Tony refilled the glass, and Daniel drank again. He could feel some strength coming back into him.

"I warned you," Tony said, "those Hunkies was gonna get you."

"It wasn't them," Daniel mumbled. "It was the sergeant. I quit tonight when I found out they 'spected me to act as a strikebreaker. They was waitin' fer me roun' the corner from the mill."

Tony was silent.

"Got a place fer me to clean up?"

"You need a doctor," Tony said.

"I don't need no doctor," Daniel said. "I got to clean up. Then I got things to do." He reached for the bottle of whiskey. "This is all the medicine I need."

"Come with me." Tony led him to the washroom in the back. This was the private washroom, not the one used by the customers of the bar. He turned on the light. "I'll get some clean towels."

While he was gone, Daniel stared at himself in the mirror. His nose looked crooked on his face, squashed flat; his cheekbones were split and cut and also his temples. His eyes were beginning to develop shiners, and his jaw was already swollen, and his face was covered with a mask of streaked blood. "Jesus!" Daniel said half aloud.

Tony had come back into the room. He nodded. "They really work-a you over."

Daniel turned on the water in the sink. "They'll pay fer it," he said quietly. Then he stripped off his shirt and began to wash. When he straightened up, he saw that his ribs and sides were black-and-blue.

Quickly he soaped the whole upper half of his body and wiped it off with a damp towel. Then he held his head under the cold tap until the fuzziness was gone. He began to dry himself. "There should be another shirt and pair of pants in the bag," he said.

256

"I'll get it." Tony went back into the bar.

Daniel got out of his pants. "Get me a clean union suit too," he called through the open door. There were additional bruises on his sides and thighs, but fortunately he had managed to escape being kicked in the groin. It had to be the way he had fallen; he wasn't conscious of having done anything to protect himself.

He wiped the rest of himself down with the damp towel, then dried himself. By the time Tony came back with the clothing, he was drinking the whiskey right from the bottle.

"You bag is a mess," Tony said.

Daniel nodded. "The stuff was all over the street. I jes' picked it up and stuffed it in."

"What should I do with these?" Tony asked, gesturing to the pile of torn clothes.

"Throw 'em out," Daniel answered. There was nothing else to do with them. They were beyond repairing. He dressed quickly.

Tony looked at him. "You better see a doctor. You-a nose is broke and some o' your cuts might need stitches."

Daniel turned and looked in the mirror. "It's not that bad. There's nothin' he kin do about the nose, an' the cuts will heal theirselves. I had worse when I was a kid."

He took another swig of the whiskey and carried the bottle back into the bar. Silently he began to repack his duffel bag. When he was finished, he looked at Tony. "Where's the union headquarters?"

"State and Main," Tony said. "Why?"

"I'm goin' over there."

"You-a crazy. It's-a one o'clock in the morning. They be closed. Nobody there."

"Then I'll be there when somebody comes in in the mornin'."

"Why don't you stay out of it?" Tony asked. "You a nice boy. You don't have to get mixed up in things like-a that."

Daniel looked at him. "I already am." He paused for a moment, thinking. Jimmy, his sister, his family, the mines. "Mebbe I always was and didn' know it."

Chapter 6

IT WAS two o'clock in the morning when Daniel reached the corner of State and Main. The sign was still over the storefront. Amalgamated Association of Iron, Steel and Tin Workers. But the store itself looked dark and deserted, and when he pressed his face against the window he could see nothing in the store, not even a chair or a desk. Just a pile of paper littering the floor. He went past the window to the door. On it was a small typewritten notice. Moved to 303 Magee Bldg.

He took a deep breath. The Magee Building was two miles across the city. He looked up and down the street. All the windows were dark. There was no place around here that he could find a room or bed even if he wanted to. He opened his duffel bag and took out the bottle of whiskey that Tony had given him. He took a deep drink, then put it back in the bag, slung the bag over his shoulder and began to walk again.

It was close to three o'clock when he got there. The building was dark, and the entrance doors were locked. He stepped out into the street and looked up at the building. There were some lights on in the third-floor windows. He went back to the building entrance and found a bell to summon the night porter. He kept pressing it until a sleepy Negro came to the door about ten minutes later.

"Cain't you see the buildin' is closed?" the Negro demanded.

"I got business in the union office," Daniel said.

Reluctantly the Negro opened the door. "You guys must be sho'-nuff crazy. Comin' an' goin' all hours o' the day an' night. It's gettin' so a body cain't get no rest no more."

Daniel looked at him without speaking.

"The staihs to your lef'," the Negro said quickly. "Thu'd flo'. Three-oh-three."

Daniel went up the steps. He had been right. The lights he had seen from the street were in the union office. He put his hand on the door and turned the knob. The door swung open. There was no one in the reception hall. He went through another door into a corridor. A sound of voices carried up the hall toward him. He walked toward it. The sound came from behind a closed door at the end of the corridor.

He paused, placing his duffel bag on the floor, and knocked once, then opened the door. There were four men seated around a desk in a cigar-smoke-filled room. They stared up at him in surprise.

One of them leaped to his feet and advanced threateningly toward Daniel, his fists balled and ready to strike.

Daniel stared at him. "Don' do that," he said quietly. "They done that once to me tonight, an' I'll kill the next man to try it."

The man stopped. "What the hell do you want? What do you mean breaking in here?"

"The door was open," Daniel said. He looked past the man to the others still seated behind the desk. "I came to see the boss o' this yere union. I got important information fer 'im."

This time it was the man who sat in the center seat behind the desk that spoke. His voice was soft. "I'm Bill Foster, executive secretary of the union."

"Are you the boss?"

Foster glanced at the men next to him. He nodded with a

faint smile. "I guess that is what you might call me. What is it you want to see me about?"

Daniel walked in front of the desk. "My name is Dan'l B. Huggins. Until tonight I was special guard on duty at Plant 5, U.S. Steel."

One of the other men started to interrupt Daniel. Foster silenced him with a gesture. "Yes?" he said softly.

"Tonight we was tol' that they 'spected a strike an' that we was supposed to help the strikebreakers git th'u the picket lines even if it meant usin' clubs and guns to do it. We was tol' that we wouldn' be alone, that a lot of men had already been deputized by the sher'f an' would be out there to help us."

Foster's voice was soft. "We already know that. What else can you tell us?"

Daniel shook his head. "I don' know. Nothin', I guess. Sorry I bothered you." He turned and started for the door.

"Just a moment." This man's voice was one used to command. Daniel turned back. He was a thin-faced man with an almost patrician nose and mouth and dark hair and deep-set eyes. "Why did you come here?"

"I quit an' was tol' to pack up and git out. Mebbe I wouldn't o' thought o' comin' here. After all, your fight was none o' my business. But they was waitin' fer me aroun' the corner from the plant. After that I knew it was my business."

They were silent for a moment while they stared up at his battered face. Finally the thin-faced man spoke again. "It looks like they did a pretty good job on you."

" 'Twon't be nothin' compared to what's gonna happen to that sergeant when I git my han's on him," Daniel said. "Where I come f'om, we don't take to things like that 'thout gittin' our own back."

"Where do you come from?"

"Fitchville, sir."

"Fitchville." The thin-faced man's voice was thoughtful. He glanced up sharply. "What did you say your name was?"

"Huggins, sir. Dan'l B."

The man nodded suddenly. "You're the boy who worked in the mines at Grafton, who—"

"Yes, sir," Daniel said quickly. "I'm that one."

The man was silent for a moment. "Would you mind waiting outside for just a few minutes?" he asked. "I would like to talk to my friends."

Daniel went back into the hall and closed the door behind him. The low hum of conversation rose behind him. He didn't bother trying to listen to what they were saying. He pulled the bottle from the duffel bag and took another swig. One wasn't enough; he was beginning to wear out. He took another.

The door opened and the man who had first come toward him beckoned him inside. He went into the room, still holding the bottle of whiskey in his hand. They stared at the bottle, then up at him.

He looked down at them. "It's the on'y thing that's keepin' me goin'. Otherwise I'd fall on my face."

The thin-faced man spoke. "My name is Philip Murray, United Mine Workers, A.F.L. I spoke to my friend Mr. Foster about you, and if you want to help, I think he has a place for you."

"Thank you, Mr. Murray." He turned to look at Foster.

"You won't get the kind of pay you got from the mill," Foster said quickly. "We haven't that kind of money. Eight dollars a week and found is the best we can do."

"That's fine with me," Daniel said. "Jes' what am I supposed to do fer this yere money?"

"You know the guards; you know their methods, the way they work. When the strike comes, you're going to have to be on the picket lines with us, telling us what we have to do to whip 'em."

"I don' know whether I can, Mr. Foster, but I'll certainly give it a try," Daniel said. "But it seems to me that if you fellers don' git off your ass real soon, by the time you call the strike they'll have the whole United States Army against you."

Foster looked at him. His voice grew testy. "We're just as aware of that as you are. The strike call is going out tomorrow."

Daniel looked at him without speaking.

"Now you better go home and get some rest," Murray said quickly.

"I have no place to go," Daniel said. "I lived in the barracks at the plant." He felt himself beginning to weave slightly and put his hand on the desk to support himself.

Foster got to his feet quickly. He gestured to the man who had come to the door. "There's a cot in the next office. Help him in there and see to it that the doctor comes to see him first thing in the morning."

"Thank you," Daniel said. The room was beginning to spin around him. "Thank you." He felt the man's hand take his arm. He managed to make it to the cot in the next room before he passed out. The date was September 22, 1919.

A week later, more than three hundred thousand men were on strike, spread over eight states. But the key was Pittsburgh, the headquarters of the biggest company of them all, United States Steel.

The day after the strike began, Elbert Gary, president of U.S. Steel, issued a statement which was widely reprinted in the newspapers in Pittsburgh and around the country.

> The Reds, anarchists and agitators have seduced a portion of American workers to abandon their jobs in an effort to disrupt the steel industry and undermine the political stability of the United States. Fortunately for America, there are enough of us who remain steadfast to our patriotic duties and defend our country from the encroachment of these vipers. I hereby issue an appeal to all the workers who have been deluded into joining this false strike to return to their jobs and I give my word as President of U.S. Steel that no recriminations will be taken against them and no discrimination shown in their desire to work. Under no circumstances will any of the steel companies bow to the dictatorship of foreign Communist anarchists. The Strike is already

lost, it is a doomed cause. Return to work and
show your patriotism and faith in our glorious
country.

Two days later there were advertisements in all the papers
and posters on walls all over the city, each proclaiming essen-
tially the same message. Under a cartoon drawing of Uncle
Sam showing a clenched fist and bare-muscled forearm and
biceps, the message Return to work was printed not only in
English but in seven other languages so that all the workers
could read it.

Each day Daniel stood in the street in front of the steel mill
as the pickets paraded. At first it was very quiet. The guards
remained inside the gate; the police stood watching the pickets, who marched silently back and forth. Every now and
then the strikers would look up to see if smoke was still issuing
from the chimneys of the great blast furnaces. It was still
coming out—thin and gray, which signified that the fires were
still banked. When steel was being produced, the smoke
belched forth thick and black with soot which settled over the
entire area.

Almost a week had passed when one of the pickets came
over to Daniel, who was standing against the corner building,
a cigar clenched between his teeth. "I think we're going to
win," the picket said. "The furnaces haven't worked for a
week."

Daniel crossed from the corner to where he could look into
the entrance yard of the mill. There were more guards on
duty than usual. The picket followed him. "What you think,
Danny?"

"I don' know," Daniel said thoughtfully. "Somethin's
gonna happen. They been waitin' long enough to see if we'd
come back. Now they're gonna have to begin work again."

"They can't," the man said. "They can't run the furnaces
without us."

Daniel didn't answer. He didn't have anything to say. He
just felt that it was all going to come to a head. Real soon.
That evening back in union headquarters, he sat silently, listening to the bustle around him. There were reports coming

in by telephone from various strike centers in the different states. They were all the same. Quiet.

Then one telephone call changed the whole picture. Four hundred Negroes were heading for Pittsburgh from South Carolina on a train that was due to arrive at eight o'clock the next morning.

Chapter 7

AT SIX o'clock in the morning, the picket line that had kept vigil through the night in front of Plant No. 5 began to grow. The thirty-odd men gave way to their comrades who began to steadily fill the streets leading to the mill. Tired as they were from the long night, there was a tension in the air that kept them from making their way home to their beds. By eight o'clock there were four hundred men on the picket lines that moved slowly up and down the streets past the foundry gate. At nine o'clock there were more than seven hundred of them, and there was no longer room for a line: there was just a solid wall of pickets from the far side of the street to the mill gate; they moved slowly in place without room to go forward or backward.

Daniel was standing on the north corner of the street across from the mill gate. On the steps of a small building behind him were the union leaders, Bill Foster and some of his assistants. Daniel climbed up the steps beside them so that he could see over the heads of the pickets. Behind the mill gate, the sergeant had all his men lined up in military platoon fashion. There were ten squads of eight men each, dressed in the guard's uniform, each with billy club and gun.

Daniel leaned toward Foster. "They brought in forty extra men," he said. "There was no more'n forty in all when I was there."

Foster nodded grimly, his lips clenched tightly on an unlit cigar.

"The sergeant is gonna use 'em as wedges once the gates is open, to clear the way fer the strikebreakers."

"I figured that," Foster said tersely.

"If'n we move the picket line up against the gates, they ain't no way they kin open 'em," Daniel said. "The gates opens out into the street."

Foster looked at him in surprise. "You sure? Nobody told me that."

"I'm sure," Daniel said.

Foster turned and whispered to two of his assistants. "Pass the word: Move up against the gates."

A few minutes later, the small open sidewalk in front of the gates and fence was packed with pickets as well as the street. Daniel could see the sergeant staring at them. He turned to his men, and a moment later each one of them held his billy club in his hand.

A man wearing the big union button on his lapel came from around the corner and pushed his way up to Foster. His voice was guttural with a Middle European accent. "They got the scabs loaded into eight trucks. There's about forty Cossacks on horses and two hundred sheriff's deputies in front of them. The sheriff an' some man in an army uniform are in a car in front of them. They should be turning up the street any minute now."

Almost as soon as the words were out of his mouth, a roar came from down the street. "They're coming! They're coming!"

The mass of the picket line surged toward the street away from the gates. "Tell them to stay put!" Daniel shouted.

Foster stood up, waving his arms. "Stand fast, men!" he shouted. "Don't move away from the gates!"

But it was too late. The striking ironworkers, in their eager desire to see who was coming, had already left their positions and were moving up the street. The first group of mounted police turned the corner six abreast, each policeman holding his nightstick up in one hand. Both the strikers and the police stopped and stared at each other silently. Behind them was an open touring car.

The sheriff and the man in the army uniform got out of the car and walked past the mounted police to confront the strikers. The sheriff took a paper from his pocket, unfolded it and began to read in a loud voice that carried down the street to where Foster and the others were standing: "This is a court order signed by Judge Carter Glass, Commonwealth of Pennsylvania Superior Court, ordering you strikers to disperse and let these men who want to work go to their jobs."

There was a moment's silence. Then a guttural roar seemed to rise from the throats of the crowd. The words were indistinguishable, because of the many languages spoken at the same time, but the meaning was clear. There was no way they were going to let the scabs through. They began to move menacingly toward the sheriff.

For a moment, the sheriff held his ground. "This here's Brigadier General Standish of the Pennsylvania National Guard with me. He has direct orders from the Governor to call out the Pennsylvania National Guard if there is any trouble."

"They won't be no trouble if you don't make it, Sheriff," a voice roared from the back of the strikers. "Jes' you turn them trucks aroun' an' send them niggers back where they came from!"

The strikers picked it up. They began to chant. "Send the scabs back where they came from! Send the scabs back where they came from!"

"This is my last appeal to you men!" the sheriff shouted. "Disperse peacefully now an' nobody'll get hurt."

For an answer, the strikers closest to the sheriff locked arms and began to chant, while moving rhythmically in step side to side. "Solidarity forever! Solidarity forever!"

The sheriff tried to shout over them, but their voices drowned him out. He stood there staring at them.

Daniel looked at Foster. The union leader's face was pale, his lips clenched. "You better tell the men to pull back, Mr. Foster. Those police are gonna ride right over 'em."

"They wouldn't dare," Foster said tensely. "That would

show the whole world what they really are. Tools of the capitalists."

"That ain't gonna he'p the strikers they beat up on," Daniel said.

"Maybe it will make the country wake up and pay attention to what's going on under their noses," Foster replied. He turned to the strikers and shouted. "Stand fast, men! Solidarity forever!" He held up his clenched fist, arm bent in a Communist salute.

"Solidarity!" the strikers shouted.

The sheriff turned and, followed by the soldier, went back to his car. The strikers began to laugh and jeer, thinking they had forced the sheriff to retire. A moment later, their laughter turned into instant panic and fear.

Without so much as a signal, the mounted police charged their horses directly into the front of the strikers, their clubs swinging and flailing about, hitting men indiscriminately. In less than a minute there were fourteen men lying in the street, semiconscious and bleeding. Unconcerned, the police drove their horses over them into the next rank of strikers. Behind the mounted police came hundreds of uniformed deputies swinging their clubs. More strikers began to fall in the street, and the screams of pain and fear began to rise over the noise. Suddenly the strikers broke and began to run toward the sides and the other streets. Relentlessly the police followed them. Now there was a clear path to the gates.

Daniel saw the sergeant give the order, the gates begin to swing open. A moment later the guards came out at the back of the strikers who remained, they too swinging their clubs.

Daniel turned to look at Foster. The union leader seemed paralyzed, incapable of motion. "We better git our ass outta here!" Daniel said.

Foster didn't move. Daniel turned to two of Foster's assistants. "Better git him out."

The two men grabbed Foster by the arms and they went down the steps, dragging him around the corner. He moved with them unresisting, almost as if he were in a daze.

Daniel watched as the first truck began to roll through the steel-mill gates. The blacks stood about fifty in a truck like herded sheep, their faces gray with fear. The sergeant came outside the gate and began waving the rest of the trucks in. Daniel came down the steps and moved quickly through the straggling strikers and came out of the crowd just behind the sergeant.

The sergeant was waving his billy club in the air, directing the trucks. Daniel reached up and picked the club from his hand. The sergeant turned in surprise. "What the hell?"

"Howdy, Sergeant," Daniel said with a smile. Then before the sergeant had a chance to react, Daniel smashed the billy club full across the sergeant's face. The man's mouth, nose and chin dissolved into a mess of blood and broken bone. He began to fall. Daniel kicked him as he went down, and the sergeant fell backward under the wheels of the passing truck. There was a popping sound almost like a ballon bursting as the wheels went over the sergeant's chest, collapsing the ribs and crushing his spine, and when the truck had passed, Daniel knew he was looking down at a dead man. Still holding the billy club in his hand, he turned away and began to walk slowly toward the side street.

A deputy sheriff came running toward him. He saw the club in Daniel's hand and took him for one of the private police. "What happened back there?"

Daniel looked at him. "I think one o' the trucks jes' run over some prick."

"Jesus!" the deputy swore. "Did yuh ever see anythin' like it?"

"Nope," Daniel said, and continued walking away. When he turned up the side street, he threw the billy club into the gutter. He walked five blocks to the nearest saloon. Once inside, he ordered a bottle of whiskey all for himself. He took three quick drinks. Then the bartender came over to him. "Know anything about how the strike is going over at the mill?"

Daniel poured himself another drink. "What strike?" he asked. "I'm a stranger aroun' here myse'f."

Chapter 8

IT WAS later in the afternoon when Daniel got back to the union office. He had expected to find an attitude of despair after the ignominious defeat of the morning. But that wasn't the way it was.

Instead there seemed to be an attitude of excitement, almost an exultation, as Foster and his assistants jumped from one telephone to another, talking rapidly to strike centers in other cities. Daniel stood in the doorway listening to Foster talking on the telephone.

"The story is going out on the wire services all over the country," he was saying. "Tomorrow the whole world will know about us. Already offers of help are coming in, from New York, Chicago, even as far away as San Francisco. We're planning a big demonstration in front of the mill the day after tomorrow. Sidney Hillman is coming from New York, Lewis and Murray from Washington, Hutchinson of the Carpenters too. Mother Jones said she would be there, and Jim Maurer, head of the A.F.L. here in Pennsylvania, will be with her. The steel companies will soon discover that we can't be intimidated, and the country will know that all labor is behind us. Not only that: by tomorrow about forty volunteer workers are coming down from New York to help out with the campaign and see that the newspapers get a steady flow of stories about us." He paused for a moment. "Good. The five hundred dollars will be a big help. I knew I could count on you. Thanks."

He put down the telephone and looked up and saw Daniel in the doorway. "Where the hell have you been?" he asked angrily. "I've got men out all day checking the hospitals to find out what happened to you."

"I'm here now," Daniel said.

"You should have seen that we were better prepared for what happened," Foster said. "That was your job."

"I tol' you the best I could," Daniel said. "You couldn't control the men. There was no discipline down there."

"Discipline?" Foster's voice was scornful. "They're workers, not soldiers. What do you expect from them?"

"Nothin'," Daniel said succinctly, "but better leadership. It seemed to me like they was jes' bein' set up to become patsies."

Foster rose angrily. "Are you accusing me of deliberately sacrificing those men?"

Daniel's voice was even. "I'm not accusin' you of anythin'. I'm jes' tellin' you how it looked to me."

Foster stared into his eyes. "Where were you when the head of the plant guards went under the wheels of the truck?"

Daniel met his gaze. "Why do you ask?"

"Some of the men said they saw you near him just before it happened."

"Who?"

"Some of them." Foster was deliberately vague.

"They're full o' shit," Daniel said. "I was busy runnin' up the street behin' you, but it did no good. You was too fast fer me."

"The police are bound to turn up here looking for you," Foster said.

"Tell 'em to go lookin' fer the men who put our poor bastids in the hospital instead," Daniel answered. "Right now the mounted cops is ridin' up and down the streets o' Hunky Town bustin' the head of any poor bastard who's standin' out in the street talkin' to his neighbors. By the time night comes, there ain't a man down there won' be afraid to come outta his house."

"How do you know that?" Foster demanded.

"I jes' come f'om there."

"How come I didn't hear about it before now?"

"All your assistants is too busy playin' important up here in the office to go out an' fin' out what's happenin'."

"You sound like you think you can do it better than we can," Foster said balefully. "Pretty smart, aren't you?"

"Mebbe I'm not smart enough," Daniel said. "I jes' don' know how things like this is s'pose to be done."

Foster relaxed, leaning back in his chair. "Well, take my word for it. We're handling it right. This is a big strike. It covers almost eight states. It's not going to be won or lost by one incident at one lousy mill here in Pittsburgh. Believe me, when the news of this gets around, we'll come out stronger than ever."

Daniel looked at him without answering.

"I'm going to put two or three men with you. Go out on the streets and bring me back written reports of specific police harassment. Names, places, times. I want to get this out on the news wires tonight."

Daniel nodded. "Yes, sir."

Daniel never filed the report. That night he and three hundred other strikers spent the night in jail. The two men whom Foster had sent with him developed good reasons to go back to the union office at their first glimpse of the mounted police riding up on the sidewalk to roust three customers out of the chairs in a Hunky barbershop. "We're gonna need more help," they said.

Daniel watched with contempt as they darted up the street. Then he turned and walked into the barbershop. One of the policemen, in the process of hauling a Hunky worker out into the street, lather still on his face, blocked Daniel in the doorway.

"Where the hell do you think you're goin'?" he barked.

"To git a shave an' a haircut," Daniel replied. "What the hell do you think a man goes to the barber fer?"

"Wise guy," the policeman snarled.

Another policeman stopped near him. "Wait a minute,

Sam," he said. "This guy sounds like an American, not like no Hunky." He turned toward Daniel. "Look, feller, you go back to a barber uptown. This ain't no safe place fer an American to be walkin' aroun'."

"These men ain't Americans?" Daniel asked.

"They're goddamn Hunky Commies," the policemen said. "They're the ones that're causin' all that trouble over at the steel mills."

Daniel looked at the Hunky standing there with the lather beginning to drip down the sides of his face. "Is that what you are?"

The Hunky stared back at him with a blank expression.

"See?" the policeman said. "The son of a bitch don't even speak English."

"He don' look like a man makin' trouble over at the steel mills," Daniel said. "He looks like some poor jerk who jes' came in fer a shave an' a haircut."

"What the hell are you tryin' to do? Make trouble?"

"No, sir," Daniel said ingenuously. "I'm jes' tryin' to git the fac's straight. Fer the record, so to speak."

"The *Record?*" The policeman said. "You a reporter with that newspaper?"

Daniel looked at him. "You mought say that. I'm down here tryin' to find out what's goin' on."

"Well, you just mosey right back to that rag newspaper of yours an' tell 'em to mind their own fuckin' business!"

"Why, Officer, ain't you never heard o' the freedom o' the press?" Daniel asked sarcastically.

The policeman shook his nightstick under Daniel's nose. "You just haul your ass outta here real quick, or I'll give you a taste of this here freedom."

Daniel looked at him for a moment, letting his eyes deliberately wander down over the policeman's blouse and looking at his shield. "Yes, sir," he said, backing out of the doorway. "I'll go right back to the paper an' tell 'em what I saw."

"You didn't see nothin'," the policeman said.

"That's right," Daniel said, still backing out. "I didn' see nothin'. That's jes' what I'm gonna tell 'em back at the office."

He saw the look flash between the two policemen. He moved quickly, but he had forgotten about the third man in the street. A nightstick creased his skull, and when he came to, he was in the tank with about sixty Hunkies.

The Hunky he had seen in the barbershop was sitting next to him. Daniel turned his head and tried to sit up. A groan escaped him.

The Hunky turned and put an arm under his shoulders, helping him sit up, his back against the wall. "Okay?" the Hunky asked.

"Okay." He rubbed the back of his head. There was a bump back there the size of a duck's egg. "How long was I out?"

The Hunky looked blank. Then he remembered: the man did not speak English. He moved his head slowly, looking around. Most of the men seemed to be sleeping or trying to sleep. None of them were talking.

"What time is it?" he asked, making a gesture as if he were looking at a watch.

The Hunky nodded and held up two fingers. Two o'clock in the morning. The Hunky stuck his hand in his pocket and came out with a pack of cigarettes. He took one out and carefully broke it in half, offering half to Daniel. Daniel took it, and the Hunky lit both of them with one match. Daniel sucked on the cigareete, its acrid smoke helping to clear his head.

"They'll let us out in the mornin'," he said.

The Hunky didn't answer. Just nodded.

"Where's the toilet?" he asked.

That the Hunky understood. He pointed across the room, then held his nose with two fingers and shook his head.

Daniel looked across the cell. There was one toilet in the corner, and there were fifty men at least in the cell. Daniel knew what the Hunky meant and didn't even bother to get up. He could wait. He finished the clincher, then leaned his head back against the wall and dozed.

The next time he opened his eyes, daylight was streaming through the small cell window and two policemen were standing outside the cell, the door open, and shouting, "Okay, you Hunky bastards, you're getting out."

Silently they filed past the policeman and left the building

274

through a small side door leading into an alley. For a moment, the men shuffled around, looking at each other; then, without conversation, they scattered, each toward his own home.

Daniel held out his hand to the Hunky. "Thanks," he said.

The Hunky smiled, taking it. He said something in a foreign language while shaking Daniel's hand vigorously.

Daniel didn't know what the man was saying, but felt the warmth both in his hand and in the man's smile. He smiled. "Good luck."

The Hunky nodded again, then hurried off down the street, and Daniel headed for the union office. He passed a diner, and suddenly he realized he was hungry. He went inside, sat down at the counter and ordered a big breakfast.

The girl behind the counter looked at him and smiled. "I'll hold the eggs for a few minutes if you want to wash up first."

"Okay," he said. He made his way to the washroom, but it wasn't until he looked in the mirror that he understood why she had made the offer. There was blood caked across part of his cheek and in his hair and down the side and back of his neck. Rapidly he washed, drying himself on the roller towel. Breakfast was ready just as he came out.

The waitress smiled at him. "It must have been a hell of a fight."

He shook his head ruefully. "I never saw what hit me."

She put a steaming cup of coffee in front of him. "Ain't that the truth?" she said. "Nobody ever does."

Chapter 9

THE UNION offices were crowded with people Daniel had never seen before. They were spread throughout the various rooms, men and women, who spoke with refined Eastern accents and were busy writing and scribbling notes and looked as if they had never done a day's work in their lives.

Daniel saw one of the regular organizers. "Who are they?" he asked.

The organizer grinned. "The do-good brigade. They always show up when something happens that will get into the papers."

"They don' look like union people to me."

"They're not," the organizer replied. "But it's fashionable to say you're with the liberal causes. It shows that they don't let their money interfere with their sense of social justice."

Daniel caught the note of sarcasm in the organizer's voice. "Do they do any good?"

The organizer shrugged. "I don't really know. But Foster thinks it's important to have them around. After all, they don't only come themselves, they all have money and bring it with them." He reached into his pocket for a cigarette and lit it, his eyes watching one of the fashionably dressed young girls walking by with a handful of notes. "But I'm not complaining. It's sweet, clean pussy, and they all put out for the cause. That's another way they have of demonstrating their solidarity with the workers."

Daniel grinned, watching the girl. "I see what you mean. Is Foster in 'is office?"

"He should be. They're getting ready to go over to the picket line at the mill for photographs. Mother Jones and Maurer are already over there."

Daniel walked down the corridor to Foster's office and went in. Foster and Phil Murray were alone in the office. Foster looked up, an expression of annoyance on his face.

" 'Scuse me," Daniel said, starting to back out the door. "I thought you was alone."

It was Phil Murray who spoke. "Come in," he said. "We were just talking about you."

Daniel closed the door behind him and stood there.

"The police were here last night and earlier this morning looking for you," Foster said.

Daniel grinned. "They should have looked in the Fifth Street jail. They had me in the tank there all night."

"Were you alone?"

He shook his head. "They had about fifty other men in there with me. The Cossacks was pickin' 'em off the streets last night. They got me when I followed 'em into a barbershop where they took two Hunkies right out of their chairs."

"The men who went with you came back and said you disappeared. They said they didn't know where you had gone to."

"You kin believe that," Daniel said sarcastically. "They took off like geese flyin' south the moment they saw the Cossacks ridin' up on the sidewalk. They was goin' back for he'p, they told me."

"They said you left them and went off on your own."

Daniel didn't answer.

"The police want to talk to you about that guard that was killed. The papers are making a big stink about it." He pushed a few newspapers across the desk.

Daniel looked down at the headlines. The *Times* and *Herald*

Tribune from New York, the *Star* from Washington and the *Bulletin* from Philadelphia. The headlines and stories were pretty much the same in each. The lead headline: "Guard Killed by Strikers at Steel Mill." After that they went into the story, and buried somewhere near the end of the story was the additional fact that almost thirty strikers were in the hospital. There was nothing in the story that even mentioned how the police and deputies had begun the attack.

"They make it sound like that was what started the whole thing," Daniel said.

"The steel company was waiting for something like that to happen," Foster said. "They jumped right on it."

"Seems to me they was better prepared than us. In every way," Daniel said.

Foster knew what he meant. "Not anymore," he said quickly. "We have the help now to get our side of the story out first."

"It's gonna have to run pretty fas' to catch up to this one. By the time you git your stories out, this will have gone all over the country," Daniel said.

Foster was annoyed. He took out his watch and looked at it. "It's getting late. The photographers should be all set up. We better get down there for the pictures." Murray got to his feet, and Foster turned back to Daniel. "You find one of the reporters outside and tell them about the night in jail. I'll talk to you when I get back."

Daniel looked at him. "I won' be here."

Foster shot a sharp glance at him. "Where will you be?"

"I'm leavin'," Daniel said. "I don' cotton to the idea o' the police takin' me in. I got the feelin' I cain't expect much support from the boys aroun' here."

"If you run, it would be like you were admitting you were guilty."

"I'm not admittin' nothin'," Daniel said. "I jes' don' like the idea o' hangin' up on a cross between the two of you."

Foster was silent for a moment. "Okay, go down to the paymaster and draw down your salary to the end of the week."

"Thank you," Daniel said. He turned to leave the office.

Murray's voice stopped him. He held out a key in his hand. "This is the key to my room over at the Penn State Hotel. When you get your things together, you meet me in my room. I'm driving up to Washington this afternoon. You can ride up with me."

"Thanks," Daniel said. He took the key from Murray's hand. "I'll be waitin' fer you."

It was just after four o'clock in the afternoon when the big black Buick pulled out of the city onto Interstate 5 with Daniel sitting next to Murray, who was driving. It wasn't until they were a half-hour out of the city that Murray spoke.

He didn't turn his head, keeping his eyes on the road. "Did you kill that guard?"

Daniel answered without hesitation. "Yes."

"That wasn't very smart," Murray said. "If the police could hang that on you, it could hurt us very seriously. Maybe even lose the strike for us."

"The strike is lost already," Daniel said. "I knew that the minute Foster lost control of 'is men. He jes' froze, an' atter that he couldn' do nothin' right. For a while I was beginnin' to think the strike didn' mean nothin' to 'im atall. That it was somethin' else he was atter."

"What?"

"I don' know," Daniel answered. "I don' know enough about strikes an' politics to have an opinion—but sure as hell, I kin smell when somethin' ain't what it's s'pose to be."

"Do you think that battle could have been avoided?"

"No, sir, but there wasn't a need fer all them men to git the shit kicked out of 'em. If I was him, I would of come down from the platform and jawboned the sher'f into goin' slow. The sher'f didn' seem that anxious to me to start anythin'; he was lookin' as much fer an excuse to back down an' go slow —but we didn' give 'im the chance."

"Do you really think the strike is lost?"

"Yes, sir," Daniel said earnestly. "The steel mills has ever'thin' too well organized. From what I been able to fin' out, they have over eight thousan' men depitized aroun' the

279

country to put the strikers in their place. The cops is runnin'
up and down all over Hunky Town, harassin' an' arrestin', an'
they won' stop till it's over. An' I can't believe that Foster
don't know it. But there's somethin' else stickin' in his craw
that's keepin' 'im goin'."

Murray glanced at him. "What are your plans?"

"I don' rightly know," Daniel said. "Amble aroun' the
country. Fin' a job."

"How would you like a job with the U.M.W.?"

"Doin' what?"

"Going to school for the first two years. Getting yourself
some education and knowledge that will help you approach
the problems that confront labor in a more intelligent manner."

"What kin' o' school?"

"College in New York. The New School for Social Re-
search. Even wind up getting yourself a diploma. We pay for
everything."

"What's the hitch?"

"There isn't any," Murray said. "You have a job with us
when you come out. If you don't like the job, you can always
quit."

Daniel thought for a moment. "I never had much formal
schoolin'. Do you think I kin handle somethin' like that?"

"I think so. You just have one lesson to learn before you
begin."

"What's that?" Daniel asked.

"The important thing about what we do is try to benefit the
workingmen who entrust their representation to us. We can't
afford to indulge in the personal luxury of taking revenge on
people who may or may not have injured us or made themselves our enemies. The people we represent don't deserve
that."

Daniel was silent for a moment. "You mean—like what I
did?"

Murray's voice was direct. "Yes. There can be no more of
that."

"But in spite of it, yer still willin' to take a chance on me.
Why?"

Murray cast a sidewise glance at him, then looked back at the road. "Because I've got a hunch. More than that, I think you have the right instincts. Without knowing why, you've been hitting every nail on the head. I have the feeling that someday you'll be an important man in the labor movement. In some ways you remind me of John L. when I first met him. All guts and instinctive knowledge."

"He's a great man," Daniel said respectfully. "I don' think I kin ever be like him."

"Nobody knows," Murray said. "But then, you don't have to be like him. Maybe if you're just yourself you might turn greater than any of us."

"I'm not twenty yet."

"I know that," Murray said. "You'll be twenty-two when you get out of school. That's just the right age to start."

"You mean it?" Daniel asked.

"I wouldn't have made the offer if I didn't," Murray replied.

"I'll do it," Daniel said, holding out his hand. "I hope I won' be a disappointment to you."

Murray took his hand, holding on to the wheel with the other. "You won't be."

"Thank you," Daniel said.

"Don't thank me," Murray said. "Just do good." He took his hand back and placed it on the wheel. "Damn! It's beginning to rain."

That had been a long time ago. Like seventeen years ago. And now Daniel sat in a hot tub in a California motel, smoking a cigar, sipping from a bottle of whiskey on the chair next to the tub and waiting for Tess to come back from the market with two steaks. And back East, it was starting all over again. A strike at the steel mills. But this time it was different. Lewis had signed Big Steel just the year before. Now Phil Murray was going to take on Little Steel. And the only thing that bothered Daniel was the feeling that Murray was walking into the same kind of disaster that Foster had walked into seventeen years before.

281

Chapter 10

"WE'VE BEEN here almost three months," she said, putting the last of the dinner dishes away. "I think it's time we found ourselves an apartment."

Daniel put down the evening paper. "What for? I'm perfectly happy here."

"Fer the money we're payin' in this hotel we could have a real nice place of our own."

He picked up the paper and began to read again without answering.

She sat down opposite him and turned on the radio. *Fibber McGee and Molly* was just coming on the air. She listened for a few minutes, then turned the dial impatiently. Nothing seemed to interest her, and she turned it off in disgust. "Daniel," she said.

He lowered the paper and looked at her over the top.

"Aren't you going to get a job?" she asked.

"I got a job," he said.

"I mean one you go out to work at," she said. She knew that the check from back East came every week.

"I work at it," he said. "I had three meetings this week with different unions."

"That's not work," she said.

He folded the paper and put it on the table next to his chair. He was silent.

"Other men go out to work every morning and come home at night. You don't do that. Instead, *I* go out every morning and come home every night. And each day it's the same thing. I leave you sittin' in that chair readin' the mornin' paper and when I come back you're sittin' in the same chair readin' the evenin' paper. It's not normal."

He reached for the bottle of whiskey and poured himself a drink. He swallowed it and poured another.

"That's another thing," she said. "You drink a bottle of whiskey a day."

"You ever see me drunk?" he asked.

"That's not the point. That much whiskey ain't doin' your guts any good."

"I feel fine," he said.

"Someday it'll get to you," she said. "I seen that happen."

He swallowed the second drink and stared at her for a few seconds, then finally spoke. "Okay. Out with it. What's troubling you?"

She began to cry. Several times she tried to speak, but each time the sobbing became stronger, until the tears began flooding down her cheeks. He reached across and literally lifted her out of her chair and put her on his lap.

He turned her face against his shoulder and stroked her hair gently. "Take it easy, baby," he said softly. "Ain't nothin' can be that bad."

"No?" She looked at him with tear-blurred eyes. "It's bad enough. I'm pregnant."

His voice was even and without surprise. "How far gone are you?"

"The doctor says between ten or twelve weeks," she answered. "He can't be more exact until the next examination."

He was silent for a moment, his hand still absently stroking her head. "If he's right, then you're too far along to get an abortion?" It was more a statement than a question.

"That's the first thing I asked him. He said he wouldn't take the chance. He also told me there's some doctors in Tijuana who would do it, but he didn't recommend it."

He looked down at her. "How come you didn't notice any-thing earlier?"

She met his eyes. "I've always been irregular. Sometimes two months before I came aroun'. 'Specially when I've been fuckin' a lot."

"We've *been* fucking a lot," he agreed.

She got to her feet and went to the kitchenette and came back with a glass. She held it out to him. "I think I need a drink."

He looked up at her. "I read somewhere that drinking isn't good for the baby."

"A small one won't hurt," she said.

He poured less than a finger of whiskey into her glass and filled his own. He raised his glass and clinked it against hers. "Here's to Daniel Boone Huggins, Junior."

She had the glass already to her lips before the import of what he had said reached her. The glass froze in her hand. "You mean that?"

He nodded.

"You don't have to," she said. "I'm not blamin' you. It's my fault."

"It's nobody's fault," he said. "I'd been thinking about it even before you told me about this."

"Honest?" Her voice was incredulous.

"Honest. You're a good woman. My kind of people. We'll do good together."

She sank to her knees in front of him and put her head in his lap, the tears welling into her eyes again. "I was so frightened, Daniel. I love you so much."

He turned her face up to him. "There was nothing to be frightened about. I love you too," he said, and kissed her.

They were married the next morning before a justice of the peace in Santa Monica.

It was a small house on a side street just off San Vicente, north of Santa Monica Boulevard in Hollywood. Two bed-rooms connected by a bathroom, a living room and a large kitchen with a dining alcove. A small driveway leading to a

284

carport attached to the side of the house separated it from its neighbor. Both the front and back yards seemed to be about the same size: thirty feet across the width of the house and about twenty-five feet deep.

The real estate agent discreetly left them in the living room to let them discuss it. "What do you think?" Daniel asked.

"I like it," she said. " 'Specially with the room on the other side of the bathroom. We kin fix it up real nice fer the baby. An' I kin make new covers fer the rest of the furniture, and with a little paint it could look real good. On'y thing is the cost. Fourteen hundred dollars is a lot of money."

"They're throwing in everything. Furniture, kitchen stove, refrigerator."

"We kin rent a place like this fer about twenty-five a month," she said.

"But then you spend three hundred a year and at the end of it you've got nothing. This way we have an equity. It's like an insurance policy."

"How much mortgage will the bank give us?"

"No bank will give me a mortgage," he said. "They don't particularly like union men."

She looked at him. "I have that money I got from sellin' my house back East," she said. "Four hundred. That should he'p."

He smiled. "I don't need your money. I can manage it. That is, if you like it."

"I like it," she said.

"Okay, then let me make him an offer," he said, calling the agent back into the room.

They closed the deal at one thousand two hundred and seventy-five dollars and moved into the house at the end of the month. It took them a little more than a month after that to do everything to the house that they wanted to do. Daniel repainted the house and the furniture; she made new curtains and draperies with an old sewing machine that one of the former owners had left in the attic.

He was sitting in the living room reading the evening paper as usual when she came in from work. He put down the paper and looked at her. She was in her fifth month and was beginning to get large. Her face looked drawn and tired.

"I was stuck late," she said. "We was busy an' the boss wouldn't let me out. I'll get right on dinner."

"Don't bother," he said. "You get yourself a nice bath and rest a bit. I'll take you out for dinner. We'll have some Chinks."

"You don't have to," she said. "I don't min' makin' dinner."

But he could see that she liked the idea. "You do what I said."

Later, over dinner, while they were spooning into their chicken chow mein, he said very casually, "I think it's about time you quit your job. It isn't fair to Junior that you should be on your feet all day like that."

"The money comes in real handy," she said. "Twelve, fourteen dollars a week covers a lot of the house bills."

"I spend more'n that on whiskey and cigars," he said.

She was silent.

"Besides, I'm figuring on going back to work. If I do, we'll have a lot more than that comin' in."

She stared at him. "What are you gonna do?"

"The same as I've always done," he said. "Organizing."

"I didn't know you kin git a job like that out here."

"It's not out here," he said. "It's back East. Phil Murray himself called me. He wants me to head up the Steelworkers Organizing Committee in Chicago. They'll pay me fifty-five dollars a week and expenses."

Dismay came into her voice. "That means we'll have to move back there jest after we settled in here."

"No," he said. "It's nothing permanent. The whole job shouldn't last more than a few months at the most. Then I'll be back."

"I'll be alone," she said. "What if you're still there when my time comes?"

He laughed. "I'll be back long before that," he said confidently.

"Wouldn't you be better off takin' a job here?"

"You know what the jobs out here pay. There's nothing that pays even half that much. And with a baby on the way, the more we make now, the better off we are. With them paying my expenses, we can sock the whole salary into the bank."

She met his eyes. "That's what you want to do, isn't it?"

"Yes," he said simply.

She took a deep breath. "Okay. But I'll miss you."

He smiled and reached across the table, touching her cheek. "I'll miss you too," he said. "But I'll be back before you know it."

She reached up, pressing his hand to her cheek. She wanted to believe him, but in her heart she knew it would be longer than he thought.

"Is it dangerous?" she asked.

He shrugged his shoulders. "No more than any of the other jobs."

"I don't want nothin' to happen to you."

He patted his jacket under the shoulder where the gun rested comfortably. "Don't worry about that. What happened before is never going to happen again. I've got a friend."

She looked into his eyes. "That's okay. But jes' don't you fergit one thing. You got a wife too."

Chapter 11

Two DAYS later he stood on the platform preparing to board the train back east. He turned to Tess. "You take care of yourself. Do what the doctor says and stay on the diet. I'll be back in six weeks."

She put her arms around his neck. "You be careful. I don't want anything happenin' to you like when the time we met."

"Nothing like that will happen," he said. He kissed her. "Just take care."

"I love you," she said.

"I love you too," he said, and boarded the train. He stood on the steps and waved to her as the train began to move. She blew him a kiss just as the train began to curve away from the platform and was gone from sight. He mounted the steps and picked up his valise just as a porter came from the car.

"Let me he'p you, sah," the porter said, his white teeth shining in a big smile. He took the bag from Daniel's hand. "Your ticket, sah."

Daniel gave him the ticket. The porter looked down at it and nodded. "Follow me, sah."

Daniel followed him down the aisle, swaying slightly as the

train began to pick up speed. The porter checked the ticket again and stopped at a seat near the center of the car. He gestured to the seat and carefully placed the valise in an overhead rack. "You kin have both seats, sah," he said. "We're not busy, an' Ah'll make sure that nobody sits next to you. That way you kin stretch out at night."

"Thank you," Daniel said, giving him a half-dollar coin.

"Thank you, sah," the porter said enthusiastically. "Anythin' you want, jes' you call me. George is my name."

Daniel looked at him. "Is the bar open?"

"Yes, sah. The smoker is three cars back, jes' behind the sleepin' cars." The porter began to leave. "Enjoy youah trip, sah."

He saw the girl as he walked through the second sleeping car. A porter was just coming out of one of the private compartments. Automatically he looked in through the open door. She was standing there, her hand on the top button of her blouse. She glanced up. For a moment their eyes met; then she half-smiled and with the other hand pushed the door shut. He went on to the smoking car.

The bar was already crowded. There was one small table left against the window, with two chairs. He sat down. The waiter came up to him. "Yes, sah."

"How much is a bottle of bourbon?" Daniel asked.

"One fifty a pint, two sixty a fifth, sah."

"I'll take a fifth."

"Yes, sah. Ice and ginger, sah?"

"Just water, thank you."

He was on his second drink when she came into the car. Her eyes searched the car looking for a table. There was none. For a moment she seemed to hesitate, as if she were going to turn back; then she saw the empty seat at his table and came toward him.

"Do you mind if I sit here?" She had a soft, educated voice.

He rose to his feet. "It would be my pleasure, ma'am."

She sat down as the waiter came up. "What are you drinking?"

"Bourbon and water," he said. "Shall I get another glass?"

She shook her head. "A very dry martini," she told the

waiter. She turned back to him. "I didn't fancy the idea of drinking alone in the compartment."

Daniel smiled.

She held out her hand. "I'm Christina Girdler."

The waiter brought her martini. She raised the glass. "To a pleasant journey."

He tossed the shot of bourbon down his throat. "A pleasant journey, Miss Girdler."

"My friends call me Chris," she said.

"Daniel."

"I'm going to Chicago," she said. "I was just visiting some friends on the Coast."

"I'm changing trains in Chicago and going on to Pittsburgh, but I'll be back in Chicago in about two, three weeks," he said.

"What line of work are you in, Daniel?"

"I'm a labor organizer. Right now I'm on a special job for the Steelworkers Organizing Committee, C.I.O."

"The S.W.O.C.?"

"You heard about us?" His surprise showed in his voice. Usually people in her society knew nothing about unions.

She giggled. "My Uncle Tom would have a fit if he knew I was sitting here talking to you. Mention S.W.O.C. to him and he explodes."

Girdler. The name fell into place. President of Republic Steel. At the spearhead of Little Steel's antiunion drive. "*That* Girdler?"

She laughed again. "*That* Girdler. Do you want me to leave the table now?"

He chuckled. "Not at all."

"Even if I told you that I work in the public relations division of his company and I'm one of those people who send out all the antiunion information?"

He shook his head. "It doesn't matter. Right now, neither of us is working."

"You people aren't going to win. You know that, don't you?"

"I'm not working," he said.

"What do you want to talk about, then?" she asked.

290

"You," he said.

"What about me?" she asked.

"I've been sitting here with a hard on from the moment you sat down," he said. "I want to fuck you."

She caught her breath. A sudden light moisture broke out on her face and she flushed slightly. She stared at him.

"Are you all right?" he asked.

She moistened her dry lips with her tongue. "I just came."

He laughed. "That puts you one up on me."

She laughed with him. "May I have another drink, please?"

He signaled the waiter. When the drink had been brought and the waiter had gone, he said, "We'll have dinner first. Then we'll go to your compartment."

"Why not yours?"

He laughed. "I don't have any. Union men ride coach."

The train took almost forty hours to Chicago from Los Angeles, and the only time they ever left her compartment was for meals. In Chicago, she clung to him as he prepared to change to the train to Pittsburgh and would not let him leave until he promised that he would call her as soon as he returned.

He never knew how she had found out, but when he got off the train in Chicago two weeks later she was waiting for him, and she stayed with him until he was ready to return to the Coast.

One day in the car driving back to Chicago from Gary, Indiana, where he had gone to complete a field survey, she put her hand on his arm. "I love you," she said. "I want to marry you."

He glanced at her. "You're nuts."

"I mean it," she said.

"You know I'm married. That Tess is expecting in less than a month."

"I can wait for you to get a divorce."

"You forget the kind of money I make. I can't afford to support Tess and a baby and have another wife."

"I have money."

"No, thank you," he said.

"You don't have to stay with the union," she said. "You

291

and Uncle Tom would get along great together. I'm sure he'd give you a job in a minute. At a lot more money than you're making now."

He glanced at her again. "We're doing great. Why press and spoil it?"

"I love you," she said. "I've never known a man who could make me feel the things you make me feel."

"You're confusing love with fucking. Just because we fuck great together doesn't mean we have to fall in love."

"But I do love you," she insisted like a child.

"Good," he said. "I want you to love me but don't fall in love with me."

"Do you love me?" she asked.

"Yes," he answered. "But I'm not in love with you."

"I don't see the difference. Are you in love with your wife?"

"No. But I do love her."

"Then I don't see the difference."

"Give yourself time," he said. "You will."

She was silent for a moment. "Why do you stay with her if you're not in love with her?"

"We're the same kind of people," he said. "Same background, same ideas. It's easy. I'd never fit in your society and you'd never be comfortable in mine. And since there's no way we can spend the rest of our lives in bed, it just won't work."

"You're wrong," she said. "You'd fit in very well anywhere. Uncle Tom is no different from you. He began with nothing and worked his way up. He fits."

"Our basic philosophies are different," Daniel said. "I've seen my whole family die because of men like your Uncle Tom. I've seen too many people hurt and hungry because of something called company policy. I could never be a part of it."

"Maybe if you were you could change it."

He laughed. "Now you're being naive, and you know it. It isn't only your Uncle Tom or any one man that makes the policy. It comes from a lot of places. Banks, Wall Street, something called stockholders' profits. They put pressures on that you either go with or they find someone else to do it. If your uncle tried to change the policy, he wouldn't last a week in his job. He has no more choice to go with what he wants —that is, if he wants to change anything—than the man in the moon."

"I still want to marry you," she said.

He took a hand from the wheel and placed it over hers. "It's beautiful the way it is," he said quietly. "Let's keep it like that."

Her voice was suddenly tense. "I want to fuck. I saw a sign for a hotel about ten miles up the road. Let's stop there for the night."

"But I have to be in Chicago in the morning."

"I don't care," she said harshly. "I want your cock inside me."

He looked at her, and after a moment he nodded. They pulled off the road, and he didn't get to Chicago until late the next afternoon.

Chapter 12

FIVE MONTHS later, Daniel walked into the office of Philip Murray, president of the United Steelworkers, C.I.O., carrying his valise. There were several men sitting in the office with Murray, but he quickly dismissed them and turned to Daniel. "What did you find out?" His voice was right to the point.

Daniel put his valise on the floor. He was equally direct. "You won't like what I'm going to say." He paused for a moment. "Do you have a bottle of whiskey?"

Silently, Murray turned to the bottom drawer of his desk and placed a bottle of bourbon on the desk between them and one glass. He waited until Daniel had taken one drink and refilled his glass. His voice was quiet. "Tell me."

"I've been on the road six weeks. I've been in fourteen cities in eight states, and I don't like what I saw. We're being suckered into a trap. They're all ready and waiting for us. Girdler of Republic Steel has a fucking army waiting for us, and where he hasn't got his own army he's got the local police sewed up to do the dirty work for him. He's pushed the harassment of the workers and the union members as far as he can go. Now he's waiting for a strike call so that he can teach the union a lesson."

"It's that bad, is it?" Murray asked.

Daniel nodded, taking another drink. "Maybe worse."

"How did you find out so much about what he's doing?"

"From a member of his family."

"A girl?"

Daniel nodded. "She also works in his office."

"Does she know who you are?"

"Yes."

"Then why would she talk to you?"

Daniel was silent. He took another drink.

Murray stared at him for a long time. "She could be laying it on you."

"I don't think so," Daniel said. "She wants to marry me."

"Does she know you're married?"

Daniel nodded. "That doesn't bother her. She thinks divorces are easy."

"And what do *you* think?"

Daniel shook his head. "I'm married. In another week or so I'm going to be a father. I told her that. She says she can wait until I'm ready."

Murray was silent.

Daniel continued. "You said I could go home in time for the baby to be born. I'm planning to leave tomorrow."

"I don't know whether I can spare you right now," Murray said.

"You gave me your word," Daniel said.

Murray nodded. "I did."

"Then I'm going."

Murray was silent again. His face was drawn and white. He began to tap a pencil against his desk. "I'm under a lot of pressure to call this strike."

"Don't do it," Daniel said. "Remember what you told me a long time ago about Bill Foster. Don't start a strike unless you know you can win it. Now you're ready to do the same thing. And there's no way you can win this one."

"You really believe that?"

Daniel nodded silently.

"Damn!" Murray snapped the pencil in half between his fingers. "Everybody's after my ass. Lewis settled with Big Steel almost a year ago, and they're blaming me for letting Little Steel hang out there so long. Even the membership drive seems to be losing its momentum. The men want action."

"If they want action, that's what they'll get," Daniel said. "But that won't win the strike for them. All it will get them is time in the jails and hospitals."

"Reuther settled with General Motors. That's a big one. Now they're saying *we* can do it."

"Ford is still out," Daniel said. "Reuther's a long way from home there. And Girdler is just as organized as Ford is."

Murray stared at him. "What do I do?"

"What does Lewis say?"

"He doesn't say anything. Deliberately. He's just laying back there like a fat cat waiting for me to make the move. If we win, he'll jump on the bandwagon."

"And if we lose?"

Murray shrugged. "He can always say that we moved without asking him."

"Then why don't you ask him directly?"

"I tried to. But you know the way he is. There's no way you can get him to talk about anything he doesn't want to."

The bottle was half empty now, but Daniel refilled his glass again. "Stall," he said.

"I can't stall much longer," Murray replied.

"Two weeks," Daniel said. "I'll be back from the Coast by then. I want to be in South Chicago when it comes. If I can keep the lid on there, it may not be too bad."

"How can you be sure?" Murray asked. "Babies have been known to come as much as three weeks late."

"This one won't," Daniel said. "If it looks like that, I'll get the doctor to do a caesarian. I'll be back here by the middle of March."

Murray stared at him. "Two weeks?"

Daniel nodded.

"Okay. But I won't be able to hold back much longer. The Commies are already beginning a campaign to get me out of this job."

"Lewis has to know about that," Daniel said.

"Of course he does," Murray said angrily. "But you know his policy. Hands off. He'll take help from anywhere as long as he can build membership. That's why he let them in when Green wouldn't take them into the A.F.L."

"They're doing good with the Textile Workers?"

Murray nodded. "Hillman's flooding them with support out of New York. They're going to stonewall in the South, but they're a year away from that. Right now they're riding high."

Daniel got to his feet. "I'll be back in two weeks. Thanks for the drink, boss."

Murray rose behind his desk. "Do you honestly think we can't win this one?"

"We haven't got the chance of a snowball in hell."

Murray held out his hand. "I hope everything goes all right at home."

"Thanks," Daniel said, taking his hand. "I'll give you a call as soon as it happens."

It was sleeting when he came out of the building, his valise in his hand. He peered up the street, looking for a taxi. There was a black Chrysler limousine parked at the curb. Its door swung open and a girl's voice called him. "Daniel!"

He stared for a moment, then walked toward it. Standing in the sleet, he stared down at her. "What the hell are you doing here?"

"Get in the car," she said. "It's stupid to stand there in the snow."

He threw his valise into the car and followed it. The door closed and the car began to roll. He turned to her. "You're supposed to be in Chicago."

"I was getting bored there," she said. She leaned over and kissed him. "Surprised?"

"How'd you get here? You weren't on the train."

"Plane," she said. "There's regular service now between Chicago and the East."

"Drop me at the Chelsea," he said. "I've got to get some sleep."

"I have a suite at the Mayfair," she said. "You're staying with me."

"I said I've got to get some sleep."

"You have a two-day train ride tomorrow. You can catch up on your sleep then."

He was silent. "You're crazy. You know that, don't you?"

"I'm in love with you. You know that, don't you?"

"Look, Chris, it was great. But it's no good chasing it. We live in different places. There's no way we can ever get it together."

"I can live in your world. I don't need the family's money."

He looked at her. "What about this car and the Mayfair?"

"We can leave the car, take a taxi and go to the Chelsea. I don't care. As long as I'm with you."

He shook his head slowly. "You shouldn't have come. If your uncle finds out about it, he'll raise holy hell."

"I don't give a damn about what Uncle Tom thinks. Let him run his steel companies. He's not going to tell me what to do."

The car pulled up in front of the hotel. A doorman opened the door. He reached in and took Daniel's valise, then stood there while they got out of the car.

"Send the bag up to my apartment," Chris said.

"Yes, Miss Girdler," the doorman answered.

Daniel followed her into the hotel. They took the elevator up to the fifteenth floor. She pressed the doorbell. A butler opened it. "Miss Girdler." He bowed.

"They're sending a valise up," Chris said. "Put it in the guest room."

"Yes, Miss Girdler."

"And I'll have a dry martini." She looked at Daniel. "The usual?"

He nodded.

"A bottle of bourbon for Mr. Huggins."

"Yes, Miss Girdler." The butler bowed.

"Thank you, Quincy," she said, leading the way into the living room. She gestured Daniel to a seat on the couch. "Make yourself comfortable. We'll have some lunch in a little while."

298

Daniel looked around the hotel suite. He had been in many hotels, but he had never seen a setup like this. It was like a private house right in the middle of the hotel. "Not bad," he said.

"It's Uncle Tom's," she said. "He keeps this apartment all year round."

"Of course," Daniel said. "It's the only way."

"He says it's cheaper to do that than to try to get a good suite each time."

"Economical too," he said. "I didn't think he paid attention to things like that."

"You're being sarcastic," she said.

He feigned innocence. "Of course not. It's just in keeping with his character. After all, his average steel-mill worker makes less than five hundred and sixty dollars a year for a sixty-hour week. This can't be much more than that. Per day."

"Now you're not being pleasant," she said.

The butler brought them the drinks on a silver tray and placed it on a coffee table in front of the couch. "May I pour, sir?"

"I'll take care of it," Daniel said.

"Thank you, sir," the butler said, and left the room.

Daniel filled his glass. He held it up toward the girl. "I apologize. I have no right to talk like that about the man and drink his whiskey at the same time."

"And don't forget one other thing." She grinned.

"What's that?" he asked.

"And also fucking his favorite niece."

He laughed and tossed the drink down his throat. "You've made your point."

She drank her martini in one swallow. He saw the flush rise into her face as the drink went down and began to pour himself another drink. She put out a hand to stop him. "My cunt is soaking. How about a fuck before lunch?"

"Mind if I take a shower first? I stink from sitting up in that train all night."

"Don't," she said. "I love the smell of the sweat that comes from your balls."

Chapter 13

HE SAT at the coach window staring out as the train rolled slowly out of the Pasadena station. Forty minutes more and they would be in Los Angeles. Around him the passengers were already busy gathering up their belongings, lifting down their suitcases and getting ready to leave. A trainman came walking through the coach. "Los Angeles, next stop. Los Angeles."

The bright sun hurt his eyes, and he leaned his head against the seat back and closed them. It had been two months since he had been home and seen Tess.

She had been at the end of her sixth month and already huge, her belly swollen, her breasts like overripe giant grapefruit and the strong, stocky body already gone to fat, even her face round and heavy.

He had spent almost five days at home that time, and when he'd mentioned that maybe she should check with the doctor, that she had been gaining too much weight, she had replied it didn't matter. She would lose it as soon as she could begin to move around again. The only reason she had gained the weight was that there was nothing else for her to do but eat and go to the movies. Besides, she was lonely, and she didn't even see the few friends she had made because she was too big to get behind the wheel of the car and drive anywhere.

That night when they went to bed she reached for him. He was flaccid. After a moment: "What is it? Usually you're hard as a rock."

He couldn't tell her that she didn't excite him. "I'm tired. I've spent five weeks working day and night, and the train trip didn't help. The only thing I could get was a coach seat all the way from Chicago."

"It has to be more than that. I don't excite you the way I look."

"That's not it," he said. "Besides, I'm afraid to hurt you. It could do something to the baby."

"The doctor said we could go right up to the last month," she said, still stroking him.

He forced himself to feel the touch of her fingers. One thing she could do was manipulate him. She was expert at that. The sensuous stroking of his cock and cupping of his testicles. He felt himself growing hard.

After a while he tried to mount her. But the position was too awkward because of the size of her belly. Finally she rolled over on her side and he took her from the rear. She began to moan and climax almost immediately, but he couldn't feel her at all. It was as if he were putting his prick into a giant barrel filled with warm oil. There was no way he could reach a climax, but he kept driving until she climaxed herself into exhaustion, panting heavily like a bitch running in heat.

She turned to face him and kissed him. "You don't know how much I needed you. No one ever could do it for me the way you do."

He didn't speak.

"Was it all right for you?" she asked anxiously. "I didn't feel you come."

"How could you?" he lied. "You were so busy coming yourself you wouldn't have felt anything if the roof fell in."

"I love you," she said, and was asleep almost before the words were out of her mouth.

The next day he went to the doctor's office with her. The

doctor came out of the examining room while she was dressing. "Mr. Huggins?"

Daniel got to his feet. "Yes?"

"There's nothing to be alarmed about," the doctor said. "But there is a strong possibility the baby might be breeched."

Daniel stared at him. "Exactly what does that mean, doctor?"

"If it proves out, we may have to take the baby via a caesarian section," the doctor said. "But that's nothing to be alarmed about. We do operations like that every day."

"If there's nothing to be alarmed about, why do you keep telling me that?" Daniel asked.

The doctor smiled. "We find that prospective fathers need a lot of reassurance too."

"I'm reassured," Daniel said. "You mentioned that it was a possibility. When will you know for sure?"

The doctor assumed a pontifical air. "We have a problem. Your wife is much too heavy. I'm placing her on a strict diet. From now until the baby is born, she must lose weight—or at least, not gain any more. You'll have to see that she sticks to the diet."

Daniel didn't answer. There was no way he could do that from the other side of the country. He nodded.

"Another thing," the doctor said. "And again, I must repeat that there is nothing to be alarmed about, but I notice that Mrs. Huggins has developed a mild coronary fibrillation. That is, a heart flutter. It could be a result of the excess weight she is carrying, and I think it might correct itself if she loses the weight I ask."

"She still has another two months to go?" Daniel asked.

"Roughly," the doctor said. "My guess is six, seven weeks. By then we will know the exact condition of the child and prepare to do whatever is necessary. If the baby is in a difficult breech position, I would prefer to take the child before she enters labor."

"Six weeks?" Daniel said.

The doctor nodded. "I would prefer that. But please feel reassured. There's nothing to be alarmed about. The baby is fine, and your wife is in generally good health. There should be no problem whatever happens."

Daniel looked at him and nodded. "Thank you, Doctor."

The doctor went back into the examining room, and a few minutes later Tess came out. "What did he say?" she asked.

"He said there was nothing to be alarmed about. You were in good shape. You just have to lose some weight, that's all."

That had been almost two months ago, and now the train was pulling into Los Angeles. He got to his feet as the trainman came through the aisle. "Los Angeles. Last stop. Everybody off."

He took his valise from the overhead rack and went out on the platform and was off the train almost before it came to a stop. He had asked Tess to wait for him at home; he didn't want her caught in the press of the railroad station. He walked rapidly through the terminal to the cab rank. Once in the cab, after giving the driver his address, he leaned his head back against the seat wearily.

"Coming in from the East?" the driver asked.

"Yes," he answered.

"New York?"

"No, Pittsburgh."

"Lot of snow back there?"

"Some."

"Can't beat the weather here," the driver said. "Nothing but sunshine. Best weather in the world, I always say."

Daniel didn't answer. He closed his eyes. Suddenly he was very tired. No way for him to come home. He straightened up and tapped the driver on the shoulder. "Stop at the first liquor store."

When he came out of the store, the small bottle of bourbon in his pocket, he saw the flower shop next door. He picked out a large bouquet of roses, then got into the car and pulled the cork from the bottle with his teeth. He finished the half-pint of whiskey, and by the time the taxi pulled up in front of the house, he didn't feel tired anymore.

"You've changed," Tess said as he sat down at the dinner table. "When I talk to you, you don't even seem to be listenin'."

303

"I have things on my mind," he said. "Murray's going to call a strike, and I think we're all going to wind up in the outhouse."

"That's goin' to be bad for you?" she asked, taking his steak from the grill and placing it in front of him.

"It's not going to do anybody any good." He cut into the steak and tasted it. It was medium rare and juicy, just the way he liked it. He smiled up at her. "Nothin' beats home cookin'."

She was pleased. "How about home fuckin'?" she laughed.

He looked at her swollen belly. "Let you know just as soon as you're back in business," he teased.

"Won't be long," she said. "Doctor said mebbe just a few weeks after the baby." She sat down opposite him and began to eat her own steak, helping herself generously to the gravy-covered mashed potatoes.

He watched her. "How about your diet?"

"I had to go off it. I was gettin' too nervous," she said. "Besides, some of my friends said that doctors are always after women to lose weight just to make their own work easier, not because it does any real good."

He didn't answer.

"*You* lost weight," she said.

"I've been moving around a lot," he said.

"It would be nice if you could find work closer to home," she said. "A man called Browne has been calling you. He says he's with the movie union, the I.A. something. He wants you to call him."

"He leave a number?"

"I have it written down. Mebbe he wants to give you a job."

"Maybe."

"That would be good," she said. "Then you wouldn't have to go back."

"I have to go back," he said. "I gave Murray my word."

"But if you're gonna lose, what difference does it make?"

"I still gave my word." He looked at her. "Besides, even if George Browne offered me a job, I wouldn't take it. He's nothing but a cheap crook, taking orders from the mob.

There's a guy named Willie Bioff who's the real boss, and he gets instructions straight from Chicago."

She stared at him. "If that's true, why don't they do something about it?"

He shrugged his shoulders. "I don't know. But it's none of my business anyway. It's an A.F.L. union. Its up to them to police their own locals and affiliates. There has been some talk at C.I.O. headquarters about coming in and challenging them, but we have enough on our plate right now. Maybe later, when some of our own things are cleared up, we'll try to do something about it."

"You should talk to him anyway," she said. "Maybe it's not as bad as you think."

"I'll call him," he said.

She picked up the empty plates and put them in the sink. "I have apple pie and ice cream for dessert."

"I'll pass," he said. "I'm stuffed."

"I'll just take a small piece," she said. "I never feel satisfied unless I have somethin' sweet after eatin'. Coffee?"

He nodded. He waited until she put the cup of coffee in front of him. "What time is the doctor's appointment for tomorrow?"

"Ten o'clock," she said.

He got out of his chair and went over to the sideboard and poured himself a shot glass of whiskey. He brought it back to the table.

"You ought to cut down on your drinking," she said. "It's bad for your liver."

"I feel okay," he said. He swallowed the drink, then sat there with his coffee while she finished her dessert. "Mind if I turn in early? I'm beat from the trip."

"You go right ahead," she said. "I'll clean up, mebbe listen to the radio a little. *Rudy Vallee Hour* is on tonight, an' the *Lux Theatre*. Then I'll come to bed."

"Okay," he said. He went into the bedroom and began to undress. He folded his pants neatly over the back of a chair and placed his shirt over it. He placed his wristwatch and money on the dresser next to the vase of roses that he had brought home. In the dim light of the room the roses were a soft dark red, and their faint perfume hung in the air. He sat on the edge of the bed and unlaced his shoes and pulled off his socks. Then, still in his underwear, he stretched out on the bed.

Slowly he let his eyes wander around the room. She was right. But it wasn't only he who had changed. Everything had changed. Or maybe it hadn't. Right from the beginning she had never pretended to understand what he was doing. And she still didn't.

It came to him, the moment before he closed his eyes and fell asleep. That he had realized it all along but had never admitted it to himself. They were strangers. And always would be.

"There's no point in waiting," the doctor said. "She won't stop eating, and every day that passes she just puts on more weight."

"Did you tell her?" Daniel asked.

The doctor nodded. "She said she couldn't help it. She had nothing else to do but listen to the radio and eat. Without you home, she was just bored."

"When do you want to do it?"

"Tomorrow morning," the doctor answered. "You bring her into the hospital tonight. I've reserved a semiprivate room."

"She agreed?"

"Yes," the doctor said. "Matter of fact, she says she feels better now that she knows it's going to be over."

Daniel was silent.

"There's nothing to be alarmed about," the doctor said. "We do caesarians every day. Many women even prefer it to going through the pain of normal childbirth. Afterward, she'll be perfectly normal. She can have other children. Nothing will change."

"We don't have any choice, do we?"

The doctor shook his head. "I'm afraid not. Not with this kind of breech."

"Okay," Daniel said.

306

"My nurse will give you an admission card to the hospital," the doctor said. "Have her there by five o'clock. And don't worry, we'll take good care of her."

The Sunnyside Maternity Hospital was on Pico Boulevard near Fairfax, a pink stucco three-story building, surrounded by a pleasant lawn and garden. Daniel drove the car into the parking lot just behind the building and into the section marked PATIENTS AND VISITORS. They got out of the car and he took the small valise she had packed.

She looked at him as she got out of the car. "I feel funny. I never been in a hospital before."

"This place looks real nice," he said as they walked toward the entrance. "Not like the hospitals I've been in. They were all gray and dirty."

"Still a hospital," she said.

"A special kind of hospital," he said. "A place for kids to be born in. That makes it better."

She was silent as they went through the entrance. The halls were soft pink and there were pleasant paintings and pictures on the walls. The receptionist in a white uniform smiled up at them. "Welcome to Sunnyside. The admitting office is straight down the hall."

The admitting office was as pleasantly decorated as the entrance. There were several desks with chairs behind and in front of them. Comfortable couches lined the walls.

A nurse in white came into the office from a room next door. She sat down behind the desk and gestured them to the seats in front of her. "Welcome to Sunnyside," she smiled. "You're Mr. and Mrs. Huggins?"

"Yes," Daniel answered.

"We've been expecting you. We have a nice room all reserved for you," she said. "But first, there are some forms to be filled out."

The forms took about twenty minutes. When she had completed them, she excused herself and went into the next room. A few minutes later she returned. "Everything seems to be in order," she said, pushing several papers across the desk to them. "If you and Mr. Huggins would be kind enough to both sign each of them. They're standard consent forms giving us permission to take care of Mrs. Huggins and do whatever is necessary to ensure her well-being."

They signed. She picked up the papers and checked the signatures, then clipped them to the file in which the other forms had already been placed. "Just one more thing, Mr. Huggins," she said. "A deposit check of two hundred dollars is required in advance. This covers the room for eight days, use of the operating room, anesthetist and other hospital services. Of course, when you leave you will receive an exact accounting, and any refund due you will be made immediately."

Daniel took out his wallet. He counted out two hundred dollars in twenty-dollar bills. She counted the bills and placed them in the folder, then pressed a button on the desk.

"A nurse will be down in a moment to take you to your room," she said. She looked at them and smiled. "What will it be, a boy or a girl?"

"Daniel says it will be a boy," Tess said.

"I'm sure he won't complain if it's a girl," she said.

They laughed just as a nurse came in, pushing a wheelchair. Tess looked at it for a moment. "There's no need for that. I kin walk."

"Hospital rules, Mrs. Huggins," the admitting nurse said. "You're our patient now and we're responsible for you. Sometimes those floors are slippery."

Awkwardly Tess got into the chair. "Kin Daniel come with me?"

"Of course," the admitting nurse said. She smiled again as they started from the room, Daniel following the wheelchair carrying the small valise. "Good luck. I hope it's a boy."

They took the elevator to the second floor. The nurse stopped in the corridor outside the room and turned to Daniel. "There's a waiting room just down the hall. If you'll give us just a few minutes, I'll call you just as soon as we make Mrs. Huggins comfy."

Daniel nodded, and the nurse took Tess into the room. He walked down the hall to the waiting room. There were three men in the room. Two of them were playing cards, the third sitting back in his chair, a bored, weary expression on his face. The cardplayers didn't even look up.

Daniel sank into a chair. He felt like a cigar, but decided against it. The nurse had said only a few minutes, and the halls were filled with NO SMOKING signs.

After a moment, the third man sat up in his chair and looked at Daniel. "Just bring your wife in?"

Daniel nodded.

"I been here since last night," the man said. "I hope you have better luck."

Daniel didn't answer.

"Doctors are full of shit," the man said. "Every time they tell me it'll only be a few hours, an' each time I wind up spendin' two days here."

"Been here before?" Daniel asked.

"Three times," the man answered in a disgusted voice. "This is our fourth kid. I got to be a glutton for punishment. But this one is the last, I promise you."

One of the cardplayers let out a horse laugh. "Only if they cut his pecker off first."

"Shit," the man said. He looked at Daniel. "When did the doctor tell you yours would come?"

"Tomorrow morning."

"You sound sure."

"She's having a caesarian," Daniel said.

The man stared at him. "Hey, why didn't I think of that? I wind up blowin' three days' pay every time. I'm goin' to talk to the doctor."

The nurse appeared in the doorway. "You can see your wife now, Mr. Huggins."

Tess was sitting up in bed, a small silk bed jacket over her shoulders, as he came into the room. She was in the bed near the window; the other bed in the room was empty. He crossed the room and kissed her. "You look comfortable."

She smiled. "They're really very nice here." She giggled self-conciously. "They made me pee in a bottle. And look . . ." She held up an arm. There was a white cross-patch bandage in the crook of her elbow. "They also took some blood. It didn't hurt at all."

Daniel nodded without speaking.

"They won't let me have any dinner," she said. "They said they're gonna clean me out. My stomach has to be empty."

"That's right, Mrs. Huggins," the nurse said, coming into the room. "We're going to do that right now." She opened a cabinet next to the bed and took out an enema can and hose, then looked at Daniel. "You'll have to leave now, Mr. Huggins. We want her to sleep afterward, so that she'll be strong and fresh in the morning."

A note of fear came into Tess's voice. "You mean I won't see him until afterward?"

The nurse smiled. "Of course you'll see him. In the morning, before you go upstairs. But now it's more important that you rest." She looked at Daniel. "If you get here at seven o'clock, you'll be in plenty of time."

"I'll be here," Daniel said. He bent over Tess and kissed her. "Be a good girl and do what they tell you. I'll see you in the morning."

"You won't be late?" Tess said anxiously. "You better set the alarm clock."

"I will," he said reassuringly. "You just don't worry about a thing. Everything's going to be just fine."

310

Chapter 14

THE TELEPHONE was ringing as he opened the front door. Leaving the door open behind him, he went into the living room and picked it up. "Hello?"

It was a man's voice. "Mr. Huggins?"

"Yes."

"This is George Browne," the voice said.

"Yes, Mr. Browne."

"Did your wife mention that I had called?"

"She did."

"I would like to see you," Browne said.

"That's what Tess told me."

"You didn't call," Browne said.

"I just came back from the hospital," Daniel said. "My wife is going to have a baby."

"I see." Browne said. "I hope everything turns out well."

"Thank you."

"When do you think we can meet?"

"Maybe after the baby is born," Daniel said.

"It's important," Browne said. "Hold the phone a minute." Daniel heard him talking to someone else at his end of the line; then he came back. "Have you any plans for dinner tonight?"

Daniel looked around the house. It seemed depressingly empty. "No."

"Good," Browne said. "Do you know Lucey's on Melrose?"

"I'll find it," Daniel said.

"I can send a car for you."

"I have a car."

"In an hour. Okay?"

"I'll see you there."

"Just ask for my table," Browne said. "I look forward to seeing you."

Daniel put down the telephone and went back to the front door and closed it. The telephone began to ring again.

This time it was Chris. Her voice was hushed as if she didn't want it to be heard past the earpiece of the telephone. "I had to call you."

"It's okay," he said.

"If your wife answered I was going to hang up."

"She's in the hospital."

"Is she okay?"

"Fine."

"I'm glad," she said. "Christ!"

"What's the matter?" he asked.

"I can't even talk to you on the telephone without my cunt getting wet."

He laughed. "A lot of good that will do you back in Chicago."

"I'm not in Chicago," she said.

"Where the hell are you?" he asked, knowing what her answer would be almost before he asked the question.

"Here," she said. "I'm at the Ambassador Hotel on Wilshire Boulevard. I have my own bungalow."

"You're crazy."

"No, I'm not," she said. "*You* are if you think I'm going to leave you alone for a week while your wife is in the hospital with all that movie pussy floating around."

"I've never seen any of it," he said.

"I'm taking no chances anyway. What are you doing for

312

dinner? I've got a great setup here—dining room and everything."

"I have a date."

"I don't believe you."

"True," he said. "With George Browne, president of the I.A. out here."

"Then come over after dinner," she said.

"No. I have to be at the hospital at seven in the morning."

"I'll wake you up in time."

"No."

"I'll play with myself all night and I'll get crazy."

He laughed. "Think of me."

Her voice suddenly turned serious. "Daniel, your voice sounds different. Are you all right?"

"I'm fine," he said.

"Then what is it? Are you worried about Tess?"

"Yes," he said. "They're doing a caesarian tomorrow morning."

She was silent for a moment. "Oh. But don't worry about it. My older sister has had two babies that way. She said it's a lot easier than having babies the regular way. And she's just fine."

"I'll be okay when it's over," he said.

"I'm sure you will," she said. "Will you call me then?"

"Yes."

"Good luck, Daniel," She hesitated for a moment. "You know I really mean that, don't you?"

"I know," he said.

"I love you, Daniel."

He was silent.

"Daniel?"

"Yes?"

"Call me tomorrow."

"I will," he said, and put down the telephone. He crossed the room into the dining area and took the bottle of bourbon from the sideboard. He poured himself a tumblerful and sipped it slowly, thinking. She was crazy, but there was one thing he could do with her that he never could do with any other woman. He could talk to her.

He rubbed his jaw reflectively. The stubble scratched under his fingers. He needed another shave. Taking the whiskey with him, he went into the bedroom and began to undress. In the bathroom, he stared at his face in the mirror.

He was thirty-seven years old and about to become a father. Being a father changed things. Already he found himself thinking more about the future. About where he was going, about what he was doing. It wasn't going to be easy bringing up a kid on the kind of money he made. Sooner or later he would have to get Murray to give him a local of his own. At least, he could build from there. That was the way all of them did it. Lewis, Murray, Green; even Browne out here had a platform from which he could move. He had just been made a vice president of the A.F.L.

Also, it wasn't good for a kid to grow up without a father around. Maybe Tess was right. If Browne came up with the right kind of deal, he should take it. It had to be better than getting his brains beat out the way he was going.

Or what Chris had said. Jump the fence. Many labor men had done that and were getting good money. He finished shaving, still thinking. Finally he washed the rest of the soap from his face, used a little talc to hide the understubble that always showed blue on his cheeks. He put on his shirt, still thinking, still undecided.

As the headwaiter led him to the table near the back corner of the restaurant, Daniel wondered why it was that so many of the customers seated at the tables seemed to be familiar to him. Then he understood why. Most of them were film actors and actresses, and he had seen them on the screen so many times. There were a few whom even he could recognize. At one table, Joel McCrea; at another, Loretta Young; the others had names he could not remember.

There were two men seated at the table. They got to their feet. The bigger man, slightly balding, held out his hand. "I'm George Browne. Say hello to Willie Bioff, my executive vice president."

After they shook hands and sat down, Browne looked at him. "I hear you're a drinking man. Is that true?"

"I've never been known to turn one down," Daniel said.

"I'm a beer drinker myself," Browne said. "Ulcers. I can't take the hard stuff. You go ahead and order.

"Thank you," Daniel said. He looked up at the headwaiter, who was still hovering over them. "Jack Daniels, please."

"Single or double, sir?"

"Neither," Daniel said. "A bottle. And bring a pitcher of water. No ice."

Browne stared at him. "If the rest of what I've heard about you is as true as that, you have to be quite a man."

"What have you heard?" Daniel asked.

"That you're the best organizer Murray has with him. That he keeps you moving from trouble spot to trouble spot, pulling the locals together. That you as much as anyone are responsible for the success of the S.W.O.C.'s recruiting drive."

"Not true," Daniel said. "We have good men everywhere. I just help coordinate their efforts."

"Also that you're a big man with the ladies."

The headwaiter came back with the whiskey. Daniel didn't reply until after the waiter had poured him a drink and had gone. He held up the glass of whiskey. "Cheers," he said, downed it and immediately poured himself another. "I heard a lot about you and your friend here too," he said, smiling.

"What's that?" Browne asked.

"That you're both on the take. That you kick back half to the boys back in Chicago. That you'd sell out your own grandmother for a dime." Daniel was still smiling.

"What the hell—!" Browne started to sputter. Bioff's hand on his arm stopped him.

"Did you also hear that our members are getting the highest salaries and job-protection benefits they ever got in their lives?" Bioff asked.

"Yes."

"Why didn't you mention that?"

Daniel sipped at his whiskey. "I figured that I didn't have to. You would." He finished the drink and poured another. "Now that we're finished with the compliments, maybe you can tell me why you want to see me."

"Let's order first," Bioff said. "The spaghetti is very good here."

"I'll have a steak," Daniel said.

They ate quickly, almost silently. Daniel cleaned his plate; the other men simply toyed with their food. At the end, when the waiter brought them coffee, Daniel took out a cigar. "Mind if I smoke?"

They didn't object. He lit the cigar and leaned back in his chair. "Gentlemen, that was a fine meal. I usually don' git to fancy places like this. I git most of my meals in hash houses and greasy spoons. Thank you."

Bioff looked at Browne. "Mind if I talk?"

Browne nodded. "Go ahead."

Bioff turned to Daniel. "There are some seven thousand office workers in the film business. About three thousand of them here in the studios, the rest scattered in film exchanges around the country and the home offices in New York. We've just begun to organize them, but we have a lot of prejudice to overcome, a lot of it from the office workers themselves. They think that white-collar workers are above that. The companies know that and encourage them. We're beginning to make a little headway, but it's slow. Now we hear that District 65 is getting into the act and they have a lot of money to spend. They already have the screen publicists sewn up in New York, but that's a Commie operation and we can handle it. We just don't want them to go any further."

"Why don't you do what you did before? Put the squeeze on the theaters and they'll get the companies to sign up the people for you?"

"We can't do that," Bioff said. "First, we got contracts we got to respect and we can't endanger our members there. Second, if we get pushed into an N.L.R.B. vote, we don't have enough members signed to make it. That's why we've come to you."

Daniel was silent.

"You've got a big reputation," Bioff said. "You've been a Lewis and Murray man all your life. You know how the C.I.O. and District 65 operate. If you come in with us, I'm sure we'll sew the whole industry up."

"Exactly what are you offering me?" Daniel asked.

"The presidency of the National Film Office Workers

Union, I.A.T.S.E., A.F.L. Fifteen thousand dollars a year and expenses for openers."

Daniel looked at him. "You know how much I'm making now?"

"Six thousand a year," Bioff said.

"That's right," Daniel said. He poured himself another drink. "I'd like to take your money, gentlemen. But I'm the wrong man for the job." He tossed the drink down his throat. "You're trying to buy me for all the wrong reasons. Because I'm C.I.O. and I've got a good reputation. What you forget is that I have the reputation because I'm working with the same people I came from. The Hunkies and Polacks and mountain men I grew up with. I talk their language; they understand me. Comes to office workers, I'm a fish out of water." He emptied the rest of the whiskey bottle into his glass. "They wouldn't know what I'm talking about and I wouldn't understand a thing they'd tell me."

"Don't you think we've thought of that?" Bioff asked. "But we also know that you're bright enough to learn. Anyone who can graduate that labor college in New York top man in the class can't be as plain as you make yourself out to be. I think you're making a mistake."

"I don't think so," Daniel said.

"Suppose we make it twenty thousand?"

"No. Your best bet is to find a man out of your own organization for the job. Someone they can look up to and respect. He'll do a lot better than I can."

"We won't take your answer as final," Bioff said. "Why don't you sleep on it? Tomorrow when you're a father and you think about the advantages you can give your family with a job like this, maybe you'll change your mind."

"I doubt it," Daniel said. He got to his feet. "Again, gentlemen, thank you."

Bioff looked up at him. "Sometimes you can be too smart."

"I agree with you," Daniel said in a flat voice. "But you can never be too honest."

Chapter 15

SHE SEEMED to be sleeping when he entered the room. The nurse turned to him and held a finger to her lips so that he wouldn't talk. "We gave her a mild sedative to relax her," she whispered. "She'll be drowsy."

He nodded to show that he understood and pulled a chair next to the bed and sat on it. Tess's face was strangely child-like and vulnerable as she slept. She was breathing slowly, the sheet over her rising and falling. He looked past her out the window. The sky was blue and the sun bright and streaming gold into the room.

He felt rather than saw her move and looked down. Her eyes were open and she was looking at him. A moment later she closed them again without speaking. But her hand crept across the sheet toward him. He took her hand and felt it close tightly around his fingers.

It was five minutes before she spoke. "I'm afraid," she murmured, her eyes still closed.

"Don't be," he said in a soft voice. "Everything is all right."

"It's hard to breathe," she whispered. "And sometimes there's a sharp pain in my chest."

"Relax," he said. "It's just nerves."

She pressed his hand. "I'm glad you're here."

"So am I," he said.

The nurse left the room, and they sat there silently for a while. Suddenly her eyes were open and she was looking at him. "I'm sorry," she said.

"There's nothing to be sorry about."

"I lied to you," she whispered. "I knew I was pregnant six weeks before I told you."

"It doesn't matter now," he said.

She closed her eyes again and rested for a moment. "I felt you were getting ready to leave me and I didn't want you to go."

"I wasn't about to leave you," he said. "But all of that is over now. Forget it."

"I didn't want to have the baby without tellin' you the truth." She paused for a moment. "If somethin' happens to me up there, I wanted you to know that I loved you so much I couldn't let you go."

"Nothing is going to happen up there except that you're going to have a baby and you're going to be all right."

She was looking at him again. "You're not angry with me?"

"I'm not angry."

"I'm glad," she said, and closed her eyes. She slept until the nurse came back into the room, a male attendant pushing a gurney bed into the room behind her.

"Mrs. Huggins," the nurse said in a cheerful voice. "Time for us to go upstairs now."

Tess's eyes opened. She saw the gurney, and a look of fear came into her eyes. "What's that?"

"A rolling bed," the nurse said, moving the gurney against her bed. "We give you a first-class ride upstairs." She moved behind Tess's head. In a moment, she and the attendant had expertly moved Tess onto the gurney. Quickly, they wrapped the sheet over her and fastened the canvas straps that held her to the gurney.

Tess looked up at the nurse. "Can he come upstairs with me?"

"Of course," the nurse said, smiling. "He'll be waiting right outside the room in which you're having the baby. You'll see him as soon as you come out."

They moved the gurney out into the hall and Daniel walked alongside, still holding Tess's hand. In the elevator going up, she looked up at him. "I feel funny," she said. "Like I'm floating, dizzy-like."

"That's normal," the nurse reassured her. "It's the Pentothal. Don't fight it. Just relax and drift with it. Its just like sleeping. And when you wake up you'll be a mother."

They came out of the elevator and went down another corridor. The nurse stopped the gurney in front of the operating room. "Here's where we leave you," she said to Daniel. "There's a waiting room just at the end of the hall. The doctor will see you there afterward."

Tess turned her face toward him. "Promise me, Daniel. If anythin' happens to me. That you'll take care of the baby."

"Nothing will happen to you."

Her voice was insistent. "Promise me."

"I promise," he said.

She seemed to relax. "I love you. You won't forget that, will you?"

"Just you don't forget that I love you," he said. He bent over the gurney and kissed her. He watched them push the gurney through the swinging doors, then went down the corridor to the waiting room.

It seemed longer, but it was less than an hour later that the doctor came into the waiting room. He held out his hand, smiling. "Congratulations, Mr. Huggins. You have a son. A big boy, like yourself. Ten pounds four ounces."

Daniel grinned, shaking the doctor's hand enthusiastically. "I can't believe it."

"You'll believe it when you see him," the doctor said, smiling.

"And Tess—is she okay?"

"Just fine," the doctor said. "She's in the recovery room right now. She should be back downstairs in about two hours. That will give you time to go out and get a box of cigars and make a few calls. When you come back, you'll be able to see the two of them."

Daniel let out a deep breath. "Thank you, Doctor."

He crossed the street in front of the hospital to the restaurant and bar on the opposite corner. No one was in the place when he entered except the man behind the bar, who was busy polishing glasses. Daniel stepped up to the bar. "Double Jack Daniels straight, water back."

Expertly the bartender poured the whiskey and placed it in front of him. With his other hand he brought a glass of water up from beneath the bar. "What was it?" he asked. "A boy or a girl?"

"A boy." Daniel stared at him. "How did you know?"

The bartender laughed. "The only customers we get here at nine o'clock in the morning are from the hospital across the street." His hand went down behind the bar and came up with a cigar. "Congratulations. Compliments of the management."

"Thank you." Daniel looked at the cigar. It had a gold-imprinted wrapper. IT'S A BOY!

"We also sell them by the box of twenty-five," the bartender said. "Two dollars."

"I'll take a box," Daniel said. "And let me buy you a drink."

The bartender grinned at him. "I make it a rule never to take a drink before twelve o'clock. But this time I'll make an exception. I'm from New York, anyway, and it's twelve there already." He poured himself a shot and put the box of cigars on the bar all in the same motion. "What's the kid's name?"

"Daniel. Daniel B. Huggins, Junior."

The bartender raised his glass. "Here's to him."

They put away their drinks. Daniel ordered a refill. He drank half, then chased it down with some water.

"If you want to make any calls," the bartender said, "there's a phone booth in the corner."

Daniel looked down the room, then shook his head. "I've got time," he said, picking up his glass. "Give me another. You have one too."

The bartender shook his head. "No, thanks, Mr. Huggins. I still have another eight hours to go. If I begin putting them away now, I'll never make it through lunch hour."

Daniel nodded. He pulled the wrapper off the cigar and lit it. He blew a cloud of smoke toward the ceiling. It wasn't bad. "Good cigar."

"The kitchen's open if you'd like some breakfast," the bartender said.

Suddenly, Daniel realized he was famished. "Steak and eggs with hash brown."

The bartender smiled and turned, yelling, toward the kitchen in the back. "Hey, Charlie! Getcha ass out here and set a table. We got a live one."

He bought a bouquet of spring flowers on the way back to the hospital. The door was closed as he came down the corridor. Cautiously he turned the knob and opened it.

Tess was lying in the bed, propped up by the pillows behind her. She had already put on some makeup and lipstick, but her skin seemed pale and almost translucent beneath it. Her eyes were closed and she seemed to be resting, not paying attention to the nurse on the other side of the bed who was straightening the sheets.

He tiptoed quietly across the room and stood at the side of the bed, looking down at her. She opened her eyes. He smiled, holding the flowers toward her. "Congratulations, Mother."

She looked at the flowers. "They're beautiful," she said. Her voice seemed to have no strength.

He kissed her. "How do you feel?"

"Okay," she said. "Weak. I can't catch my breath. It's like there's a band across my chest."

"You'll be all right after you get some rest," the nurse said. "Sometimes the bandages we have around your abdomen make you feel like that." She turned to Daniel. "I'll put the flowers in a vase for you, Mr. Huggins."

Daniel gave her the flowers, and they watched as she took a vase from the closet, filled it with water from the sink and arranged the flowers in it.

"Did you see the baby yet?" Tess asked.

"No," Daniel answered. "Did you?"

She shook her head.

"The doctor said he's a big one," Daniel said. "Ten pounds four ounces."

"My brothers were all ten pounds or more," Tess said. She looked at the nurse. "Can we?"

The nurse smiled. "That's just what I was about to do. I'll be back with your son in just a minute." She closed the door behind her.

Daniel pulled a chair to the side of the bed and took her hand. "I bought a box of cigars. Look." He held one up. "See the band? It says, 'It's a boy.' "

She smiled wanly. "Were you here this mornin' before I went upstairs?"

"Of course I was—don't you remember? I even walked you upstairs to the operating room."

"I thought maybe you did, but everything was so fuzzy. They gave me a shot before I went upstairs and I don't remember too good." She looked at him cautiously. "Did I say anything bad?"

He shook his head. "No. Only that you loved me. Maybe you think that was bad."

"That was good." She pressed his hand. "I do love you. You've always been so good to me."

He laughed. "You didn't treat me too bad either."

The door behind him opened and the nurse came in carrying the baby, all covered with a blanket. She went around the bed across from Daniel. She lifted the cover from the baby's head and held the infant toward Tess. "Mrs. Huggins, your son."

Wonderingly, Tess took the baby. Gingerly, she moved him close to her and peered into his tiny face. She looked up at Daniel, a radiant smile on her face. "Oh, Daniel, he's so beautiful. He looks just like . . ."

A sudden agony contorted her face. "Daniel!" she screamed. "Oh, my God!" The baby began to slip from her nerveless fingers, and Daniel caught it just as she slumped back against the pillows, a light froth bubbling from her mouth. She turned to look at him, her eyes bright and staring.

Her lips moved as if she were trying to speak. Then her eyes went blank and her face fell sideways on the pillow, her eyes staring into eternity, her mouth open with the words she would never speak.

The nurse tore around the bed to his side, roughly pushing him out of the way as she hit a button on the wall. A bell began to ring in the hall outside the room. A moment later the room was filled with nurses and doctors; oxygen tanks were being rolled in with other machinery.

Daniel stood against the wall, watching them for a moment. The nurse looked up, catching his eye for a moment. He shook his head. "It won't do any good," he said to no one in particular in a flat voice. "She's gone."

Then gently he hid the baby's face in the blanket. "Come, my son," he said, carrying the child with him into the hall.

Chapter 16

DANIEL PULLED his coat collar tight against his chest as he stood bareheaded in the slanting rain. The minister's voice was as rich and full as if there had been a crowd of mourners instead of just one lonely man. "Ashes to ashes, dust to dust . . ."

Daniel stared at the reddish mahogany coffin, the rain beading on its highly lacquered surface and dripping down its sides into the open, yawning grave beneath it. So small, so very small. Somehow it didn't seem right. She had never been a small woman.

The minister's voice stopped. He turned to Daniel. "You may add your own prayer," he said.

"I was never very much of a praying man, Reverend," Daniel said.

"It doesn't matter; the Lord will hear whatever you say."

Daniel took a deep breath. "You were a good woman, Tess. May the Lord make you welcome."

The two gravediggers looked expectantly at the minister. It was their last job of the day and they were anxious to get it over with. The minister glanced at Daniel to see if he had finished his prayer, then turned to them and nodded.

Expertly, the two men moved away the steel poles on which the coffin had been resting, then began to lower it into the open grave until it settled with a squishy sound on the already water-soaked bottom. They reached for the shovels.

"I'll do it," Daniel said, stepping forward. In answer to the questioning looks: "Back home, we always buried our own."

Silently, they stepped back and watched him. The feel of the shovel was good in his hands; it took him back in time. He was just a boy, and the mines were dark. He looked into the grave as the first shovelful of dirt fell upon the coffin and scattered over the flowers lying upon its closed cover. Soon she too would be covered by the dark. The rhythm picked up. The earth was rain-soaked and heavy, and soon he felt the sweat coming up under his clothing and with it a sense of lightness and strength. Suddenly he was once again together with the earth. Then, almost before he knew it, it was over, the earth lying neatly in a mound over the grave.

He handed the shovel to one of the men. "Thank you," he said. The man nodded without answering.

The minister walked back to the car with him. At the door of the car Daniel stopped and took a twenty-dollar bill from his pocket.

"You don't have to do that," the minister said. "Forest Lawn has already included my services."

"Take it anyway," Daniel said. "I'm sure that someone in your parish could use the help."

"Thank you," the minister said. Daniel got behind the wheel of the car. "Don't be bitter, my son," he said.

"I'm not bitter, Reverend," Daniel answered, starting the engine. "Death and I are not strangers. Nor will we ever be."

He had to pull around the big black limousine parked against the curb in order to get into the driveway between his house and the next. He glanced at the chauffeur sitting imperturbably behind the wheel of the limousine, then ran through the rain to his open doorway.

There were neatly closed and tied cardboard boxes in the living room, stacked as if awaiting pickup. He walked through the empty room to the bedroom. Chris was there together with another woman—middle-aged, heavyset, with blond hair pulled neatly back on her head in a bun. They turned as they heard his footsteps.

Chris's voice was without surprise. "There's a fresh bottle of bourbon on the table," she said. "Help yourself to a drink. We'll be through here in a minute."

He looked at her for a moment, his eyes falling to the open drawer of the dresser and the cardboard box next to it. The last bits and pieces of Tess's clothing were being packed. Without speaking, he went back into the living room.

When she came into the room, he was standing at the window, staring into the rain, half-empty glass of whiskey in his hand. "Someone had to do it," she said.

"You know, it was raining the first day we came to California," he said. He turned to look at her. "Seems only fitting its raining now."

"The Goodwill truck should be here in about a half-hour to pick up the things," she said. "I've also ordered some new furniture for the baby's room and a new convertible couch for the living room, one that turns into a bed."

"I was the only one at the cemetery," he said. "I never knew any of the friends she made while she was working, so I didn't know whom to call. I never knew where any of her family back home were either."

"The painters will be here first thing in the morning. They said they'll need only a day. The new furniture will be delivered the day after."

"She had nobody but me," he said.

"Daniel," she said sharply.

He looked at her.

"She had a son. Your son. But now she's gone and there's nothing that can be done about it. So get off it. You have a responsibility toward your son and you have to plan for it."

There was pain in his eyes. "I'm scared. I don't know where to begin."

"I'll help you," she said. "That's why I had Mrs. Torgersen come out here."

"Mrs. Torgersen?"

"The woman in there. She's an experienced baby nurse and nanny. She will take care of the child for you."

He looked at her with a growing respect. "Chris."

She smiled.

"Thank you."

She stood on tiptoe and kissed his cheek. "I love you. And that's more than just fucking."

He looked into her eyes for a moment, then nodded slowly. "I'm learning." He reached for the bottle and poured more whiskey into his glass. "But I have other problems. I don't know whether I can afford all this. I may have to take the job out here that Bioff and Browne offered me."

"But you said they were crooks."

"That doesn't mean I have to be one."

"You know better than that," she said. "At least be honest with yourself. If you're going to jump the fence, jump clean over it. Take a job with Uncle Tom. Don't climb halfway up and try to straddle it."

"Maybe I'd be better off if I brought the baby back East with me."

"Don't be stupid," she said. "What will you do? Keep the baby in a suitcase? And how will you take care of him?"

He didn't answer.

"You have a perfectly good home here, and it's a comfortable place for a child to grow up. And the way you move around, there's no way for you to take care of the child. The best thing for you to do is go with Mrs. Torgersen. She's got the experience to deal with all the things you know nothing about. She took care of my sister's kids for years."

"How much do I have to pay her?"

"It won't be much. She wanted to come out to California. She's had it with the cold and ice back East. She'll take two hundred a month. My sister was paying her three fifty."

"That's twenty-four hundred a year," he said. "I figure food and other expenses at least sixteen hundred, two thousand. That doesn't leave me very much."

"What do you need money for?" she asked. "The union pays your expenses while you're on the road. And you're always on the road."

He took a sip of his whiskey. "You've got it all figured out, haven't you?"

"Not all of it," she said.

"What did you leave out?"

A touch of temper came into her voice. "If you're too stupid to know, I'm not about to tell you."

He was silent for a moment, searching her eyes. Then, abruptly, he turned away from her, back to the window. His voice was tight with emotion. "I'm not ready to talk about that yet."

She walked to him and placed her hand gently on his arm. "I know that," she said softly. "But in time you will be."

Mrs. Torgersen was a take-charge lady. Just approaching fifty, she had been widowed twenty years before when her husband, a second mate in the merchant marine, had gone down with his ship, blown in half by a torpedo from a German submarine. She spoke an almost perfect English, only the faintest trace of her original Swedish sounding in her voice, and there was almost nothing she couldn't do. Cook, sew, drive a car, clean house, laundry, garden. And she did it all with an efficiency that made everything seem almost effortless.

"You don't have to worry, Mr. Huggins," she said. "I'm a good woman, a responsible woman. I don't fool around. I will take good care of your child. As if he was my own."

"I'm sure of that, Mrs. Torgersen," Daniel said. "I just want to make sure you have everything you need."

"I can't think of anything," she said. "The house is very comfortable. I feel very good here."

"Tomorrow morning, before we go to the hospital to pick up the baby, we'll stop at the bank. I want to open an account for you so that you don't have to wait for money each week," Daniel said. "I'll be moving around a lot, and there will be times I may not be able to send money as easily as I would like to."

"Whatever you say, Mr. Huggins," she said. "And when you do come home, I can sleep on the new couch here."

He smiled. "You don't have to do that. I think I can stand it for a few days."

She hesitated a moment before she spoke. "Is Miss Chris coming to the hospital with us?"

He looked at her in surprise. "I didn't think of it. She never said anything about it."

"You must excuse me, Mr. Huggins," she said, almost apologetically. "But I have known Miss Chris for almost ten years, since she was fifteen years old. She would never say anything. But I think she would like to come."

He nodded slowly. "Thank you, Mrs. Torgersen. I'll ask her at dinner tonight."

"No," she said. "I'm going back to Chicago in the morning."

He was surprised. "I thought—"

She interrupted. "I'm sorry. I've done all I can. I just can't take any more." She rose from the table in her bungalow and ran into the bedroom.

He followed her. She was standing in a corner of the room, her hands over her face. He put his arms around her shoulders and turned her to him. "Did I say something wrong?"

Wordlessly she shook her head.

"Then what is it?"

"I just took a good look at myself. I have to be nuts to put myself through the things I have." She looked up into his face with moist eyes. "It was one thing to talk about our being together. But that was before I came here. It was almost in the abstract. But being here with you was not abstract. It was real. I saw your hurt. I saw your care. I love you. I know what you told me is true. That you need time. But I'm human. I hurt too much. I'll be better off home, away from you. Maybe it won't be as bad then."

Silently, he moved her close to him and held her tightly. "I didn't mean for it to be like this."

"It's not your fault. I did it all myself. You never said anything to make me think differently." Her voice was muffled in his jacket.

The telephone began to ring. She looked up at him, then moved across the room and picked it up. "Hello?" she said into it, then listened for a moment. "I'll tell him," she said, putting the telephone down.

"It was Mrs. Torgersen. She said Mr. Murray just called and wants you to call him right back. He said it was an emergency."

"I can't stall any longer. There's too much pressure on me." Murray's voice was taut. "When will you be back?"

"I can leave Sunday," he said.

"Come to Chicago," Murray said. "I'll meet you there."

"Okay."

"Everything all right?" Murray asked. "What was it? A boy or a girl?"

Suddenly Daniel realized he hadn't let him know what had happened. "A boy."

"Congratulations," Murray said. "Give my best to your wife, and I'll see you in Chicago on Monday."

He put down the telephone and turned to Chris. "Maybe I'd better go home," he said heavily.

"No."

He looked at her.

She met his eyes. "I told you I was nuts. No way are you getting out of here without giving me a farewell fuck."

Chapter 17

THE NEWSPAPER headlines were already proclaiming the strike against "Little Steel" by the time Daniel got off the train at Union Station. He bought a *Tribune* and read it silently in the taxi that took him directly to the union offices.

There were two interviews featured on the front page. One, prominently displayed near the top of the page, was with Tom Girdler, president of Republic Steel; the other, smaller, in a little box in the bottom corner of the page and continued into the back pages, where it was almost impossible to find, was with Phil Murray, president of the S.W.O.C., C.I.O.

> The Commies, anarchists and agitators who are trying to take over this country and deliver us intact into the greedy hands and power of the Soviet Union will awaken to a rude shock when they come face to face with the mass of real Americans ready to protect their ideals and the American way of life for themselves and their children. We will not shirk nor shrink from our task. We are ready for them and we will fight them in the fields and the streets even unto the

gates of our plants and beat them, just as the
American soldiers beat back the threat of the
Boche in the war. I say to the misguided strikers,
"Listen not to false prophets who will betray you
unto your enemies. Come back to your jobs and
work. We are Americans, always ready to forgive
and take our neighbors in as our brothers."

In contrast, Murray's statement was restrained, even tem-
perate.

All we ask for the workingman is justice, the job
security and the benefits already granted to his
compatriots working for U.S. Steel and the other
companies who have already recognized that
their demands were simply fair and equitable.
We have no intentions to deliver anything into
the hands of any foreign power or ideology, only
to make life better for the American workingman
whose labor makes our American way of life possible and a reality.

Daniel left the paper in the taxi as he got out in front of the
union headquarters. Carrying his valise as he walked through
the whole floor that served as the S.W.O.C.'s regional offices,
he could not help thinking of the difference in organization
between the present and the last attempt to unionize the steel
industry in 1919. Then everything had seemed haphazard and
improvised. Now all was planned. There were a complete
information section, with over forty employees, who serviced
the newspapers and wire services with up-to-date reports on
the organizing activities; a statistical section, which kept
abreast of all economic trends that might affect the union's
position; a striker's help-fund section, which supplied aid,
financial and otherwise, to the members. There was no doubt
about it. It was very different. But was it?
Despite the application of the most modern business tech-
niques and the solidest financial support any union organizing
effort had ever had, something was missing. Daniel could feel

it but could not quite put his finger on it. Perhaps it was just that the union itself, moving forward on the crest of the pro-union wave of the past few years, was overconfident and did not recognize the determination of the opposition. The sudden collapse of Big Steel last year, the success of the Textile Workers' drive in the South, the organization of the automobile workers at General Motors represented a trend which perhaps led to an illusion. In each of these victories it was the largest companies with which agreements had been reached, the companies whose share of their respective markets was so great that the net results could not affect them more than just a little. But the smaller companies, to which the differences had a major effect on their profit margin, had good reason to battle on. The Ford Motor Company was as far from agreement as it had ever been And so was Little Steel. And each of these companies' individual managements had translated this into a personal battle to retain what it felt was control of its own business and freedom. Neither Henry Ford nor Tom Girdler was about to bend his knee to the serfs. On the contrary, they felt that those who worked for them should be grateful to them for the opportunity to serve in their vineyards, especially after all they had given to them.

The executive offices were at the back of the floor, away from the elevators. Each with windows looking out on the city, respectably if not expensively furnished, rugs on the floor, in contrast with the mass grouping of most employees in large open rooms with as many as thirty or forty desks crammed into space big enough for half as many. Now the union leaders were as effectively isolated from the rank and file of their organization as any executive of the companies with which they did battle. Suddenly Daniel knew what it was. A new hierarchy was in the process of developing. Sooner or later, the man inside that office, behind the closed door, had to lose touch with the people outside, those whom he represented. No longer was there an emotional relationship. Now it was a calculated representation of an ideal that itself had turned into another form of big business.

Now Daniel could understand the pressure on Phil Murray to perform. Their organization was much like any division of

General Motors. They had goals to reach, and if for some reason, whatever that might be, they were not achieved, new managers would be found who could reach those goals. The battle had to be joined. even if the outcome was in doubt. Murray had to prove that he was not afraid, nor was he shirking his task. And all the while, he was aware that Lewis was sitting back there in Washington, careful to maintain his position as the man who had settled Big Steel without a strike, and because of that carefully avoided taking a position within the union councils either pro or con regarding a strike effort. He was quite willing to leave it to Murray. If he failed, he would hang himself; if he won, Lewis could come in and share the glory because he had shown the way and had confidence that Murray could do it.

Daniel stopped in front of the door that had MR. MURRAY painted on it in gold letters and turned to the secretary seated at the desk just outside. She was a new girl, one he had never seen before. "Is Mr. Murray in?"

She looked up from her typewriter. "May I ask who wishes to see him?"

"Daniel Huggins."

She picked up the telephone. "Mr. Huggins is here to see you, Mr. Murray." A moment later she put it down, a new respect coming into her voice. "You may go right in, sir."

Daniel thought Murray looked drawn and tired as he rose from behind his desk and came toward him. He shook Daniel's hand warmly. "I'm glad you're back."

"I am too," Daniel said. And meant it.

"Grab a chair," Murray said, going back to his own seat. "How's the baby?"

"Fine."

"Your wife must be very proud. Apologize to her for me for having to pull you back so fast."

Daniel met his eyes. "My wife is dead."

A stunned look came into Murray's eyes. "You never said anything."

"There was nothing to say. It happened, and it's over."

Murray was silent for a moment. "I'm sorry, Daniel. If I had known, I wouldn't have pressed you."

"It's okay," Daniel said. "I did the things I had to do and now I'm back to work."

"Is your child in good hands?"

"I've got a fine woman to take care of him and the house. It's going to be all right."

Murray took a deep breath. "If there's anything I can do to help, you let me know."

"Thank you." Daniel waited. The amenities had been disposed of quickly, but from the moment he had come into the office he had felt there was something wrong. It was nothing he could put his finger on, just the feeling that Murray did not seem completely comfortable with him.

Murray shuffled some papers on his desk, finally coming up with the one he sought. Holding it in his hand, he glanced at it for a moment, then spoke. "I've got a new job for you. I'm bringing you into the office here as coordinator of the sub-regional offices in the Midwest. It will be up to you to see that none of them go off half-cocked on their own."

"I don't know if I'm an office man," Daniel said. "I'm used to being out in the field. Why can't I just stay on my old job?"

"You're becoming too important to be running around in the field with the organizers. We need someone in here to keep an eye on the overall picture for us."

"Who do I report to?"

"David McDonald in Pittsburgh. He's taking over day-to-day operations. I'm moving back to Washington, where I can keep pressure on the government."

Daniel nodded. McDonald was a good man, a veteran of many years in the steel industry. There had been talk that he was Murray's heir apparent, just as the talk had been that Murray was Lewis' heir apparent. Now, at least, the first part of the rumor had been confirmed. But Daniel could find no fault with it. McDonald was the logical candidate.

"Do I have any specific authority in the new job?"

"I thought you would get together with Dave and work that out between you," Murray answered.

Daniel took a cigar from his inside coat pocket. He bit off the end and lit it sowly, his eyes fixed on Murray all the while. Finally, when the cigar was going, he leaned back in the chair. "Okay, Phil," he said quietly. "We've known each other a long time. You can tell me the truth. Why am I being kicked upstairs?"

Murray flushed. "It's not exactly that."

"It's not exactly anything else either," Daniel said.

Murray shook his head slowly. "You won't let me off the hook, will you?"

Daniel was silent.

"Too many people have heard you say you were against the strike. Too many people know of your affair with the Girdler girl. They just don't trust you."

"Do *you* trust me?"

"That's a stupid question," Murray flared. "If I didn't trust you, I wouldn't give you another job."

"Maybe I'd better quit anyway," David said. "I don't like running up blind alleys."

Murray's voice was forceful. "You're not quitting. I don't want it, David doesn't and Lewis doesn't. You're the only man we know who has worked in all the subregional offices, the only one we can depend on to give us a clear picture of what's happening there. Besides, it won't be for long. When this strike is settled, we've got something in mind for you."

"It's not going to be settled for a long time," Daniel said. "I can't seem to make any of you understand just how tough Girdler is. He's managed to forge an unholy alliance with the other independents, and they're going all the way with him."

Murray was thoughtful. "An unholy alliance. I can use that phrase in the press conference I'm holding in Washington next week."

"Be my guest," Daniel said.

"Memorial Day is about three weeks off. We're planning mass demonstrations all over the region. I think that unholy alliance you talk about might have second thoughts when they see the mass of workers behind us."

"I don't think they'll give a damn," Daniel said. "They're out to break this strike no matter what it costs."

"Daniel, stop fighting me." Murray's voice was suddenly weary. "I have enough people on my back now. Don't make it impossible for me to keep you. Just help me."

It was the first time Murray had ever come out and spoken so bluntly to him. It was only friends who talked to each other that honestly. Murray had been there when he needed help. For almost twenty years Murray had been there. Now it was his turn. "Okay," he said. "What's the first thing you want me to do?"

"Work on the Memorial Day demonstrations. See that they go off without any trouble."

"I'll do my best," Daniel said. He got to his feet. "If I'm going to stay in Chicago, I'd better go out and find myself a place to live."

Murray looked up at him. "Thanks, Daniel."

"You don't have to thank me, Phil," Daniel said. "I owe you."

Murray smiled wearily. "We can argue about who owes whom someday. Right now the important thing is to get the job done. And incidentally, I forgot to mention that the executive board approved a salary of eighty-five hundred dollars a year to go with your new job."

Daniel laughed. "You should have mentioned that first. Maybe I wouldn't have given you such a hard time."

Murray laughed with him. "If it were the money you wanted, you could have taken that job with the I.A. But I knew better."

Chapter 18

THE OFFICE assigned to him was small, with just enough room for his desk and two chairs, one behind it and one in front. In the corner of the room was a small coatrack. The walls, painted white, were bare. But he did have one window, and if it had not been for that he might have gone completely mad in his first week.

Frustration was the game. He began telephoning all the subregional offices to align his contacts with the local organizers. They were friendly enough, but not about to relinquish any of their power or authority to anyone without specific instruction, and they had received no communication as yet from the central office as to his position. He had placed innumerable calls to McDonald in Pittsburgh, but had never reached him. Each time, he was assured by the secretary that McDonald would return his call, but at the end of the week, he accepted the fact that it was not about to happen.

The papers on Friday afternoon played up Murray's press conference in Washington. The phrase "Unholy Alliance" caught on. It was jingoistic journalese. The newspapers loved it. Even Gabriel Heatter used it on his national evening radio newscast. Daniel picked up the telephone and called Murray in Washington.

He felt a minor surprise when Murray came to the phone. "Congratulations," Daniel said. "The press conference went down well. The newspapers here gave it a big play."

Murray was obviously pleased. "Good. I think we're beginning to make some headway. Public opinion is beginning to move our way. How are you doing?"

"Going crazy," Daniel said shortly. "I'm not doing anything. I'm being locked out."

"I don't understand." Murray sounded genuinely puzzled. "You talk to Dave?"

"Can't get him on the phone. And the subregionals haven't been officially notified as to my position. I'm out here in left field with nothing coming my way."

"I'll talk to him," Murray said.

"I don't want to make things difficult for you," Daniel said. "You have enough on your mind. Maybe it would be better if I moved on."

"No." Murray's voice was emphatic. "Stay with it. I'll get it straightened out."

"You don't owe me anything," Daniel said. "Besides, I have the feeling I should be back in California with my kid. Bad enough he has no mother; he shouldn't be without a father too."

"Give me until the end of the month," Murray said. "If we can't straighten it out by then, you can go where you want."

"Fair enough," Daniel said. He put down the telephone and took the bottle of whiskey from the bottom drawer of his desk. He poured himself a drink and turned to the window and stared out while sipping his drink. Rain and dusk were falling on Chicago, and as he watched the buildings disappear and the lights come on, he began to feel closed in and trapped.

He got to his feet and threw open his office door. To his surprise, the big office was empty except for one lone girl huddled over her typewriter at the far end of the room. He glanced at his watch. Five o'clock.

Times had changed. It hadn't been so long ago that union workers never went home. After hours they would sit around talking about what they were doing and what they hoped to achieve. But now it was like any other business. Five o'clock and everyone went home.

Holding the drink in his hand, he walked down the room to the girl. She looked up as she heard his footsteps. "What are you doing?" he asked.

"Mr Gerard wants this report on his desk when he comes in first thing Monday morning," she answered.

"Mr. Gerard?" It was a new name to him. "What department is that?"

"Legal," she said.

"What's your name?"

"Nancy."

"Nancy, do you like working for a union?"

She glanced down at her typewriter. "It's a job."

"Why the union?" he asked. "Do you feel you're making a contribution to the labor movement and the betterment of working conditions?"

"I don't know anything about that," she said. "I answered an ad in the paper, even though they were only paying fifteen dollars a week."

"Is that a fair salary for your job?"

"Most places pay about nineteen a week for the same job," she answered. "But there aren't any other jobs."

"Maybe what you need is a union," he said, grinning. He finished his drink. "Want a drink, Nancy?"

She shook her head. "No, thanks. I have to finish this."

"Okay," he said, and started back to his office.

Her voice stopped him. "Mr. Huggins." He turned to look at her. "Can I ask you a question?"

"Sure."

"Ever since they put your name on the door and you moved in, everybody's been wondering exactly what is it you do and what department you're with. You're kind of a mystery man around here."

He laughed. "Ever hear of the limbo department?"

"Limbo?" she was puzzled. "I don't think I have."

"That's where I'm at," he said, and went back to his office and closed the door.

It was still drizzling when he left the office and walked to the parking lot for his car. He started the engine and switched on the headlights, then sat there with the motor running. The idea of going back to his empty apartment didn't attract him at all. He had read all the papers to come out that day, and the prospect of sitting alone with a bottle of whiskey, listening to the radio, wasn't his idea of spending an evening. He thought about going to the movies, but that too was empty and offered no real escape from his restlessness.

Impulsively he drove down into South Chicago, to a bar near the Republic Steel mill, which he had helped organize. The bar was crowded with men, steelworkers, who had spent the best part of their day on the rainy picket line. Against the wall, neatly stacked, were their picket signs. REPUBLIC STEEL ON STRIKE! FOR A LIVING WAGE, GO C.I.O.! Some were printed, but there were many that had been hand-lettered by the men themselves.

He pushed his way up to the bar and ordered a double whiskey. While waiting for the drink, he glanced down the bar. There were maybe two whiskey shot glasses in a field of beer glasses. The strike had already made changes in the workers' drinking habits. Steelworkers drank whiskey. Beer was usually nothing but a chaser.

The bartender put the whiskey in front of him and picked up the dollar bill. He put the quarter change on the bar as Daniel raised his glass. Daniel took his drink and was about to walk back to a booth at the side of the room when a voice called from the end of the bar. "Hey! Big Dan!"

He recognized the man, a grizzled veteran of many years in the mill, one of the first to join the union. "How're y' doin', Sandy?"

Sandy picked up his beer and worked his way up the bar to him. "Okay, Big Dan," he said. "I didn't expect to see you down here again."

"Why not?" Daniel asked.

"We heard you went out to California."

"I did. But I've been back more than a week now."

"You haven't been down to the union office." He was referring to the subregional office.

"They've been keeping me back at headquarters in Chicago," Daniel said. "They gave me a new job."

"There's been talk about that too," Sanday said dourly.

Daniel looked at him. "I didn't know that people were so interested in me. What other talk did you hear?"

Sandy was embarrassed. "Things."

"Give me another whiskey," Daniel said to the bartender. When he got the drink, he took the two glasses in his hand. "C'mon, Sandy, let's sit down."

The steelworker followed him to a booth and sat down opposite him. Daniel pushed the other glass of whiskey toward him. "Cheers." They drank. "We've been friends, Sandy," he said. "You can tell me what they've been talking about."

Sandy stared into his glass, then looked up at him. "Mind you, I didn't believe what they were saying."

Daniel was silent.

Sandy took another sip of his drink. "They said you were against the strike an' that you were very cozy with someone in the Girdler family. And because of that, they're keeping you in headquarters."

Daniel nodded toward the men at the bar. "What do *they* think?"

Sandy's voice was contemptuous. "Hunkies, Swedes and niggers. They don't know how to think. They believe what they're told."

"And they're told that I'm not to be trusted?"

It was Sandy's turn to be silent. Daniel gestured for refills. When the drinks came, he swallowed another shot. "How does it look from the line?" he asked. "The mill shut down?"

"Not completely. It's running at about forty percent. A lot of men were afraid to come out after Girdler said that no striker would ever be rehired." He took a sip from his glass. "How does it look from headquarters?"

"I spoke to Murray today," Daniel answered. "He feels it's beginning to swing our way. He's counting on the demonstrations across the country on Memorial Day to really bring public pressure on the steel companies to settle."

Sandy nodded. "We got a big meeting scheduled for that day. All of us out of the Republic mill will be there. We expect a turnout of maybe three hundred people over at Sam's Place."

"That's the big meeting hall we used before?"

Sandy nodded and lifted his glass. "I'd feel better if you were back here with us."

"So would I," Daniel said.

"This guy Davis they sent down to replace you. He's a bookkeeper type. College man. I don't think he ever swung a shovel in his life." Sandy finished his drink. "I know he's supposed to be good. He says all the right things. But I have the feeling that they're all things he learned in school somewhere. Do you think there's a chance they might send you back?"

Daniel got to his feet. "I don't know," he said heavily. "I really don't know what they're going to do." He held out his hand. "Good luck."

"Good luck to you too," Sandy said.

Daniel crossed the street in the rain to his car and opened the door. Three men appeared from the shadows of a building and came toward him. Daniel felt the hairs on the back of his neck tighten.

They stopped a few feet from him. "Big Dan?"

"Yes," he said.

"Don't come back here," one of them said. "We don't like finks or stoolies."

"I'm still a member in good standing," Daniel said. "And my job says I can go where I want."

"We don't give a shit," the man said. "You're a fucking spy who sold us out for a piece of Girdler pussy. We don't need pricks like you around."

They began to move toward him. Daniel slipped his gun from the shoulder holster. "Stop right there," he said quietly. "Unless you'd like to get your balls blown off."

The men froze, staring at him.

"Now go back across the street to the other side," he said. "And don't do anything you might be sorry for."

He watched the men cross the street, and as they went up onto the sidewalk, he got into the car and started the engine.

They turned as they heard the motor and ran out into the street after him as he drove off. He heard them shouting. "Fink! Cuntlapper!" Then he turned the corner and he could hear no more.

The steel mill was on the road home. He drove past it slowly. The night picket line was only a few men marching forlornly in the rain. Behind the gates were the uniformed guards, smart and dry in their rainproof slickers. He counted at least twenty guards to the four men on the picket line. He turned at the next corner and drove back to Chicago.

He was about to insert the key in his apartment door, but it swung open even before he touched it. He pushed it the rest of the way open and stepped inside, his gun again in his hand.

Chris's voice came from the kitchen. "Where the hell have you been, Daniel? I've been trying to keep this dinner warm for you for almost three hours."

Chapter 19

IT WAS about two o'clock in the morning, and his eyes suddenly opened. He closed them for a moment. No use. He was wide awake. He moved quietly in order not to awaken her. As he turned, he could see the faint outline of her sleeping form, the scent of her perfume mingling with the odors of their lovemaking. He slipped out of bed and, closing the bedroom door quietly behind him, went into the living room.

He didn't turn on the light. He knew where the bottle was, took it and poured himself a shot. He swallowed it and sat down at the window and stared out at the rain splashing like gold drops against the yellow street lights. He took another drink. But it didn't help. There was a hollow, drained, empty feeling deep inside him. Even the thought of the loving didn't completely take it away.

The bedroom door opened, and light spilled into the room from behind him. He turned and saw her standing there naked. "I didn't mean to wake you," he said gently. "Better get a robe on. It's damp."

"What's troubling you, Daniel?"

"Put a robe on first," he said.

She disappeared and came back a moment later, still naked. "You don't have a robe, and I didn't bring one with me."

He laughed. She was right. He had never owned a bath-robe, nor a pair of pajamas. If he slept in anything, it was his B.V.D.'s. "Take one of my shirts."

The shirt fell to her knees. "I feel ridiculous."

"Better than catching cold." He poured another drink. "Want one?"

She shook her head and waited until he swallowed the whis-key. "What is it, Daniel? I've never seen you like this."

"It's like I suddenly became the invisible man," he said.

"Is it the new job?" she asked.

He stared at her. "You know about it?"

"Yes, of course."

"How did you find out about it?"

"The same way I found out where you were living. From the confidential files in my Uncle Tom's office."

"They know things like that?"

"They keep a record on everything and everybody," she said.

"He knows about us?"

She nodded.

"He ever say anything?"

"He was angry at first; then he calmed down. He still didn't like it, but he said it could have been worse. You could have been A Jew Commie or a nigger."

His laugh was bitter. "Would you be surprised to learn that he knows more about my new job than most of the union members?"

"He told me they were moving you out of the way because you didn't think they should call the strike. He also said if they hadn't gone out on strike they would have fired you outright, but they're afraid to rock the boat at this time. They feel getting rid of you would upset too many of the men you organized."

He shook his head. "Then they figured wrong. I found out tonight that nobody really gives a damn. Somebody really did a hatchet job on me. Everything I said got twisted out of shape and thrown into the rumor mill. Even about you and me. That I was selling them down the river because of you."

"They have to know you better than that."

"I think Phil Murray does. But I doubt if any of the others share the same conviction."

"I'm sorry," she said. "What are you going to do?"

"I honestly don't know," he said. "Murray wants me to wait. He says it will all get straightened out. But I'm not sure that I can wait the way he wants. I'm not used to sitting in an office not doing anything."

"Why don't you talk to Uncle Tom?" she asked "I know from what he said that he respects you, even if he might not like you."

He looked at her. "I can't do that. I've been living on this side of the street so long there's no way I could cross over. Besides, if I did, then everything they're saying about me would be true."

She moved closer to him. "I love you. I don't like seeing you on the rack like this."

He didn't say anything, just looked at her.

"I know I said I would wait for you to call me," she said. "But I couldn't. I missed you too much. Daniel, I want to stay here with you."

He took a deep breath. "I would like that too. But it would only make things worse."

"Then what are we going to do?"

"Wait," he said. "The way Phil Murray told me. Maybe when this is over, things will be better."

"What if you can't wait the way he wants and decide to go away?" she asked.

"I'll make you a promise," he said. "If I should decide to go away, I'll take you with me."

He saw the tears jump into her eyes and pulled her to him. "Don't be silly," he said, kissing her cheek.

"I'm not being silly," she snuffled. "I'm just being happy." She looked up into his face. "You do love me, don't you?"

He smiled, teasing. "Don't get personal."

"Just a little?" she asked in a small voice.

"Not just a little," he laughed, kissing her on the mouth. "A lot."

He looked down at the calendar on his desk. Friday, May 28, 1937. The two weeks just past had dragged interminably. He had waited for the call that never came. Despite Murray's promise, McDonald had never called. Meanwhile, he felt the rising excitement swirling in the office around him. He knew plans were being made for the Memorial Day demonstration, but no one spoke to him or included him in the conversations about it. He found out more about the progress of the strike from the newspapers than he did in the office. He glanced at his watch. It was after five thirty.

He opened the door of his office and looked out. The big outer office was empty. He closed the door and went back to his desk. He reached for the telephone and placed a call to Phil Murray in Washington. Mr. Murray had gone to Pittsburgh and would not be back in the office until Monday. He tried Murray's home in Pittsburgh, but there was no answer.

He took the bottle of whiskey from his desk. It was almost empty. He held the bottle to his mouth and drained it. There wasn't enough to warrant a glass. Again he stared down at the calendar. Murray had asked him to wait until the end of the month. For all intents and purposes, this was the end of the month. A thought ran through his mind.

Monday was the thirty-first. Could it be that they were keeping him here, safely out of the way, until after the demonstrations on Sunday? That what Girdler had told Chris was right? They were afraid that he might rock the boat?

He wondered what would happen on Monday. Would Murray call and tell him regretfully that he couldn't work anything out? Or would they then feel he was safe enough to give him a real job? Either way, it didn't matter now. He spread his hands flat on the desk top and stared at them. Something had changed inside him, but nothing showed in his hands. They were still the same. Big, square, a workingman's hands. Not the hands of a man supposed to think or feel. And that was all he had ever been. Working hands. Moved and directed by someone else's brains and thoughts and desires.

A choking wave of anger rose inside him. He clenched his hands into fists and smashed them down on the desk. Pain rose sharply up through his arms. He held his fists up to his face and stared at them. His knuckles were white, and blood seeped through the broken skin. Slowly he unclenched them. Whatever it was he thought they were holding, it was time now for him to let go.

Time for him to leave, time for him to move on, time for him to discover what was going on in his own head. He had begun to open the desk drawer when a knock came at the door.

"Mr. Huggins?" It was a girl's voice.

He went to the door and opened it. Nancy stood there, a wide-eyed look on her face. "Yes?" he asked gruffly.

"I came back to get something from my desk," she said quickly. "Then I heard a crash from your office. Are you all right?"

He nodded slowly. "I'm okay."

A faint relief came into her face. "I'll go, then. I'm sorry to have disturbed you."

"That's all right, Nancy," he said. "Thank you for your concern."

She turned to leave. He stopped her. "Nancy."

She turned back. "Yes, Mr. Huggins?"

"Would you have time to type a letter for me?"

"Will it take long? I have a date tonight and have to get home to change."

"It shouldn't take long," he said. "But it's very important to me."

"Okay. Give me a minute to get my steno book."

He watched her walk toward her desk, then went back to his own desk and began to empty the drawers.

Chapter 20

IT WAS just after lunch when she arrived at the apartment. She came into the bedroom and saw him bent over the open suitcase. "Need any help?"

He shook his head. "I'm almost finished. There wasn't much." He emptied the last of the bureau drawers and snapped the valise shut. "That does it."

She stepped aside as he carried the suitcase into the living room and put it down next to the other one near the front door. "My bags are in the car," she said.

He straightened up. The train didn't leave until six o'clock. "I've got a half-bottle of whiskey. There's no point in leaving it."

She nodded, and he took the bottle of whiskey and two glasses. He gave her one glass and held the bottle toward her. "Just a little," she said.

He splashed some whiskey into the glass and filled his own. "Luck," he said.

She sipped it and made a face. "How can you drink this stuff? It tastes awful."

He laughed. "You'd better learn to like it. It's poor man's liquor. Them dry martinis costs twice as much."

She was silent.

He looked at her. "Sure you want to come? It's going to be a very different life for you. You can still change your mind. I'll understand."

She smiled. "I'm not letting you off that easily." She took another sip. "This whiskey really is not that bad."

He laughed.

"Did you speak to Mrs. Torgersen?" she asked.

"Yes. She's already moved into the baby's room so we can have the other bedroom. She sounded very pleased that you were coming with me. She likes you."

"She's known me for a long time," she said. "How's the baby?"

A note of pride came into his voice. "She says he's just fine. Getting bigger. Gained almost a pound and is no trouble at all. Sleeps right through the night."

"Anxious to see him?"

He looked at her, then nodded. "Yes. Funny, I never thought of myself as a father. But when I held him and looked down at him and realized that I was part of making him, I felt I was going to live forever."

She held her glass toward him. "I'll take a little bit more."

He covered the bottom of the glass. "What's it like outside?"

"Sunny and warm," she said.

"Good," he said. "At least the strikers are in luck. It's not easy to look confident with the rain pissing in your face. The girl who typed my letter told me that her boss was very pleased. Paramount movie newsreel is coming out to cover the South Chicago demonstration. It'll be in six thousand theaters next Tuesday."

"I'm glad you won't be with them," she said. "At breakfast this morning, I heard Uncle Tom on the phone. He was talking to someone in the South Chicago police headquarters. He said he was expecting trouble at the mill, and he asked for a hundred and fifty policemen to help protect it. When he came back to the table, he was smiling and told my aunt that if the Commies came looking for trouble they were going to get more than they bargained for."

He stared at her. "He's got almost a hundred men inside the gates. Why does he need the cops outside?"

"I don't know," she answered. "I was too busy figuring out how to leave the house with my bags without their finding out."

"He's going to be disappointed," Daniel said. "The meeting is in a hall a few blocks away. They're not even going near the mill."

She didn't answer.

A thought flashed through his mind. "Your Uncle Tom seemed sure that they were going to be at the plant?"

She nodded.

He put down his drink. "I'd better get right over there to make sure they don't go anywhere near the mill."

"It's not your business anymore, Daniel," she said. "You resigned. Remember?"

"I remember Pittsburgh in 1919," he said. "A lot of men got hurt because nobody had the guts to talk sense to them."

"This is 1937," she said. "And it's not your fight anymore."

"Maybe it isn't," he said. "But I got a lot of those men out there today into the union, and I don't want it on my conscience if any of them get hurt."

She didn't answer.

"Give me the keys to the car," he said.

"Let go of it, Daniel," she said. "We're going to start a new life. You told me that yesterday."

"Chris. There's no way I can start a new life over the dead bodies of my friends. Not if I have a chance to prevent it. Give me the keys."

"I'll go with you," she said.

"No. You wait here for me."

"You said you would take me with you wherever you go." Her voice was steady. "It starts here."

The streets in front of Sam's Place were crowded with cars and people, and there was no place that Dan could park the car. He stopped in the middle of the street and got out. "You park the car in the next block and wait for me."

Chris's face was pale. She nodded.

Dan turned and made his way toward the meeting hall. It had turned unexpectedly hot, and the crowd overflowing the street seemed more like a group of people at a family outing than a serious group of strikers. Many of the men had brought their families to the meeting, and women and children were moving around in the crowd of shirt-sleeved men.

Daniel pushed his way through the crowd into the meeting hall. It was packed solid with people. On the small platform at the far end of the hall several men were sitting, while one man was at a lectern shouting.

"There is only one way to show the cops that they do not intimidate us, that Girdler is not the law. They must see that we, the people, the strikers, are strong enough, brave enough to look them in the face and spit in their eye!"

A roar of approval went up from the crowd.

The speaker looked down at a piece of paper in his hand. "Be it resolved that we, the members of the Steelworkers Union, Local ———, condemn the arbitrary and oppressive tactics of the Chicago Police Department in their attempts to frighten and intimidate the workers from exercising their consitutional right to free speech and strike for a better way of American life, All in favor say 'Aye.' "

The roar of Ayes deafened the ears.

"Let's show 'em now!" a voice yelled from the crowd.

"Yeah," another voice shouted. "Let 'em see what a real picket line is. Not just ten men but a thousand!"

Daniel made his way to the platform just as the hall rang with approval for the suggestion. He pushed the speaker away from the lectern. "Hold it!" he yelled at the crowd. "Hold it!"

The meeting was still in a turmoil. The speaker turned to Daniel. "Get out of here, Huggins. We don't want you here," he said in a voice that reached only to Daniel.

"You're Davis," Daniel said. "You've got to listen to me. I found out there are a hundred and fifty cops out there spoiling for trouble. You keep the meeting here. If they get outside in front of the mill, a lot of people are going to be hurt. Not only men, but women and children too."

"Workers have a right to express themselves," Davis said.

"Their leaders have a responsibility to see that they don't get hurt. In 1919 I saw what happened when leaders abdicated that responsibility. It can happen here."

"No," Davis said. "There are too many of us. Besides, the cops wouldn't dare try anything with the newsreel cameras out there. That's why we arranged to get them here."

"Cameras don't stop bullets," Daniel said. He turned back to the crowd. "Brothers!" he shouted. "You know me. Many of you were brought into this union with me. More than anyone else I want to win this strike. But we're not going to win it by demonstrating against the Chicago police. We're going to win it by closing down production at the mills, by getting the rest of the workers to join us. Let us turn our efforts here to that end, to find ways and means of persuading our brothers that our battle is their battle. Here, in the union hall, is where the battle will be won. Not out there in the fields in front of the mill."

A sarcastic voice shouted up from the crowd. "We know you, Big Dan. We know how you sold us out for a piece of Girdler pussy. We know you didn't want us to strike."

"That's not true!" Daniel shouted.

"If it's not true," another voice shouted, "then join us. Don't fight us."

Daniel looked down at the suddenly silent hall. "I'll join you," he said. "But only the men will go. Make sure that your women and children don't follow us."

A roar came from the crowd. Two young men leaped on the platform and, picking up the American flags, turned and started up the aisle.

Daniel looked at Davis. "You've got to help me, man. Let's try to stop them at least a block from the mill." He didn't wait for an answer but leaped from the platform and marched up the aisle between the two flag bearers.

The sun outside had turned bright and hot. Daniel tore off his jacket and held it over his arm.

"Across the field," A voice shouted. "The streets are blocked by the police."

Slowly, purposefully, they began walking toward the plant, about a mile across the open field. Daniel turned and looked behind him. Men were streaming behind them, in an unorganized, shapeless form. Despite Daniel's warning, women and children had joined them. There was an air of almost childlike gaiety in the crowd, more like people going to a Sunday-school picnic than a picket line.

"Get rid of the women and children!" he shouted back at them. His voice was lost in the noise. A hand pulled at his arm. He turned.

"Big Dan." Sandy was next to him with Davis. "I knew you'd show up."

Daniel didn't answer. He looked at Davis. "Look over there. There's an army of cops waiting for us. Now do you believe me?"

Davis stared. "I see them. But they won't do anything. The newsreel truck is right behind them. We got to get in close enough so they can film how big a crowd we are."

"What's more important? People's lives or movies?"

"The movies will take our message all over the country," Davis said.

Daniel looked at him. It was no use. It didn't make sense. They were going like lambs to the slaughter. "A block away," he said heavily. "Try to stop them a block away."

But there was no stopping them; the press of the crowd behind pushed them on. Daniel saw the police begin taking out their guns and clubs. For a moment, a picture flashed through his mind. The Boche were waiting just across no-man's-land.

They were halfway through the last open field, about two hundred feet away from the police, when Daniel turned his back on them and help up his hands to stop the crowd.

"Now!" he shouted. "Form your picket line here!"

An unexpected voice joined him. "Yes," Davis shouted. "Form the line here. One flag to the right, one to the left and spread out behind them."

The crowd milled around uncertainly, not knowing what to do. Daniel pushed at one of the flag bearers. "Get going, man!" The flag bearer began to move off. "Okay, now," Daniel shouted to the crowd. "Follow him!"

"Follow him!" Davis shouted.

Daniel glanced at him. "Thanks."

Davis' voice was grim. "Don't thank me. I'm scared."

"With some luck," Daniel said, "we may still be okay."

But luck was not to be with them. He heard the first few sounds of the shots. Then a sledgehammer hit him in the back, and he pitched forward to the ground. He tried to pick himself up on his hands, but his legs wouldn't support him. He heard the sounds of women screaming and men shouting in their panic. Then there were blue-uniformed police all around him, lashing out indiscriminately with their truncheons and billy clubs. He saw Davis and Sandy fall to the ground under a hail of men in uniform, beating them long after they were inert and prostrate.

He felt the tears spring to his eyes. "Oh, shit," he cried, the hurt in his soul greater than the one in his body. "Shit, shit, shit."

Then his arms gave way, and he fell into an eclipse of the sun.

Now

MAYBE BECAUSE it was Sunday. Or lunchtime. Or maybe the Arab oil embargo of last spring had left its imprint on the psyche of the American motorist. But I had been sitting on the low stone wall for almost an hour and not one car had passed.

I remember my father's indignation as the lines formed at the gas stations and factories began to close, laying off thousands of workers. He held a news conference at which he blasted everybody. The President, the Congress, the oil companies. "The same old story," he had growled. "They're all in cahoots to bring up prices and pick the pockets of the American workers who built the very oil fields the fruits of which they are now denied. We gave the Arabs the power by developing their resources at the expense of our own and the American worker because we were told it would be cheaper. Now we find out how cheap it really is. The cost is blackmail and extortion. And there is only one way to deal with blackmailers and extortionists. Exterminate them. We have all the valid and legal reasons. Our national security, our very lives and welfare are threatened. Send in the marines!"

Accused by many of the papers and commentators of old-

361

fashioned jingoism and warmongering, of being pro-Zionist and anti-Arab, he replied in scornful tones. "We didn't fight two major wars to make the world safe for the Arabs and the oil companies so that they could enrich themselves at our expense. Our country has a history of standing up and fighting for its rights. If we don't do that now, we may turn around five years from now and find we have delivered up ourselves and maybe all of Western civilization into the hands of Cain."

It wasn't that long ago; but now, it was forever. At least for my father. He was gone, and no one heard his voice anymore. Maybe. Except me. I wondered how long it would take for me to stop hearing him.

"When you know me, Jonathan."

"I know you, Father. I've always known you."

His voice was gentle. "You only thought you did. But now you're beginning to learn."

"Learn what?"

"Where I come from. Who I am."

"Who you were," I said pointedly.

He chuckled. "A point of view."

"Nothing's changed. You're still what I always thought you were."

"I never claimed to be anything else. I will always be whatever you think I am. Just as you will always be whatever you think you will be."

"I'm getting ready to go home, Father. I'm getting tired of sitting on walls and fence posts and standing at the sides of roads. I'm not discovering anything anymore."

"You're lonely. But be patient. The journey will soon be at an end. Then you will go home and put all you have learned together."

"I don't know what it is I'm supposed to learn."

"Love, my son. And that only a fool throws it away."

"I'm tired of all that shit, Father. I'm going home. Now."

No." His voice was strong and sharp. "Look up the road, my son, and discover why no cars have passed in this last hour and why you have been sitting on this particular wall at this particular moment in time."

A mile down the road a car had crested the hill and was moving rapidly toward me. I watched it, the sun sparkling brightly from its silver radiator. It sped past me, a white Rolls Corniche convertible, top down, driven by a girl with sun-yellow hair streaming behind her in the wind. Several hundred yards down the road I saw its brake lights go on, then, as the car stopped, the white backup lights as it reversed toward me.

The car backed off onto the side ramp and came to a stop in front of me. The girl in the car and I just sat there looking at each other. We didn't speak. Just looked at each other.

She was beautiful. Suntanned bronze, almost white hair falling down below her shoulders now that the wind was not taking, high cheekbones, wide mouth and firm chin. But it was her eyes that did it. Pale gray with a splash of blue. I had seen them a thousand times before. But I didn't know where.

Finally she smiled, her teeth white and crinkles at the corners of her eyes making them even bluer. Her voice was low and soft but very clear and distinct. "Humpty Dumpty sat on a wall."

"Humpty Dumpty had a great fall," I answered.

"All the king's horses—"

"And all the king's men—"

We finished together. "Couldn't put Humpty Dumpty together again." We laughed.

"Are you Humpty Dumpty?" she asked.

"I don't know," I answered. "Do you think I am?"

"You could be," she said seriously.

"No. That's a nursery rhyme."

"Then why are you sitting on the wall like that?"

"I didn't know until you came along. Now I do. I've been waiting for you. I almost left but I was talked out of it."

Her eyes glanced around quickly. "By whom? I don't see anyone."

"A friend. But he's gone now."

Her eyes came back to me. "I thought I heard you call me. That's why I stopped."

I didn't say anything.

"I did hear someone call me," she said.

I climbed down from the wall. "I called you, Princess." I

picked up my backpack and slung it over the side of the car into the back seat, then got in beside her.

"Princess," she said thoughtfully. "Only my mother has ever called me that. My name is—"

I cut her off. "Don't tell me, Princess. I don't want to know."

"And what do I call you? Humpty Dumpty?"

"Jonathan."

She nodded her head. "I like it. It suits you." She put the car into gear and it moved silently, effortlessly onto the road. We were doing 60 before I could count that far. "I'm taking you home."

"Okay."

She glanced at me. "How old are you?"

"Eighteen," I answered. I wasn't pushing too far. Only two months.

"You look older," she said. I didn't answer as she reached into the well between the two bucket seats and came up with a gold cigarette case. She flipped it open. "Light one for me."

Machine-rolled, chocolate-brown paper, gold-tipped thin marijuana. I was impressed. I lit the joint. It was good shit, maybe the best I'd ever had. Two tokes and I was up there. I passed the cigarette to her. She stuck it in the corner of her mouth and let it hang there. Two seconds later when I looked at the speedometer, we were doing 85. I reached over and took the joint from her mouth.

"Why did you do that?" she asked.

I gestured at the speedometer. "You said you were taking me home. I just want to make sure we get there."

The car slowed down to 60. "I can handle it."

"I'm sure you can," I said, pinching out the joint. "But I'm the cautious type."

She was silent. A few minutes later she turned into the West Palm Beach exit ramp and coasted to a stop at the toll-booth.

The toll collectors all seemed to know her. She gave her card with a five-dollar bill attached to it to the man in the booth. He stepped out of the booth with the change in his hand. The red light on the meter showed $3.50. "Fine day, Mrs. Ross," he said. "How's the new car running?"

"Real good, Tom," she said.

"Highway Patrol radar clocked you at ninety back there, but you came down real quick. We told them to clear you."

"Thanks, Tom," she said, holding out her hand to him again. This time there was a twenty-dollar bill in it.

It disappeared as he turned back to his booth. "Don't push it, Mrs. Ross," he said in a polite voice. "Never can tell when someone who doesn't know you might be on duty."

"I'll remember that," she said, starting the car again. We rolled on down the ramp and onto the highway. Ten minutes later we crossed a small bridge over a waterway and down a small private street. She pressed the Genie on the sun visor in front of her and a pair of electric gates opened before us as we turned into the driveway. They were closed by the time we pulled to a stop in front of the house.

She turned to look at me. "We're home."

"Okay," I said. I got out of the car and walked around to her side and opened the door for her.

"You'll have to carry your own bag," she said. "It's August and all the servants except the gardener are on vacation."

"I'll manage." I pulled the backpack from the car and followed her into the house. She led me down a hallway and opened a door. I followed her into the room.

"This is your room," she said. "The door over there is to the bathroom. The door next to the window leads you right outside to the pool or the beach, whichever you prefer. The closets are on the near wall."

There was one door she hadn't explained. "What about that one?" I asked.

"That's the door to my room," she said. "This room was my ex-husband's. Anything else you want to know?"

I looked at her for a moment. "Where's the washing machine? I've got some laundry to do."

I rolled over in the bed and opened my eyes. The sun had gone and dusk shadowed the room. I moved slowly, feeling the luxury of real sheets against me. It had been a long time since I had slept in a bed. I hadn't known how good it would feel until just now.

I sat up in the bed. I had thrown all my clothes into the washing machine. I still had time to get them into the dryer so that I would have something to wear tonight instead of the one pair of shorts I had kept out. I was out of the bed and into my jean shorts before I saw the clothes, all neatly pressed and folded, lying on the couch against the wall.

I really must have been out, because I hadn't heard her come into the room at all. I touched the clothes. It couldn't have been that long ago, because they were still warm. I rubbed my cheek. A shave now and another shower and I could feel almost human again. The shower I had taken just before I fell into bed had been just to get me clean.

I stood in the shower stall luxuriating in the hot water. Steam obscured the glass of the shower door, and when I came out, the faint scent of marijuana hung in the air and there was a large bath sheet hanging where I could reach it. I took it down and began to dry myself and walked back into the bedroom. Her door was still closed. I went over to the window and looked out toward the front driveway. The Rolls was gone. I finished dressing and knocked at her door.

There was no answer. I knocked again. Still silence. I opened the door and went in. The room was empty. I went back into my room, then out into the hall. I went all through the house. She was nowhere in it.

I took a can of beer from the refrigerator, snapped it open and went through the living room onto the veranda. I sank into a chair looking out over the ocean. On the horizon a freighter slowly made its way south, and while I was watching, night fell and it was gone. Slowly the stars began to come out, and soon the sky was blue velvet filled with diamonds. It all belonged together. The Rolls Corniche, this house, now a diamond-filled sky. Rich was rich.

Her voice came from behind me. "Hungry?"

I got to my feet and turned around. She had a large white bag with the Colonel's smiling face imprinted on it in each arm.

"I've got ribs, chicken, salad and French fries," she said. "I didn't feel like cooking."

"I'm not complaining," I said. I reached for the bags. "Let me help."

There was four times as much food as we could eat. Finally I pushed myself away from the table. "I'm gonna bust if I don't stop."

She laughed. She hadn't eaten much at all. Maybe one rib and one piece of chicken. No more. "We'll put the rest in the fridge. Maybe you'll feel like some later."

We put the dishes into the dishwasher. Then she took a glass of red wine, I took another beer and we went back outside to the veranda. She sat down in a chair next to mine. From nowhere the gold cigarette case appeared. I watched while she lit the chocolate stick.

"You do a lot of that?" I asked.

She shrugged. "It's better than Valium."

She passed it to me. I took a few tokes. It was even better than before. Floaty and clear and very up. "Can't argue with that. But why?"

She didn't look at me. "It eases the pain of loneliness."

I took another hit and gave it back to her. "Why should you be lonely? You seem to have everything."

"Sure," she said She dragged on the chocolate stick again. "Poor little rich girl."

"I didn't mean that," I said quickly. "You're beautiful; you don't have to be alone."

Her voice was bitter. "I'm not in the habit of picking up young boys on the Sunshine State Parkway."

"Hey, cool it," I said. "You're going off on the wrong track. I called you, remember?"

"I was stoned," she said. "I imagined it all and you went along with it."

"Princess."

Anger seeped into her voice. "Don't call me that! My name is—"

I leaned toward her. With one hand I took the chocolate stick from her fingers; with my other hand holding the back of her head, I covered her mouth with mine. At first her lips were hard, then they were soft, then they were warm, and when I took myself away from them, they were trembling. There were liquid blue shadows in her eyes.

"You have your mother's eyes, Christina," I said.

I could hear the catch in her voice. "If you knew my name all along, why did you call me Princess?"

I said the words, but my father spoke them. "If you had been my daughter, that's what I would have called you."

Her fingers clutched at my hands in fear. "Jonathan, what's all this about? Either I'm going crazy or there's something in this dope that's making me hallucinate."

I put her hands together and held them to my lips. "Don't be frightened," I said. "We're just playing catch-up."

"Catch up?" She was puzzled.

"We're finishing something our parents never did." I got to my feet and drew her up after me. "Are your mother's scrapbooks still in the library?"

She nodded. "On the top shelf in the corner."

There were five books. Large, leather-bound, one on top of another. I took them all down and placed them on the desk. But I opened only the second and went right to the page I sought. "Here we are," I said, pointing to the photograph.

She stared at the picture of the young woman and the man smiling at each other in quarter-profile. Wonder crept into her voice. "It could be you and me."

"It could be. But it's not," I said. "It's your mother. And my father." I began to turn the pages. "There are more pictures."

Her voice was suddenly angry. "I don't want to see any more!" She ran from the room, slamming the door behind her.

I closed the book carefully and followed her. I found her sobbing on the bed in her room. I stood there for a moment. "I'm sorry," I said. "I think I'd better go."

She turned, sitting up on the bed. "No."

"I didn't come here to upset you," I said.

"I know that. I'm upset with myself. I'm ten years older than you are. I should be able to handle the way I feel."

I didn't speak.

"Daniel," she said. And when I looked into the familiar depths of her eyes, I know it wasn't she who was speaking. It was her mother. "I still love you. And I still want you."

I had all I could do to keep myself from being sucked into the vortex of her eyes. I leaned over the bed and kissed her forehead gently. "Try to get some sleep."

"I don't want to sleep," she said. "I have so much to tell you." Her hands drew me down to the bed beside her. "You were filled with anger. I never knew a man so filled with anger. That's why I left you."

I pressed her slowly back against the pillow. "You didn't leave me," I said quietly. "You never left me."

Her hand found mine and squeezed it tightly. Her voice was a whisper. "Yes, in a way that's true. I never left you." Then she was asleep.

I waited for a long moment, then quietly, so that I would not awaken her, went back into my room and began loading my backpack.

"Jonathan."

"Stop messing with my head. Let go, Father, You're dead."

"I'm not messing with your head. I need you."

"It's over for you, Father. You don't need anything or anybody now."

"I love her, Jonathan."

"You're mixed up, Father. She's not her mother."

"She is as much her mother as you are me."

"I can't help you, Father. Go away and let me lead my own life." A thought flashed through my head. *"Is she your daughter, Father?"*

"No." There was a sighing sibilance in his voice. *"If she were, I wouldn't need you to tell her how I feel."*

"Her mother is dead, Father. Why don't you tell her yourself?"

"The dead cannot talk to the dead, my son. Only the living can talk to each other."

"Were you talking to someone, Jonathan?"

She was standing in the open doorway connecting our

rooms. I didn't answer. She came into the room. "I thought I heard voices."

"There's no one," I said.

She looked down at the half-packed backpack on the bed. "You're not going?"

I picked up the backpack and spilled my clothing over the bed. "No," I said. "I'm not going."

There was a curiosity in her voice. "What happened between my mother and your father?"

"I don't know. I just feel things. But something led me here because it's important that I do know."

"I feel that too," she said. A sudden comprehension came into her eyes. "My mother kept a diary. Maybe—"

"That could be what we want to know," I said quickly. "Do you know where it is?"

"Yes," she said. "This was my mother's home. After her death all her personal things were boxed and put away. The scrapbooks were never touched because they were on the top shelf of the library and we didn't find them until afterward. By then it didn't pay to bother."

"Can we get to them?"

"Everything is in storage in Miami. We could drive down there tomorrow."

I began to feel better. "At fifty-five miles per hour."

She smiled. "At fifty-five. I promise." She turned back to her room. "Good night, Jonathan."

"Good night, Christina," I said. I watched the door close behind her, then undressed and got into bed. I felt exhaustion seem through my body and dived into a deep sleep.

June 30, 1937
Philip Murray came to the hospital today to see Daniel. It was the first time anyone had come from the union in the month he had been there. It was almost a week after the doctors had told Daniel he would never walk again. Two men came with him. Mr. McDonald and Mr. Mussman. I was sitting beside the bed, so I was the first to see them as they walked down the ward past the curtains that separated the patients from each other. I got to my feet when they stopped in front of Daniel's bed.

Daniel introduced us and there was an awkward pause when they heard my name, so I excused myself and walked down to the end of the ward. They remained there about fifteen minutes. Then they left, walking silently back down the ward, never once looking back to see me. I went back to Daniel.

There was an expression on his face I had never seen before. As if all the muscles had turned to stone and only his eyes were alive, burning with a coal-black anger. There were papers lying on the bed sheet in front of him, but his big hands were clutched into fists so tight that I thought the knuckles would burst through the taut white skin. After a few moments, he picked up one of the papers and held it toward me, with hands he could hardly restrain from trembling.

It was on the stationery of the Steelworkers Organizing Committee. In view of his past and valuable services, the executive board had agreed not to accept his letter of resignation dated before his injury. Instead, they had voted to retire him with one month's severance pay and a pension of twenty-five dollars a week for a two-year period beginning thereafter. In addition, they would assume the hospital expenses over and above what was supplied by the public services and wished him every success in whatever future endeavor he might undertake. It was signed by Philip Murray.

I looked at him. There was nothing I could say.

"The strike is lost," he said. "You know that."

I nodded.

"Ten dead on Memorial Day in Chicago; less than a month later, twelve dead in Youngstown, over a hundred men crippled and injured; and now it's over. They walk away from it, while the men drift back to work like beaten dogs. We'll get them next time. Meanwhile they go back and play their games of power, and the men who went on the line for them, bled for them and died for them are nothing but junk. To be thrown away like a lemon squeezed dry for which they have no further use."

His eyes had gone from coal black to glacial. His voice had a passion I had never heard before. "They think I'm finished. That I won't walk again, that I won't function. And that's another mistake they can chalk up to their credit. Just like the strike they should never have begun. A strike they knew they could not win."

His eyes tore into mine. "I'm going to walk again. And you're going to help me."

371

I nodded.

"The first thing you have to do is get me out of this place where the only word you hear is 'Sorry.' "

"Where will we go?" I asked.

His voice was suddenly very soft. "Home."

July 16, 1937

We got off the train at Fitchville. I left him sitting in a wheelchair surrounded by valises on the station platform while I went down the street and bought a '35 Dodge touring car for two hundred and ninety-five dollars. Then we drove up the back roads far into the hills to the place he called home. It was not even a ramshackle cabin anymore. It was a blackened, burned-out hulk. He stared at it impassively for a moment, then turned to me.

"Tomorrow morning, you go back into town, hire the four biggest colored men you can find at a dollar a day and found. Then go over to the general store and buy each man a hammer, a saw, an axe, some lumber and a barrel of twopenny nails. Then get enough victuals to keep them for a week. Beans, fatback, coffee and sugar. Get whatever you like for us."

He saw the expression in my eyes when he turned to look at me. "Don't worry," he said. "It's going to be all right."

"You sure you want to do this, Daniel?" I asked. "We can still take Uncle Tom up on his offer." It had been just a few days ago that Uncle Tom had agreed to pay for all the therapy, but only on the condition that Daniel sign an agreement whereby he would never work in the union movement again.

Daniel had refused. "No more deals with anyone. For or against the unions. I'm keeping my options open. The only man I trust is me."

He ignored my question. "We'll sleep in the car tonight. Tomorrow we'll move into the house after the men clean it up."

He stretched out on the back seat as comfortably as he could. I used the front seat because it was easier for my legs to go under the steering wheel. Sometime during the night I woke up. He was sitting on the back seat, looking out at the house. When he heard me, he turned his face to me.

"Are you all right?" I asked.

He nodded. "Will you do me a favor?"

"Of course. What?"

"Think you can manage to sit on my face?"

"Only if you let me suck you afterward."

For the first time in a long while I heard him laugh. That was when I knew it would really be all right. He held out his arms toward me. "Come here, baby," he said. "We're home."

August 28, 1937

Dr. Pincus, the orthopedist, finished his examination. All afternoon, he had tapped and probed and checked. He had watched Daniel walking. With crutches. Then on the long runway of parallel bars, moving his legs stiffly, but moving them nevertheless, while supporting himself with his arms. Then on crutches again, with a brick tied under each shoe to give them extra weight so that greater effort was needed to make each leg take a step. Finally the examination was completed and Daniel stretched, exhausted, while Ulla began to massage and knead his legs from thigh to toe.

The doctor walked out into the field with me. "I can't believe it. A month ago I would have said what he just did was impossible."

"You don't know Daniel," I said.

"But everything he's done was wrong. It goes against the theory of musculature repair under which we work."

"Maybe there's something wrong with your theory," I said.

He looked at me. "Where did Daniel get his ideas?"

"From two books he ordered by mail. Bernarr MacFadden's Body Building *and Charles Atlas'* Don't Be a Ninety Seven Pound Weakling.*"*

"And the therapist? Where did she come from?"

"Mrs. Torgersen, who takes care of Daniel's son in California. She used to work with her in a hospital and wrote us about her. She was an expert on orthopedic massages in her own country."

Dr. Pincus shook his head. "I saw it, but I still don't know whether I believe it. But I'm not going to fight it. It's working. At this rate, in another month he'll be walking."

"That's what Daniel said. By September thirtieth he's going to walk out of here."

Dr. Pincus nodded. "I think I'd better come down every week now to check him out. I wouldn't want him to overdo it and run into a real setback."

September 10, 1937

Daniel threw away the crutches. He is now walking around with the support of only two canes. He is beginning to try to walk even without them, but when he takes more than a few steps his legs go out from under him. Ulla picks him up as if he were a baby and chides him for trying to move too quickly. He must move slowly at first. He shakes his head stubbornly and starts out again. This time she catches him even before he falls. Then, as if he were a child, she holds him up with her hands under his armpits and puts him down in a chair and makes him rest. I don't know which of us was more surprised when she did that, Daniel or me. She is a big woman, almost six feet, massive-breasted, broad-hipped, strong legs.

She knelt at his feet, unlacing his shoes. "Unbutton your pants," she commanded.

He looked up at me. I laughed. "Better do as she says or she may beat you up."

He opened his belt and unbuttoned the pants. Expertly she slid them off and stretching his legs across her knees, began to massage them. "The trick is to keep the circulation up so that the muscles do not get stiff and tight."

"Sure," he said, looking at me uncomfortably.

I laughed and went inside. It was almost time for me to start dinner. Ulla and I take turns cooking. Today was my turn.

September 27, 1937

I suppose subconsciously I knew that he was fucking Ulla but I wouldn't admit it. Ever since that day I saw her pull his pants off to massage his legs and noticed the swelling in his underwear. But I didn't face it until I walked in on them. I returned from Fitchville, where I had gone to take Dr. Pincus to the train station. The doctor had been continually amazed at Daniel's progress. He had never seen anything like it before. Already Daniel was beginning to take short but still shaky walks without the cane.

"The human willpower," Dr. Pincus had said on the drive

374

down. *"I don't think we'll ever understand it. Bones were broken, nerves, muscles, tendons torn apart in both legs. According to the book there is no way he could ever do what he is doing."* He glanced at me, his eyes twinkling. *"I'll never believe anything anymore. Not even the nursery rhymes. Humpty Dumpty can be put together again. Only he has to do it himself."*

Then the car stalled on the way back and I had to walk the last quarter-mile to the cabin. They were naked on the floor. She was on her back, her massive white breasts thrusting upward like twin mountains while she held her legs apart and back against her belly with her hands under her knees. He was poised over her, supported by his arms, hands flat against the floor, his legs straight out behind him. She groaned with pleasure as he slammed into her again and again until he collapsed in orgasm, coming to rest against her Junoesque body.

She stroked him gently, speaking almost as if he were a child. *"That vass very gut. Ven ve are finished, your legs vill be ass strong ass your prick."*

I tried to close the door quietly before they could see me, but he looked up just at the last moment. I finished closing the door and sat down on the small porch. About ten minutes later, he came out, walking with the help of his two canes, and sank into a chair next to mine.

We didn't speak for a long while. Then he finally spoke. *"I suppose you wonder what we were doing?"*

"I know what you were doing. Fucking."

He laughed. *"That's right. But what else?"*

"What else could it be?" I asked sarcastically. *"Fucking is fucking."*

"Its part of my rehabilitation," he said.

"Oh, sure," I said, skeptically. *"But your cock was never broken —only your legs."*

"It's a kind of push-ups."

"I could see that."

"Really. It's a way of exerting pressure on the legs."

I couldn't help it. I began to laugh. *"The pleasure was just incidental?"*

He grinned. *"You know me. I never could resist a little pussy."*

"That wasn't a little pussy," I said. *"That was a lot. Even for you."*

He laughed and reached for my hand. Then he was serious. "I'll send her away if you want."

"No." I said. "There's just one change I'm going to make."

"What's that?"

"If you have to exercise, you're going to do it with me. I've been too easy on you. Always on top so that you wouldn't strain yourself. Now you can go back to work and I'll lie back and enjoy it."

October 10, 1937

He's walking. When he's tired, with one cane. But he's walking. Today I took Dr. Pincus and Ulla to the train. The doctor was so impressed with her that he was taking her back to Washington to work in his office. He didn't know it, but with the kind of physical therapy she was ready to give his patients he would have to become the busiest orthopedist in the country.

When I got back to the cabin, Daniel was sitting on the porch, a drink in his hand, puffing on a cigar. A bottle of whiskey and another glass were on the table next to him. He poured some for me. "We did it."

"You did it," I said, holding the glass toward him. We touched glasses and drank. "Now what do we do?"

"First, I'm going out to California to see my son. Then I got to get me a job."

"Going back with Murray?"

He shook his head, black anger flashing in his eyes. "He can go fuck himself."

"Lewis?"

"Not as long as Murray is with him."

"You can still talk to my Uncle Tom."

"You know better than that. I'll find something. Maybe even start my own union."

"Your own union? In what industry? It seems to me that everything is covered now."

"Not everything," he answered. "I've been thinking that the union members themselves need some kind of protection against their leaders."

"That doesn't make sense," I said. "A union within a union."

He laughed. "Who knows? It might come down to that. When

I see the things done to the union members by their leadership, I begin to wonder exactly for whose benefit the whole thing is run. But I'm in no hurry. There's time for that. I've got to get around more. There's still lots I have to learn."

"And what about me?" I asked. "What am I supposed to be doing while you're doing all this?"

He refilled his glass. "You have your job with your uncle."

"I left that," I said. "I can't go crawling back to him now. You know that."

"Well, you don't need the money anyway. You have money of your own."

"You're not answering my question, and you know it." I was getting angry. "I'm not talking about a job, I'm talking about you and me."

He didn't answer.

"You know I want to marry you."

He still didn't answer.

"I'm two months pregnant. Dr. Pincus confirmed it."

The glass shattered in his hand. Angrily, he flung it away from him, the whiskey and the blood from his fingers spattering against the wooden rail. His voice was thick. "No, godammit! You're not going to do that to me. All you women are alike. You think your cunts can nail a man down. Tess did that to me and fucked up my life. I'm not going to let it happen again." He got to his feet and went to the door. "You get yourself an abortion or do whatever the hell you want. It's your baby, not mine."

The door slammed behind him, and I heard the crash as he stumbled and fell. I opened the door and looked down at him stretched out on the floor. He turned his head, and his eyes stared up at me angrily.

"Fuck you!" I said, and closed the door on him. It was the first time there was no one there to pick him up when he fell.

October 15, 1937

I had my abortion today. The doctor wouldn't tell me whether it was a boy or a girl. It's raining in Chicago. I haven't heard from Daniel. I don't know why I can't stop crying. The doctor says he's coming back to give me a shot so I can sleep.

377

There were few entries in the diary after that date. She began a new diary the next year, but after the first few entries that too seemed to have been given up, and there were no further diaries for the following years. Neither was there any further mention of my father.

Christina stared down into the red wine in her glass. "I wonder if she ever saw him again afterward."

"I don't think so." I put the diaries back into the box we had brought from the warehouse. "When were your parents married?"

"Nineteen forty-five. After the war. My father was a colonel in Eisenhower's headquarters in London. He met my mother there when she was working in the office of procurement. They were married when they came back to the States. I was born the next year. And yours?"

"Nineteen fifty-six. Ten years after my father founded C.A.L.L. It took him almost nine years to start the union he talked about to your mother."

"What was he doing those nine years?" she asked.

"I don't really know," I said. "But then, I never knew anything about him. We never talked much."

"You talk to him now," she said.

"What makes you say that?"

"I feel it." She sipped at the wine. "Sometimes you are a completely different person, and when I look at you I don't see you at all. I see someone else."

I looked at my watch. It was past two in the morning. "I think we'd better get some sleep."

"I'm restless. Want to share a joint first?"

I hesitated.

"Just a few tokes," she said. "It will calm me down."

"Okay."

I walked outside onto the veranda while she went for the chocolate sticks. It was a blue velvet night, a warm salt breeze coming in from the ocean. I stretched out on the lounge.

She sat down on the lounge at my feet. I lit the chocolate stick while she sipped at her glass of wine, took a few tokes and passed it to her. She hit it pretty good—long deep tokes, filling her lungs and holding it, then slowly exhaling the residual smoke.

I took another few tokes, and my head began to spin out. I gave it back to her. "I think I've had it."

She smiled. "You have to get used to it."

"I don't know whether I could afford it."

She laughed and dragged on the chocolate stick again. She looked down at me. "Where do you go from here, Jonathan?"

I put my arms under my head and rested back against my hands. "I was thinking about going home. But now, I don't know."

"Did you find what you were looking for here?"

"I don't know what I'm looking for," I said. "That is, if I'm looking for anything at all."

"Your father," she said.

"He's dead. Too late for that now."

She dragged on the chocolate stick again. "You know better than that."

I took the cigarette from her fingers. This time I really took it down. The top of my head came off. My tongue went all fuzzy. "Let's not talk about him anymore. Okay?"

"Okay. What do we talk about, then?"

"Being rich. What's it like?"

"I don't know any other way."

"Your husband? Was he rich too?"

"Yes."

"And your father?"

"Yes."

"You were born batting a thousand."

She thought for a moment. "I suppose you could put it that way."

"Why did you get divorced?"

"The truth?"

I nodded. "That's why I asked."

"He was guilty rich. I wasn't."

I laughed.

"Not funny," she said. "He didn't know how to relax and enjoy it. He was always uptight."

"So you got divorced. How long ago?"

"Last year."

"Better now?"

She shrugged. "In some ways. At least he's not always looking down his nose at me. Putting me down because I don't make any contribution to society by not working. The way I look at it, at least I'm not taking a job away from someone who needs it."

"Can't argue with that point of view." I hit the chocolate stick again and passed it back to her. "My whole head is spinning. I've never had a buzz like this."

"Feel good?"

"The best."

"Then enjoy it." She leaned over and kissed me. Her mouth was warm. I pressed her tightly against me. After a moment, she raised her head and looked at me. "I want you to stay with me for a while, Jonathan. Will you?"

"I don't know if I can."

"As long as you can. I need you."

I went deep into those familiar eyes. "It's almost incest. It's my father you want, not me."

"There's nothing wrong in that. You are your father just as much as I am my mother. You said we were playing catch-up. At the time I didn't know what you meant. Now I do. We have to finish out the game."

I didn't speak.

"Have you ever been in love, Jonathan?"

I thought for a moment. "I don't think so."

"Neither have I," she said. "But I know it's there some-where. My mother found it with your father. Maybe we can find it together."

This time I went all the way into her eyes. And suddenly I wasn't myself any longer. I opened my arms and she came into them, her head pressed against my chest. Slowly I stroked her long, soft hair. "I think we've already found it, Christina." I turned her face up to me. "But it's not ours. It never will be ours. You know that."

"I know it," she said softly, her eyes filling with tears. "But it doesn't matter whose it is. As long as we can feel it."

380

Book Three

Another Day

Chapter 1

"You're a fucking crook, Big Dan."

Daniel laughed easily as he refilled his glass from the bourbon bottle in front of him. He looked at the other of the two men sitting opposite him. "What do you think, Tony?"

"The same thing."

Daniel laughed again. He finished his drink in one swallow and got to his feet. He towered over the table, a shock of his iron-gray hair tumbling over his forehead. "I guess the meeting is over."

"Wait a minute," the first man said quickly. "I didn't say that. Sit down. We can talk it over."

Daniel looked at him for a moment, then nodded. Slowly he sank back into his seat and refilled his glass. "Okay. Talk."

"You're asking too much," the man said.

"Too much what? Money? That's nothing compared with what I can do for you. I can make you respectable."

"We are respectable," the man said stubbornly.

Daniel fixed him with a look. "But for how long? As long as you sit in the shadows. The minute you come out, they're going to take after you.

"I look at it very simply. Dave Beck is going to fall. Logically, Jimmy, you're the next international president of the Teamsters. But will you be? Suppose Meany doesn't like it? You can't jump from the A.F.L. to the C.I.O., because they're all together now. You're fucked. You have no place to go."

He turned to the other man. "That goes for you too, Tony. John L. is not going to appoint you president of the U.M.W. when he steps down. Tom Kennedy gets first crack. He's been around longer. But you can get executive v.p., and with a guy like Kennedy that's even better. You're still safe in the shadows, and it will be time for you to make your move when Kennedy goes."

"You got it all figured out," Jimmy Hoffa said.

"I've been around a long time," Daniel answered.

Tony Boyle laughed. "So why ain't you rich?"

"I was in no hurry," Daniel said, smiling. "I was waiting for you guys to grow up."

"You know I couldn't get Lewis to go along with a dime-a-member assessment for C.A.L.L.," Tony said.

"I know that," Daniel said. "But the individual locals can do it if they want. You can see to that. It's the same thing."

"The old man'll go through the roof," Tony said. "He hates your guts after what you've said about him."

"What else is new?" Daniel said, smiling. "Meany, Beck, Reuther—none of 'em like me any better. They're all members of the same club. They've been after my ass for years, but I'm still around."

Boyle shook his head in wonder. "I don't know how you do it. You haven't that many members—maybe forty, fifty thousand."

Daniel smiled. "Closer to a hundred thousand. But the numbers don't matter. They're all small unions. Independents. Which the big boys never bothered with because there wasn't enough in it for them. But they add up to something nobody else has got."

"What's that?" Hoffa asked.

"Balance of power. We've never had any trouble, any scandals. Nobody's made off with any money."

"There wasn't enough there for anybody to take," Boyle said, laughing.

"Maybe," Daniel said. "But the fact remains. The public trusts us. We're the only labor group they approve of, and we have the surveys to prove that. And I speak for them."

"The Teamsters won't go for the deal either," Hoffa said.

"Local 299 will," Daniel said. "It's your local, and they do what you tell them. Two hundred thousand members is enough to start the ball rolling. In time they'll all come in."

"Okay, so we know what you're getting. What do we get?"

"Help and advice," Daniel said. "You're both young and ambitious men. I can help you achieve your ambitions. I can protect you against everything except yourselves."

"Talking to any other unions?" Hoffa asked.

"I plan to," Daniel said. "You two are the first."

"Why us?"

"Because you both are in businesses that are vital to the country's existence."

The two men were silent for a moment. Then Boyle looked at Daniel. "Can we think about it?"

Daniel nodded. "Of course."

"What do you do if we don't go along with you?"

"There are other men, just as young and just as ambitious, in other locals of the same union."

"That's blackmail," Hoffa said, without rancor.

"That's right." Daniel nodded agreeably.

"Do we have a week?" Boyle asked.

"You have a week," Daniel said.

They shook hands, and Daniel watched them leave the bar together. Through the open window he could see them go to their separate cars. When the cars had gone, he looked down at his glass. He wondered if they knew just how desperate he really was. Ten years he had struggled to build up his power base, and in one stroke last year it had all been wiped out. The A.F.L.-C.I.O. merger had put it away. And now bit by bit, the individual unions he had signed up were drifting away. There was enough left in the treasury to carry them another month or two. Then it would all be over. The past twenty years down the drain. The dreams, the hopes, the ideals shattered beyond repair.

He rose wearily to his feet. "Put it on the tab, Joe," he said to the bartender on the way out. "And add ten bucks for yourself."

"Thanks, Big Dan," the bartender called after him.

He blinked as he went into the sunlight of the street, waited a moment until the traffic cleared, then cut across to the two-story office building. He looked up at the spotted aluminum letters over the building entrance. C.A.L.L. They were clouded and pitted by time. He made a mental note to have the janitor polish the letters.

He went into the building, bypassing the big general office on the ground floor and going up a back stairway that led directly to his private office.

Daniel, Jr., was waiting for him. "How did it go, Father?"

"They listened," he said, sitting down behind his desk.

"Think they'll go for it?"

"I don't know," he said. "I don't know anything anymore." He opened his desk drawer, took out a cigar and lit it. "Any word from the school?"

Daniel, Jr., smiled. "I've been accepted at Harvard as an economics major."

Daniel got to his feet. His hand almost crushed his son's. "Congratulations. I'm proud of you."

"I feel good about it," the boy said. "But—"

"But what?"

"I don't have to go, Father." Junior hesitated. "I know the money situation. I'm old enough to go to work."

"You are going to work," Daniel said. "Someday, you're going to have to take all of this over. You have to be ready for it."

"But what if Hoffa and Boyle don't come through? You'll have to fold."

"I'll find a way," Daniel said. "You're going to school. That's your job." The telephone rang. "You get it, Junior. I got to take a piss."

Though Junior tried not to show it, his voice showed how impressed he was when Daniel returned to the office. "That call was from the White House. A Mr. Adams."

"Sherman Adams?"

Junior nodded.

"What did he want?"

"You're invited to a breakfast meeting with the President on September sixth. They want you to call back to confirm."

"Did he mention who else was invited?"

Junior shook his head. "I didn't ask."

Daniel picked up the telephone and asked his secretary to return Adams' call. While waiting for the answer, he looked up at Junior. "Eisenhower must be getting worried. Practically every union in the A.F.L.-C.I.O. has come out for Stevenson." Adams came onto the phone. "Sherman, what's up?" Daniel asked.

"The President thought it might be a good idea if you sat down and had a chat."

"Who else is coming?"

"John L. Lewis. Maybe Dave Beck."

"Don't invite Beck," Daniel said. "There are some things going on there that might turn up to embarrass you."

"Can you talk about them?" The President's assistant asked.

"Not on the telephone."

"I see." Adams' voice sounded thoughtful. "Will you be able to come?"

"I'll be there."

"Good. The President will be pleased when I tell him."

"Give him my best," Daniel said. "And I'll see you on the sixth."

"Eight o'clock." Adams said, and clicked off.

Daniel looked across the desk at his son. He smiled. "I guess the White House hasn't heard yet that we're in trouble." He looked down at the papers on his desk. "I've got to get to work."

"I'll get out of your way, Father," Junior said. He went to the door and looked back. "Will you be home for dinner tonight?"

"I don't know yet," Daniel answered. "Tell Mamie I'll call her later to let her know."

He stared at the closed door for a moment after his son had gone. Then he took a bottle of whiskey from the bottom drawer of his desk and took a long pull at it. Carefully he screwed the cap back onto the bottle and returned it to the drawer, then reached for the telephone and asked for his messages.

Chapter 2

"It's DOWNHILL the rest of the month," Moses said. "If we can't get our hands on some money, we're finished."

Daniel looked up at his executive assistant. "I thought we were good for at least two more months."

"Collections aren't coming in. Apparently they're not even bothering to notify us that they're quitting." The black man's face was worried. They had been friends for over twenty years and he was the first man Daniel asked to join him at C.A.L.L. "I think we'd better start giving our people their notices."

Daniel thought for a moment. "We can't do that. The word gets out that we're closing down and it's really all over."

"I don't know what to do, then," Moses said.

"We'll have to borrow."

Moses laughed wryly. "Who's going to lend us money? They won't accept our membership lists for receivables. Especially when they see the collection record for the past year."

"I know where we can get the money," Daniel said. "Lansky."

The black man was silent.

Daniel met his eyes. "You don't approve?"

"Do you? You know what that means. Once you let them in, they never get out. I've heard you say that many times."

"Sure," Daniel said bitterly. "And where did it get us? Maybe it's time we just faced the facts of life. The others did it. I don't see where they're hurting."

"You're not them," Moses said.

"Maybe it's time I changed," Daniel replied wearily. "The whole world can't be out of step but me."

Moses was silent.

"Don't stand there like Mr. Righteous," Daniel said in a suddenly angry voice. "Even God had to make a deal with the Devil to divide the Hereafter."

"We're talking about the now," Moses said.

Daniel's voice was hard and flat. "If you don't like it, you can always quit."

"You know I won't do that." There was hurt in Moses' voice.

"I'm sorry," Daniel said contritely. "I didn't mean that. It's just if I can nail down the deal with Boyle and Hoffa, we'll put through. Meanwhile, I've got that White House meeting next week. That won't hurt. At least it will show that we're still alive and that the President thinks we're still important."

Moses was silent for a moment. "Okay. When do you plan to see Lansky?"

"Tomorrow, if it can be arranged. I can fly down to Miami on a morning flight and be back here in the evening."

It was almost six o'clock, and he was getting ready to leave the office, when his secretary buzzed. "Miss Rourke is here."

He drew a blank. "Miss Rourke?"

"She telephoned last week. You spoke to her. Something about her father not collecting his pension from his union. You asked her to bring in the details. I put her down for six today."

He remembered. The girl's father had been run over by a tractor and had lost the use of one leg. Now he was having trouble collecting his pension. "Okay," he said wearily. "Send her in."

The door opened and the girl came into the office. He struggled to his feet. "I'm Daniel Huggins."

She was very young. Not more than nineteen, he thought. Soft black hair to her shoulders, blue eyes and Irish pale skin. "Margaret Rourke," she said, taking his outstretched hand. Her voice was soft and cool. "Thank you for seeing me."

He gestured to the chair opposite his desk as he sat down. "That's what I'm here for. Now, what's the problem?"

She opened a large manila envelope and took out some papers, which she placed on his desk. "I told you about my father's accident. Here are all the details you asked me to get."

He picked up the papers and went through them quickly. She was thorough. Everything was in there, from the accident report to his paid-up membership card, indicating his dues were up to date. There was only one thing wrong. The local he belonged to was bankrupt. Money that was supposed to have been paid into the pension fund had disappeared along with the union's president and treasurer.

He looked up at the girl, who had been watching him intently. "There is a problem."

"They have no money," she said.

He nodded. "That's right."

"But my father said that you were the one who set up the pension plan for them and that they weren't supposed to be able to touch that money."

"That was the way it was set up," he said. "But the local itself changed it."

"How can they do that?" she asked. "If you people are responsible—"

He interrupted her. "We can only advise them. We cannot order them to do anything. We haven't the authority. We set up what we think is a safe, foolproof plan. If the union wants to go along with it, good. If they don't—"

"It's not fair," she said angrily. "My father said the union paid you to take care of it. You have to be responsible."

"They never paid us to administer the pension plan. We would have had they requested it, but all they wanted was our advisory services."

She looked down at the papers on the desk. "Then those things aren't even worth the paper they're printed on."

He didn't speak.

She looked up at him, tears of frustration in her eyes. "What do we do now? My father can't work, and there are two more kids at home, younger than I am. We even applied for welfare but were turned down because I'm working. But there's no way we all can live on the thirty dollars a week I make."

"What about the union? Did your father ask if they could find a watchman's job in one of the plants for him?"

"There's no one down there that can do anything," she said bitterly. "All they could tell me is that they're still trying to find out what happened after the president took off with their money."

"Let me see what I can do," he said.

She rose from her chair angrily. "You're all alike. Great when you're collecting dues, but none of you are there when it's your turn to pay."

"That's not true," he said quickly. "Most unions take their responsibilities seriously. It's unfortunate that your father belonged to one where the president was a thief."

"You're all thieves," she said. "You can't make me feel any different."

He was silent for a moment. "Getting angry won't help," he said gently. "Why don't you sit down while we try to figure something out?"

Slowly she returned to her chair, her eyes on his face. "Do you really think you can do something?"

"I don't know," he admitted. "But we can try." He reached for the telephone. "Let me make a few calls."

It was almost an hour later when he put down the telephone for the last time. He looked across the desk at her. "At least we have a few possibilities started. Now we'll wait and see what happens."

Her eyes met his gaze. "I apologize, Mr. Huggins. I shouldn't have said what I did."

"It's all right. I understand. You've had enough provocation." Suddenly he was tired. "If you don't hear from me by the beginning of next week, call me."

A concern suddenly came into her voice. "Are you all right, Mr. Huggins?"

392

"Just tired," he said wearily. "It's been a rough day."

"I'm sorry," she said. "I suppose you have lots of problems like this. I didn't mean to make it worse, but there was nowhere else for me to go."

"It's okay, Margaret," he said. He opened the bottom desk drawer. "Do you mind if I have a drink?"

She shook her head and watched as he took out the bottle and two glasses. He poured himself a shot and looked over at her. "No, thanks," she said.

He swallowed the drink, and she could see the color come back into his face. He refilled his glass. "Where do you work?"

"I'm in the typing pool at the housing agency," she said.

He took the second drink. "Good job?"

"It's okay," she said. "I'm still on temporary. But I grabbed it. It was the first thing I could get."

"Do you live far from work?"

"Two-hour bus ride," she said. "But it's not so bad. I get through work at four o'clock and I'm usually home in time to get dinner ready."

"What about your mother?"

"She's dead."

"I'm sorry," he said. "Maybe I'd better let you go. Dinner will be late enough as it is."

"It's okay. I've made arrangements for a neighbor to do it."

He finished his drink and returned the bottle to his desk. He got to his feet. "My car's outside. I can drop you at the bus station."

"I can walk," she said. "The next bus doesn't leave until nine o'clock."

He looked at his watch. It was just past seven o'clock. "Would you like to have a bite of dinner with me? I'll get you to the bus in time."

She hesitated. "I've put you to too much trouble already."

"Don't be silly," he said, smiling. "I had nothing planned. Just an early dinner and then to bed." He reached for the telephone. His secretary answered. "Call home and tell Mamie I'm having dinner out." He saw the questioning look on her face. "Mamie's my cook."

She nodded without speaking.

"I'm not married," he said.

"I know that," she said.

"What else do you know about me?"

She was silent.

"You can tell me. I won't be angry."

She hesitated, then spoke. "My father didn't want me to see you. He said you have a lot of women."

He laughed. "What else did he say?"

"He said you would probably offer to take me to dinner."

"He was right. That's exactly what I did. Did he say anything else?"

"He said if I went to dinner with you, I should be careful."

"Well, we haven't gone to dinner yet, so we don't know about that, do we?" He was smiling.

After a moment, she too smiled. "That's right."

"Well, you've got a chance to check that out."

She was still smiling when she met his eyes. "I'll take that chance."

"We won't go anyplace fancy," he said. "The restaurant across the street has good steaks."

"That sounds good to me." She got to her feet. "Is there a ladies' room?"

"Through my secretary's office. In the hallway to the right." He watched her go through the door, then sat down and took the bottle out again. He took a quick drink. It was something about the way she walked. It was another kind of walk than the one she had used coming in. Then she had seemed like a young girl. Suddenly, she was a real woman.

Chapter 3

HE CAME down the ramp into the Miami airport, already sweating in his summer suit, a small briefcase in his hand. Two young men moved toward him purposefully, one tall and blond, one short and dark, both dressed in cotton seersucker suits. The short man spoke. "Mr. Huggins?"

"Yes," he answered.

"We have a car waiting outside. Do you have any luggage?"

"No."

The short man nodded. "Okay. This way, please."

They fell into step alongside him and went through the airport, crowded with summer package vacationers on tour. Outside, a Cadillac limousine was waiting, the motor running. They held the door for him. Then the blond man got in beside him, while the dark man got in front beside the driver.

"We'll be there in fifteen minutes," the blond man said. The car began to move. "Did you have a good flight?"

"Very nice," Daniel answered.

"It will be even better in a few months. They expect to have the new jet planes flying by the time the winter season starts."

"I thought they had them already."

"Only a few," the blond man answered. "By fall, the whole schedule will be jet."

Daniel looked out the window. The car was moving rapidly toward the causeway leading to Miami Beach. There didn't seem to be much traffic. They paused for a moment at a tollbooth, then continued, beginning to pass small islands in the bay that separated the mainland from the beach. As the car approached the last few islands it began to slow down. finally turning off onto the causeway leading to one of the islands.

Daniel noticed two uniformed armed guards at the foot of the ramp. They knew the car, because it went past them without slowing down. They drove past several low-built Florida homes, green rolling lawns of zoysia grass behind cropped hedges, finally turning into a private street, at the end of which was a high iron gate. The car stopped in front of the gate.

A man came out of the small gatehouse and looked at the car. A moment later, he went back into the gatehouse and the iron gate swung back. The car went through, the gate closing behind it, and around a long, rolling driveway to the house, which had been hidden from the road.

The two men got out of the car and waited for Daniel. "Just a moment, sir," the tall man said politely. "We have to do this."

Daniel nodded silently and held out his hands while the man expertly patted him down. The tall man straightened up. "May we see your briefcase, please?"

"It's open," Daniel said, giving it to him.

The blond man riffled through the papers quickly and checked the sides for any hidden compartments, then gave it back to Daniel. He nodded politely. "This way, please."

The house was cool and air-conditioned as Daniel followed them through the house to a room with two floor-to-ceiling windows looking out at a pool. Beyond it he could see a small pier on the bay, at which a forty-five-foot cabin cruiser was docked.

"Mr. L. will be with you in a minute," the blond man said.

He gestured to a corner. "The bar is over there. Help your-self."

"Thank you," Daniel said. The men left the room as he went to the bar. It was completely stocked with every kind of liquor one could want, pitchers of orange and tomato juice, buckets of ice, cuts of lemon peel, olives, pearl onions, Tabasco and Worcestershire sauce. Daniel was fascinated by the liquors. There were no open bottles. Every bottle was sealed and full. He took down a bottle of Old Forester, cracked the seal and poured himself a drink, adding just a touch of water from the pitcher. He sipped the drink and walked toward the window.

The view from the window was beautiful. The sky and water blending shades of blue, speedboats and sailboats lazing their way back and forth. He sipped at the drink. Good whiskey. The voice came from behind him. "Mr. Huggins."

Lansky stood there, a small man, old before his time, a Florida tan over his pallor. Daniel was shocked for a moment. They were about the same age, but Lansky seemed much older.

"Mr. Lansky." Daniel held out his hand.

Lansky's grip was light but firm. He went to the bar and poured himself a glass of orange juice. He sipped it slowly and looked at Daniel. "Florida oranges. You can't beat them. I have them squeezed fresh every hour."

Daniel nodded and followed him to a couch, then sat down opposite him. "How are you feeling, Mr. Lansky?"

"Better, but not that good." He tapped his chest. "The old ticker isn't what it should be."

"You'll live to piss on all our graves," Daniel said.

Lansky smiled wanly. "If they don't bother me I'll be okay, but they're always pushing."

"One of the dangers of success," Daniel said.

Lansky nodded, his voice suddenly turning firm. "I heard you have big problems."

"That's right," Daniel said.

"I told you that would happen four years ago. I warned you that when the A.F.L. and C.I.O. merged, you would be out of business."

"You did."

"You should have listened to me." Lansky sounded as if he were reprimanding a recalcitrant child.

Daniel didn't answer.

"No point looking back," Lansky said. "What's the situation now?"

Quickly Daniel brought him up to date. When he had finished, Lansky nodded his head wisely. "Your idea is a good one, but Hoffa and Boyle don't really need you. Respectability don't mean a shit to them. They're both street fighters. They're going to need some persuasion to help them make up their minds to go along with you."

"A good word from you might be all that's needed," Daniel said.

Lansky nodded. "Maybe. But you have other problems. Even if they go with you, where does the money come from? Dues alone are not enough to pay the freight."

"If they buy my plan, we'll have a good portion of their pension-fund administration and insurance."

"They won't turn it over to you completely."

"No," Daniel said. "I didn't suggest that. Only that we become coadministrators. There will be enough there for everyone to play with."

Lansky was silent for a moment. "And where do I fit in?"

Daniel began to feel more confident. Lansky knew damn well how he could fit in. He had insurance companies, banks, construction companies all under his thumb. He took his best shot. "If I have to explain that, Mr. Lansky, then I've wasted my trip down here."

Lansky was silent for a moment. "The word is out that you're having a meeting at the White House."

Daniel nodded. There seemed to be very little that Lansky had not heard. "Breakfast September sixth with the President."

"You spoke to Adams?"

Again Daniel nodded.

Lansky's voice was approving. "Good contact. Stay close to him."

"I plan to," Daniel said.

Lansky was silent for a while. "Eisenhower will get in again. You can be sitting pretty if you play your cards right."

"I've got my fingers crossed."

Lansky laughed for the first time. It was a dry, almost mirthless chuckle. "You seem very relaxed for a man on the edge of disaster."

Daniel laughed aloud as he poured himself another drink. This time he didn't add water. "The worst thing could happen is that I fall off."

Lansky looked at him. "How much do you think you'll need?"

"Two hundred and fifty thousand. That will carry us for a year until things start falling into place."

"It's a lot of money."

"It's cheap considering the table stakes. U.M.W.'s pension fund must have more than sixty million dollars in it already, and the Teamsters' can't be far behind. Commissions on just twenty percent of that can bring in better than two million a year."

Lansky had made up his mind. "Okay. You got it."

"Thank you, Mr. Lansky."

"Don't thank me," Lansky said quietly. "Just remember the rules. We're partners. Fifty–fifty."

"Too much," Daniel said. "There's no way I can wash that much money and not get picked up."

"How much do you think you can handle?"

"Twenty-five percent."

"That's not much."

"Maybe," Daniel said. "But it's your companies that will be doing business. There's heavy leverage right there."

Lansky thought for a moment. "You drive a hard bargain."

"Not hard," Daniel said. "Just practical. Both of us have enough trouble as it is. We don't have to look for any more."

"Deal," Lansky said. He pressed a button on the side of the couch. A moment later, the tall man who had met Daniel at the airport came into the room, carrying a black attaché case. He placed it on the coffee table between them and left the room. Lansky gestured. "Open it."

Daniel pressed the buttons and the case flew open. The

inside was neatly packed with rows of bills, still encased in their original bank wrappers. He glanced at Lansky.

"A quarter of a million dollars," Lansky said casually. "You can count it."

"I'll take your word for it," Daniel said, closing the case. He rose to his feet. "You had it all ready, Mr. Lansky."

Lansky smiled. "I have to. Never can tell when an opportunity might come along."

Chapter 4

MICHAEL ROURKE looked up from his Sunday newspaper as his daughter came into the room. He noticed she was wearing a new dress and had put on fresh makeup. "Going out tonight?" he asked.

Margaret nodded. "I've got everything ready. The roast is in the oven. It will be ready by six o'clock. The kids know when to take it out."

He was silent for a moment. "Big Dan?"

"Yes."

He put down the newspaper. "Did you read where he met with the President at the White House this week?"

"He told me about it," she said.

"You saw him?"

"Thursday night. Remember, I told you I was having dinner out."

"You didn't get home until after midnight. You didn't tell me you were having dinner with him."

"There's nothing wrong with it, Daddy. He's a very nice man."

"He's older than I am."

"If you talked to him, you wouldn't think so. He's so interested in everything."

"I don't like it," her father said. "I think you're seeing too much of him. You ought to be going out with more boys of your own age."

"Boys of my own age don't interest me, Daddy. They're so immature. And all they want from you is one thing."

"And he doesn't?"

"He's been a perfect gentleman."

He shook his head. "Did he say anything about a job for me?"

"Only that he's working on it and expects something real soon."

"Sure," he said sarcastically.

Margaret looked down at her father. "Don't you believe him? Why should he lie?"

"Because he wants to get into your young hot pants, that's why," Michael said bitterly.

"Daddy!" she said sharply.

"Don't Daddy me," he said. "You know as well as I do that's what he wants." He looked up at her shrewdly. "And maybe that's what you want too."

"I won't listen to you talking like that," she said. She started from the room.

"Margaret!" he called after her.

She turned at the doorway. "Yes?"

"I didn't mean it the way it sounds," he said apologetically. "It's just that I'm worried about you. I told you about his reputation. His drinking, and all those women. I don't want you to become just another one of his women, that's all. I don't want to see you hurt, girl."

"I'm not a child anymore, Daddy," she said in a stiff voice. "I can look after myself."

He stared at her for a moment, then picked up the paper again. "Okay," he said. "Just remember that I warned you."

The door closed behind her, and he stared into the corruption of futility. If only he could get around as he used to, it wouldn't be like this. But there was nothing he could do. The whole of the burden was on her shoulders—the house, the other children. Maybe she was right. She wasn't a child any-more. She didn't have the time.

John L. Lewis sat in the chair behind the massive desk in the heavy oak-paneled office, the windows behind him looking over the white marble buildings of government in downtown Washington. Dressed as usual in a heavy dark suit, stiff white collar and tie, he reflected a stolid, single-purposed sense of power. On either side of his desk were his two chief aides— Tom Kennedy, now approaching seventy, with white hair and gentle manner, and Tony Boyle, young, aggressive and pushing. Daniel looked at the two men. Kennedy, thinking and planning, meticulous in his approach; Boyle, flamboyant, using power and strength to bulldoze his way through oppo-sition. And at the center was John L., who was equal to the two of them; he was all the things they were and more, with an aura of natural leadership that brooked no refusal.

Lewis was talking. "The T.V.A. is the largest coal cus-tomer in the world. Because of their inexhaustible demand, we are faced with the countless number of independent mines' opening without union contracts and selling coal below the prices fixed by the union mines. Not only does this cause union mines to sell less coal, but it affects workers who are laid off who are union members and creates jobs for many who are not.

"We have exhausted every reasonable means of request for the government's assistance in this problem, and our pleas have fallen upon deaf ears. The situation is steadily growing more desperate and, if it continues, threatens the entire back-bone of the union structure built so laboriously by us over the years. If we allow this situation to continue, I can foresee the time when our members will question themselves as to the benefit of remaining with us. If that time should come, it will be the end of the United Mine Workers as we know it."

Kennedy nodded solemnly without speaking. Boyle was more positive. "We have no choice. We have to hit them with everything we've got."

Daniel looked at him. "The violence did you no good in

District 19 in '46 and '47, nor did it do any good in District 23 from '48 to '52. All we succeeded in doing was forcing the closing of the mines that signed with the union because the price of coal climbed out of the economics of doing business. Even U.M.W. financial participation in some of the mines did not prevent their bankruptcy, causing the union to lose not only membership but a great deal of money as well as prestige. And we still don't know what liabilities the courts will assess the union as damages in the lawsuits against us due to the activities of those years. If all the potential liabilities are assessed, the union will be bankrupted and shut down as effectively as if every member resigned in one day."

Boyle was belligerent. "You have a better idea? What are we supposed to do? Lay down while those scabs and operators put the shaft to us?"

"I haven't an idea right now," Daniel said. "But I know what you can't do. This is an election year. We can't afford to do anything that would force Eisenhower into taking a position against us, which he will do if he has to in order to maintain his support from the conservatives."

"What you're saying, then, is wait?" Boyle asked.

"That's right," Daniel said flatly.

"Then what the hell do we need you for?" Boyle asked irately. "You were asked down here to come up with some answers for us."

"Sorry to disappoint you," Daniel said. "I never said I had any answers. And you are right. You asked for the meeting. I didn't." He got to his feet. "Mr. Lewis, it's always an honor to see you."

John L. scowled up at him. "Sit down, Daniel. I didn't say that the meeting was over." He waited until Daniel had returned to his seat. "The one thing that came out of our meeting with the President was the impression I got that he has an extremely high regard for you."

Daniel was silent.

"I think it would go a long way to establish our credibility with the government if we could find a way to work together. I think an announcement that U.M.W. had signed with C.A.L.L. to engage in a number of feasibility studies covering new organizing, pension-planning, health and welfare programs would go a long way to convince the President that we're not engaged in reckless behavior."

Daniel looked directly at the old man. "What you mean is that we create a smoke screen behind which you can continue on your own path."

Lewis cleared his throat. "That's putting it rather vulgarly."

"But it's the truth."

Lewis looked at his associates, then nodded. "Yes."

"Mr. Lewis, you know my reputation," Daniel said. "I'm not noted for remaining silent when I feel strongly about what is good for the union member."

"We'll take that chance," Lewis said. "Don't forget that I too have fought all my life for the betterment of the workingman. We may have differences of method and opinion, but none of motivation. And in the final run, the decision must still remain the right of the union which employs your services."

"Mr. Lewis, I thank you for the opportunity, and it's an honor for me to be of service to you and the U.M.W." Daniel held out his hand. "When do you want us to start?"

Lewis took his hand, smiling. "Yesterday. You work out the details with Tony and Tom."

Boyle followed him out to his car. "You're going to be working with me—you know that."

"I know that."

"It was my idea. John L. went for it, hook, line and sinker. He's getting old. All he wants to do now is keep his hands clean."

"I'll help him do that," Daniel said. "But I can't keep them away from the financial deals. He's got the union into too many things. The National Bank in Washington, West Kentucky Coal and the Nashville Coal companies, all bought with union money out of the pension and welfare funds. Sooner or later, the government is going to get into that, and when it comes, it could spell disaster. It isn't only the union-sponsored organizing campaigns that he has to think about."

"Are you going to tell him?" Boyle asked.

"In due time," Daniel said.

405

"He won't like it."

"I can't help that," Daniel said. "He asked me to help him. I'll try to do that. He also told me that he will still do exactly what he wants. I got the message."

"And what we talked about. That hasn't changed?"

Daniel looked at him. "No change. I'll be working with you to see that you become the president. But I'll give you some free advice right now. You're not John L., and you never will be. That means you won't be able to get away with ninety percent of what he does. When he dies, the shit's going to hit the fan. You better see to it that you stand there with clean hands."

"You leave that to me," Boyle said confidently. "I know what I have to do. You can't run this union by being Mr. Nice Guy."

"I'm not arguing," Daniel said. "Just some friendly advice."

"The first thing I'd like you to do is send a team down to Middlesboro and get us a report on all the new mines and tipples that are springing up all over the area. We'll need estimates on their production and labor force. I have a feeling if we don't get on it real soon, they'll undercut the sales of the union-operated mines to the T.V.A. to practically nothing."

"I'll get on it," Daniel said. He got into his car. "It will take money."

"You tell me how much," Boyle said. "And you get it the next morning."

Chapter 5

SHE WAS waiting in the street in front of his office building as he pulled his car to a stop at the curb. He got out of the car and walked toward her. "Why didn't you go inside?" he asked.

"Your office was locked and there was no one there."

"You could have waited in the reception room."

"The girl there was leaving, and she said they didn't know if you were coming back."

"I'm sorry," he said, opening the door and holding it for her. They walked up the stairs to the second-floor offices. "Been waiting long?"

"Since six o'clock."

He glanced at the wall clock. It was after seven. "I was stuck at a meeting." He took a key from his pocket and opened the door. She followed him into his office. He went to his desk and took out the bottle of whiskey. He poured himself a drink.

"I didn't mind waiting," she said. "I knew you wouldn't forget."

He swallowed the drink. "I should have called."

"I didn't mind. Really."

He smiled at her. "You look very pretty today."

She felt the heat rising in her face. "Thank you."

"I think I've got a job for your father if he's interested. We're getting busy here, and we could use a night man to keep an eye on the place and cover the telephones."

She smiled. "I think he'll be real pleased."

"The hours are long. Seven at night until seven in the morning."

"He won't mind."

"You bring him next week and have him see Mr. Barrington. He'll arrange everything."

"Thanks, Mr. Huggins."

He poured another drink. "Isn't it about time you called me Daniel?"

She was suddenly shy. "If you want me to."

"I want you to, Margaret."

She was almost whispering. "Okay, Daniel."

"That's better," he said. "I have a few calls to make. Are you in a hurry for dinner?"

"I have time."

He picked up the telephone and dialed a number. Moses answered the call. "Barrington." Behind his voice came the shouts of children.

"Am I interrupting dinner?"

"Not yet," Moses answered. "That's why you hear the kids hollering."

"I won't keep you," Daniel said. "I just thought you would like to hear some good news for a change."

Excitement came into Moses' voice. "Boyle came through?"

"Better than that. John L. wants us to do some work for them."

Moses was incredulous. "You're kidding. Don't fool with me, Daniel. My heart can't take it."

Daniel laughed. "It's legitimate. He wants us to undertake impartial studies of all areas. We're beginning with a survey of the Middlesboro and Kentucky districts. You'll have to put together a field team and get down there right away."

"I'll need more men," Moses said.

"Then get them. And take Junior down there with you as your number two. I want him to get his feet wet."

"But what about Harvard?"

"He'll have to pass that. It's more important that he get some real experience. He can pick up on college later. Once you feel he has the idea, then leave him there and you come back to the office."

"Okay, Big Dan." His voice lowered. "You got a call from Miami. He wants you to call him right back."

"I'll take care of it."

Moses' voice went back up. "Congratulations. Its like pulling a rabbit out of a hat. I don't know how you did it."

Daniel was pleased. "It's only the beginning. See you first thing in the morning."

He put down the telephone and looked across the desk. "Just one more call and we can go."

"I'm in no hurry."

He gave the long-distance operator the number. He put a hand over the mouthpiece while the call was going through. "Is that a new dress, Margaret?"

She shook her head.

"It's very pretty," he said. "But then, so are you."

She blushed. "Thank you."

A voice came on the wire. Just the number. "Seven six three three."

"Daniel Huggins calling."

"One moment, sir." There was a click on the line. Lansky came on. He came right to the point. "I need a favor."

"Just ask it," Daniel said.

"There's an election coming up in the New Jersey Teamsters. I want you to see that the right man wins it."

"I'll do my best." Daniel said. "What's his name?"

"Tony Pro."

Daniel was silent for a moment. Tony Pro; Anthony Provenzano. One of the Family. "You don't pick easy ones," he said. "You know Dave Beck is against him."

"That's your problem," Lansky said flatly. "Just tell Hoffa that if Tony Pro becomes president of that local, he'll never have to worry about the Teamsters on the Eastern Seaboard."

"I'll get on it right away," Daniel said.

"Keep me posted." Lansky went off the line.

Slowly Daniel put down the telephone. He began to dial

Moses' number again, then changed his mind. That would keep until the morning. It was either feast or famine. From nothing to do to too much. Suddenly he was tired.

"Anything wrong, Daniel?" she asked.

He looked at her. "Just tired, I guess. It's been a long day."

"You don't have to take me out to dinner. If you'd rather just go home and rest, I won't mind."

"I have an idea," he said. "Why don't we go to my house? I'll have Mamie fix us a nice dinner, and afterward we can sit around and watch television."

She felt the heat rise in her face again, but her eyes were ready. "If that's what you want."

He smiled suddenly, the smile seeming to drop the years from him. He picked up the telephone and dialed home. "Mamie, big steaks and all the trimmings. I'm bringing a pretty girl home to dinner."

It was a small house, not at all what she had expected. Cape Cod style, in a development where each house on the street looked almost like its neighbor. There were no driveways, and he parked the car in the street. They crossed a small patch of lawn to the front door.

Before they reached it, the door was opened by a heavyset black woman, a smile showing her large white teeth. "Evenin', Mistuh Dan."

"Mamie, this is Miss Rourke," Daniel said as he led the way into the house.

"Miz Rourke," Mamie said.

"Pleased to meet you, Mamie." Margaret smiled. "I hope we didn't make any problems."

"Oh, no, Miz Rourke. You work foh Mistuh Dan, you git used to things like that. No tellin' who he comin' home with. You jes' make yohse'fs comf'table an' I'll go on gittin' dinner ready." She looked at Daniel. "You got time foh a shower an' to git changed if'n you want."

"Okay, boss lady," Daniel said. He turned to Margaret. "Mamie thinks she's my mother. She runs my life."

Mamie pretended anger. "Somebody's got to take charge.

Now you git goin'. I'll see that this purty li'l thing is made comf'table."

Margaret nodded. "Go ahead. I'll be all right."

He went up the stairs, and Mamie led her into the living room. "Now you jes' set down heah an' I'll bring you any drink you like."

"I don't need anything. Can I help with anything?"

Mamie smiled. "Ev'ything's done. You jes' relax." She started from the room, then stopped and turned back. "You know Mistuh Dan a long time?"

Margaret shook her head. "Not long. Maybe two months."

Mamie grinned. "You must sho have somethin'. This is the fust time he ever brought any of his girls home."

Margaret stared after her as she left the room. From upstairs she heard the sound of a door slamming. Slowly she looked around the room. The furniture was old-fashioned, heavy-framed and dark wood. The chairs and couch crowding the small floor space. There was a desk with a telephone in one corner, and on the wall opposite the couch there was a television set, over which were bookcases, filled with books that looked as if they had never been read. There were several nondescript paintings on the walls. Nothing else.

Suddenly a thought came to her. Quickly she looked around the room again. Strange. Nowhere in the room was there a picture or photograph of anyone. This was the first time she had ever been in a home that did not have at least one photograph around. Her own little house was filled with them.

She heard his footsteps on the stairs and turned toward him. He had changed into a sport shirt, open at the throat, revealing the heavy matting of hair across his chest, and a pair of dark slacks. His hair was still wet from the shower, and he grinned as he saw her staring at him. "Anything wrong?"

He looked younger somehow. She shook her head. "It's the first time I've seen you without a suit and tie."

"I also take them off to go to bed," he said.

She blushed.

"I'll see if dinner's ready," he said. "Want to eat in here or in the kitchen?"

"Wherever you want."

"The kitchen," he said. "That's where we usually eat. It's easier."

After dinner, they came back to the living room. He turned on the television set and placed a bottle of whiskey on the table in front of them. He poured a drink for himself.

They watched as the set warmed up, bringing a quiz show into the room. She watched it with interest. She had no television set at home. He seemed bored with it but watched it silently, working steadily at the bottle of whiskey. Later they watched a movie for a while, then the news at eleven o'clock. During the evening they had scarcely exchanged more than ten words and had sat on the couch respectably distanced from each other.

Finally he got to his feet. "It's getting late," he said. "Time I got you to the bus station."

She looked up at him without moving.

"Didn't you hear me?"

"I heard you," she said.

"We'd better get going, then."

She rose silently and moved toward him. "Daniel."

"What is it?"

"I didn't have to come out here just for dinner."

He looked at her. "I'm old enough to be your father."

"But you're not my father."

"You've heard all those stories about me. Even your father warned you."

"That's right."

"Doesn't that mean anything to you?"

She nodded. "Yes."

"Then you'd better let me take you to the bus station before we do something we'll both regret."

Her eyes looked directly at him. "Don't you want me?"

He didn't answer.

"I want you," she said. "From the moment I first walked into your office, I wanted you."

"I don't pick on children," he said harshly.

412

"I'll tell you the same thing I told my father. I'm not a child anymore."

Again he was silent.

"I'm not a virgin, if that's what you're worried about," she said. "But this is the first time I've ever really wanted anybody. So much that the fire between my legs turns them into jelly and I'm afraid to walk."

He stared at her for a long moment, then turned and walked across the room away from her. "Get yourself together," he said gruffly. "I'm driving you home. I want to talk to your father."

"No," she said firmly. "Anything you have to say to my father, you can say to me."

"How old are you?"

She hesitated a moment. "Almost seventeen."

"Then I will have to talk to your father," he said. "You see, I want to marry you."

Chapter 6

THE RAIN had turned into falling sleet that slicked the black surface of the road leading into town. Daniel looked across the seat at Moses, who was driving. "Where's Junior?"

"He's at the Green boardinghouse waiting for us," Moses answered, his eyes squinting through the windshield as the wipers clicked back and forth.

"The others?"

"They're with him."

Daniel glanced at him again. Moses was silent. It wasn't normal for him. Usually he never stopped talking. Daniel took a cigar from his inside pocket and lit it. "When do you think you'll have the report ready?"

"We've got it all together. We're just waiting for you to go over it, maybe take a look around for yourself before we put it on paper."

Daniel nodded. This was not the usual pattern. Moses had never waited for him before. "How did Junior do?" he asked.

"Good." Moses looked at him. "He's got something of you in him. Cuts right through the bullshit."

"I'm anxious to see him," Daniel said. "I've got news for him."

"If it's about Margaret being pregnant," Moses said, "I think he's already heard."

"But I only found out last week." Surprise echoed in Daniel's voice.

"She's two months gone," Moses said. "Congratulations."

"Thanks," Daniel said drily. "Looks like the whole world knows. What have they got? Microphones in my bedroom?"

Moses grinned. "You know better than that. Women just can't keep a secret."

"Shit." Suddenly Daniel understood. Mamie. Junior called her once a week for his messages. He laughed. "I bet you all were as much surprised as I was."

"We weren't surprised," Moses said. "Matter of fact, we couldn't figure out what took you so long." They passed the sign at the side of the road.

WELCOME TO JELLICO

POP. 1200

"Five minutes," Moses said, turning the car into the main road. They began to drive past houses clustered on either side of the street. The lights of the town center loomed in front of them. Despite the sleet, the streets were filled with people walking, looking in shop windows.

"Busy town," Daniel said. "Looks like more than twelve hundred people."

"Most of them aren't from here," Moses said. "You won't find many locals on the street right now."

"Who are they?"

"Miners."

"They don't look like miners to me," Daniel said. "They're too clean. And miners are generally too tired to be walking around like this."

Moses was silent.

"Where do they work?"

"Not here," Moses said. "They're from out of town. But they're miners, all right. They all hold union cards." He made a left turn on the far side of the town center and pulled the car to a stop in front of a large house. "We're here."

Daniel waited while Moses locked the car, then followed

him up to the house. Junior was waiting just inside the door. "Father," he said, a smile on his face.

Daniel took his hand. Junior had filled out. Somehow he didn't look as boyish as he had looked three months ago. "How are you, son?"

Junior nodded. "Fine. You?"

"Real good."

"Come with me," Junior said. "Everybody's waiting in the dining room."

There were five men waiting around the table. Two of them Daniel knew. They worked for C.A.L.L. Jack Haney, the young new labor lawyer who had joined them last year, and Moses' assistant, a bright statistical analyst just recruited from the Wharton School of Finance. Daniel shook their hands, and Junior performed the introduction of the others.

Max Neal and Barry Leif, sent up from the U.M.W. headquarters in Middleboro, and Deputy Sheriff Mike Carson, a veteran U.M.W. activist. To all intents and purposes, they were spearheading the U.M.W. drive in Jellico.

Daniel sat down at the head of the table and looked around. He came right to the point. "You all know why I'm here. I've been asked by John L. Lewis to give him a report on certain aspects of our organizational efforts in this area, so let's get right down to it. The first order of business is Who's got the whiskey?"

They all laughed. Deputy Sheriff Carson answered while bringing up a jug from underneath the table. "Never thought you'd git aroun' to askin', Big Dan." Glasses appeared almost magically. He filled a glass and passed it to Daniel. "This is down-home product. The best."

Daniel tasted it. It was liquid fire going down. He smiled. "You're right, Sheriff. Haven't tasted squeezin's like this since I used to he'p out my paw with our still."

"Thanks, Big Dan. Comin' from you, I regard that as a real compliment." Carson filled the other glasses and passed them around. He raised his glass. "Welcome home, Big Dan."

Daniel nodded and took another drink. "Now fill me in."

Jack Haney looked around the table. "Any objections if I just do a quick summary?" There were no objections. He glanced down at a sheaf of papers. "The principal problem here is the Osborne mines. They're the biggest in the area and operating through a series of tipples, and blind trucking companies are avoiding union contracts and selling coal to the T.V.A. at less than the prices union mines can afford because of two factors.

"One, he pays less than union-scale wages. Two, he doesn't have the forty-cents-a-ton contribution to the union welfare fund. He claims that if he paid either one or both, he would not be able to bid in T.V.A. contracts and he would go broke. Because of his leadership, there are about thirty to forty other smaller mines following the same patterns. And that's the nub."

"You have his figures?" Daniel asked.

Moses answered. "Yes." His assistant gave him a set of papers. "Right here."

"You've done an extrapolation?"

Moses nodded.

"And?"

"Basically, he's right. The way he's operating, he'd go broke if he paid out."

"You said the way he's operating?"

"He's old-fashioned," Moses said. "HIs productivity is about eight tons per man, as against completely equipped union mines' getting thirty tons per man. If he could make the equipment change, he could afford the salaries and welfare-fund payments. But he claims he hasn't the capital to do it."

"Has he?"

"No." Moses said. "The way he operates, he's marginal."

"And the others?"

"They're as bad off as he is or worse." He put down the papers. "They're mostly family-type operations."

Barry Leif spoke up. "The end result is that we're all gittin' screwed. Unionized mines can't meet their prices, so the result is that they're layin' off workers while the others are puttin' them on. We got four big mines, employin' over a thousand members, about ready to shut down right now."

"Driving through town," Daniel said, "I saw a lot of men on the streets. They all miners?"

Leif nodded.

"Working around here?"

"No," Max Neal said. "They're volunteers we brought up from Middleboro to help us straighten out this here mess."

"How do you expect to do that?" Daniel asked.

"We'll turn the heat on the scab bastards. They'll either join up or we'll bust 'em up."

Daniel looked around the table. After a moment, he nodded. "I've got the picture," he said. "Suppose tomorrow you take me around so I can get a firsthand look at the problem."

"What time?"

"Right after breakfast. Eight o'clock okay?"

After the U.M.W. organizers and the deputy sheriff had gone, Daniel looked around the table. "Okay. Now give it to me straight."

Moses was the first to speak. "We're sitting on a volcano that's about ready to erupt. Yesterday they began stopping the trucks coming into town to pick up coal. If they didn't turn away, the sheriff gave them a warrant for operating without proper equipment. Then on the way out of town, the drivers were hauled out of the trucks, had the shit kicked out of them and the coal was dumped. Now we hear that Osborne has hired armed guards to ride the trucks to the state line. Carson says he's ready for them, and he's deputizing over a hundred of the U.M.W. volunteers and issuing gun permits. Plans are being drawn to dynamite some of the smaller mines and to have flying squads go to others and force the men to sign up. Some of these mines are owner-worked-and-operated; they're mountain people and they're not going to take it lying down. They're armed and ready. All the makings are here for a bloodbath."

Daniel turned to Jack Haney. "What's the legal position?"

"Not good," the young lawyer said. "As the law now reads, the U.M.W. is liable for any damages that result. Even if they succeed in forcing unionization of all the mines, they're still liable for a lot of money. It may take years for the courts to assess the penalties, but when they do, it can have a genuine damaging effect on the U.M.W. financial structure."

"What about an N.L.R.B. election?"

"U.M.W. doesn't want it. They haven't the local membership and they know they'll lose."

"What about direct negotiation?"

"Completely broken down. Neither side trusts the other."

"Any ideas on a possible compromise that would get them together?"

There was silence for a moment. Then Junior spoke. "I have one. But I don't know enough as to whether it's practical."

"Let's hear it, then, son."

"U.M.W. has brought in at least five hundred men, and they're not paying their own way. It's costing U.M.W. at least twenty-five hundred a day to keep them. I think the mine owners would go for union-scale wages if the welfare tonnage payments could be cut."

"Lewis wouldn't go for that. It would prejudice every other deal he's made."

"On the surface, the forty cents a ton wouldn't have to be changed. Supposing they paid ten cents a ton as mined and accepted a payment plan for the balance based on audited profits at the end of each year. If there aren't enough profits in the kitty, just carry it over to the next year. Meanwhile, the union shows the total forty cents a ton due to the welfare fund, with the unpaid portion as a receivable. Over a three-year period, based on present production of these mines, even if the union never collected the balance, it would come out cheaper than maintaining these men here for another sixty days as well as the liabilities that could result from the present situation."

Daniel looked at his son. He nodded slowly. He didn't show the pride that he felt. There might be flaws in the plan, but it was a step in the right direction. It was a face-saving compromise for both sides. But more than that. It was his son who had thought of it. No one else. His son. He looked around the table. "What do you think?" he asked of the others.

Moses answered for all of them. "It's a good idea. It just might work. But you'd have to sell it to Lewis first."

"How much time do we have?"

"Not much. A few days at the most. Neal and Leif are ready to blow the lid off."

"Any chance of slowing them down?"

Moses shook his head. "None."

Daniel poured himself another drink. He gulped it down. "If it does blow, is there any way in which we can support and justify the U.M.W. position? After all, that is what we were hired to do."

Moses looked around at the others. Again he spoke for them. "I don't see how we could. Even with both sides wrong, we can't say that makes one side right."

Daniel was weary. "If we can't do that, we lose Lewis and the U.M.W. Then we're practically back where we started. We lose their payments and we're broke again."

"We don't have to do anything, Father," Junior said. "All we have to do is take our time getting the report ready. By the time we get it into Lewis' hands, there will be nothing that can be done. Meanwhile, we've done what we're supposed to do."

"On the surface, yes," Daniel said. "But we all know better. We're not being honest."

"Nobody's asking us to be honest, Father."

Daniel looked at his son without speaking.

"The way I see it right now, it's a question of survival. Maybe the next time we could afford to be honest. If we ever expect to be anything at all, we have to be around to do it."

Daniel shook his head. "That's not the way I do it. I'm going up to Washington tomorrow to see Lewis."

"Why, Father? Why don't you just let us finish our report and then take it up there in the usual manner? You don't have to charge up there like a knight on a white horse. What do you hope to accomplish?"

"Once this starts, a lot of people are going to be hurt. On both sides. It doesn't matter. Maybe we can prevent that."

"It's not our war, Father," Junior said. "All your life you've been fighting other people's wars, and where did it get you?"

"I'm sorry, son," Daniel said. "But your idea is a good one. I'm sure that when Lewis hears what is happening down here, he'll do something about it."

Junior met his father's eyes. "What makes you think he doesn't know? This has been the pattern of every U.M.W. drive since '44. Meadow Creek mines in Sparta, Tennessee,

1948. Dynamite, violence, terror. The same tactics in Hopkins County, Kentucky, against the West Kentucky Coal Company in 1949. I've got a list as long as your arm. John L. Lewis is the United Mine Workers, and he will be until the day he retires or dies. And just because he delegates the dirty work to Tony Boyle and his other assistants, do you think he doesn't know exactly what is happening?"

"You might be right, but I still have to do it."

"No, Father. You're not being fair. To yourself or the men who stuck with you all these years, sacrificing themselves and their families and their careers in pursuit of an ideal that simply doesn't work in our society. You recognized that yourself when you made your proposition to Boyle and Hoffa, when you took that money from our friend in Florida. You yourself made the deal. You can't walk away from it now."

Daniel's voice was gentle. "It's easy for you to speak, son. And maybe you're right. It's not our war. But I've been there. In the midst of violence, with the hurt and the dead lying around me. I can't let it happen as long as there is a chance I can prevent it."

They were silent. Daniel looked around the table. "That was personal," he said. "We still have to do the job we're supposed to do. After this is all over, we're going to have to supply the U.M.W. with the justification they'll feel they needed to do all this." He rose to his feet. "Cancel my appointment to go out tomorrow. Tell them I was called back on an emergency." He turned to his son. "Do you think you can drive me back to the airport?"

The sleet had stopped, but the road was slippery. For a long while they were both silent, until the car was near the airport; then Daniel turned to his son.

"You made me very proud, son."

"I thought you were angry with me, Father. I don't want that to happen. Ever. I want to please you. Even if we don't agree."

"I wasn't angry. What you said was true. But I'm old-fashioned, I guess. I remember the way it used to be. The dreams we had when I was young. But you're right. It's another world."

"It's the same world, Father. It's just that there are different ways of doing things."

"When this job is finished, I want you to go back to college," Daniel said.

"Do you think it's necessary, Father? I can do a lot to help you."

"You said it was a different world, Junior. You're going to have to know a lot more about it than I did." He reached for a cigar, then put it back in his pocket. "No point in lighting this. They'll only make me throw it away when I get on the plane."

Junior laughed as they turned into the airport road. "How's Margaret?"

"She's fine."

"She happy about the baby?"

"I think so." Daniel glanced across the seat at him. "Are you?"

Junior nodded. "If you are."

"I am. Margaret's a good girl."

"She's young, Father."

Daniel smiled. "I guess she is. But I'm still a mountain man at heart. We pick 'em young."

Junior was silent.

"You don't approve?"

"You're fifty-six, Father. It isn't as if you didn't have girls. All my life I've seen you with them. I just didn't understand why, that's all."

"Maybe it was because she reminded me of the girls I knew when I was young. Girls who grew up before their years. Girls who were used to taking care of their families."

Again Junior was silent.

"Or maybe it was because I loved her, son."

Junior turned to look at him as he stopped the car in front of the terminal building. "That's the best reason of all, Father. You don't need any more than that."

Daniel got out of the car. He leaned back into it. "You know, son, that I love you too."

Junior's eyes were moist. "And I love you, Father."

Chapter 7

HE TURNED over in the bed and opened his eyes. Margaret was watching him. He smiled, leaning across the pillow, and kissed her.

"You were dreaming last night."

"I don't know," he said.

"You were crying in your sleep," she said. "Are you unhappy?"

He shook his head. He swung his feet off the bed. "How are you feeling?"

"All right. I think the baby moved."

He turned, looking back at her. "You should have wakened me."

"I wasn't sure. It's not five months yet."

"It could be possible," he said. "Especially if it's a boy."

"Is that what you want?"

He nodded and rose to his feet. "Yes."

"But you have one son already," she said. "Are you unhappy with him?"

"No. It's just that . . ." He thought for a moment. "Junior is only one side of me. The practical side. He's very good, and in time he'll be better than I am in what he does."

"Then what is it?"

"I would like a son who feels as I feel. Who dreams the way I used to when I was a boy, who senses the beauty in people and things around him, for whom living doesn't have to be a series of logical explanations."

"Couldn't a girl feel like that?"

He smiled. "I suppose so. But it will be a boy."

"Will you be unhappy if it is a girl?"

"No."

She was silent for a moment. "It will be a boy." She got out of bed and looked at herself in the mirror. "My stomach isn't very big, but my breasts are."

He smiled. "Beautiful."

"You like big breasts?"

He laughed. "I like your breasts."

She reached for a robe. "I'll go downstairs and get breakfast started."

"Mamie will do it."

"I like to do breakfast for you. She does everything else."

He walked over and put his arms around her. "Not everything."

"I hope not," she said, kissing his cheek.

He slipped his hands inside her robe, cupping her breasts. They were strong and heavy in his fingers; he felt her nipples hardening and the corresponding surge in his loins. "Come back to bed."

She felt herself flowing toward him. "You'll be late for work."

He pulled the robe down from her shoulders, exposing the milky whiteness of her breasts. He lowered his head to them, his tongue licking at the circle of her flushed aureole. "Not if you let Mamie get the breakfast."

Her hand found his ready strength as they moved back to the bed. They sank back on the bed, her legs climbing around his waist as she guided him into her. "Daniel," she whispered, her eyes half closed. "It's so good. So good. So good."

Only Junior was at the table when she came into the kitchen. "Good morning, Maggie Mother," he said, smiling.

"Morning, D.J.," she said, smiling back as she went to the stove and helped herself to a cup of coffee. She came back to the table and sat down. "Your father gone to work?"

He nodded. "He's dropping Mamie off at the market."

She sipped at her coffee. "You're going back to school on Monday?"

He laughed. "If you two lovebirds can be trusted to manage alone."

"D.J.," she said in protest. She had begun calling him that after they met. Short for Daniel Junior, it sounded better to her than Junior alone. He retaliated by calling her Maggie Mother, but there was a genuine liking between them, a respect for each other's love of the man that bound them together. "He didn't sleep well last night."

D.J. looked at her.

"Something's worrying him," she said. "Ever since last week, he's taken to wearing a gun in a shoulder holster under his jacket."

"He say anything to you?"

She shook her head. "No. If I ask, he says he's always done that."

"That's true. I remember seeing that ever since I was a kid."

"What's going on, D.J.? I'm not a child, no matter what he thinks. I'm his wife."

"Father doesn't confide in me either." He thought for a moment. "He's made a lot of enemies coming out in support of the U.M.W. after the riots and trouble in Jellico a couple of months ago."

"Do you think they would threaten him?"

D.J. shook his head. "I shouldn't think so. That's the kind of war he's been in all his life."

"What could it be, then?"

D.J. looked at her. "Now you've got me worried."

"I didn't mean to do that," she said. The tears came to her eyes. "I worship him. You know I do. He's the most wonderful man I've ever known."

He spoke awkwardly. "Maybe it's nothing. He's always carried a gun. Maybe we're creating something that doesn't exist."

She was crying now. Softly. Quietly. "I want to help him. I want to talk to him. But I don't know how. He knows so much more than I do. I don't know what to say."

He reached across the table and patted her hand gently. "You just relax, Maggie Mother. Getting yourself all upset isn't going to do the baby any good."

"You're just like your father," she sniffed, the beginnings of a smile tugging at her lips. "That's just what he would say."

"Maybe that is what he would say," D.J. admitted. "But I'm afraid I'm not just like him, though I wish I were."

Daniel parked the car in the alley behind the warehouse, walked up the rickety back stairs and knocked on the iron fire door. Three times quickly, then one knock.

The door opened quickly. A heavyset man stood there looking at him. "Mr. Huggins?"

Daniel nodded.

"This way."

Daniel followed the man through the long empty warehouse, its storage bins gathering nothing but dust, then up another staircase at the far side of the building. He went through another steel door and now they were in an office. At a long table were a number of men and women sorting slips of paper. They didn't look up as the two men walked past them into another room. Here too was a long table around which were gathered men and women. Only at this table they weren't sorting slips of paper, they were counting money. Bills and coins, the coins set in a machine that rolled them into neat, banklike stacks. They were ignored as they continued through into the next room.

Lansky was seated behind a desk in the barely furnished white-walled room. There were several nondescript chairs and couches in the room. The other two men in the room were the bodyguards Daniel had met when he visited Lansky in Florida. At a gesture from Lansky, they left the room, leaving him alone with Daniel. "Pull up a chair," Lansky said.

Daniel sat down in front of the desk. He didn't speak.

"You've done a good job," Lansky said. "I think this is the

426

first time union members ever got their fair share of insurance and pension-fund benefits. They're so used to getting screwed by their officials I wonder if they really understand what you're doing for them."

Daniel remained silent.

"We haven't done too badly either," Lansky said. "Though some of the insurance companies complain to me that you drive too hard a bargain."

"Let them bitch," Daniel said. "There's enough there so that nobody has to steal."

Lansky looked at him; he seemed puzzled. "You're a strange man, Big Dan. As far as I can see, there's been nothing in it for you except hard work. Your loan repayments are made on schedule, the commissions go into the union funds, you draw nothing down except your regular salary, your expense account is minimal. Where's your payoff?"

Daniel smiled. Lansky evidently had checked everything. "Money isn't everything. I'm an idealist."

Lansky laughed. "Ideals, shmideals. Everybody likes money."

"I didn't say I didn't. I only said it wasn't everything. You have all the money you need, Mr. Lansky. Why do you keep working?"

Lansky looked at him thoughtfully. He didn't answer.

"Why don't you retire and just enjoy the rest of your life?"

"It's not that easy," Lansky said. "I have obligations."

"Money can pay them off. It has to be more than that. There is one thing you don't want to give up."

"What do you think that is?" Lansky asked.

"Power," Daniel said simply.

Lansky stared at him for a moment. "And that is what you want?"

"Yes. But I won't pay for it at the expense of the people I'm supposed to represent."

"Then how do you expect to get it?"

"Simply. I make deals with the devils."

"Isn't that betraying your trust?"

"No. The way I see it, I minimize their capacity for evil. Because of what I did the last six months, more than six hundred thousand union members are getting twenty-percent greater benefit from their insurance and pension funds. And if I hadn't kept pressing, the U.M.W. would never be opening those ten hospitals in Virginia and Kentucky next June."

"But isn't that helping to perpetuate the devils in power?"

"I'm not a policeman, Mr. Lansky. I didn't elect them to their positions. It's up to the union members themselves to decide who they want to represent them." Daniel took a cigar from his pocket and put it in his mouth. He didn't light it. He looked at it thoughtfully. "I've spent my life in the labor movement, Mr. Lansky. I've seen all the injustices. On both sides. And I've come to the conclusion that I can't improve it from outside. The only way to improve the system is to work within it."

Lansky looked at him. "I don't mind if you smoke." He waited until Daniel had lighted his cigar. "Then I suppose you wouldn't be interested in floating five million dollars a year through your pension funds even if you were to get a five-percent commission on it for yourself personally?"

"You're talking about the money out there?" Daniel jerked his head at the door behind him.

"Yes."

"You supposed right, Mr. Lansky."

Lansky was silent for a moment. "But you wouldn't object to working with any union even if the A.F.L.-C.I.O. were to expel them for corruption?"

"You're talking about the Teamsters, the Bakery Workers, the Laundry Workers specifically?"

"About them. And the Building and Maintenance Workers and the I.L.A., as well as others. I'm talking about two and a half million more union members who might within the next few years be looking for a new home."

"Only on the same conditions that I'm working now. I have no intention of starting another labor organization to counter the A.F.L.-C.I.O. As I said before, my purpose is to gain more benefits for the working people by working with their elected officials, not controlling them."

Lansky smiled. "Remember the story, The Devil and Daniel Webster? Are you sure your name isn't Daniel Webster Huggins?"

Daniel laughed. "No. It's Daniel Boone."

"And I am not the Devil," Lansky said softly. "You don't have to plead with me for the soul of labor."

"I'm glad to hear that, Mr. Lansky," Daniel said. "I was beginning to feel concerned."

"You've been making enemies, Big Dan," Lansky said. "Some of the people you've been helping the most are beginning to resent the appeal you're gaining among their own unions."

"I've been making enemies all my life, Mr. Lansky," Daniel said. "I've learned to live with it."

"So have I, Big Dan," Lansky said softly. "And I would like to suggest that you take some of the same precautions that I do to stay alive."

Daniel was silent. This was the point of the meeting. After a moment, he got to his feet. Some whisperings had already reached him, which was why he had taken to wearing the gun again. In a strange way, he was glad that the threat was not coming from the little man in front of him. He felt a strange kinship with him. They were both outcasts of a sort. "Thank you, Mr. Lansky," he said. "I'll do what I can."

Lansky smiled and pressed a button on the desk. The men came back into the room. The meeting was over.

Chapter 8

"Two HUNDRED thousand dollars a week, and that's only the beginning," Hoffa said. "An' Dave Beck ain't gonna get his sticky fingers on it."

Daniel sat watching him. He didn't speak.

"I want Central States to set up their own pension fund, and you're gonna help me," Hoffa continued. "That's why I called you guys down here."

Daniel glanced at Moses and Jack Haney, who had come with him, then across the room at Hoffa's two associates, Bobby Holmes and Harold Gibbons. "Exactly what is it you expect of us?" he asked.

"I want you to set up a foolproof system so that we can administer our own fund for the benefit of our own members."

"Who's going to run the fund?" Daniel asked.

Hoffa was surprised. "I am. Who else do you think I'd trust with all that money?"

Daniel kept a straight face. "You may run into problems. There could be a conflict of interest. Personal and union."

"No problem," Hoffa said. "What's good for me is good for the union."

"I'm not arguing that," Daniel said. "But it might be hard to convince others."

"That's your job," Hoffa said. "Now, how do we do it?"

"You want an answer right now?"

"Damn right I do," Hoffa snapped. "We been collectin' this money for almost a year now, and there's over ten million dollars layin' there in the bank doin' nothin'."

Daniel smiled. "The money beginning to burn a hole in your pocket, Jimmy?"

For the first time, Jimmy laughed. "You better believe it. We got some propositions in front of us that can make a lot of money."

"What kind of propositions?"

"A couple of old friends of mine from Detroit are very big in Vegas. They can use some buildin' capital. They pay big premiums for money because the banks are very sticky with 'em."

Daniel nodded, remembering his conversation with Lansky last month. It made sense. The little man's connections went far and wide. "Sounds reasonable. But you're going to have to diversify your investment portfolio. You can't just go into things like that. How's the insurance package working out?"

"It's okay," Jimmy said. "They gave my friend the exclusive agency, so everything's in order."

"Glad to hear that," Daniel said. "Supposing you give us all the information you have available, and we'll get back to you with a workable plan within the week."

"No later?" Hoffa said.

"No later."

Hoffa turned to Gibbons. "Turn the papers over to him."

"Copies be okay?" Gibbons asked, looking at Daniel. "I don't like losing originals."

Gibbons left the room. Hoffa leaned across his desk. "Can we talk privately for a minute?"

Daniel nodded. At a gesture, the other man left the room. He waited until the door closed behind them. "What's on your mind?"

"Dave Beck," Hoffa said. "It don't look good."

"True," Daniel said.

"How long do you think it will take 'em to put him away?"

"With all the appeals open to him, another year, fifteen months maybe."

Hoffa picked up a pencil and worried it for a moment. "There's talk that he might sing to get a lighter sentence."

"I don't think he will," Daniel said. "All they have him on is a lousy income-tax rap. Nothing there to keep him forever. He's too smart to blow the whistle, because he knows that will blow his pension and agreements under his Teamster employment contract."

"Then I should be ready to make my move for the fall '57 convention?"

"Yes."

"Think I can make it?"

"You can make it. There's nobody else," Daniel said. "But you might as well know this, if you don't already. You're the next target. They're going to come after you like gangbusters."

"Fuck 'em," Hoffa said. "They're not going to get anything on me."

"That's what Dave Beck thought. They found a way."

"I'm not an idiot. I pay my taxes."

"There's a great deal of heat on the Teamsters. A political attack on the union can exploit the public's fear of the power the union has over our economy. Sooner or later, some politician's going to jump on it. There've been too many statements made by Teamster officials that they can close the whole country down with one strike."

"We can," Hoffa said.

"You do and that's the end of the union," Daniel said. "The government steps in and takes over."

"I know that," Hoffa said. He put down the pencil. "Where do you think Meany stands on all this?"

"The Teamsters are out as far as the A.F.L.-C.I.O. is concerned. They're jumping on the corruption bandwagon that came up in the course of Dave Beck's examinations and trials."

"But the government hasn't proved a case."

"For Meany they don't have to. All he needs is an excuse and you're out."

"He's afraid that we'll move in and take over," Hoffa said. "Maybe."

"I'm not interested. Maybe you can tell him that."

"I will. But there's no reason for him to believe me. He doesn't like me any more than he does you." Daniel looked at him. "The big difference between us is—he can't do anything to me. C.A.L.L. is not a union; we're a union service and consultation group, available to any union that wants to employ our services. And even then, we do not make policy, we only recommend. The individual unions have to decide for themselves what course they want to follow. And they're free to discharge us at any time for any reason."

"I've heard that he's told a number of unions that if they employed C.A.L.L. he would regard that as a violation of A.F.L.-C.I.O. confidences and information."

"I've heard that too," Daniel said. "But I have no proof. Besides, that's not my problem."

"I guess not." Hoffa smiled. "From what I hear, you've been signing up quite a few unions around the country."

Daniel nodded. "Maybe they're beginning to find out that we're doing the job we promised."

"If you should decide to form another national labor organization, you could count on the Teamsters."

"Thank you," Daniel said. "But there isn't room enough for two separate labor organizations. The A.F.L. and C.I.O. recognized that and merged. I'm satisfied the way things are."

Hoffa laughed. "Big Dan, you're either the smartest man in the labor movement—or the dumbest."

Daniel joined in his laugh. "Ever think I might be both?"

Later, in the car on the way to the airport, Moses leaned toward Daniel, speaking in a low voice. "You know, Hoffa lied to us."

"About what?"

"He said they had about ten million lying around. It's more like fifty million. He forgot to mention some of the other major locals he controls."

"I figured that," Daniel said.

Moses' voice was hushed, almost in awe. "In three years, they'll have over a billion dollars to play with."

"So?"

"That makes the U.M.W. kitty seem like the corner grocery store. Lewis can't hold a candle to that."

"The money they have is none of our concern," Daniel said.

"It has to be," Moses said. "They're asking us to tell them what to do with it."

"No, they're not," Daniel said. "They're asking us to recommend procedures on the investment and protection of that money for the benefit of their members."

"What they're really looking for is for you to give them a license to steal."

"They won't get that from me. They'll get exactly what they asked for."

"You won't be able to stay out of it," Moses said. "If they get into trouble, they'll come to you to defend their actions."

"I can't worry about that at this time," Daniel said.

"We'd better start thinking about it all the same," Moses said gloomily.

"Okay," Daniel said. "What do you think is the first thing we ought to do?"

"Central States is paying us ten cents a member. If we take on this pension-fund assignment, I think they ought to pay us another ten cents."

"I don't see how that will help us solve their problem."

"We're going to have to add to our staff. That's going to cost money. Somebody's going to have to pay for it."

Daniel looked at him. "And you think they ought to?"

Moses nodded. "It seems only fair to me. They can afford it. We can't."

Daniel thought for a moment. "I don't object to it. Include it as part of the proposal we make them."

"And if they don't agree?"

"We do the job anyway. Whether I like it or not, I made a deal with Jimmy Hoffa, and I don't intend to go back on my word."

Chapter 9

THE SOUND of the automobile horn came through the open window. Daniel looked up from the morning paper. "The car's here already."

"I heard it," Margaret said.

He gulped at his coffee. "I've got to run."

"Will you be home for dinner tonight?"

"I don't know," he said. "We're up to our ass in work. I never should have taken on the additional work for the Teamsters. We wound up processing and checking out all the loan requests, and there's a lot of them which we have to forward with our recommendations for their executive-committee meeting the day after tomorrow."

"You've only been home for dinner two nights out of the last ten days," she said.

He looked at her. "It can't be helped. I have responsibilities."

"You have a responsibility to me too," she said.

He got to his feet. "I know that. But you knew the work I do before we were married."

"You weren't as busy then. You had more time for yourself. And me."

"We were also on the verge of bankruptcy."

"And the money makes it better?"

"At least we can pay our bills," he said. "And the new house we're getting up in Scarsdale, New York, isn't exactly poor man's life-style."

"I'm happy here," she said. "Why do we have to move up to New York?"

"I've explained that to you already," he said patiently. "More and more we're getting into the fund-management business. New York is where the money is. That's why we're moving our offices down near Wall Street."

She was silent as he put on his jacket.

"Relax," he said. "It will okay. The last month is always the worst. After the baby comes, you'll feel better."

She shook her head. "I look so ugly."

He walked around the table and kissed her. "You're beautiful."

"I'll never get my figure back."

He laughed. "You will. Don't worry about it."

"I'm afraid you're going to meet some girl and she'll take you away from me." She looked up at him.

"No chance."

"It's been more than a month," she said. "And I know you. I see the way you are when you wake up each morning."

"A piss and a cold shower takes care of that," he said, laughing.

"How many cold showers do you have to take during the day?" she asked.

He shook his head. "What am I going to do with you?"

She didn't answer.

"Come on," he said. "It's not that bad."

"I can't even take you in my mouth anymore," she said. "I get nauseous all the time."

"You're being silly," he said.

The tears began to roll down her cheeks. "I'm scared. I'm going to lose you. I know it."

He lifted her to her feet and kissed her, taking care not to press against her belly. "You won't lose me." The auto horn sounded through the windows again. "I'm late. I've got to run."

436

She followed him to the door. "What about dinner?"

"I'll try to make it," he said. "I'll call you later in the afternoon."

She stood in the doorway and watched him walk down the path to the car. The driver got out and opened the door for him. He got into the back seat. She waited there until the car had turned the corner at the end of the street, then went back into the house.

Mamie was just coming from the kitchen, her shopping bag in hand. "I was jes goin' to the store. Anything I can get for you, Miz Huggins?"

"No," Margaret said. "I'm all right. I'm just going up to bed and lie down for a while."

They hadn't driven for more than a few blocks when George, the driver, glanced back at Daniel. "There's a car following us, Mr. Huggins."

"Sure?" Daniel asked.

George glanced in the rearview mirror. "Positive. The blue Dodge. There are two men in the front seat. They picked me up when I came out of the garage this morning."

Daniel looked out the rear window. Traffic was heavy behind them, and he didn't see the car. "Where?"

"About seven cars back," George said.

Daniel saw them now. It was an ordinary-looking car. He could make out two men in the front seat but couldn't tell what they looked like. "Recognize any of them?" he asked.

George shook his head. "Never saw any of them before."

"Did you come right to my house from the garage?"

"No, sir," George answered. "I had to pick up Mr. Gibbons from the hotel first and take him to the Teamster office for a meeting with Mr. Beck. I dropped him off, then came to get you."

Daniel nodded. It was a Teamster car and driver. Only normal that they take care of their own first. Hoffa had arranged for the car and driver to be available to him when he needed it. "Who do you think they are?"

"I don't know," George said. "Could be cops. They use crummy cars like that."

"Did you mention it to Mr. Gibbons?"

"No. I wasn't sure then. It wasn't until after I dropped him off and they still followed me that I was sure."

"Do you carry a gun?" Daniel asked.

"No, sir."

"Who else knew you were picking me up this morning?"

"Everybody," George answered. "The drivers' assignments are posted on the bulletin board the night before."

Daniel looked back through the window. The Dodge was still there about five cars behind them. He turned back in his seat. "Jump the next red light and make a right turn. Then duck up the first alley you come to. Stop there and lie down on the front seat."

George glanced back in time to see Daniel taking the gun from his shoulder holster. His voice went dry. "Do you think there'll be any shooting?"

Daniel checked the cylinder of the revolver. "I don't think so, but I learned a long time ago not to take any chances."

George's hands tightened grimly on the wheel. They went three more blocks before George had his chance. He shot through the red light and made a sharp right. Daniel, watching through the rear window, didn't see the blue car as they turned again into an alley. Halfway through to the next street, George stopped the car. He turned to look back.

"Get down," Daniel said sharply.

George disappeared, and Daniel looked back at the street from the window. About a minute later, the blue car sped past the alley.

"Okay," Daniel said. "Let's shag ass outta here and get me to my office."

George spun the wheels of the car getting out of the alley as Daniel returned the gun to its holster. "Jesus!" George said.

"Do you have any other assignments after you drop me off?" Daniel said.

"I was told to stay with you all day."

"No. Drop me off and then go back to your garage. As soon as you get there, call and let me know if they're still following you."

George glanced in the mirror. "They're behind us again."

"I expected them," Daniel said. "I just wanted to make sure

of what they were doing." He caught a glimpse of George's worried face in the mirror. "Nothing to be afraid of," he said reassuringly. "They know we're on to them now. They won't make any trouble."

The car stopped in front of the two-story taxpayer building that housed the offices. Without looking around, Daniel walked into the building and went directly to his office. He was in the midst of his morning mail when the call came.

"This is George, Mr. Huggins. I'm at the garage. They didn't follow me."

"Okay, George. Thanks."

"Is there anything else you want me to do?"

"No, George. I'll call you if there's anything. Thanks again." He pressed a button on his phone. A moment later, Moses and Jack were in his office. "There's a blue Dodge sedan parked somewhere on the street outside with two men in it. They've been tailing me since I left the house this morning."

"Do you know who they are?" Moses asked, concern in his voice.

"I haven't the faintest idea. Have someone get the license-plate number for us, then see if we can find out who the car belongs to through our friends in the police department."

"I'll do it myself," Moses said quickly.

"No. If they know me, they know you. Send one of the office boys or a stenographer. Tell them not to be obvious. Just walk by and get the number. That's all."

"Okay," Moses said. He left the office.

Daniel turned to Jack. "What's our position if we're questioned on any of our clients' affairs?"

Jack looked at him. "If they have exercised proper legal procedures and you're required to testify under oath, you have no choice but to answer the questions."

Daniel was silent.

"You don't enjoy the protection of a lawyer–client or even a doctor–patient relationship, if that's what you're thinking," he added.

"What about files that have been entrusted to us by our subscribers?"

"If they're subpoenaed, you have to turn them over."

Daniel nodded and stared thoughtfully down at his desk. "Better get everything we have in the place that comes from outside and make arrangements to get them back to whichever unions are concerned. I want nothing in our files by tonight except our own papers."

"You're making it tough on us," Jack said. "We need a lot of those papers so that we can do our job."

"I don't give a damn," Daniel said. "I'm not going to be the back door for any son of a bitch that wants to get to one of our subscribers. You get those files out of here. Tomorrow we'll start planning small task forces to work in the sub-scribers' own offices. It may be a little inconvenient, but we'll get the work done."

"It's also going to cost money," Jack said.

Daniel looked at him. "Can you tell me what doesn't?"

Moses came back into the office. "We know who the car belongs to. We didn't have to call the police. It's stamped right on the plates. U.S. Gov't. G.S.A."

Daniel looked up at him. "Know anybody over at General Services who will tell us what department the car is assigned to?"

"I think so," Moses said. He picked up the phone and dialed rapidly. He spoke into the telephone in a quiet voice, then covered the mouthpiece with his hand. "He's checking for us." A moment later, he said, "Thank you" and put down the telephone. "It's signed out to the McClellan committee," he announced.

The Senate Select Committee on Improper Activities in the Labor or Management Field was the full name. "Okay," Daniel said. "At least we know now what we're dealing with. There's only two unions they're targeting. The United Auto Workers and the Teamsters. And since we're not signed with the U.A.W., we have to assume they're tying us into the Teamsters." He looked up at Jack. "You make sure that the Teamsters' files are the first you get out of here."

Chapter 10

"WE'RE FOOLS," Daniel said, pushing the elaborate report on the table away from him.

"What's wrong?" Moses asked anxiously.

"Nothing," Daniel said. "We've just been sitting on a gold mine and we never knew it. Here we are recommending investments for the Teamsters' pension fund and we're doing nothing about it ourselves."

"What can we do about it?" Jack asked.

"We can start our own fund," Daniel said.

"We haven't got that kind of money," Moses said.

"We can get it." Daniel lit a fresh cigar and blew a gust of smoke toward the ceiling. "Union Mutual Funds. We open it up so that individual union members as well as locals can subscribe. There are hundreds of small independent locals who haven't enough money to go into a plan on their own who will jump at an opportunity to join in."

"We'll still need a lot of money to get it off the ground," Jack said. "Maybe as much as ten or fifteen million dollars, for openers."

"I can get it," Daniel said confidently. "Between the Teamsters and the U.M.W. it will be easy. And what's more, it will be a good public relations move for them. Some of their investments, while they may be profitable, are beginning to smell a little bit. This could freshen the air for them."

"It's very interesting," Jack said cautiously.

"I don't know," Moses said cautiously. "It could change the whole nature of our operation. We move from the position of adviser to manager."

"I can't see anything wrong in that," Daniel said. "It's consistent with our purpose. To provide better security for the union man."

"It could be tricky," Moses said. "We don't know anything about running a fund like that."

"We hire experts. There isn't a stockbroker in the world who wouldn't jump at a chance to come in on a deal like this. Right now we have over three million union members in unions affiliated with us. Just one hundred dollars from each member gives us three hundred million dollars to invest. You don't have to be an expert to know that if you invest only in blue-chip stocks, you'll average an eight-percent return on the money. That's twenty-four million dollars a year, and if our service fees for management are only half the commercial rate, we'll be earning three million dollars a year."

"That's almost twice what we're collecting in affiliation dues right now," Moses said. "And we don't have to go around hat in hand."

"You're beginning to get the idea," Daniel said. He picked up the report on the desk. "Jack, you get started on this right away. I want to know everything we need to set up shop."

"Right."

He turned to Moses. "Get the statistical department to make up a list of members of each affiliated local. Names and home addresses."

"We'll have to get that from the unions," Moses said. "Right now we collect on the per capita reports sent us by the unions."

"Get it, then."

"What will I tell them?" Moses asked. "You know how touchy they are about giving out members' names."

"Tell them we're doing a study on members' living conditions. Anything. Just figure out something, but get the information."

"Okay."

The two men got to their feet. Jack gestured at the report. "Do you want me to send that on to Hoffa?"

"No," Daniel said. "I think I'll deliver this one myself."

"Something's on your mind," Hoffa said shrewdly. "Otherwise you wouldn't have come down here yourself just to bring these."

"That's right," Daniel said. "In addition to our recommendations in that folder, I want you to invest fifteen million dollars in a mutual fund that we're starting."

Hoffa looked at him. "What makes you think I'm gonna give you money to start up a mutual fund when we can start our own?"

"Good public relations." He smiled. "It will show that your concern for labor transcends jurisdictional lines. That you're concerned not only with the welfare of the Teamsters but with all union members equally."

What kind of crap is that?" Hoffa asked.

Daniel laughed. "Want the bottom line?"

Hoffa nodded. "You bet your ass I do."

"For the last two weeks I've been under surveillance by agents of the McClellan committee. Our friends up on the Hill tell me the reason they're watching me is that they're after you and they figure our association will lead them to something they can use against you. Any day now they're going to come marching in here to look over your records."

"What the hell are they looking for?"

"I don't know. And I have a hunch they don't know either. They just figure with the kind of money pouring in, there has to be something illegal going on."

"They ain't gonna find nothin' in my files."

"They won't in mine either," Daniel said. "I had every piece of paper I received from the Teamsters sent back to you two weeks two."

"How come nobody told me about it?"

"I don't know. I had everything sent back to Gibbons."

Hoffa reached for the telephone. "I'll get Gibbons in here."

"That can wait," Daniel said. "It's not important now. You better do what I did. Get hold of your legal department and find out exactly what rights you have if they do come in."

Hoffa stared at him. Then he nodded. "Yeah."

Daniel was silent.

"Who else is putting money into this mutual fund you're starting?" Hoffa asked.

"The U.M.W. is coming in for five million."

"Then why should I kick in fifteen?"

"Because you're three times as rich as they are."

Hoffa laughed. "You lay it right on the line, Big Dan." He opened the report and glanced through the pages. "What makes you think that will be a better investment than any of these you recommend?"

"I don't know whether it will be better. I only know it will be safer. Every deal in there involves a degree of speculation. You might make a lot of money, or you might blow it. We're staying in blue-chips. Nothing fancy—just straight-line steady growth. You might not make as much money, but you won't get hurt."

"Do we get any special consideration for coming in early?"

"You can put a man on the investment committee."

Hoffa laughed. "A lotta good that will do us. I got those assholes on my committee and I still have to make every decision myself." He leaned back in his chair. "For fifteen million bucks we ought to get some extra points."

Daniel shook his head. "That's exactly what I want to stay away from. This is going to be a public fund. I don't want politicians to be able to turn this into another political football. We're going to play this one by the rule book."

"Okay, Big Dan," Hoffa said. "We go by the book."

"Five million dollars," Lewis said thoughtfully. He glanced across the desk at his associates. "What do you think, Tom?"

Kennedy nodded his head. "It has good possibilities."

"Tony?" Lewis asked.

"I think it could do what Big Dan says. It opens the door

for all union members to get in on the American market for peanuts, and it makes good p.r. for us to associate with it."

"Five million dollars is a lot of money," Lewis said.

Daniel was silent. Considering that Lewis had bought a Washington, D.C., bank for the U.M.W. which now had assets of over two hundred million dollars and that the U.M.W.'s cash deposits in that bank were in excess of fifty million dollars at this very moment, the old man was doing a good job of poor-mouthing it.

Lewis leaned across the desk. "How much capital have you already got committed to this project, Mr. Huggins?"

Daniel smiled. "If you give me the five, I'll have twenty million dollars to start up."

"And if I don't?"

"Nothing," Daniel said flatly.

"Where are you getting the other fifteen?"

"From the Teamsters."

Lewis's voice held disbelief. "Dave Beck?"

"No, sir. Central States. Jimmy Hoffa."

"So if I don't give you the money, Jimmy Hoffa won't?"

"No, sir. He attached no strings to his investment. It's just that if you don't come in, I won't take his money."

"Why not?"

"I need a broader base in the labor movement than just one union. I want to begin something that transcends all union lines. Something that could be of benefit and opportunity to every union member, no matter what union he happens to be part of."

John L. Lewis looked at him. "That sounds idealistic."

"It might be, sir. But there's nothing wrong with ideals. If you hadn't had them, the mine workers would still be where they were when I first went down into the mines as a boy forty-five years ago."

Lewis nodded slowly. "That's true. We sometimes forget the struggle that made all this possible. A struggle that will never end, one that will forever demand our vigilance." He turned to Tom Kennedy. "Tom, work out the arrangements with Mr. Huggins. In my opinion, he's embarking on a very constructive step for the labor movement in America."

Chapter 11

"THE KEY to the success or failure of the fund will be the individual investors. Otherwise we leave ourselves open to the charge that we're just another branch of the big unions' drive to monopolize their treasuries' money." Jack Haney's voice was clinical. "It will also make a difference in the way Wall Street looks on us. Right now, they're not too happy about our plan."

"Screw 'em," Daniel said. "Who gives a damn what they think?"

"You can't say that," Jack replied. "Without their help we go nowhere in a hurry. They have to invite you into the club; just money won't buy your way in."

Daniel was silent for a moment. "We need the funding of the Teamsters and the U.M.W. or we can't get started."

"They recognize that," Jack said. "And they're not against it. It's just that they feel the fund should have a broader base at the beginning. They'd be satisfied if we had as little as fifty thousand shareholders with minimal investments."

"It's going to take time to get them," Daniel said. "By the time we get the mailings out, the prospectuses, process the replies and finally sell shares, at least six to ten months will go by. I don't want to wait that long."

"I don't know any way to speed it up," Jack said.

Moses, who had been silent until now, spoke up. "I know how it can be done." He turned to Jack. "You weren't around here when Big Dan traveled the country picking up memberships for C.A.L.L. when we were starting out. He's the greatest salesman in the world. They love him out there. He's one of them."

Daniel looked at him. "I don't know. This is something else."

"It's the same thing, Big Dan," Moses said. "You got to go out there where your strength lies. You let them see you, they'll follow you."

"It will still take time," Daniel said.

"I can set things up. You can cover the whole country in two months," Moses said. "We still have a lot of friends out there. And if we sweeten the deal by offering officers and stewards a ten-percent commission payable in shares based on the subscriptions by their locals, we can't miss."

Daniel thought for a moment. "How long would it take for you to get that program in motion?"

"I can have you on the road as early as next week," Moses said. "In two months you'd be back here with all the shareholders we need to make everybody happy."

"I have to be here by the middle of next month at the latest," Daniel said. "Margaret's expecting the baby about then."

"We can work our schedule around it," Moses said. "It's up to you."

Daniel looked at Jack. "Do we have any druthers?"

Jack shook his head. "I don't know any other way."

Daniel thought for a moment, then finally agreed. "Okay," he said. "Start working on it. But remember, keep the middle week of next month open." He looked at his watch. It was after seven o'clock. "I'd better be getting home. I promised Margaret I wouldn't be late for dinner."

There were two men waiting for him as he came down the steps into the lobby of the office building. He recognized one of them as Lansky's bodyguard, the tall blond man he had first met at the Miami Airport.

"Mr. Huggins," the blond man said politely. "The boss would like to see you."

"Fine," Daniel said. "Ask him to give me a call at home. We'll set up an appointment."

"He wants to see you now," the blond man insisted.

"I'm already late for dinner," Daniel said. "My wife is expecting me."

"So is the boss" came the noncommittal answer.

Daniel looked at him. "He'll have to wait."

"No, he won't."

Daniel looked down and saw the outline of a gun in the man's pocket. It was aimed at him. Daniel laughed. "I guess he won't."

"We have a car outside." The other man led the way to the black limousine parked in front of the building, the blond man staying at Daniel's side. A driver was behind the wheel. The two men climbed into the back seat with Daniel. The car pulled out into traffic.

Daniel looked back out the rear window and saw the blue Dodge sedan move out after them. He turned to the blond man. "Mr. L. is not going to be too happy about this," he said. "You're taking the Feds right to his door."

"What are you talking about?" the blond man asked.

"Look back," Daniel said. "The blue Dodge sedan with government plates. F.B.I. They've been tailing me for weeks."

The blond man looked at him, then at the driver. "Lose them."

"I wouldn't do that either," Daniel said. "They've already got your plate number. The minute they don't see you, they'll put out an All Points."

The blond man looked worried.

"I think you better get to a phone and let Mr. Lansky know what's happening," Daniel said.

"Okay, hold it," the blond man said quickly. "Pull over to the drugstore on the corner."

As the car came to a stop, he got out of the car. "Wait here with him," he told the man sitting next to Daniel, then went into the store. He was out in a few minutes and got back into the car.

He looked uncomfortably at Daniel. "Mr. Lansky says for us to take you home."

"That's more intelligent," Daniel said as the car moved out into traffic again.

"He says he will call you later tonight."

"I'll be in," Daniel said. "I'm not going anywhere."

Fifteen minutes later, the car came to a stop in front of Daniel's house. Daniel got out. He turned back to the blond man. "Thanks for the lift."

The blond man scowled silently.

Daniel smiled. He didn't seem to move, but suddenly the gun was in his hand and he pushed it into the blond man's face. "The next time you come for me," Daniel said softly, still smiling, "you'd better come shooting. Because the minute I see your face I'm going to blow your head off. Tell Mr. Lansky that for me."

The gun disappeared from his hand as he slammed the door shut and, turning his back on them, walked up the path to his front door. By the time he went inside, the car was gone.

The telephone began to ring as they sat down to dinner. Mamie answered it. "They's a Mr. Miami on the telephone for you."

Daniel looked up at her. "Tell him I'm just sitting down to dinner, to call me back in an hour."

Margaret looked at him. "Who's Mr. Miami?"

Daniel cut a piece of his steak. "Lansky."

"Why doesn't he use his real name?"

Daniel shrugged.

"What does he want?"

Daniel glanced up. "His pound of flesh."

"I don't understand," she said in a puzzled voice.

"He's probably heard by now we're starting a mutual fund," he explained. "He figures he's entitled to a piece of it."

"Is he?" she asked.

"No."

"Well, that settles it," she said. "You'll just tell him."

Daniel controlled his smile. "He's not the easiest man in the world to say no to."

Margaret was silent for a moment. "Daniel, you're not in any kind of trouble, are you?"

"No."

"I've read about this Mr. Lansky in the papers," she said. "He's a gangster, isn't he?"

"That's what they say."

"Then why are you doing business with him?"

"My business is legitimate. Whatever else he does is none of my business."

"I wouldn't do any more business with him if I were you," she said.

He smiled at her. "I don't intend to." He finished his steak and pushed it away from him. "That was good."

She got heavily to her feet. "Go into the living room and put your feet up. I'll bring you the coffee."

She leaned over him, picking up his plate. He patted her belly. "Won't be long now."

"Eight weeks, the doctor said."

"Watching your weight?" he asked.

"I haven't gained an ounce this last month."

"Good," he said. He went to the sideboard and took out a bottle of bourbon and a glass. "Bring some cold water with you," he said as he walked into the living room.

He sat in the chair, the half-empty whiskey glass in his hand, while she put the coffee on the cocktail table in front of him. "I'm starting a series of meetings around the country next week."

She was surprised. "What's that all about?"

"I have to sell the mutual fund to the different unions and locals."

"Do *you* have to do that? Couldn't Moses or Jack?"

"*I* have to do it," he said. "I'm the only one they'll come out for."

"How long will you be gone?"

"I'll be in and out," he said. "I'm working out the schedule so that I'll be here when the baby comes."

Suddenly she was angry. "That's real nice of you," she said sarcastically.

"What's eating you?" he asked. "I told you I'd be here when the baby comes."

"And what am I supposed to do when you're out on the road having all those meetings? Sit here waiting, holding my belly in my hands?"

"This is business," he snapped. "Stop acting like a child."

"I may be only seventeen, but I'm not acting like a child," she said in a hurt voice. "I'm acting like a woman who is going to have a baby and wants her husband to be near her."

He looked at her without speaking for a moment. He had almost forgotten. Seventeen. He was fifty-six. There was a long spread of years between them, and maybe there would never be a way to build a bridge across time. He reached for her hand. "I'm sorry, Margaret," he said slowly. "I wouldn't do this if there were anyone else who could do it. But it's my job."

The telephone began to ring. She withdrew her hand from his grip. "That's your friend Mr. Miami Lansky Gangster, whoever the hell he is," she said coldly. "You better go answer it. There's nobody else to speak to him."

Chapter 12

Lansky's voice was guarded. "Do you remember where we met the last time?"

"Yes."

"Do you think you can get there without being followed?"

"I can try. If I can't shake them I won't show up."

"I have to see you," Lansky said.

"Will you be there for long?"

"Two hours."

"Okay."

"If you don't make it, call me tomorrow morning in Florida. Use a pay phone."

"Okay."

Daniel put down the telephone and walked back into the living room. "I have to go out," he said.

Margaret looked at him. "I'm afraid."

"Don't be," he said "It's just business." He walked to the window and looked out. It was already dark outside, but the blue sedan was still there, parked under a street light. He didn't understand that. Apparently they wanted him to know he was under surveillance; otherwise they would have taken pains to park the car where he would not see it. It was more as if they were trying to frighten him than anything else.

The telephone rang again. It was Hoffa, calling from Detroit. "You were right about your tip," he said. "I got my first visit from the McClellan committee today."

"What did they want?"

"They started for my files. I threw them out. They got nothing."

"Who were they?"

"Some kid named Bob Kennedy who says he's the chief counsel. A real jerk. He had two flunkies with him." Hoffa paused. "They still on your tail?"

"Parked right outside my house," Daniel said. "Out in the open where I can see them."

"What do you think?" Hoffa asked.

"They're fishing. They don't know what they're looking for. They're hoping we'll do something that they can make a case out of."

"I took your advice and spoke to my lawyer. He says sit tight and give them nothing unless they come with a subpoena. Then, even with that, he has ways to make it tough for them."

Daniel thought for a moment. "I think my mutual-fund idea is even more important now than ever. It will be a clean operation that no one can throw a stone at. Open and aboveboard."

"The word out of Florida is that it won't be so clean. They want in, and they're pissed off you didn't talk to them."

"Too bad," Daniel said. "I'll straighten them out."

"They play rough," Hoffa said.

"We don't?" Daniel laughed.

Hoffa laughed. "If you need help, holler."

"If I need help it will be too late to holler," Daniel said.

"Just be careful," Hoffa said. "Good luck."

"Thanks." Daniel put down the telephone. He stood there for a moment, then called Moses at home. "Bring your car over and park it on the street behind my house. Wait there for me."

"What's up?"

"Nothing to worry about. I just have to get out of here without my watchdogs following me."

"I'll be there in fifteen minutes."

Daniel went back into the living room. Margaret was sitting on the couch. "Moses is coming for me in about fifteen minutes. I'm going out the back door and through our neighbors' yard to the street behind us."

"Why can't you go out the front door?"

"Because there are some men out there from the Senate Labor Committee. They've been following me for weeks now and I don't want them to know where I'm going."

She was silent, watching him pour another drink for himself. She waited until he drank it. "Why didn't you tell me about those men before?"

"I didn't want to worry you. Besides, it's not important."

"Not important? Is that what you want me to think? Because it's not important you carry a gun on you all the time. What do you expect me to think? I'm going out of my mind thinking you're in some kind of danger I know nothing about."

"I've always carried a gun."

"D.J. told me that, but I thought it was only to make me feel better."

"It's true," he said. "It's habit more than anything else." He refilled his glass. "A long time ago I was kidnapped, beaten up and held prisoner for three days, then dumped on a deserted highway in the middle of a freezing storm. I swore I would never again allow that to happen to me."

"Are you going to meet Lansky?"

He nodded.

"Will it be dangerous?"

"No. We just have some business to talk."

"How long will you be?"

He looked at his watch. It was almost ten o'clock. "Not long. I'll be back here before midnight. I'll call you if I see it will be later."

"I'll wait up for you."

He smiled and bent, kissing her cheek. "Don't worry, Margaret. I'll be all right."

Moses pulled the car into the parking lot behind the warehouse. "Want me to go with you?" he asked.

Daniel shook his head. "No. Wait here in the car for me." He went up the steps and knocked on the iron door. The door opened and the same man who had let him in before nodded to him. Daniel followed him inside.

It was exactly the same as it had been before. The counting tables were busy, and no one looked up as they walked through the rooms and into the office. As before, Lansky was behind the desk.

The blond bodyguard stepped in front of Daniel as he started forward. "You packing a gun?" he asked in a cold voice.

"No. I don't carry guns when I visit friends," Daniel said.

The bodyguard glanced over his shoulder at Lansky.

"If he says he's not carrying a gun," Lansky said softly, "he's not carrying a gun."

The bodyguard nodded, then, turning swiftly, dug a hard right fist into Daniel's stomach. Daniel bent almost double, fighting the pain and sudden nausea that clutched at him. He stayed bent over, forcing himself to breathe slowly, until the nausea subsided, then straightened up.

There was a faint smile on Lansky's face. "My boy doesn't like having guns shoved in his face."

"I don't blame him," Daniel said. He started as if to walk around the bodyguard to the desk. The bodyguard turned to watch, and so he never saw Daniel's hamlike fist coming up almost from the floor. Daniel felt the shock run up through his arm as the old-fashioned uppercut tore into the bodyguard's chin, lifting the man almost straight up into the air, across the corner of the desk, tumbling backward until he came to a stop against the wall and slid to the floor. The bodyguard's chin hung crookedly from his face, broken teeth impacted into his lower lip, blood pouring from his nose and mouth, his eyes dazed and vague.

Daniel stared down at him for a moment, then turned back to Lansky. He spoke as if there had been no interruption. "I don't like having guns shoved at me either."

Lansky stared at him for a moment, then glanced down at the bodyguard. He gestured to the two other men in the room. "Better get him out of here and clean him up."

"If I were you," Daniel said. "I would get him to a doctor. Your boy's got a glass jaw. I felt it break in at least three different places." He moved toward the chair. "Mind if I sit down?"

Lansky gestured silently. They didn't speak until they were alone in the room and the door had clicked shut.

"Now what was that all about?" Daniel asked.

"I'm sorry," Lansky said. "But you know how it is. I had to let him prove himself."

Daniel shook his head. "What did he prove? Nothing."

"He proved himself out of a job," Lansky said. "I don't need bodyguards with glass jaws."

Daniel laughed. His voice turned serious. "So much for the fun and games. You wanted to see me?"

Lansky came right to the point. "The mutual fund. My feelings are hurt. You didn't ask me in."

"That's right."

"I want in."

"It's not part of our deal," Daniel said.

"I didn't say it was," Lansky replied. "I just told you I wanted in."

"Then let me make it simple for you, Mr. Lansky. The reason you weren't asked in is that I don't want you in. This is one operation that's going to stay clean."

"You're being naive," Lansky said. "You're asking for trouble. We can blow you away like that." He snapped his fingers.

Daniel smiled. "Then you have nothing. Not the mutual fund nor the business we're already operating."

"You have a pregnant wife and a son at school," Lansky said.

"And what do you have, Mr. Lansky?" Daniel asked softly. "A life you live in the shadows, surrounded by glass jaws to keep you from being blown away? Did you stop to think that every time the butcher and grocer come to your house, every electrician and telephone man, every delivery that's made to you is made by a man who wears a union button? There's twenty million of them. And if I say the word, there is no way on God's earth you can escape them short of dying of natural causes."

Lansky stared at him without speaking. Daniel got to his feet. Lansky finally spoke. "I'm not alone in this. I'll have to explain it to my associates."

Daniel looked down at him. "You speak Yiddish don't you?"

Lansky nodded.

"When I was going to the labor school in New York many years ago, I picked up a few phrases that really said it all. This is one of them. You tell your associates that I'm the shabbes goy. That I'm the one man who can help keep the labor movement respectable and legitimate in the public eye. And they don't want to fuck with that, because if they do, they might very well kill the goose that lays the golden egg."

"I don't know whether they'll buy it."

"If they don't," Daniel said. "we'll both be sorry."

Lansky stared up at him thoughtfully. Finally a slow smile crossed his face. "Are you really sure you're not Daniel Webster?"

Chapter 13

DANIEL STARED down at the reports piled on the desk in front of him. Quickly he flipped through them, a sinking feeling of despair going through him. Finally he put them back on the desk and brought his hand down hard. "It's not working, God damn it."

Moses and Jack stared back at him. They were silent. D.J. leaned against the wall looking at his father. It was the end of June, and there were no more classes until fall.

"In the last ten days, I traveled four thousand miles, spoke to fifteen different union locals with a membership of at least eight or nine thousand men and all we got is a lousy five hundred and seventy subscriptions. How do I make those idiots understand that this is the best thing that ever happened to them? The only time in their lives they have a chance to get an honest count?"

Moses was consoling. "That old saying about a prophet being without honor in his own country has to be true."

"That's no help," Daniel said. "We need at least eighty to a hundred thousand subscriptions."

"You've got to come on stronger with them," Jack said.

"They want to hear blue sky and a pot of gold at the end of the rainbow."

"That's not my style," Daniel said. "I'm not a con man." He bit the end from another cigar. "Where do I go next?"

"It's a big one," Jack said. "Detroit. We expect fifteen thousand men at this one. In addition to the Teamsters, Reuther promised us a big turnout from the United Auto Workers. It's so big that we've even got network television and radio coverage."

Daniel chewed on the cigar for a moment. "Maybe we'd better cancel it. I don't feel like having the whole country watch me fall on my ass."

"Father." D.J. came toward the desk. "I have an idea, but I don't know whether it will work."

His father looked at him. "Let's hear it. Right now I'm ready to listen to anything."

"It may not be a practical application for this," D.J. said. "But one of the courses I just finished was on credit and installment buying. You know—automobile, appliances, home furnishings, things like that."

Daniel was suddenly interested. "Tell me more."

"They pay so much down and so much a week or a month until it's all paid off. The minute the contract is signed, the seller discounts the contract with a bank and he's got his money right away. And the buyer has the merchandise."

"It's not quite the same thing," Daniel said.

"Maybe. But in our case, a share in the mutual fund is our merchandise. And you know as well as I do that the average man will think twice about shelling out a hundred dollars at one clip, but two dollars a week doesn't sound so bad."

Jack spoke quickly. "I think D.J. has a good point there."

"We're not set up to do business like that," Daniel said.

"We can handle it," Moses said. "They can make their payments directly to their union, which can then forward it to us each month."

"That's right." Jack nodded. "And if we draw up the right kind of purchase contract I'm sure we can find a bank to discount it."

Daniel finally held a match to his cigar. He was nodding to

himself. It could just work. "I've got the bank. The U.M.W. is the major shareholder of the National Bank of Washington. I'm sure John L. will tell Barney Colton, who's running the bank for them, to give us the money."

He looked up at D.J. "You've come up with a very good idea, son."

D.J. flushed. "We don't know yet, Father. It might not work."

"We have to make it work," Daniel said. He turned to Jack. "How come the television and radio people are covering this meeting?"

"They think it's an interesting story. First time it's ever happened that union members are beginning a mutual fund to invest their money in capitalism."

Daniel looked at him. Suddenly he smiled; his voice boomed again with confidence. "It's going to work. Everything's falling into place. They don't know, but they're giving us an opportunity to organize the whole country."

"You're nervous," Margaret said as she watched him pack the small valise he was taking to Detroit.

He took a deep breath. "If this doesn't work, we have to put away the whole idea and we're right back where we started."

"Is that really too bad?" she asked. "We're getting along."

He turned to her. "You don't understand. Once you begin to stand still in the labor movement, you might as well quit. All you can do is go backward."

"There's enough money coming in from the regular memberships, isn't there? We can live comfortably on that."

"Now there is," he said. "But how long do you think it will last? Sooner or later we'll run out of jobs to do for the unions we have. Then unless we get others to join us, we're out of business. It's a vicious circle, but success breeds on success. The moment our people begin to realize we're not attracting new members, they begin to wonder why they need us. The minute they start thinking that, we're finished."

She was silent as he closed the valise. "Is it that important to you, Daniel?"

460

"Yes," he said. "All my life I'd dreamed of doing something important in the labor movement, and every time I tried I wound up with shit thrown in my face. The name of the game was politics. I needed a union local of my own for a base, and they would never let me have it because I had a mind of my own and they were afraid I wouldn't play ball with them. This is a chance to go around all of them and force them to listen to me. In the only language they understand. Money and power."

He picked up the valise, and she followed him downstairs. He left the bag in the hall and went into the living room. He took the bottle of whiskey from the sideboard and poured himself a drink.

"Have you finished your speech yet?" she asked.

"No. I'll work more on it. I'll have it finished by the time I have to deliver it tomorrow afternoon."

"I wish I were going with you," she said.

"I wish you were too." He took a sip of his drink. "But we won't have to wait long now. Two more weeks."

"It seems like forever."

He smiled. "It will pass quicker than you think." He put down the glass. "You know where to get me if you need me?"

She nodded. "I have the hotel number written next to the telephone."

"I'll call and let you know how we're doing."

"I'll be watching you on television," she said. "Jack told me the evening news will be carrying a clip from your speech."

"I hope it will be all right. TV does funny things to people."

"You'll be okay," she said.

"You're prejudiced," he said, smiling.

"Maybe. But you'll still be okay. I worry enough now about the way women come on to you. After this I'm going to have to worry double."

He laughed. "Don't double your trouble, double your pleasure."

She laughed with him. "I can't wait. I feel like a virgin again. I think the first time we make love after this I won't be able to stop coming."

"Promises, promises. I'll remember that."

461

"Daniel."

He looked at her. Her voice had suddenly become serious. "Even if it doesn't work, it's not that important. We still have each other. I don't need very much."

He kissed her cheek. "I know that, baby. That's one of the reasons I love you."

She smiled gently. "I'm glad to hear that. Until just a little while ago I thought all you cared about was my beautiful body."

"That too." He laughed. An automobile horn sounded from outside. "The car is here. I've got to get going."

She followed him to the door, where he picked up his valise. "Give my best to D.J. and the others."

"I will." He looked down at her. "I forgot to tell you. If there's anything you need, Jack Haney is staying in town. Don't hesitate to call him. He'll be at home or at the office."

"I thought he was going with you too," she said.

"We had to change our plans at the last minute. He's waiting for the new purchase contracts to come back from the printer so that he can check them and get them out to us in time for the meeting."

"Then only D.J. and Moses will be with you?"

"I don't need any more from here. Hoffa has placed some of his office staff at my disposal." He bent over and kissed her cheek. "Take care of yourself. I'll be back the day after tomorrow."

"Good luck." She kissed him. "And stay away from them bad women. I love you."

"I love you too," he said, laughing.

She stood in the doorway and watched him get into the car. He leaned out the window and waved to her. She waved back, and the car started from the curb. She watched until it had turned the corner and gone out of sight. The telephone began to ring. She closed the door and went to it.

It was Jack Haney. "Big Dan gone already?"

"He's just left."

"Okay. I'll call him when he gets to Detroit."

"Are there any problems?"

"No. I just wanted to check some agreement language with him." He hesitated a moment. "Will you be home tomorrow?"

"Yes."

"I'll give you a call to see how you are. Big Dan asked me to check in with you."

"He told me," she said. It was her turn to hesitate. "Look, if you're not doing anything tomorrow, why don't you come over and have supper here and we can watch him on television together?"

"I don't want you to go to any trouble."

"It's no trouble," she said. "Mamie takes care of everything. And I won't feel as alone as I usually do when he's away."

"Okay," he said. "I'll check with you tomorrow in case you should change your mind."

"I won't change my mind."

He hesitated again. "Okay. What time do you want me?"

"Seven o'clock all right?"

"I'll be there," he answered. "Thanks."

She put down the telephone and went upstairs to the bedroom. Slowly she got out of her dress and picked up her robe. She caught a glimpse of herself in the mirror. Her belly looked so big. She couldn't be sure, but she thought it was beginning to drop slightly. She slipped into the robe and went to the bed.

She leaned back against the pillows. She was glad she had asked Jack to dinner. It was the first time she had ever spoken with him without many people around. He seemed like a nice young man—a little shy perhaps, but maybe that was because she was the boss's wife. But he had always been very nice and polite to her. Not like so many of the others, whose very attitudes made her feel that they thought she was nothing but a clever young girl who had used her youth and sex in order to trap Daniel into marriage.

She let out a deep breath. To hell with them. After the baby was born she would show them all how wrong they were.

Chapter 14

Daniel stood in the wings of the stage at the end of the convention hall. The pressure of the mass filling the hall beyond weighed heavily in the air. The U.A.W. and the Teamsters had done their job well. They had turned out the members. Now it was all up to him. If he couldn't sell the new purchase concept, it was his failure.

He looked down at the notes he held in his hand. They were typed in capital letters on medium-sized index cards. Each card made a point. Security. Saving for retirement. Increase in capital. Additional current income. All the pluses. Plus an easy payment plan. Two dollars a week for a unit.

It was all there. If he bombed, there was no one to blame it on. The failure had to be his and his alone. He took a deep breath.

For the last half-hour, various speakers had been talking about and explaining the mutual fund to the audience. The last speaker was the head of one of the U.A.W. locals. His voice carried through the loudspeakers to Daniel.

"And now, to tell you more about this great opportunity for all of us to participate in the growth and increasing wealth of our country, here is the man whose genius thought up the plan, a man whose lifelong dedication to union labor is known to everyone, a man I am proud to call my friend: the president of the Confederated Alliance of Living Labor, Big Dan Huggins."

Daniel walked onto the stage. The speaker came toward him, a big smile on his face. They shook hands while the speaker whispered. "Go get 'em, Big Dan. We softened them up for you."

Daniel smiled and went to the lectern. He placed his speech cards on the lectern in front of him. He held up his hand, waving and smiling to the applause. Then he turned his hand palm out, and slowly the applause died down and the hall became quiet.

Daniel stood there silently for a moment as his eyes surveyed the audience. A good fifty percent of the men were still in their work clothes. They had probably come directly from their shift. The other men were in their shirt sleeves. It was over eighty degrees outside, and there were very few jackets in evidence. Between the very first row of seats and the stage, the television cameras began to move into position in front of him.

Daniel looked at the audience again. The workingman. He almost could feel and touch every one of them. He had grown up with them, eaten and drunk and slept with them. He felt himself all of them and each of them.

He looked down at his speech cards again. Something was wrong. He was the same man sitting out there in the audience; he was not a securities salesman. No matter how valid the idea was, those men had not come here to listen to a sales pitch. They had come to see him. They had come to hear him and renew their faith in labor and the union. They had come to hear him say just one thing. That he still cared, that he still believed.

Slowly he picked up his speech cards from the lectern and held them out so that the audience could see them. "My brothers, my friends. These cards I hold in my hand are the speech I'm supposed to make. I'm supposed to tell you how important it is for each and every one of you to join with us. I'm supposed to tell you how much money you will make with it and about the comforts that money will buy for you."

He paused for a moment. "But I've changed my mind. I'm not going to make that speech. Others can do that far better than I. Besides, each of you has been given a sheet of paper when you entered the room which tells you everything you need to know about it. So that speech I'm not going to make at all."

He opened his hand and let the cards drop to the floor. He looked at them for a moment, then back at the audience. "The little time we have together is much too important to waste on that. Instead, I want to talk to you about something I feel is much more important, about something so important that it affects our lives each and every day of our existence. I want to speak to you about the way we live—something I call The Challenge to Democracy."

He paused and searched the faces in the audience. They were his people. He began to speak very slowly, very clearly.

"A man is born, he works, he dies. Then there is nothing. . . . This has been the life of all of us who have been born into the society of those who labor. We have accepted it. Because traditionally this is the way it has always been.

"But one day, some time ago, a group of men gathered to set down the principles of something they called democracy under which all men would be created equal. In race, in opportunity. And these goals became the challenge of democracy. Because it is always easier to state the ideal than to achieve it.

"The achievement becomes the struggle, and the struggle is ours. Because we are the people who labor, and we are the people who must accept the challenge of democracy and make it work."

He paused and gazed slowly around the audience again. "My brothers, we have accepted that challenge. We have created unions to help us better our living conditions. And we must continue to improve our unions and create others to help those who need them. But there is more to the challenge than just unionism. The real challenge is life. We deserve more than just birth, work and death. We deserve more than being nothing. Because the world in which we live is our world too.

And each and every one of us by his actions must leave his mark on it. So that each and every man here will be remembered forever. Not forgotten."

He reached for the glass of water on the lectern. For a moment the silence in the hall made him feel as if they did not know what he was trying to tell them. Then the applause began to roll over him and he knew that he had reached them. He held up his hand and the applause died down.

"We are warriors in the battle. We must create as well as meet the challenge to democracy. Because only by searching in ourselves for our aims will we be able to help others to achieve theirs."

The applause came up again. He held up his hand. "And that is exactly what we must do. Care for one another as we care for ourselves. . . . "

He stood on the platform for more than an hour. He spoke of youth gone by and dreams that had been lost and faiths that had vanished, and then he shared with them his dream of the future. His dream of the world, which they and they alone could make come true because it was their dream too. And he said that the only way they could make it happen was to accept the challenge. And if they did not accept that challenge, they were placing in other hands the responsibility for their lives, and in time they would go backward until all the newfound gains would be irretrievably lost.

When he finished, the audience was silent. He turned and started from the stage. Then the roar broke over him. The applause. The audience began to chant. "Big Dan! Big Dan! Big Dan!"

He turned back to them. They could see the tears running down his cheeks. He could hardly speak anymore. "Thank you."

There was a strange silence backstage as he came off. None of the usual handshaking or backslapping of enthusiasm. Instead there was a strangeness, a kind of watchfulness, among the men who just before his speech had so exuberantly predicted that he would easily collect a half million dollars' worth of subscriptions from this rally alone. He could read the expression on their faces. He had blown it.

Even Moses and D.J were strangely silent in the car on

their way back to the large suite they had reserved in the hotel for a postmeeting reception for the local union officials who had cooperated in the planning. Silently they went up in the elevator. They opened the door to the empty suite.

Daniel stood in the center of the large living room and stared at the preparations they had made for the reception. The large bar set up, the tables filled with sandwiches for those men who would be hungry.

He turned to Moses. "I guess you better make arrangements for the hotel to take this stuff back. I'm going to start packing. There's no use hanging around. I'm going to see if I can make a plane home tonight."

Moses nodded silently.

"D.J., you better start gathering up the papers. Don't bother sorting them out. Just dump them into a box and leave 'em here. Doesn't look as if we're going to need them now."

"Yes, Father."

The telephone began to ring as he went into his bedroom. He closed the door behind him and the sound of the ringing was blocked out. He walked to the bed and sat down heavily. Why the hell had he done it? He had had it all in his hands and he had thrown it away. And for nothing. Merely to tell them how he really felt, something they would forget by the time they sat down for dinner that evening. How the hell could he have been so blinded by his own vision that he could have deluded himself into believing what he said was really important? Ideals were pretty words. They no longer moved people. Nor did people really believe in them. Power and money was the only faith that moved them.

The bedroom door opened and Moses stuck his head into the room. "The President wants to talk to you," he said in a hushed voice.

"The President?" Daniel asked stupidly.

"The President of the United States," Moses said.

Daniel stared at him, then turned and picked up the telephone at the side of the bed. "Hello."

A woman's voice came through the line. "Mr. Huggins?"

"Yes."

"Just one moment for the President of the United States."

There was a click on the line, then the familiar sound of

Eisenhower's voice. "Mr. Huggins, I called to congratulate you on your magnificent speech. I just saw it on television."

"Thank you, Mr. President."

"It was a magnificent reaffirmation of all the basic truths that have made America great. A restatement of the ideals with which we all grew up, ideals that far exceed the boundaries of labor but reach out and touch the core of all Americans who love their country and their fellowman. I want you to know that in that speech you not only spoke for all Americans, you spoke for me as well. It is a speech I would have been proud to make myself."

"Thank you, Mr. President."

"Congratulations again, Mr. Huggins. Goodbye."

The telephone clicked off in Daniel's hand. He looked up and saw Moses and D.J. in the doorway. "The President liked it," he said in a wondering voice.

Then, suddenly it seemed, all the phones in the suite began to ring at the same time and people began pouring into the room.

The pains began somewhere in the middle of his speech. They were sitting in the living room watching him on the television screen. A moment after Daniel had begun to speak, Jack looked at her in surprise.

"That's not the speech we had worked on. Did he tell you he was going to change it?"

She shook her head. "He never told me about any speech. I wouldn't know whether it's the same thing or not."

A few minutes later the first pain came. A spasm cutting through her like a knife. She tried to control it. She felt oddly embarrassed at letting Jack see it. She took a deep breath and it went away.

Two minutes later, it hit again. Stronger this time. Involuntarily, she gasped, bending forward in her chair.

Jack turned to her. "Are you all right?"

She felt the perspiration on her face. "The baby. I think it's coming. Call the doctor. His number is next to the telephone."

Jack got to his feet. "Mamie," he called. The black woman

appeared in the doorway. "I think Mrs. Huggins' baby is coming. You stay with her while I phone the doctor and find out what he wants us to do."

The suite in the hotel was now a madhouse. Where all the men had come from, he didn't know. But they were there and they were exuberant. At the last count there was over a million dollars' worth of purchase contracts signed, and they were still being counted.

"You foxy bastard," the speaker who had introduced Daniel to the audience said to him. "You had us all thinkin' you were crazy, but you knew all the time what you were doin'."

Moses came toward him clutching a handful of telegrams. "The calls and telegrams are pouring in. From all over the country. Everybody wants you. From Dave Dubinsky in New York, who wants to take Madison Square Garden for you to talk to the I.L.G.W.U. and places the services of their bank, the Amalgamated, at your disposal, to Harry Bridges, who wants you to speak to the longshoremen in San Francisco. Even George Meany sent a telegram of congratulations and pledges his support in the achievement of all our common goals and ideals."

Suddenly Daniel was tired. He began pushing his way through the crowded living room to his bedroom. He passed one man, already enthusiastically drunk, who clapped him on the shoulder. "Big Dan!" the man said. "You kin be the next President of the United States if'n you want to."

He slipped into his room and closed the door. He walked to the bed and sat down. He needed a few minutes' rest. Too much had happened. The highs and the lows had drained him. The door opened and D.J. came into the room.

"Are you all right, Father?"

"Just tired, son."

"It was a brilliant idea, Father," D.J. said. "You knew instinctively just the way to sell them. I don't think any of us even came close to understanding what you were doing."

Daniel looked at his son. And they still didn't. Even D.J. believed that it had been a clever plan to sell subscriptions.

He didn't speak. The telephone at the side of the bed began to ring. He gestured for D.J. to get it.

D.J. picked it up. "It's for you, Father. Jack Haney."

Daniel took the telephone. "Yes, Jack?"

"Margaret's having the baby. I just took her to County. She's up in the labor room right now."

"Is she all right?"

"Her doctor says she's just fine. Everything's normal. She should have the baby any minute." There was a sound over the phone on Jack's end of the line. "Hold on a minute." Daniel could hear the voices. Then Jack came back on the line. "It's a boy, Daniel." His voice was excited. "Six pounds four ounces. Congratulations."

Daniel took a deep breath. "I'll leave right away. Tell Margaret that I'll see her this evening." He put down the telephone and looked up at D.J. "You have a brother," he said.

D.J.'s face broke into a smile. "Congratulations." He grabbed his father's hand and held it. "I'm really happy for you. Really."

"Get Moses," Daniel said. "I want to tell him I'm going back right now. The two of you stay here and wrap up."

Moses and D.J. came back into the room just as Daniel was closing his valise. "I'll slip out through the bedroom door," Daniel said. "Nobody'll even miss me."

Moses nodded, grinning. "Congratulations, Daniel." He gestured at the valise. "You don't have to take that. We'll bring it back tomorrow."

"Good idea," Daniel said. He went to the hall door. "I'll get a cab to take me to the airport," he said, opening the door and stepping out into the hall. They stepped out after him.

There were about ten or twelve men outside the main entrance to the suite. "They're still coming in," Moses said. "You better go down to the elevators on the other side."

Daniel glanced at the crowd and nodded, beginning to turn away. A picture clicked in his mind. He whirled suddenly, one hand reaching inside his coat for his gun; with the other he pushed Moses hard back into the open doorway. Moses crashed into D.J., and they both stumbled back into the room just as the first shot rang out.

Daniel felt the blow in his solar plexus, the picture of the blond man still bright in his mind. He struggled to raise his gun. The second shot brought him to his knees. He had the gun up now, holding it in two hands. It took all his strength to squeeze the trigger. Then the picture of the blond man's face exploded into a mass of blood and bone and disappeared as still another shot tore into him, tumbling him backward, unconscious, to the floor.

"*I am dying, my son. And you are being born. I will never see you. We will never know each other.*"

"*You will not die this time, Father. I have just come for the future and you are still there.*"

"*I will leave you my dreams, my son.*"

"*I will wait for them, Father. But you will have to show me the way.*"

He struggled up through the maze of pain. He could feel the hands lifting him onto a stretcher. He opened his eyes just as they picked up the stretcher and saw D.J. and Moses bending anxiously over him. He managed a wan smile. "I feel stupid. I should have expected something like this."

"Take it easy, Father," D.J. said. "You'll be okay. The doctor said none of the wounds are serious."

"I know." Daniel nodded weakly. "Your baby brother has told me that already."

Now

THE CRISP October air felt good as it went deep into my lungs. All around us the West Virginia hills were covered with the red and gold and burnt orange of the early falling leaves, and those that were left danced nervously on the branches of the trees. We crested the hill. "Here," I said.

Christina moved the white Rolls off the highway onto the shoulder of the road. She looked at me. "Are you sure you want to do this?"

"Yes. I promised myself I would come back before I went home." I reached into the back seat and picked up my sleeping bag. "I planted flowers," I said, getting out of the car.

"Eight o'clock tomorrow morning," she said. "I'll be here to pick you up. Don't be late. You promised your mother you would be home in time for the wedding."

Mother and Jack were to be married at our house tomorrow evening. Judge Paul Gitlin, to whom Jack had once been law clerk, was coming up from the city to perform the ceremony. "I won't be late," I said, slinging the sleeping bag's straps over my shoulders.

"Do you have everything you need?" she asked.

I smiled. "I've got my toothbrush. It's only overnight, Christina."

I waited until the white Rolls disappeared over the crest of the hill, then crossed the highway and went over the fence and down the embankment on the other side. She had a reservation for the night in a motel the other side of Fitchville. This time I didn't have to search for the path. I knew the way.

It took me less than an hour to reach the small cemetery at the top of the knoll. Betty May had been as good as her word. The flowers were planted neatly around its borders and between the graves, their bright reds, yellows, blues and purples smiling at the sky. I stood there for a long moment. Somehow it didn't seem lonely and forgotten anymore.

I looked down the hill. The naked stalks of the cornfield were dancing in the afternoon breeze. A faint wisp of smoke came from the small chimney of the house, and the pickup truck was still dusty in front of the door.

While I was watching, Jeb Stuart came out of the house and stood on the front steps, looking around. He looked up at the knoll and saw me, his eyes squinting against the sun. I waved to him. His face broke into a grin as he recognized me, and he waved back. I started down the knoll, and he opened the door.

His voice floated back to me on the wind. "Betty May! Jonathan's back!"

She came into the doorway behind him and stood there, waving and smiling. Something about her looked different, but it wasn't until I drew close that I knew what it was. She was slimmer than when I had left; the big belly was gone.

Jeb Stuart came down the steps and pumped my hand enthusiastically. "Howdy, Jonathan, howdy."

I smiled at him. "It's real good to see you, Jeb Stuart."

"We been expectin' you like any day." he said. "I thought you might have forgot us."

"No way," I said. I looked past him at Betty May. "Congratulations. Do I get a chance to kiss the pretty mother?"

"You shore do," he said.

I went up the steps and kissed Betty May on the cheeks. "You look beautiful. Is she as pretty as you are?"

Betty May blushed. "How'd you know it was a girl?"

"I knew," I said. "But you didn't answer my question."

"She shore is," Jeb said. "She's the spit an' image of her maw. Come an' see for yourself."

I followed them into the cabin. It was more like a small home now. There were chintz curtains on the windows, the wooden furniture had been cleaned and painted, there was a large ceiling-to-floor drape that screened off the sleeping area from the rest of the ouse and new hurricane oil lamps were on the table and on the tops of the wooden chests.

Betty May pulled back the drape. "There she is," she said proudly.

The baby was lying in an old-fashioned homemade crib cut from half of a whiskey barrel. It had been painted white and was supported on either end by two-by-fours. I bent over the crib. Her little red face was screwed up monkeylike in sleep, her hands gripped into tiny fists, her almost white hair made it seem as if she were bald. "She sure is pretty," I said. "How old is she?"

"Six weeks now," Betty May said. "She came the day we finished harvestin'."

"It was almost like she knowed not to come until Betty May had finished helpin' with the work," Jeb Stuart said.

"Have you named her yet?" I asked.

"We been thinkin'. But we ain't decided yet. We want to take her down to Fitchville an' get her rightly baptized," Betty May said. "We jes call her Baby."

I smiled. "That's good enough. I brought a present for her." I went back to the door and unrolled my sleeping bag. Inside it was the box Christina had bought for me in a shop on Worth Avenue. I gave the box to Betty May.

"You hadn't oughter done it," Betty May said.

"Open it," I said.

Carefully she took the paper from the box. "This paper's so pretty I'm goin' to save it," she said shyly as she lifted the cover. Inside was a complete layette—dress, hat, socks, booties, sheets, blanket and pillow, all in pink. Betty May looked at me, then back at the layette. "It's so beautiful. I never seen nothin' like it."

"It's for her to wear at her baptism," I said.

Jeb Stuart had been standing there silently. He touched my arm and I turned to him. "Betty May an' me ain't too good with words, but we want you know that we're moughty grateful to you, Jonathan."

"That's right, Jonathan," Betty May said. Just then a cry came from the crib. Betty May turned quickly. "It's her feeding time. She's like an alarm clock."

I followed Jonathan outside as she went to the crib. We sat down on the steps. "Everything go all right?" I asked.

"Jes' fine," he said. "The crop was real good. I jes' drew the bead off the mash an' barreled it. There's thirty barrels of top corn up there right now agin' natural style in wood. I kin sell it right now fer a hundred a barrel. If'n I hold it until next spring I kin git maybe double that or more."

"What are you going to do?"

"I been thinkin' maybe I'll sell off ten barrels. That should take us through the winter, an' next spring sell off the rest."

"That makes sense," I said. I took out a package of cigarettes, offered him one, then held a match for the two of us. "Hear anything more from the sheriff?"

He shook his head. "Not a word. I thought maybe he'd be comin' on by, but he never did."

"Did he quash that warrant in town like he said?"

"I guess so," he answered. "But it don't matter none now. My ol' wife got herself a divorce up at the county seat an' married up with some storekeeper. So I figger when we go into Fitchville to git the baby baptized, me an' Betty May kin git hitched proper."

"It's all working out, isn't it?" I said smiling.

"Yep," he said. "But none of it would have if it weren't for you bein' here when the sheriff showed up."

"That's over now," I said.

"Plannin' on stayin' awhile?" he asked.

"Only overnight. I'm leaving early in the morning. I have to be home tomorrow night."

"Maybe you kin come back for the baptizin'. Me and Betty May would be right proud if you would be Baby's godfather."

There was a sudden tightness in my throat. "I'd be honored. You just give me the date an' I'll be here."

478

Betty May came out of the door behind us. "I'll have supper ready in a half-hour."

"That's jes' fine." Jeb Stuart got to his feet. "Want to take a quick look at the still?"

I nodded. We followed the almost invisible path through the small forest. It was just as I remembered it. Only one thing was different. The small wooden barrels were stacked neatly against the cords of wood. Carefully Jeb Stuart drew a long tarpaulin over the barrels.

"Don't want the wood to get damp," he explained.

I walked over to the small stream and scooped a handful of water from it and ran it over my face. The water was cool and sweet.

"Next year when I git the money I'm goin' to pipe that water down to the cabin," Jeb said.

"That's a good idea." I walked back to the still. The daylight was beginning to fade. I saw the shelves built against the wall of the small open shed behind the still. "My grandfather used to keep a gun up there on the top shelf."

Jeb Stuart stared at me. "How do you know that?"

I shrugged. "I just know."

He walked over to the shelves and reached up to the top shelf. "So do I," he said. "But he never had a gun like this."

I stared at the automatic rifle, the clip already locked in place. "Where'd you get a gun like that?"

"A friend of mine was in Vietnam. I bought it fer ten dollars with four clips of ammunition. They's thirty rounds in each of these clips." He held the rifle down and turned swiftly. "Brrrr-p! One quick squeeze kin cut a man in half."

I didn't speak.

"Ain't no hijackers goin' to git this whiskey," he said.

I felt a chill. "Let's go back."

"Okay." He returned the gun to the shelf and we started down the hill.

Supper was boiled smoked cally, greens and beans. Hot corn muffins and steaming black coffee finished it off. Betty May apologized. "I'm rightfully sorry we didn't have somethin' better fer supper fer you, but we ain't been down to Fitchville since the baby was born."

"There was nothing the matter with this supper," I said. "It was real good." I picked up my sleeping bag. "I think I'll get some sleep now. I have to be back on the highway early."

"You don't have to go out in the cornfield," Jeb Stuart said. "You kin sleep right here on the floor now that we got the curtain up."

"It's okay," I said.

"No, it ain't," Betty May said firmly. "It ain't summer no more an' the groun' is too cold and damp. You'll catch your death."

"You heard the lady." Jeb Stuart smiled. "You spread your bag out there on the floor near the stove where it's warm."

I didn't realize how tired I was until I crawled into the sleeping bag and the warmth from the stove hit me. I closed my eyes and was asleep before I knew it.

I felt the hand on my shoulder and opened my eyes. Jeb was kneeling over me. I could barely see him in the gray tinge of light just before dawn. He put a finger on his lips so that I should remain silent. I sat up suddenly wide awake.

"There's about five men and a pickup truck about a mile down the road," he whispered.

"Who are they?"

"Dunno. Could be revenooers, could be hijackers. I jes' heered some strange noises an' went to check it out."

"What are they doing down there?"

"Right now, nothin'. They seem to be jes' standin' aroun' an' waitin' fer someone."

"Think it's the sheriff?"

"Could be. I'm takin' no chances. We all movin' up to the still. Ain't nobody but us knows where that is."

I crawled out of the sleeping bag and put on my shoes. I had been sleeping in my clothes. Across the room, Betty May had already wrapped the baby in some blankets.

She turned to us. Her voice was calm. "The baby's ready."

Jeb nodded. "We'll go out th'u the back window. No sense takin' chances, case they got somebody watchin' the front door already."

We moved across the room to the window. Carefully Jeb opened it. "You go out first," he told me. "Betty May will give you the baby."

I went through the window. The crack-of-dawn chill bit into me. I turned and Betty May gave me the baby. A moment later she was beside me, and Jeb came through the window as she took the baby back into her arms.

"Keep youah heads down," Jeb whispered as he reached back into the window and lifted out his long hunting rifle. "We go out behin' the cornfield an' then up the hill. Follow me."

Bending half over, we began to run behind the cornfield. We reached the edge of the forest just as the gray of dawn cracked the sky and the first pink of the sun came from the east.

We started up the path. I saw how heavily Betty May was breathing and held out my arms for the baby. She shook her head grimly and continued on up the path.

Jeb dropped back to me. "Y'all go on. I'm jes' goin' back a li'l way to mess the ground up a little. I don' want them trackin' us."

I nodded. He dropped back down the hill and we went on up to the still. At the heavy clump of bushes that concealed the still, Betty May dropped to her knees. "You go through the bushes first. I'll han' the baby to you."

I went through the bushes and turned around. She placed the child in my hands, then came through herself. She took the baby back almost immediately, and we went into the underhang of the side of the hill against the shelves. She sat down, cradling the baby in her arms.

"Are you all right?" I asked.

She nodded. "Right fine, thank you." She seemed as calm and polite as if nothing out of the ordinary were happening. There was a small cry from the baby. She moved quickly, opening her blouse. "She's hungry, poor thing," she crooned. "She wants her breakfast titty."

I watched the baby clamp hungry lips around the flushed, swollen nipple. She began to suck with smacking, slurping sounds. I felt the tears begin to come to my eyes and turned

481

away. I got to my feet and took a deep breath. Beauty seemed so out of place in this morning.

There was a sound in the bushes and Jeb Stuart came through them. He paused for a moment, looking down at Betty May and the baby, then reached up to the top shelf and took down the automatic rifle he had shown me yesterday. He broke away the clip, checked it, then locked it back on the rifle. He glanced at me. "It's the sher'f."

"Sure?" I asked.

He nodded. "I saw his private car. He's not up here on official business."

"How do you know that?"

"He ain't in uniform. An' if he was bringin' revenooers they would have picks and axes with 'em. He come here fer the 'shine." He reached up to the shelf and took down three more cartridge clips and shoved them into the pockets of his shirt. "I knew it was too good to last," he said bitterly.

"Maybe he won't find us," I said.

"He'll fin' us," he said flatly. "He come all prepared. He brought the dogs with 'im. When I saw that, I didn't even bother coverin' the tracks."

I looked at Betty May. She was still feeding the baby, seemingly oblivious to our conversation. I turned back to him. "What are they doing now?"

"They was walkin' up the road to the house when I started back here," he said.

"Maybe if I went down and talked to them?"

"They'll kill you. They all got guns, an' they come here for that hundred-forty proof, not talk."

"Why don't you just give it to them, then?" I asked. "It's not worth losing your life over it."

He met my eyes. "You don't know 'em, Jonathan," he said softly. "They take that 'shine, they cain't afford to leave no one 'live to point a finger at 'em."

The sound of the sheriff's voice through a bullhorn echoed in the hills. "Jeb Stuart. This y'ere's the sher'f. Y'all come outta that there house with youah han's up ovuh youah haids an' no harm'll come to you an Betty May."

Jeb had turned to listen; now he turned back to us. "It'll

482

take him ten minutes to fin' out we're not there. Then he'll turn the dogs loose. You take Betty May an' the baby an' go over the back of the hill to the highway. I'll stay here an' keep 'em busy."

Betty May had been listening after all. "I ain't goin' 'thout you, Jeb Stuart."

"You'll do as I say, woman," he said sternly.

"You cain't make me," she said firmly. "A woman's place is with her man, no matter what."

The bullhorn rang through the hills again. "Jeb Stuart, you got two minutes to come outta there or we goin' in after you."

"They wouldn't dare," I said. "They have to be bluffing. They know there's a baby in there."

"They don't know nothin'," Jeb Stuart said. "We never went down to town after she was born, so she was never registered in City Hall. Outside of us, nobody even knows about her. As far as they are concerned she was never born." He paused for a moment. "An' even if they did know, it would make no difference to 'em."

"Last chance, Jeb Stuart," the bullhorn cried. "Time's up!" A moment later the crackling sound of gunfire echoed through the forest; then the heavy shouting and cursing of men; more gunfire; then silence.

Jeb Stuart turned back to us. "By now they know the house is empty an' they'll turn the dogs loose."

He knew exactly what they were going to do. Suddenly the barking and yapping of hounds came wafting on the breeze. The sound of the dogs began to approach the hill. Jeb Stuart looked down at his wife. "Okay, Betty May, unless you want your baby murdered by those sons of bitches, you better get on outta here."

She shook her head stubbornly.

"Why don't we all get out of here?" I suggested. "Fuck 'em. Let them have it. It's only whiskey."

Jeb Stuart looked into my eyes. "It's not only my whiskey they'd be takin', but my honor. If'n a man won't fight fer his own, he ain't wu'th nuthin'."

Now the yapping of the dogs was even closer, and the sounds of the men scrambling through the brush of the path came clearly to our ears. They seemed very close when all the sounds stopped. For a moment there was silence. Then the bullhorn blasted its sound right up at us.

"We got you spotted, Jeb Stuart. You don't stand a chance. They's five men down here, so jes' come on down with youah han's up an' we'll settle ever'thin' peaceable like. Nobody'll get hurt."

Jeb Stuart was silent.

The sheriff's voice came through the bullhorn again. "I'm a peaceable man, Jeb Stuart. I'll make a deal with you."

Jeb Stuart cupped his hands. "What kinda deal, Sher'f?"

"Twenty-five dollars a barrel for that 'shine an' we part frien's."

"No deal," Jeb Stuart shouted back. "Friendship don't come as cheap as that."

"Thirty dollars a barrel," the sheriff said. "Only 'cause I don' want to see Betty May git hurt."

"No deal," Jeb Stuart shouted.

"Come on down an' we'll talk it over," the sheriff said.

"You come on up yere 'thout a gun an' we'll talk," Jeb Stuart shouted.

There was a moment's silence; then the sheriff replied. "Show yerself; I'm comin' up."

"You start comin' up 'n'en I'll show," Jeb Stuart replied.

"I'm on my way," the sheriff called.

"This is it." Jeb Stuart turned back to us. "Betty May, now you git outta here with that baby."

Betty May stared at him for a moment, then suddenly turned and thrust the child into my arms. "Jonathan will take her. I'm stayin' with you." She picked up the hunting rifle from the ground where he had left it to take the automatic.

I stared at him for a moment; then he nodded heavily. "It's not your fight, Jonathan. Take the baby an' git outta here."

I didn't move.

"Do as he tells you, son. This is what you came back for. The child you never made."

The sheriff's voice seemed to come from almost directly in front of us. "I'm out here, Jeb Stuart. Show yourself."

Jeb Stuart picked a long dead tree branch from the ground. Holding it as far away from himself as he could reach, he rustled the bushes about a yard from where he was standing. The morning air screamed as a murderous gunfire tore through the bushes where they thought he would appear.

"You sumbitches!" he yelled, dropping to his belly and pushing the automatic rifle through the bushes in front of him. He squeezed the trigger. The rifle coughed in short, rapid bursts. "Yippee!" he yelled. "Blew the sumbitch into a thousand pieces."

Then he saw me. "Git outa here. Goddammit! You think I want my baby to die?"

It was all reflex. Without another word, I began running up the path behind the still, hugging the child to my chest, just as the shooting began again and the bullets began tearing into the still behind me. I heard the automatic rifle begin to fire again. I kept running, the breath tearing in my throat, without looking back. We had just reached the crest of the hill when the explosion came.

I turned just in time to see the ball of flame climb up into the sky, followed by a cloud of smoke, then another explosion and a whirling fireball climbing upward. I stared at it, my mouth open. One hundred and forty proof, he had said. All it would take was one spark.

I sank to the ground, catching my breath. It was over. They were gone. Nothing could survive an explosion like that. I lifted the corner of the blanket from the baby's face. She was sleeping peacefully, the milk from her mother's breast still warm in her little stomach. I felt the tears rush up into my eyes and bent down, kissing the baby's tiny forehead.

"It will be all right, Danielle," I said, covering her again. "You're coming home with me." Then I got to my feet and made my way down the hill to the highway where Christina was waiting in the white Rolls convertible.

It was four o'clock in the afternoon, and the street in front of my house was parked solid with cars as I turned into it. I drove past the house, around the block and into the driveway of Anne's house, right behind mine. I looked across the seat at Christina as I turned off the engine. Danielle was asleep in the small car cradle resting on her lap. Next to her was a bottle filled with the formula the druggist had recommended at the stop we had made that morning in a shopping center in Virginia. Two more bottles, filled, were in the thermos carrier, keeping warm. I opened the door and got out of the car as Anne came down from the back porch into the driveway.

She stood there looking at me. "I knew you'd come in this way," she said. "I was waiting for you."

"Where are your folks?" I asked.

"They're over at your house," she answered. She came toward me and into my arms. I kissed her. "I missed you," she said. "I wondered if you would ever come back."

"You knew better than that," I said.

She kissed me again. "Yes."

"Come," I said, leading her to the Rolls. Christina got out of the car. "Anne, this is Christina. Christina's mother was a very close friend of my father's. Christina, this is Anne; she's my special girl."

An instant warmth seemed to flow between them. They touched hands first, then impulsively kissed. "Is he all right?" Anne asked.

"He's fine," Christina smiled.

"Anne, look." I lifted the cover of the blanket and she saw the sleeping baby. "This is Danielle."

Anne's eyes were wide. "Whose baby is she? Where did she come from?"

"Mine now, I guess. You remember her father and mother. Jeb Stuart and Betty May?"

She nodded. "Yes. Where are they?"

It was hard saying the words. It was still too new. "They're dead." She looked puzzled. I could see more questions in her face. "I'll explain it later. Meanwhile, I was wondering if you could keep her in your house until after the wedding is over. I wouldn't like to mess up my mother's wedding if I don't have to."

486

"Of course." She turned to Christina. "We'll take her up to my room." She looked at me. "You better get over to your house. They have to be going crazy over there by now. The wedding's due to begin any minute and your mother told everybody that you had promised to be there."

I went over the fence as I always had. When I went up the steps of the back porch, I looked back. They were going into the house with the baby. I opened the kitchen door and went inside.

Mamie turned from the stove. For a moment I thought she would almost faint; her face went pale and gray. Then she ran to me and hugged me against her ample bosom. "Jonathan, my baby. You come home. All grown up an' a big man jes' like your daddy!"

I kissed her, half laughing, half crying. "I don't know what all the fuss is about. I said I'd come home, didn't I?"

"Yoh mother will be so happy," she said. "I'll go fetch her."

"No. Let me go upstairs and wash up first. I don't want to scare hell out of her."

"I pressed yoh blue suit for you," Mamie said.

I went up the back stairs to my room and managed to get inside without running into anyone. From downstairs came the hum of conversation and the clinking of glasses. I headed right for the bathroom and a shave and shower. In less than ten minutes I was dressing. I looked at myself in the mirror. Mamie was right. I was beginning to look more like my father than ever. Carefully I tied the knot in my tie, slipped on my jacket and went down the hall to my mother's room and knocked at the door.

Mother's voice came from inside. "Who is it?"

"Your son," I said.

The wedding was at five o'clock promptly. By seven all the guests had gone and only the family and the closest friends were left. My brother, Daniel, and his wife, Sally; Moses Barrington; Judge Gitlin and his wife, Zelda, and Anne's parents, the Forbeses.

Daniel looked over at Moses. "Are you sure we can really

spare him for three weeks? Seems to me that big court case is coming up next week."

Moses went along with the joke. "You may be right. We'll have to go over that."

Jack grinned. "Come on, fellas."

I got to my feet. "I'll be back in a minute." I left the room and went out the back door and over the fence. I went into Anne's house and up to her room.

The baby was lying on the bed, gurgling happily. Anne looked up at me. "She's really beautiful."

Christina smiled. "We were just talking. You may not get her back."

"Forget it," I said. "Wrap her up. We're going over to my house."

Anne held the baby while I backed the Rolls carefully out of the driveway and went around the block to my house. We went up on the front porch and rang the bell.

My mother opened the door. She stood there staring in astonishment. She looked down at Danielle in my arms, then up at me. For the first time in my life, she was speechless. I carried the baby into the room and everybody went crazy. The questions came at me from all sides. It was Judge Gitlin who finally got everyone to calm down.

I liked him. In some ways he reminded me of my father. He always carried his own bottle of whiskey with him. In my father's case it had been bourbon, while the judge's drink was Scotch. And, like my father, once in a while he would forget himself and take a pull right from the bottle instead of pouring it into a glass while his wife, Zelda, yelled at him just as my mother had yelled at my father.

"Relax. Let the boy tell the story in his own way," he said, stroking thoughtfully at his iron-gray, neatly trimmed Van Dyke-ish beard. "You know," he added, "I'm tingling."

"What's that got to do with it?" Zelda demanded.

"Nothing," he said. "But I thought it was interesting." He smiled at me. I knew just what he was doing. He was taking everybody off base. "All right, Jonathan."

I gave Danielle to my mother. She gurgled happily into my mother's face. "We've got disposable diapers out in the car if she should need them," I said.

"She's just fine," Mother said, looking down into Danielle's face. "She has such beautiful blue eyes."

Judge Gitlin smiled at me. He knew what I was doing. "Take your time, Jonathan. Start from the beginning."

I looked around the room. I chose my words carefully. I was not looking to hurt anyone's feelings. "It all began at Father's funeral. How much did any of us really know about him? Somehow all of us saw him differently. Because each of us in our own way saw only what we wanted to see in him. And each of us was right. He was all those things. But he was something more. More than any of us saw. He was himself."

I had to be talking a long time. I began with the morning that Anne and I had picked up the truck on U.S. 1 and finished with what had happened this morning. The clock in the foyer chimed ten as I finished.

I looked around at them. "They had never given the baby a name, so I did. Danielle, after Father. Now I want to keep her. She has no one else, no family. She hasn't even got a birth certificate. Jeb Stuart had never gone down to Fitchville to record her birth. They planned to do it when they went down to have her baptized. But it never happened."

Judge Gitlin nodded thoughtfully and took a pull at the bottle of Scotch. This time Zelda didn't yell at him. "It's not as easy as you make it sound, Jonathan," he said quietly. "First of all, you are a minor yourself and there is no court in the land that would give you the custody of an infant child."

"Why not?" I asked. "All I have to do is file a birth certificate that I'm her father."

"You can't do that," the judge said. "There are many legal problems to surmount. A search would have to be conducted for any possible relatives or family. Then if there are any, consents would have to be obtained, and if not, she would be made a ward of the state until her disposition was settled."

"That's stupid," I said. "What's to stop me from just going off with her?"

"You know better than that, Jonathan." He looked at me thoughtfully. "But there might be a way to keep her close to you with much less of a problem. However, it would take the assistance of Jack and your mother."

"What's that?" I asked.

"If they were willing to adopt her, I could find ways to expedite things." He paused for a moment. "But that is a decision they would have to make for themselves. It's something we can't urge on them."

I turned to my mother. She was looking down at Danielle and crying. Jack went over to her and knelt by her side. He looked up into her face, down at Danielle, then up at Mother again.

He cleared his throat. "I always wanted a little girl."

There was one more task to be done. The following month, two days before Thanksgiving, my brother, Daniel, and I took my father home. The first winter chill had frozen the ground, and while the grave was being dug, I walked Daniel up the hill to where the still had been.

There was nothing there but a black hole in the ground and a mass of tortured tubing burned and melted black with the earth. I stood there for a moment, then turned away. It seemed as if only yesterday I had been there, but yesterday was forever.

We walked back down to the cabin. It was already falling apart. The curtains Betty May had been so proud of were nothing but tatters, and the new paint was already peeling off the wood. Most of the windows were broken and the cold air blew through the room.

Daniel looked at me. "So this is where it all began. I never knew."

"No one ever knew," I said. "I wouldn't have known if he hadn't shown me. And it was here I began to learn about the goodness of him and how much I really loved him."

We went back up the knoll to the cemetery. The grave was almost ready. Finally the two gravediggers climbed out and placed the two-by-fours across the open grave. They laid the heavy canvas straps across the planks, then went down the knoll to where the hearse was waiting.

We watched as they were joined by the driver and his assistant and took the coffin out of the hearse. Slowly, carefully, they made their way up the knoll. Despite the cold, I could see the sweat standing on their faces as they walked past us to place the coffin on the two-by-fours. They stepped back, each man taking up an end of the canvas strap, and looked at us expectantly.

I turned to Daniel. He and I had agreed that we did not want a minister. He nodded. The man pulled on the straps, raising the coffin slightly. I kicked one two-by-four out of the way; Daniel kicked the other. Slowly, the men lowered the coffin into the grave. Just as it settled to the bottom they snapped the canvas straps loose and brought them up.

Daniel and I bent down and each of us picked up a handful of earth and threw it into the grave on top of the coffin. Quickly the two men began to shovel back the earth. At first, it rattled hollowly against the wood, but gradually the sound grew muffled. At last they were finished, and giving the earth a few final pats with their spades, they went down the knoll, leaving the two of us alone.

Daniel looked at me. I nodded. He turned back to the grave. His voice husky and low.

> "Here he lies where he longed to be;
> Home is the sailor, home from the sea,
> And the hunter home from the hill."

I looked and saw the tears running down Daniel's cheeks. I reached for my brother's hand and held it tightly. "If you listen, Daniel, you can hear him."

It was like a whisper on the breeze.

"Thank you, my sons."